# Christmas
## at the
# Board Game
# Café

# Jennifer Page

# Christmas at the Board Game Café

HEAD
ZEUS

An Aria Book

First published in the UK in 2024 by Head of Zeus,
part of Bloomsbury Publishing Plc

9 7 5 3 1 2 4 6 8

A catalogue record for this book is available from the British Library.

ISBN (PB): 9781035905577
ISBN (E): 9781035905546

Cover design: Jessie Price

Typeset by Siliconchips Services Ltd UK

Printed and bound in Great Britain by
CPI Group (UK) Ltd, Croydon CR0 4YY

Head of Zeus Ltd
First Floor East
5–8 Hardwick Street
London EC1R 4RG

WWW.HEADOFZEUS.COM

To Rob, the best friend anyone could ever wish for

# Prologue

Everything changed when she saw the soldiers. They were lined up, gripping their firearms, their faces set with determination as they prepared to face the enemy. Whatever mission they were on, it appeared to be well planned.

For a few seconds, she marvelled at their smart uniforms. Their combat packs. Their ammunition belts. If she had any kind of military knowledge, she'd be able to tell who held the highest rank or what type of weapons they were carrying, but she hadn't a clue.

Then her mind snapped back from pondering the stripes on their epaulettes to wondering if she could escape. Could she make it to the front door and disappear into the night? No, it was futile. She was trapped here now. Just had to accept her fate. Were the warning signs there all along? Had she failed to pick up on something? She thought back over the evening, trying to spot the clues that she'd missed.

Only minutes ago, she'd been happy sitting on the sofa, blissfully ignorant of the soldiers' presence. If only she'd stayed there. But it was too late now. All she could do was wait.

There was a noise in the kitchen. The sound of running water. Footsteps. Cupboards being opened and closed. He was obviously searching for something. She took a step backwards towards the door behind her, but a floorboard creaked. She froze as he entered the room and saw her.

He handed her a steaming mug. She looked around, but there was nowhere to put it. Not a coaster in sight. Not one square inch of free space on the table.

She had hoped that this was the beginning of something – dinner then coffee back at his place. Their fifth date. She might even spend the night with him.

But she couldn't do it. She couldn't. No matter how much she liked him, she couldn't bring herself to sleep with a man who played with toy soldiers on his dining table.

# I

Four years later

If the new intern, tasked with organising the Kompleet Marketing Solutions Christmas bash, hadn't chosen that particular afternoon to allocate the names for the Secret Santa, it would never have happened. Kate wouldn't have found herself waking up in Peter Ridley's bed.

(Well, not *his* bed exactly, but a king-sized bed with luxurious Egyptian cotton sheets in an executive suite in a somewhat nondescript four-star hotel in Leeds.)

And yes, we're talking about *that* Peter Ridley.

Peter Ridley, as in the co-owner of Peter Ridley Engineering Ltd, the biggest employer in the little town of Essendale where she lived.

Peter Ridley, as in the ex-fiancé of her oldest and dearest friend, Em.

Who, she was sure, would not be too pleased about this one, even if it had been Em who had ended things with him, and not the other way round.

If she ever found out.

Kate, for one, didn't intend to tell her.

This was a major cock-up. Sleeping with your mate's ex: a violation of the girl code if ever there was one. Hardly the behaviour of a perfect friend. And Kate tried so hard to be the perfect friend.

In fact, she tried so hard to be the perfect everything. Once, she had strived to be the perfect daughter. Then the perfect student. The perfect employee. On numerous occasions, the perfect girlfriend. And always the perfect friend: the kind who listened for hours, gave advice when needed, and, in recent years, offered her extensive marketing knowledge and skills completely free of charge to help her mates with their projects. The launch of Em's board game café, for example. Jo's Scrabble festival. Taylor's upcycled fashion show. Kind, generous and always willing to muck in and lend a hand. The perfect friend.

Until now.

She'd failed spectacularly. She shuddered, imagining what Em would say. She absolutely *mustn't* find out.

Their bond was a strong one, cemented when, aged sixteen, they had both found themselves motherless within a few weeks of each other, albeit in very different ways. Em's mum had died in a traffic accident, whilst Kate's... well, she preferred not to think about how she'd 'lost' *her* mother. Suffice it to say that the two girls had seen each other through some tough times, and grown even closer during adulthood. Their friendship mustn't get ruined by this unfortunate incident with Peter.

She looked up at him now. He was lying on his side, his elbow on the pillow, his head propped on his hand, gazing down at her.

'I have never seen anyone look so fabulous first thing in the morning,' he said.

She smiled modestly. 'Thank you.'

It wasn't by accident that she looked this way. She'd got up to go to the bathroom at twenty past five. She'd run a brush through her hair, removed the mascara smudges from under her eyes, washed her face, and reapplied a little tinted moisturiser and the tiniest smidge of lip gloss. Her usual routine, in other words, when she spent the night with a bloke. She never let anyone see her without at least some make-up. Well, anyone but Em.

Oh God. Of all the people to have a one-night stand with! How had this happened?

She'd had the misfortune to draw Jeroen, her boss, in the Secret Santa, which meant she *had* to find the perfect gift – not easy with the spending limit of a tenner. Since she'd had no plans that evening, she'd decided to hit the shops straight away and get a later train home.

It was early November, but there was already a festive atmosphere in Leeds – a buzz of excitement, sparkly lights and the inevitable soundtrack of Slade, all of which left her cold. She wasn't into Christmas. It reminded her too much of what was missing in her life, but needs must – that gift had to be bought – so gritting her teeth, she headed into the glorious County Arcade, hoping something suitable would catch her eye.

Ninety minutes of fruitless searching later, she reached the station with three minutes to spare before the eleven minutes past eight train to Essendale. Perfect timing. She glanced up at the information board to check the platform number, and there it was in capital letters:

CANCELLED

Almost an hour until the next train.

Rather than hanging around on the freezing platform, she'd decided she'd rather wait somewhere warm, with a drink in her hand, and had headed back outside in search of the nearest pub.

The pub was crowded. Predictable. It was Friday night after all. She'd weaved her way through the revellers to the bar, and ordered herself a small glass of Merlot. And then a familiar voice had said, 'I'll get that,' and she'd turned to find herself looking into the handsome face of Emily's ex-fiancé, Peter Ridley.

Peter.

Kate had never really got on with Peter. She didn't like him – had never thought he was right for Em – and was fairly certain that he didn't care much for her either. When Em had arrived on her doorstep one evening and announced that she'd ended their relationship and needed somewhere to stay, Kate had offered Kleenex and sympathy, and had tried to act like she was sorry, but she'd been inwardly cheering. He hadn't made Em happy, and whilst a broken engagement was obviously upsetting, it was better than a broken marriage further down the line. And hadn't she been proved right when, a short while later, Em had got together with Ludek and was now happier than she'd ever been? Sickeningly loved up, the pair of them.

'And a vodka and slimline tonic, please.' Peter was brandishing a twenty-pound note.

They watched in silence as the barman poured their

drinks, Peter nodding when asked if he'd like ice in his vodka.

'So,' she said, as Peter pocketed his change, 'cheers.' She held up her drink, avoiding making eye contact as he clinked his glass against hers.

'Cheers, Kate. Shall we see if there's anywhere to sit?'

'We'll be lucky,' she said sceptically, looking around the busy pub.

Peter had led the way, saying, 'Excuse me,' and 'May we please squeeze through?' several times in that posh accent of his. He was Yorkshire born and bred, but always managed to sound like he was from the Home Counties. Kate suspected his mother had paid for elocution lessons.

'There we go,' he said triumphantly.

At the very back of the pub was an empty leather sofa with a small table in front of it. Ever the gentleman, Peter gestured for her to sit down first. He took off his woollen coat, and laid it carefully across the arm of the sofa, then settled himself beside her. Kate kept her coat on; she didn't intend to stay that long. She couldn't imagine what they'd find to talk about.

'How are you, Kate?' Peter said.

'Fine, thank you. How are you?'

'Yes, I'm good, thanks. How's your work going these days?'

It was the kind of stilted conversation you got on a foreign language course, Kate thought. They had nothing in common. Except Em.

'Work's great,' she said. On the whole, she enjoyed her job. 'How's the business?'

'Pretty good. I was out for dinner with a new client this evening as it happens. But then his wife called – one of the children was sick. And so I stumbled in here, and there you were.'

'And there I was,' Kate echoed.

There was a pause. This was awkward.

'Are you looking forward to Christmas?' he said.

She couldn't be honest. It didn't do to say that quite frankly, no, she wasn't, whilst the rest of the world worked itself up to a fever pitch of partying and present buying and decorating trees. She'd sound like the Grinch.

'Yes, of course.' She smiled. 'You?'

'Not really,' said Pete. 'I never do, these days. I always wonder... you know, if things had worked out with Emily, we might have had a child by now. Two even. I might have been hanging up stockings and putting gifts under the tree. Instead, I'll be sharing an M&S turkey crown with my mother and her fiancé, and lovely though Stan is, it's not easy seeing your elderly parent find love when you yourself have failed. Sorry, that sounds terribly churlish of me. I'm happy for them really. It's just... you know, Christmas.'

She did know. More than he could have imagined. Christmas had that knack of making you think of the people who should be in your life, but weren't anymore. Every year she dreaded it. It loomed on the calendar as if it were a work appraisal with the most fiendish of managers or a dentist's appointment for root canal work. When autumn arrived, Kate took no pleasure in the scrunch of leaves underfoot, or the Halloween displays that the highly imaginative folk of Essendale created in their doorways and windows, or standing on the hillside on a chilly November evening watching colourful fireworks lighting up the night sky. All of these things told her that Christmas was coming, and it was her least favourite time of year.

Her biggest bugbear was the Christmas TV ads. As a marketing professional herself, she could appreciate the high production values of those adverts, the skill and thought that went into them, but she hated them nonetheless. Several generations gathered round a huge table laden with food, trying to persuade you that your Christmas would be like this if you only shopped at [INSERT BRAND OF SUPERMARKET]. A party scene with music and laughter implying that you too could have a fabulous time if you drank [INSERT BRAND OF ALCOHOL]. Women in sophisticated evening gowns pushing the idea that you could be this attractive if you wore [INSERT BRAND OF PERFUME]. Kate knew she scrubbed up well. She could pull off the glamour of the perfume adverts, she could be the life and soul of a Christmas party, but she couldn't manage the large happy family gathered round the table, arguing amicably over who would have the last roast potato, or whether to play Cluedo or Monopoly this year.

Christmas made her ache even more than usual to have someone by her side who loved her. To have children – or at least the prospect of children – with that person. To feel like she was part of a family. Kate had never felt that, not even as a child in the good old days, as she thought of them, before her sixteenth birthday, when her mum had been around.

'An M&S turkey crown sounds great,' she said to Peter now. 'It'll be a Tesco roast-in-the-bag chicken for me and my dad.'

'Just the two of you?'

'Yes.'

She sighed. Her relationship with her father was virtually non-existent, but she felt obliged to spend the day with him. She couldn't leave him on his own on Christmas Day. Nobody, no matter what they'd done, should be alone on Christmas Day unless they chose to be.

She looked at Peter now. When he'd first got together with Em, she had tried to get on with him, for her friend's sake, but he'd always seemed cold. Distant. She'd struggled to connect. Yet now the dreaded C-word had been mentioned, and she'd seen the sadness in his eyes, she felt a flicker of empathy with him.

'One more drink?' said Peter standing up. 'To cheer ourselves up?'

One more drink had turned into three more – or had it been four? – and she'd missed the last train. Then Peter had said he'd booked a room – he'd assumed his evening out with the new client would be a late one – and somehow she'd found herself in a hotel corridor with him brandishing a key card, and saying, 'Room 103. This is me.'

He hadn't unlocked the door straight away, instead pressing her up against it and kissing her.

Then, when they'd finally got inside, he'd kissed her again, up against the wall this time, unbuttoning her shirt, which had ended up crumpled on the carpet. He'd unzipped her skirt, still kissing her, and slid it over her hips. She saw it all in her mind's eye, as if she were watching a movie. Her skirt falling to the floor. Kicking off her shoes. His fingers unhooking her bra.

And now here she was, the morning after the night before, wondering what on earth she had done. She sat up in bed a little now, pulling the duvet up with her, over her breasts. 'Did we...? We didn't...?'

'No, we didn't.'

Well, that was one thing anyway.

Peter smiled. 'You were a little inebriated, Kate, and I'm not the kind of man who'd take advantage. And in any case, you said we shouldn't. Because of Emily.'

Yes, it was coming back to her now; she vaguely remembered mumbling something about Em. But even so, she was naked under here. She looked around the room, expecting to see her clothes strewn everywhere, but they lay neatly folded on a chair. His suit was hanging up.

Just as she had got up in the night and fixed her face, he had got up at some point and sorted the clothes. Kate considered herself to be a meticulously tidy person, but even she drew the line at getting up in the night to fold up clothes that had been discarded in the heat of passion.

Good job he hadn't married Em, she thought suddenly. Her friend was notoriously messy.

Shit. Em. Sex or no sex, she mustn't find out about this.

Kate's head was throbbing, she realised. These days she wasn't accustomed to drinking quite as much as she had last night. She'd cut back in recent years, partly for health reasons – it was crazy to be careful about eating a healthy diet, if you were going to drink so much booze – and partly after that dreadful evening where she'd got completely hammered and wrecked the launch party of Em's first board game café.

If Em ever did find out about her and Peter, she would blame the Merlot.

But in truth, it hadn't been alcohol that had brought the

two of them together last night. It hadn't been lust either. It had been loneliness. They were two lonely souls, facing the loneliest season of the year, who had sought solace in each other's arms.

## 2

No-one looking at Kate later that day as she stood in the houseplant section of the garden centre would have guessed that she was lonely. And that was exactly what she wanted, because she was deeply ashamed of her loneliness.

She appeared to be the embodiment of style and confidence in her dark blue, wide-legged trousers, a classic white shirt under a tailored jacket, and a simple necklace of indigo glass beads. With her dark hair in her trademark sleek, shiny bob, she wouldn't have looked out of place on a Parisian boulevard. Her one concession to living in the quirky little town of Essendale was flat shoes; heels weren't exactly practical given the number of cobbled streets.

The key to hiding her loneliness from the rest of the world, her friends and colleagues especially, and to coping with it, was to keep busy, really busy. If she was always on the go, rushing from one appointment to another, ticking off task after task on her to-do list, she didn't have time to dwell on it. If she kept herself occupied, she could pretend to everybody and, more importantly, to herself that everything was all right and that life had turned out exactly as she'd hoped. But underneath the perfect façade she worked so hard to maintain was a woman longing for love and companionship.

Orchid or jasmine?

Kate tried to focus on the task in hand: to buy a houseplant for Jo's birthday. Razz had said that that was what his partner wanted, but hadn't specified which kind. And now, with only minutes to go until the celebratory afternoon tea at the board game café, she couldn't make up her mind. She wasn't a gardener, and her mind kept wandering back to the previous night. To waking up in bed this morning with Peter Ridley.

Peter Ridley!

She felt certain that Em would guess her secret the moment she walked into the café. They knew each other so well; could read each other like a book. She might as well wear a T-shirt that said *I slept with your ex* or have it tattooed across her forehead.

Jasmine or orchid?

They were both pretty – the jasmine with its pure white flowers, the orchid with its pink ones. There was only one way to decide when it came to Jo; Kate would add up the Scrabble score for each word.

Orchid: 12 points.

Jasmine: 16 points.

Well, that decided it. Kate smiled to herself. Her friends would laugh later when she explained how she'd made her choice; Jo would love it, Taylor would roll her eyes, and Em would say, 'There are other board games, you know, Jo.'

As she made her way through the garden centre towards the tills, she came face to face with a forest of Christmas trees, adorned with brightly coloured baubles and garish flashing lights. There was the most hideous display of mechanical giant reindeer, which nodded their heads at passers-by. At least they weren't yet playing the inevitable Christmas songs, but nevertheless, Wham!'s 'Last Christmas' began playing in her head, and she felt decidedly tetchy.

She stepped back to allow a woman with a pushchair to pass and collided with a giant inflatable Santa. She heard the mum pointing out the reindeer to the occupant of the pushchair, then the child's delighted giggle, and once again she felt that all-too-familiar longing to have a child as she hurried on.

It was unseasonably mild that afternoon in the little Yorkshire town that lay nestled between the Pennine hills. Although the leaves had already dropped from the trees, there wasn't a coat or a woolly hat in sight. Come to think of it, there weren't actually that many people about; the town had been unusually quiet in recent weeks. She vaguely recalled Peter saying something about that last night.

She dodged the hissing white geese who patrolled the streets of Essendale like an overzealous neighbourhood watch, and opened the door to the café. Em owned this place; her career as a café owner had had a bumpy start, but had got going eventually, thanks partly to her introducing her USP of having the board games on offer, partly to moving to the high street instead of the side street on the outskirts of town where she was originally based, and partly to Kate herself. She'd put in hours of unpaid labour, organising an extensive marketing campaign for the launch.

Em had been profoundly grateful, but in truth, it had been one of Kate's many ways of staying busy, of keeping the loneliness at bay. Even now, she still posted regularly on social media on Em's behalf: the latest game that had been acquired, tasteful shots of the board-game-themed cakes on offer, or an arty photo of a mug of cappuccino with a table of gamers out of focus in the background.

Ludek, Em's lovely boyfriend, was behind the counter this evening. He waved to Kate and pointed at the stairs. Fixing a smile on her face, she headed up, past the home-made cardboard sign that said, 'Sorry but this section of the board game café is closed for a private function.'

'Hey,' she said, as she walked into the upstairs room. She was running slightly late, and had expected to be the last to arrive, but instead found only Em fixing a 'Happy birthday' banner across the window with Sellotape.

An image of herself and Peter, entangled in the Egyptian cotton duvet, flashed through Kate's mind. The last thing she wanted was to be alone with Em right now; she was sure the guilt was written all over her, and subconsciously she shifted the jasmine, concealing her face.

'Hi.' Em rushed over and embraced her. Well, as best she could, given the size of the pot plant. 'Put that down, Kate, and give me a proper hug.'

Kate reluctantly parted with the plant, placing it on an empty table, and hugged her friend, feeling like a complete traitor. She would not let last night ruin this afternoon. She would *not* let it ruin their friendship. She sank into Em's embrace, pushing from her mind the thought that the last person who'd held her had been Peter.

'What d'you think?' said Em, pulling away.

Kate looked round the room. Whilst downstairs the board game café was – unsurprisingly – full of board games, the vibe was a little different upstairs. Since Taylor had lost her shop a few months back, Em had allowed the sewist to use this space to display her range of quirky, upcycled clothes, many of which were themed to match the board games. There were skirts with Scrabble fabric patches, and shirts and jackets with appliquéd steam trains on the pockets for the many fans of railway games who frequented the café. In addition to the birthday banner across the window, Em had placed a bouquet of colourful helium balloons on one table. There was an ice bucket with the neck of something sparkling poking out and a scattering of table confetti.

'Looks great,' she said. 'Are the others running late?'

Em nodded. 'I'm glad though. I wanted to ask you something, just between us. I didn't want to dampen the mood.'

Kate's heart began to thud. Em couldn't know about Peter, could she? Surely he wouldn't have confessed?

Her mouth felt dry. 'Fire away.'

She bit her lip, waiting for the question.

Waiting for Em to say, *Have you slept with Peter?*

Then she was saved by footsteps on the stairs, and Jo, the birthday girl, and Taylor burst into the room, with cries of, 'Yay, we made it,' and 'Sorry we're so late.'

'Happy birthday, Jo.' Kate picked up the pot plant and held it out. 'Razz said this was what you wanted.'

'It is.' Jo beamed. 'Lovely.'

'I nearly went for an orchid, but jasmine—'

'Scores more in Scrabble!' said Jo. 'Love it.'

In contrast to her friendship with Em, which went back

to their school days, Kate had only known Jo a short while, but she loved that they could already finish each other's sentences. Kate looked at Jo now and knew what she was thinking; she was checking Kate's maths, working out the Scrabble scores of the two words.

'There are other board games, you know, Jo,' said Em, as Kate had known she would.

'And Taylor, how are you?' Kate beamed.

'Great, thanks,' said Taylor.

Taylor was the newest member of their little friendship group, but she'd fitted in easily. In fact, Kate thought, looking at her three friends, if anyone didn't fit in here, it was herself. The others all worked here in the valley, whilst Kate commuted to Leeds. They all wore quirky clothes – Jo was wearing her Scrabble dress in honour of her birthday and Taylor was in a baggy, chiffon tunic – and they all had boyfriends. Kate was the only one who was single, which was kind of ironic, as they all viewed her as something of a dating guru. She'd read *so* many books about dating and finding love and had given advice to all of them, and yet they had found love whilst she hadn't.

There were more footsteps on the stairs and Ludek appeared in the doorway, bearing a tray with a large birthday cake and a huge pot of tea, covered in a cosy.

'Happy birthday, Jo.' He planted a kiss on her cheek and then disappeared back downstairs to resume his duties in the café.

Em removed the cosy from the teapot and began to pour.

Jo was studying the cake. 'Wow, did you make this, Em?'

Em nodded. 'Certainly did.'

The icing on the cake had been painted to look like a

Scrabble board, with the letter tiles spelling out *'Happy birthday, Jo.'*

'Beautiful,' said Taylor. 'It almost seems a shame to cut it.'

'Nonsense.' Em handed a knife to Jo. 'You do the honours.'

'Just a small piece for me, please,' Kate said.

'Not on a diet?' Jo said.

Kate shook her head. 'No, as you know, I like to make healthy lifestyle choices.'

It was hard work though. There was so much you had to do these days. Never mind five portions of fruit and veg a day, it was apparently best to aim for ten. By the time you'd eaten plenty of oily fish, nuts and seeds, along with a healthy dollop of kimchi, kombucha and live natural yoghurt to keep your gut bacteria happy, there wasn't much room for cake. There was a certain satisfaction in it though, and people often complimented her on her lovely, glowing skin.

Mind you, Taylor had glowing skin too. In fact, she was positively blooming and Kate knew for a fact that she munched her way through packets of custard creams as she sewed.

'How about I open the bubbly?' Jo suggested.

Without waiting for an answer, she retrieved the bottle from the ice bucket, and eased the cork out. It flew across the room with a pop, hitting the 'for sale' clothes rail of Taylor's garments.

There were four champagne flutes on the table already, and Jo filled the glasses, handing the first to Em and the second to Kate, before holding the third out to Taylor, who shook her head. 'Not for me, thanks.'

Kate looked at her in surprise.

Taylor was blooming.

She was wearing loose-fitting clothes.

And she'd refused alcohol.

Kate's stomach lurched, but she fixed a smile to her face and, with all the warmth and enthusiasm she could muster, she said, 'Congratulations, Taylor. When are you due?'

# 3

'Oh my goodness,' said Em as the penny dropped. 'You're pregnant!'

'Well, cheers to that,' said Jo, holding out her glass.

Three champagne flutes were clinked against Taylor's mug of tea.

'The first of us to have a baby,' said Em, a little wistfully.

'I already *was* the first to have a baby,' said Taylor. 'I have Max, remember?'

Taylor had a son – Kate thought he was about nine – from a previous relationship.

Kate knew she ought to feel pleased about Taylor's news. She *was* pleased.

But she was also envious, and she felt as ashamed of her envy as she did of her loneliness; well, it was hardly an attractive quality to be consumed by the green-eyed monster when one of your friends announced the happy news that they were having a child. She could cope – just about – with being the only single one in their group, but now Taylor was having a baby, and Kate suddenly felt sure that it wouldn't be too long before Jo and Em would be following suit, judging by how excited both of them now looked, and she'd be the odd one out in yet another respect. They'd all be going off to their NCT classes and their parents and toddlers groups, whilst she sat home alone. If only her workplace were more sociable.

And all she wanted was to find her soulmate and have a family of her own, to give her babies the happy childhood she hadn't had herself. She loved her job in marketing, but a job didn't stroke your hair or keep you warm in bed at night. A job didn't beg you for one more bedtime story or snuggle up on your knee.

'Boy or girl?' Jo was saying now. 'Or don't you know?'

'A girl. We're going to name her Esme.' Taylor's eyes were bright with excitement.

'Esme?' Em laughed. 'After the judge on *The Great British Sewing Bee*?'

'Of course not. After Harry's late mother,' said Taylor, but she winked.

'It's so exciting,' said Jo. 'A new baby!'

Kate rolled her eyes at Em, who frowned back at her.

When they'd eaten their cake – Em's sponge was the lightest – they cleared the table and Em produced a Scrabble box. It was Jo's favourite game, and since it was her birthday, they'd all agreed to play.

They took their seven letter tiles, then an eighth to decide who would play first. Jo drew an A, so it was her to start.

'N-A-P-P-Y.' Jo said the name of each letter as she laid her tiles on the board, then tallied up her score. 'Double word score so that's 24 points.'

'And a baby-themed word too,' said Em. 'In honour of Taylor's news.'

They laughed.

Taylor put two Ds down to make DAD using the A of NAPPY, then Em placed two O's make DO and POO.

'Brilliant,' said Jo. 'All baby words!'

'Let's make all the words baby words,' said Em.

Kate looked at her letters, then at the board, then back at her letters, before laying an L on the end of POO, and used that to spell LATHE going down the board.

'Kate!' Em sounded exasperated. 'They're not baby words.'

'Pool as in birthing pool,' said Kate.

'You could have made LATE instead of LATHE,' said Em. 'Since babies often arrive late.'

They continued playing, with Jo, Taylor and Em shrieking with excitement every time a baby word was played, and Kate trying valiantly to get into the spirit of things, but she felt increasingly distant from her friends as the game went on. It was almost as if she was having an out-of-body experience, watching herself from the top corner of the room.

She wanted to be pleased for Taylor – she *was* pleased for Taylor, and for Harry too; she knew how much he longed to be a dad – but she couldn't shake off her envy, of wishing it were her.

'What did you do last night?' Em said.

Kate looked up from her letter tiles in alarm, then realised that Em was addressing Jo, not her. Jo's actual birthday had been the previous day.

'Razz took me out for dinner to a new Italian in Halifax,' Jo said.

'Nice,' said Taylor, drawing new letter tiles from the bag. 'Your turn, Jo.'

They were totting up the scores – not that it mattered who'd won – when there were footsteps on the stairs and Ludek, Harry and Razz appeared.

'I've shut up shop,' said Ludek, 'so we thought we'd join you ladies.'

Em frowned, and looked at her watch. 'This early?'

'Harry and Razz were my only customers,' said Ludek, as he moved three chairs from a neighbouring table, and the women obligingly moved round to make room for them. 'The town's dead this afternoon.'

'Actually, Kate,' said Em, 'that was what I wanted to ask you about. If you had any more bright ideas for marketing.'

'Marketing,' said Kate slowly. So that had been it – nothing to do with Peter.

'Yeah, marketing. You know, that thing you're so good at. The thing you do for a living. Business hasn't been great lately, to be honest. It was busy in the spring and summer. So good that I did all this.' She gestured around her at the newly refurbished upstairs room; until a few months ago, it had been a storeroom. 'But then the school summer holidays ended, and trade has gone down every week.'

'I already post quite a lot about the café on social media,' said Kate. 'But I'll put my thinking cap on.'

'I didn't just mean for the café, I meant for the town. I think all the shops are struggling. Alessandra's has closed down. It's up for sale.'

'Someone else was saying that...' Kate began, then stopped herself, remembering who that someone had been.

Peter. Somewhere between her third and fourth glass of Merlot.

'Mother was terribly upset,' he had said. 'She bought most of her clothes there. I suspect there may be other businesses in trouble too.'

Kate hadn't paid too much attention. She'd never cared much either for Peter's mother – she'd made Em's life a misery when the two of them had been together – or for the dresses in Alessandra's shop, which had specialised in what she thought of as the mother-of-the-bride look; far too fussy for her.

'I guess it's partly because of the cost of living being so high at the moment,' Jo said. 'People are going out less.'

'I'm not selling as many clothes.' Taylor nodded.

'Another problem,' Kate said, 'is that a lot of the homes here are now Airbnbs, and the locals can't afford to live here anymore. But the visitors don't come in the winter when the weather's bad, and the local businesses suffer. A lot of seaside towns are having the same problem, only worse.'

'Have you been talking to Peter?' said Em.

Kate bit her lip. 'Peter?'

'Yeah, he popped in the other day and said much the same thing.'

Kate kept her eyes lowered, and hoped she wasn't blushing. 'I think I read it somewhere. The local paper maybe.'

'Anyway, I was wondering if you had any thought on how to boost trade,' Em continued. 'Especially in the run-up to Christmas.'

'I'll mull it over,' Kate said. 'Leave it with me.'

'You could buy Alessandra's, Taylor,' Jo said. 'For all your designs.'

'I'd love a proper shop,' said Taylor, then looked at Em in horror. 'Not that I don't really appreciate having the clothes on display up here. But you know… a window display on the high street. It'd be amazing.'

'We looked into it,' said Harry, 'but we couldn't afford the shop unless we sold the house. And the flat upstairs isn't big enough now there's going to be four of us. Oh.' He realised what he'd said, looked at Taylor and whispered, 'Sorry, I didn't mean to let that slip.'

Taylor laughed, her eyes bright with excitement. 'Don't worry. I already told them. Well, actually, Kate guessed.'

'Congratulations, Harry,' said Jo. 'Wonderful news.'

'It's fantastic,' said Em.

'Lovely that you're naming her after…' Kate felt the toe of Taylor's shoe strike her ankle '…your mum, Harry.'

'And after Taylor's favourite judge on *The Great British Sewing Bee*,' said Harry. 'I'm not daft.'

Kate looked at the smiling faces of her three closest friends and their three lovely boyfriends – fiancé in the case of Harry – and felt another stab of envy. She was delighted for them that they'd all found someone, but why hadn't she?

She'd come close a couple of times. Rob had been lovely, but he was obsessed with his training routine at the gym, and Michael was always tinkering with his computers. She always said that she'd dated men who were obsessed with their mothers, but Michael was obsessed with his mother boards; it was a joke she'd cracked a few times, but the truth was that she didn't find it funny. He hadn't had much time for her, and after the initial attraction had faded, they had grown apart. And then there'd been Xander, but that was years ago now, and she tried not to think about him.

Talk had turned to babies again. Taylor had already made three dresses for Esme; she'd embroidered bunnies onto one of them. Harry couldn't decide which colour to paint the nursery; not pink – he didn't want to conform to stereotypes.

'He's hoping she'll like model railways,' Taylor said with a laugh.

'And you're hoping she'll like sewing,' said Em. 'What's it like being pregnant?'

'It's okay,' said Taylor. 'I'm a bit tired.'

'And very grumpy,' added Harry.

'I am not.' Taylor was indignant.

'You are, but I love you anyway.'

'And I love you too, despite your terrible dress sense,' said Taylor.

'Ditto,' said Jo, looking at Razz. 'Although admittedly you have smartened yourself up a bit since we got together. And...' her eyes twinkled '...I love you despite the fact you took me potholing on our first date, then wimped out of going down the pothole yourself.'

Ludek laughed. 'And I love Em, even though I met her at running club, but she's refused to come out running with me ever again.'

'And I love you, Ludek, even though you can't move in our house for all the board games,' said Em, wiping a tear from her cheek.

'And I love you all,' Kate declared, trying to get in the spirit of it, 'despite the fact that this is the cheesiest conversation I've ever had the misfortune to witness. Stop it, now. I get it. You all love each other, warts and all.' She sighed. 'Now I hate to break up the party, but I've a client meeting at eight a.m. tomorrow, so I'll be on the early train to Leeds. Happy birthday again, Jo, and congratulations again, Taylor and Harry.'

Jo and Taylor exchanged glances.

'But Kate...' Em began, but Kate silenced her with a cheery wave.

'Must dash. Sorry.' She grabbed her bag, and hurried down the stairs before any of them could point out that the following day was Sunday.

The high street *was* quiet, Kate thought as soon as she stepped outside. In the summer, the place had been full of tourists and day-trippers, lured to the town by its quirkiness and its proximity to some of Yorkshire's most beautiful countryside. Now, there was no-one about. She glanced at Alessandra's. Not so long ago, it had been a thriving business, but now it was boarded up and abandoned.

She walked past the florist's, pondering what could be done to draw more visitors over the winter months – they had to do something; the run-up to Christmas was such a vital time for everyone in retail – and it was then that she saw him. Or at least she thought she saw him.

Xander.

The One Who'd Got Away.

Except that wasn't quite accurate. It had been Kate who'd got away from him. She couldn't get away quick enough.

She'd been on so many dates over the years in her quest to find the right man that she didn't recall all their names, let alone where they'd been on their date or what they did for a living. Yet she not only knew his name, she remembered every detail about her five dates with him.

Sometimes a few dates were all it took.

Was it Xander? Or someone who looked like him? Same kind of shabby clothes. Faded jeans. Jacket that had seen better days. An old university scarf. Similar gait too. Kind of bouncy. Optimistic. Like a spaniel.

And then the man had gone. Disappeared into an alleyway before Kate could get a better look at him.

It couldn't have been Xander. He lived over two hundred miles away. And there were lots of shabbily dressed guys in this valley, some of whom were probably optimists.

It was her mind playing tricks on her. Like when you were bereaved, you suddenly thought you saw the person trying to decide between frozen peas and petits pois in the supermarket or feeding bread to the mallards in the park or waiting for the 7.27 to Leeds. And the person in question would look up or turn round, and you'd realise it wasn't them at all, but merely a stranger who bore a passing resemblance.

As she reached her road, her thoughts were swirling round her head. Xander. Peter. Whether Em had any inkling about her and Peter. Alessandra's closing. How to attract more visitors to the town over the winter months. On automatic pilot, she unlocked her front door, not noticing the bouquet of flowers propped up against it until she was about to step inside and knock it over.

Her heart began to thud, remembering the man who'd looked like Xander. Had it been Xander himself? Had he somehow tracked her down to Essendale and left flowers on her doorstep?

She reached down for the little envelope sticking out of the flowers, opening it with trembling fingers, and bit her lip with disappointment as she read the words on the card.

*Last night was incredible. Have dinner with me? P x*

# 4

'Hi, Kate, how was your weekend?' Simone said, pausing by Kate's desk as she walked into the office on Monday morning. 'Get up to anything good?'

Like all her colleagues, Simone was always friendly. Cordial. Would ask about her weekend or chat about last night's telly by the water cooler. But that was as far as it went. No-one ever suggested popping out for lunch or after-works drinks. The office Christmas party was practically the only time she ever socialised with her colleagues. Which reminded her, she still had to find the perfect gift for Jeroen in the Secret Santa.

Kate smiled at Simone. 'An impromptu date on Friday evening with a rather lovely man.' She was surprised to hear herself describe Peter as lovely; that would never have happened this time last week. 'And then my friend Jo's birthday party on Saturday, which was made all the more special by another friend announcing she's pregnant. And then Sunday, I just chilled, you know.'

She made no mention of the fact that Peter was her best friend's ex-fiancé and that she felt dreadful about it, or of how the green-eyed monster had struck when Taylor had made her announcement, or of how lonely she'd felt on Sunday, with no plans and no-one to talk to.

It was funny how you could put a positive spin on things; she'd been doing it for as long as she could remember. As a child, she'd quickly learned that people wanted to hear positive things. So when her mum asked, 'How was school, darling?' the answer she wanted was: 'Fine, thanks', not all the details about how she'd fallen over in the playground and grazed her knee or how the mashed potato had been lumpy or how one of the boys had teased her with a spider.

'And how was your weekend, Simone?'

'Dull, really. Running the usual taxi service for the kids, you know? Football practice. Riding lesson. Mates' houses. Nightmare. You're so lucky. Enjoy your freedom whilst it lasts. It'll be you one day.'

*I hope so*, Kate thought.

As Simone went over to her own desk, Kate took a sip of green tea from her Little Miss Perfect mug and tried to concentrate on her to-do list, putting the tasks in order of priority as she did at the start of each day.

She had three of these mugs: two at home and one here in the office. They'd all been gifts in the office Secret Santa, each giver clearly oblivious to the fact that she'd received exactly the same thing in previous years, but Kate didn't mind. She was proud of her nickname. Prouder still of the pile of 'Employee of the Year' certificates that were stashed in her top drawer. Keeping them on display would look boastful, and besides, she'd won the award three times in the eight years she'd worked here, and there simply wasn't the space to display them all.

She'd worked hard to earn those certificates. And the nickname, come to think of it. She couldn't remember when – or why – her quest for perfection had started. As a child, she'd spend hours practising her handwriting, getting all her letters uniform, the loops dangling the same length underneath the line. She recalled how proud she'd felt when the teacher had held up her work in front of the entire class as an example to the other children. She'd excelled at most things, not because she was naturally gifted, but because she practised, putting heart and soul into everything. The one thing she couldn't pull off was singing. Because no matter how hard she tried, the music teacher said that she was flat. She couldn't hear it herself. The answer was simple: she didn't sing.

Kate sighed. She couldn't focus.

Hadn't been able to since Saturday.

This morning she'd done her usual twenty minutes of mindfulness meditation.

Well, sort of.

It would be more accurate to say she had spent twenty minutes sitting on a yoga mat in her pyjamas, trying to focus on her breathing whilst her mind flitted from Taylor being pregnant, to concern for the future of the board game café and all the other businesses in Essendale, and then to the man who'd looked like Xander but couldn't possibly *be* Xander, and finally on to Peter Ridley.

She'd been sorely tempted to call him, and had very nearly accepted that invitation, but instead had sent a text message thanking him for the flowers, but making it quite clear that dinner was out of the question.

Peter had replied quickly.

Understood. If you ever change your mind, you know where I am. P x

So magnanimous.

People could be so obnoxious when you turned them down – presumably because they felt rejected – but not Peter. He was far too nice for that. And to think that all that time when he'd been dating Em, Kate had completely misjudged him. To her surprise, she'd felt a pang of regret at having to decline his invitation. She couldn't remember the last time a man had taken her out for dinner. She'd taken a break from the dating apps recently, focusing all her energies on marketing Taylor's upcycled fashion show. It had kept her busy, but once it was over, she'd had far too much time on her hands.

And now Christmas was approaching and somehow it was worse being single at Christmas than at any other time of year.

Why was meeting someone so difficult? She'd read enough find-a-man self-help books to fill an entire library, marking the most relevant sections with Post-it notes and diligently applying the advice. She'd tried salsa dancing, running club, singles evenings, speed dating, all to no avail. She hadn't been on a date in ages. Maybe it was time to reactivate her profile on the Buzzz dating app; it was, after all, how Jo had found Razz, and it would help her get Peter Ridley out of her mind.

She glanced around the office. The perfect employee did not look at dating apps at work, but most of her colleagues were still chatting about their weekends or making coffee; several hadn't even fired up their computers. No-one was paying any attention to her, so she opened up the app, and clicked 'Reactivate.'

It was nearly ten to six when Kate heard the tell-tale ping of the Buzzz app, and realised she had her first message. Five p.m. was officially the end of the working day at Kompleet Marketing Solutions, but Kate always stayed late, till six at least, regardless of whether she'd completed her tasks for the day, because that was what you did if you wanted to impress your boss. In any case, it wasn't as if she had anything – or anyone – to rush home to.

She picked up her phone, opened the app and read her new message.

Fancy a drink tonight?

Straight to the point. No small talk. No 'How are you?' or 'You look nice. Can we talk?' or anything like that.

Nevertheless, she clicked on the sender's profile. A bald man with green eyes grinned at her from the main photo. Attractive, she thought.

She'd be leaving for her train soon, so needed to decide quickly. Go on this date? Or return yet again to a cold, empty house and a boring evening in front of the telly?

(Actually, the house wouldn't be cold at all, because she'd left the central heating on and had had the loft insulated, but it would be empty, and somehow that emptiness made the house seem cold, even if the thermostat said otherwise.)

She didn't bother looking at the rest of her new potential date's photos, but scanned what he'd written – the usual kind of stuff. He liked to holiday abroad, and favourite destinations included Norway, Iceland and Madeira. Not bad, she thought. She wouldn't mind a trip to any of those. He had his own business selling and fitting kitchens. Where it said 'pets', he'd ticked none. Where it said, 'Wants kids?', he'd put 'maybe'.

Not yes, but maybe. She could live with that.

Her fingers hovered over her phone. In at least one of her many 'how to get a man' books, you were advised against accepting a last-minute date. Best not to look too available. She should say no, but she wasn't exactly fending off admirers. In fact, as far as she knew, she didn't have any.

Except for Peter.

And Peter was not an option.

She tapped out a reply.

That would be lovely.

She broke another of her dating rules only five minutes later when she found herself agreeing to dinner. She never had dinner on a first date. What if, by the time the starter arrived, you realised that there was no spark? You'd have to get through the main course before you could make your excuses. She remembered advising Jo not so long ago to 'keep first dates short'.

'Just stay long enough to pique his interest,' she had said.

Mind you, Jo had gone haring off to North Yorkshire on her first date with Razz, and look how brilliantly that had turned out in the end.

\*

Kate studied Steve over the top of her menu. His photo, she decided, hadn't been exactly recent, but those eyes of his were a striking shade of green. His snug-fitting T-shirt showed off his biceps and chest muscles. Definitely attractive, but it was too early to say if there was a spark.

As usual, she'd taken care over her own appearance, removing then reapplying her make-up in the toilets at work and adding product to her hair to make it shiny. She'd dusted off a pair of heels that she kept in her office drawer for occasions such as this.

'You look lovely,' said Steve. 'Super dress.'

Kate smiled in a way that she hoped looked both pleased and modest the same time. 'This old thing? I had to come straight from work. There wasn't time to go home and change.'

Actually, the knitted cashmere dress wasn't old at all. She knew it flattered her; it was a gorgeous shade of forget-me-not blue, and showed her slim figure off to its best advantage.

When they'd ordered – roast vegetable salad with quinoa and a tahini dressing for Kate; steak and chips for Steve – he leaned across the table and said, 'Which of my photos did you like best?'

She'd only looked at the first one. 'Oh, the erm... one with the...'

'I knew it! The one with the fish!'

Kate's heart plummeted. There it was: the deal breaker. And so early in the date!

Why hadn't she checked the photos? She did not go on

dates with men whose photo showed them bearing a large fish, not – she was ashamed to admit – on animal welfare grounds, but because she might as well stay single if the man in her life was going to while away every weekend sitting by a river whilst she stayed home alone.

'Wonder why you ladies love those fish photos so much?' He was staring at her intently. 'I reckon that despite your feminism stuff, you all long for a strong hunter-gatherer, and what says hunter-gatherer more than a fish photo?'

'A dead mammoth?'

She expected a laugh, a smile at the very least, but he looked blank and sipped his beer, then proceeded to tell her in great detail about his recent divorce.

'So tell me about your holidays,' she said, trying to change the subject. 'Iceland and Norway, wasn't it? Have you seen the northern lights?'

'Nah.' He shook his head. 'I go for the fishing. You should see the size of the cod.'

The waiter arrived then with the food.

Kate thanked him. Steve, she noticed, didn't. He stabbed his steak, and blood oozed onto his plate.

'Do you always eat budgie food?' he said, looking pointedly at her quinoa.

Why did she put herself through this?

The trouble was, it was impossible to tell from a photo and a few words on a profile what someone would actually be like in real life. Whether you'd get on. Whether there'd be a spark. Over the years, she'd been on many first dates like this with a stranger off a dating app, and she could count on the fingers of one hand the ones she'd actually enjoyed.

Kate speared a piece of roasted pepper with her fork, irritated that she'd not only broken her dating rules and accepted this last-minute date, but had agreed to dinner too. She would eat her 'budgie food', as he'd called it, as quickly as possible, settle her share of the bill, then make her excuses and leave. Her empty house was beginning to seem a more appealing prospect by the minute.

On the train home, Kate's mind drifted back four years. It had been around this time of year when she'd first met Xander. He'd been in her thoughts since Saturday, when she'd imagined seeing him in Essendale. That couldn't have been him. He lived two hundred miles away in London; they had met when she'd been coming to the end of a four-month secondment in the capital.

Such a weird date.

Weird, but also lovely in a way.

And definitely unforgettable.

Not unlike Xander himself.

# 5

Four years earlier

Kate was late – not her fault; some problem with the Tube – and raced from South Kensington station at a speed that would have given Usain Bolt a run for his money. As she reached the café where Xander had suggested that they meet, she stopped in her tracks. An absolute Adonis of a man was coming out of the door. Kate suddenly understood something she'd never understood before: women swooning in costume dramas at the sight of an attractive man. Her heart pounded. Her mouth went dry.

He was in his mid-thirties, a little older than her. With a few silvery highlights beginning to show in his dark hair, he resembled George Clooney in his younger days. Well, a shabby-chic version of George Clooney at any rate. A shabby-chic version of George Clooney who didn't happen to own a hairbrush.

She realised she was staring, that he was waiting for her. He'd moved back into the café so as to hold the door open for her to go inside. She thanked him, then tore her eyes away, scanning the café to see if she could spot her date. Not easy when she hadn't a clue what he looked like. He hadn't put a photo on his profile – work reasons, he'd said.

'Kate?'

It was the man who'd held the door open. Shabby-chic George.

No. He couldn't be, could he?

'Xander?' she said.

He made no attempt to kiss her on the cheek, or even shake her hand. 'I was just leaving. I thought you'd stood me up.'

He thought she'd stood him up, yet he seemed very relaxed about it. As if he wasn't bothered.

But what a voice. Rich and chocolatey. No, velvety. Velvety chocolate.

Well, whatever. Lovely anyway. She could listen to that voice all day.

'Yes, sorry about that,' she mumbled. 'Problems on the District Line. There's always something isn't there? Signal failure. Leaves. Trespassers.'

She was rambling now. She closed her mouth and took a deep breath. Two minutes later, and she'd have missed him. Would have missed out on a date with this gorgeous bloke.

'Not a problem,' said Xander. 'These things happen.'

'I'll buy the coffees,' she said, trying to act like her usual confident self, but to her ears, her voice sounded wobbly. She had dated some attractive men in her time, but this guy…! 'To make up for being late.'

'There isn't time for coffee,' he said. 'And I've already had one. Whilst I was waiting.'

'There isn't time?'

'No, there's a lot to get through.' He was rummaging through his inside pockets, looking for something. 'I hope you haven't seen it already.'

'Seen it?'

What was the man going on about?

'The exhibition.'

'Exhibition?'

'Cold War Design—' he waved two tickets at her '—1945 to 1970. At the V&A.'

A war exhibition? On a first date?

'You've seen it, haven't you?' he said.

Seen it? Why the hell would she have seen it?

She shook her head. 'Never heard of it.'

He looked puzzled. 'What a relief! I took a bit of a gamble when I bought the tickets. I thought you might have seen the exhibition already, you know, with you saying in your profile that you liked history and design.'

Ah. Her profile.

She realised her error. In an attempt to make herself sound more interesting, she'd written that she liked history and design, even adding selfies she'd taken at Hampton Court and the Tower of London. (She'd been doing all the touristy things since she'd arrived in the capital.) With hindsight, that had been overegging the pudding, but both photos had been flattering. Now she wondered if she'd made a mistake. In the event that she was lucky enough that this George Clooney lookalike turned out to be her Mr Right, she'd be saddling herself with a lifetime of visiting ancient ruins, old battlefields and stately homes.

Unlikely though, she thought, casting a sideways glance at him as they walked. He was out of her league.

Kate's feet were already aching by the time they reached the entrance to the exhibition. Her navy heels would have been fine had they been sitting in a café or bar this afternoon as she'd assumed they would be, but they were definitely the wrong choice for traipsing round a museum.

'Now this is what I wanted to see,' said Xander.

A metal ball, about two feet across, was suspended above them. It had long metal arms, like radio aerials, coming off it, but Kate couldn't see what was so impressive.

'What is it?'

'A sputnik.'

She was none the wiser. 'Sputnik?'

'A Russian satellite,' he said. 'The first satellite, in fact, to orbit the earth.'

'You'd wonder how they could send something so small into space then get it back again.'

'They didn't. They made several. This one never went into space.'

'Doh!' Kate hit her forehead with the heel of her hand. She needed to think before she opened her mouth. The man had clearly been expecting a history buff, and here she was sounding like a complete ignoramus.

'It's amazing,' he said. 'All the things we take for granted today that wouldn't exist if it weren't for satellites. Global communications.'

'Sky TV.'

'GPS.'

'Tinder.'

'Tinder?'

'We wouldn't have Tinder if we didn't have GPS,' Kate said, feeling a little smug. 'It only works if it knows your location. So, if it weren't for sputnik here, no Tinder.'

'What a great loss to the world that would be.' He laughed. 'Although I suspect Tinder actually uses mobile phone mast signals rather than satellites to work out your location.'

Gorgeous but geeky, Kate thought.

'Did you know...' he was on a roll now '...that sputnik actually means "fellow traveller" in Russian? That's what I'm looking for. A travelling companion on life's journey.'

Geeky *and* cheesy.

Although good to know he was looking for a proper relationship, rather than a quick fling.

A small crowd gathered round one exhibit. Kate and Xander joined them, and were jostled closer together as people tried to get a better look. They were so close that she could smell him: a fresh, lightly spiced scent, not too overpowering.

'Amazing, isn't it?'

For a second, Kate thought he meant his aftershave. Then she realised he was talking about the exhibit: a small, silver car with a curved bonnet, a curved boot and headlights that stuck up like frog's eyes.

'The Messerschmidt micro-car,' he said, his eyes shining. He became aware of her watching him and smiled. Good teeth, Kate thought. Teeth were important. Kate didn't like kissing men who had poor standards of oral hygiene. She herself flossed every evening without fail.

'Messerschmidt weren't allowed to produce aircraft for a time after the war, so they made these instead,' Xander said.

How did he know this? He hadn't even glanced at the little board with information on.

She racked her brains for something intelligent to say, but heard herself coming out with: 'You'd be great in a pub quiz.'

'I love pub quizzes.'

'Yeah, me too.'

She wasn't quite sure why she'd said that; it couldn't have been further from the truth.

'It has a steering bar rather than a wheel.' He was still peering at the little car. 'Like in a plane.'

'Wonder if anyone ever drove them?'

He shrugged. 'I've got no idea. Perhaps they were a flop like the Sinclair C5.'

The Sinclair C-what?

They moved on. Slowly. Very slowly as Xander studied each and every object. Kate was expecting to find the exhibition boring, but having Xander by her side was like having her own entertaining, overenthusiastic audio guide. Normally first dates consisted of sitting in a café, bar or pub, nursing a coffee or a glass of red, and trying to make conversation. Some men tried to impress her by talking about all their achievements, and barely letting her get a word in edgeways. Others tried too hard to be interested in her, asking question after question so that she felt as if she were being interrogated.

Xander did neither of those things. She had the strongest sense that he was 'being himself', that he wasn't making any extra effort because this was a date, and was simply enjoying himself. Enjoying her company. As a result, she found *his* company relaxing; she couldn't remember feeling this chilled out with someone when she'd only just met them. She couldn't remember feeling this chilled out full stop.

She marvelled at how he managed to make this museum visit interesting with his little nuggets of information. A brightly coloured scarf with four faces and a bird in the middle: Picasso apparently. A radio with three aerials: Kate didn't hear why that was important as she was thinking what surprisingly good company this nerdy man was. A magazine cover with two images of Superman: one had USA on his chest, the other CCCP.

'The two superpowers,' he said. Kate guessed CCCP must be the USSR but didn't like to ask; she didn't want to look ignorant.

He paused for even longer at a photo showing a crowd of men looking at a kitchen.

'IKEA on a Bank Holiday weekend,' Kate said.

Xander laughed again. A sense of humour too. Another tick.

'Nixon and Khrushchev, 1960.' He read the information next to the photo. 'The kitchen debate,' he added.

'I have that on a daily basis. Do I wash up now? Or leave it till the morning?'

'The morning obviously.'

'Obviously.' Kate laughed, though in reality, she *always* washed up straight away. 'Why were they looking at a kitchen? I thought the Cold War was all nuclear weapons and the Berlin Wall.'

'It was. The U-2 incident was only a year after the Kitchen Debate.'

'U2? Was Bono even born then?'

'You're hilarious.' He looked at her for a second, as if he were trying to figure if she was joking or genuinely didn't know what the U-2 incident was. He correctly guessed the latter. 'The U-2 incident was when the Russians shot down an American U-2 spy plane. Relations between the States and the Soviet Union went downhill after that.'

From someone else, this might have felt like mansplaining, but somehow, from Xander's lips, it didn't.

His lips. What might it be like to kiss them?

They stopped at a strange yellow chair. Apparently, it could be folded up into a giant egg.

'You wouldn't get that at IKEA,' Kate said because she liked the way his face looked when he laughed and she loved how he found her funny.

'You seem to know an awful lot about IKEA. I've never been.'

'You mean, you're the one person in the entire world who hasn't got a Billy bookcase?'

'I must be. But now you've mentioned bookcases – well, I always need bookcases.'

'You seem to know a lot about the Cold War,' she said.

'I'm a history lecturer. It's my field. Twentieth-century stuff, but particularly the Cold War.'

'Oh, I see.' She remembered how he hadn't uploaded a photo to Buzzz. 'So why no picture on your dating profile?'

'Half my students are on there.'

Kate nodded. It made sense now. 'Bet they all have a crush on you anyway. Now, tell me, I don't get what Picasso scarves and an egg that turns into a chair has to do with the Cold War.'

'Propaganda,' said Xander. 'The East was competing with the West. They wanted everyone to believe their way – communism – was best. The Russians won the first part of the space race when they launched Sputnik in 1957, then wanted to compete with the Americans on the domestic front. Could a housewife in East Berlin have a better kitchen than a housewife in New York?'

'Okay.' Kate was starting to understand, but couldn't think what to say. There was something compelling about him. He wasn't saying all this to impress her; he simply found it interesting. Whereas her desire to impress him was growing stronger by the minute. She liked this guy. Really liked him.

'Design was all about showing off. Who could create the best products? Create things so perfect that you'd never want to buy another.'

'Sounds like a marketing nightmare,' she said.

'You're in marketing?'

'I am. Bit of a marketing guru if I do say so myself.'

She was hoping to impress him, but regretted the words as soon as they left her lips; it had sounded a little boastful, which wasn't what she intended.

They paused next to a black and white photo of a model, the upper half of her face obscured by a mask.

'Her swimming cap was too big so she had to cut eye holes,' Kate said. 'Or is it a gimp mask? Not that I've any experience of gimp masks.'

'A gimp mask covers the whole face, doesn't it? Isn't that the point? Not that I've any experience either.'

'Good we've got that established on our first date –
neither of us are into BDSM. Tick.' Kate mimed ticking a
box.

Their eyes met.

Xander raised his eyebrows and laughed. 'Now we've
established that all-important fact, I don't suppose you
fancy a second date sometime, do you?'

'Definitely.' She couldn't keep the enthusiasm out of her
voice, and kicked herself. All her self-help books advised
playing it cool, appearing at least a little hard to get. 'A
second date would be lovely. I've had such a good time this
afternoon. I never knew history could be so fascinating.'

Xander looked puzzled and Kate realised her gaff. She
would change that Buzzz profile as soon as she got home.
'Modern history, I mean. I like the older stuff. The Incas
and... er...'

'Aztecs?'

'Oh God, yes. I love the Aztecs. Now, tell me, why have
they got an old black and white telly on display?'

# 6

That wonderful first date with Xander four years ago couldn't have been more different from this evening's rather less wonderful one, Kate thought as she stared out of the carriage window. On the face of it, she and Xander had had so little in common. History was not only his career, it was his passion, and it was a subject that she knew little about, but his enthusiasm had been infectious and she'd found herself genuinely interested in all those strange Cold War exhibits. And she'd found herself even more interested in her unofficial tour guide. He was such easy company, and easy on the eye too.

In contrast, tonight's date had felt like pulling teeth. She shouldn't have accepted Steve's last-minute invitation; should have sussed him out by exchanging more messages first.

But on the other hand, maybe it *was* better to have cut straight to the chase and met up immediately. She'd spent days – weeks, sometimes – exchanging messages with someone in the past, her hopes rising a little further with each fact she gleaned about him, or each interesting question he posed, only to eventually meet him and discover he wasn't the one. Hopes would turn to disappointment; the longer the period of messaging first, the more crushing the disappointment. She imagined some scientist somewhere drawing a graph to show this correlation as if it were a scientifically provable fact. She'd met Steve within a few hours of his first making contact, and consequently wasn't too disappointed now that they weren't a match. The mistake had been in going out for dinner, rather than just meeting for a quick drink. Her dating rules were there for a reason, she reminded herself. Best to stick to them in future.

She was so lost in thought that she almost missed her stop, springing from the train in the nick of time as the doors were about to close.

It had been dry in Leeds, but was raining in Essendale. Kate dodged around the puddles on the platform, rummaging in her bag for her umbrella as she walked, but couldn't find it. She paused at the top of the high street, ducking into a shop doorway to keep dry. She looked at the street of familiar shops, at the '*sold*' sign on Alessandra's, at the puddles on the pavement reflecting the rather dismal Christmas lights that the council had deigned to put up this year. She didn't know why they'd bothered; better to go all out and put on a proper display or do nothing at all. No-one was expecting Blackpool Illuminations, but this half-hearted attempt at making Essendale's main thoroughfare look festive... well, it screamed 'council cuts' rather than 'Christmas cheer'.

The lights were on in the board game café. Even from this distance, Kate could see the place was half-empty, and was that the familiar figure of Harry, sitting in the window, by himself? She knew he always went in on a Thursday evening, but sometimes on a Monday too. Perhaps she'd pop in on her way home, have a green tea and keep him company.

Who was she kidding?

It was Kate, rather than Harry, who needed company. He was a family man these days, and was doubtless in the café for a bit of peace and quiet.

She retrieved her umbrella from the very bottom of her bag and walked on towards the café.

Em was standing behind the counter, chatting animatedly to a customer. She laughed at something the customer said, then spotted Kate in the doorway and waved, clearly delighted to see her. Kate knew then that even if Peter was her perfect match, there was no way she'd risk this friendship. She loved Em like a sister. It was Em who'd got her through the toughest period of her life, back when they were sixteen, even though she was going through the toughest period of her own life at the time. Em who'd supported her during their A-level years. Em who'd helped with her uni applications. Em had always been there for her, and always would be.

And she would always be there for Em, Kate thought.

She waved at Harry, gesturing that she'd order a drink then come over. The other tables, she noticed, were mostly empty. She had to think of something to help attract more visitors to the valley, and get more people through the door of this rather special café.

'Hi Kate.' Em didn't sound her usual cheerful self.

'Em! You okay?'

'Yeah, it's just...' She gestured at the empty tables. 'Are *you* okay? You made a very hasty exit on Saturday. How was your work meeting the following morning?'

Kate harrumphed. They both knew there'd been no work meeting. 'I had a touch of the green-eyed monster; that was all. You lot all loved up. Taylor expecting. When will it happen for me? *Will* it happen for me?'

'It will.'

Across the counter, Kate met Em's eyes, full of love and empathy, and the image of herself and Peter snogging in that hotel room on Friday night flashed into her mind. 'Could I have a green tea, please?' she said, trying to push it away.

'Sure, I'll bring it over.'

Kate pulled up a chair opposite Harry.

'How are you, Kate? On your way back from work? You're late, aren't you?'

She shook her head. 'No, I had a date.'

'Oh? And how was that?'

She grimaced. 'Not great. We went out for dinner, and he called my quinoa budgie food.'

Harry laughed. 'Well, he's got a point.'

'Here you go.' Em placed a green tea in front of Kate, a latte in front of Harry and a game box on the table. 'Azul.' She tapped the lid of the box.

'I'm just here for a chat,' said Kate. 'You know I'm not that into the board games.'

'Please, Kate,' said Em. 'It's a board game café. If anyone walks past, I want them to see people inside having fun playing board games.'

Kate rolled her eyes at Harry. 'Oh, go on then. Why Azul?'

'Because it's very popular, the tiles are beautiful, and it's inspired by the Alhambra Palace in Granada and you did Spanish A level.'

'*Sí*,' said Kate. '*Pero no sé como se dice* "tenuous reason" *en Español.*'

Em laughed. 'Did I overhear you saying you've been on a date?'

'Yes, it was terrible. Honestly, it feels like I'm never going to meet The One. You two are so lucky.'

'I wouldn't have met Lud if it weren't for you dragging me to running club,' said Em.

'Yeah, you would,' said Kate. 'It's a small town. You'd have bumped into each other sooner or later. You might have had some mysterious illness or nasty rash and gone to see him as a patient.'

'Yeah, that would have been romantic,' said Em, '*not. And I'd have been off limits if I'd been his patient.*'

'Love would have found a way,' said Kate dramatically, slapping her hand to her heart.

There was a sudden metallic clatter from the kitchen, followed by the sound of crockery smashing, then more metallic clattering.

'And that,' said Em, 'is the sound of my lovely man wreaking havoc in my kitchen. I'd better go and see what he's done.'

She hurried off, and Harry began laying the game out, placing five colourful cardboard circles on the table. They'd make rather good coasters, Kate thought, but Em wouldn't be happy if they went missing from the box. He placed four little tiles on each coaster – they were, as Emily had said, very pretty – and explained that they'd take it in turns to take tiles from the coasters and place them on their board.

The tiles had different patterns and colours on, and they would score points according to how they were placed on their board.

'The player with the most points at the end wins,' Harry concluded.

That much was obvious, thought Kate.

She picked up four tiles from one of the coasters, placing the two white and blue ones on her board, and discarding the others. 'Does your pregnant girlfriend not mind you coming to the board game café? Doesn't she want you to stay home and curl up on the sofa with her, or massage her back or something?'

Harry collected tiles, placing two red ones on his board. 'No, she's cool with it. Taylor's very independent. It's healthy to have different interests. We've always done some things together and some things apart. Her being pregnant hasn't changed that. Were you surprised when she told you?'

Kate's fingers hovered over two black tiles on one of the coasters. Should she opt for those? Or more of the blue and white ones? 'Very surprised and very happy.' She took a deep breath. 'And a little bit envious, if I'm honest. I wish it was me. Not with you,' she added hastily. 'I didn't mean that. I just wish I could meet someone, settle down and have a child. I felt like a gooseberry on Saturday with you lot all loved up.'

'So that's why you left in such a hurry. I was worried about you.' Harry looked thoughtful. 'Was the man this evening from one of the apps?'

Kate sighed. 'Yeah. From Buzzz.'

'Maybe Mr Right is right under your nose,' said Em.

Kate looked up to see her friend standing beside their

table again. 'Under my nose? Essendale is hardly over-run with eligible bachelors.'

'True, but there's one very eligible bachelor who you haven't dated.' Em looked smug.

She couldn't mean… could she?

'And who's that?' Kate said.

'Isn't it obvious?' Em said. 'Peter.'

'*Your* Peter?'

'He's hardly *my* Peter these days, is he? Look, I know you've never really got on with him, but wasn't that because you didn't think he was right for me? If you think about it, you two would be a brilliant couple. He's the biggest employer in Essendale and you're behind so many wonderful things round here – my café's launch event, the Scrabble festival, the upcycling fashion show. You'd be the Posh 'n' Becks, the Wills 'n' Kate, of the valley. You're both gorgeous-looking. You both dress well. You both like a tidy house.'

Em looked at Kate expectantly, clearly pleased with her idea.

Kate shook her head. 'It wouldn't work, Em.'

Since Friday night, she had a grudging respect for Peter. A liking even. Empathy too, if only over the 'lonely at Christmas' thing. And there was no doubt he was good-looking. Exceptionally good-looking. She'd tried not to think about it, but from what she could remember, they'd had a fun time between those Egyptian cotton sheets. Nevertheless, something had been missing.

Kate wanted that thunderbolt moment that happened in films. She wanted to end up with someone of whom she could later say, 'We looked at each other for the first time and we both knew.'

The first time she'd met Peter? She'd thought, *Em, why are you with this guy? He isn't 'you' at all.*

'There's no spark,' she said now.

'Does there need to be a spark?' said Em. 'I mean, I had that with Ludek. The minute I saw him. But not everyone does, do they? Look at Taylor and Harry. She wasn't that interested when she first met him.'

'Thanks for the reminder,' said Harry drily. 'It's your turn, Kate.'

Kate took the two black tiles and laid them on her board. Should she admit that she and Peter had already spent the night together? That he'd already asked her out?

'Your turn, Harry,' she said.

Harry pursed his lips, weighing up his options.

'You had a spark,' said Em, 'with Rob. And then again with Michael. And those two relationships didn't last.'

Admittedly that was a good point.

'And you and Peter both want to settle down and have children,' Em continued.

'Come on, Em. Just because they're more stylish than the rest of us and they both want children doesn't mean they'd be right for each other,' Harry said.

'It's not *just* that though,' said Em. 'I really think you'd be good together, Kate. Couldn't you go on one date with him? See how you get on?'

Kate bit her lip. She had to tell her.

'The thing is, Em,' she said slowly, 'Peter and I have already spent the night together.'

Harry stood up suddenly, pushing his chair back along the floor with a terrible scraping noise. 'I need to have a quick word with Ludek.'

The two women watched him heading for the kitchen and then looked at each other. Em slipped into Harry's newly vacated seat and leaned forwards across the table towards Kate. 'You slept with Peter?'

'We didn't... I'm so sorry, Em. I bumped into him.'

Kate scrutinised her friend's face, trying to gauge her reaction. Was she upset? Devastated by the betrayal? On the contrary. Her eyes were wide, shining. She was smiling. She looked hungry for information, for gossip, the way she had when they were teenagers, when Kate was sharing the news of her first proper snog.

'When?'

'Friday night. I'm sorry, Em. I should have told you, but I thought you'd be upset. And it was a one-off. I felt sorry for him.'

'Sorry for him?'

'He was saying about Christmas. How he wasn't looking forward to it. He looked so bereft, and I knew how he felt, Em, because it's absolutely crap being single at this time of year. Anyway, he bought me a few drinks, and one thing led to another...' She held up her hands in defeat. 'Are you upset with me?'

'Only cos you didn't tell me,' said Em. 'I thought we told each other everything. But I'm not upset about you and Peter. Has he been in touch?'

'He asked me out for dinner, but I said no.'

'I hope you didn't say no because of me?'

Kate paused. 'Partly. Mostly. I dunno.'

'Kate, you have my blessing to date my ex. If you can make each other happy, go for it. I think you'd be good together. Call him. Tell him you changed your mind.'

# 7

Kate didn't like Christmas. She didn't like weddings. And, until recently, she hadn't liked Peter Ridley.

Now here she was, sitting beside him in a freezing cold chapel at what was clearly going to be a Christmas-themed wedding. Every aisle was adorned with a small wreath: sprigs of fir and pine cones, sprayed with a light dusting of fake snow, and finished off with a white ribbon. There were tall white candles with more fir and pine cones in every window, and Kate had to admit the effect was magical.

She had called Peter from the board game café. Em had insisted on listening in and seemed ridiculously excited at the thought of her ex and her bestie getting together; she was generous like that – she was happy with Ludek and wanted everyone else to be happy too. Kate had told Peter that she'd changed her mind, that she'd like to accept his dinner invitation after all, and that Em had given her blessing. She wondered if he'd be free the following weekend.

Peter had said no, he was sorry but he was away at a wedding. Then he'd hesitated and said, 'Unless…'

'Unless?' Kate had said.

Em had pressed her face against Kate's, trying to hear every word of the conversation.

'You could come,' Peter had said. 'I did say I'd be bringing a plus-one.'

'Say yes,' Em had mouthed.

Kate had turned away from her. 'Oh, Peter, I'm not sure…'

'It's in a lovely hotel,' he'd said. 'I can book another room. I don't want to rush you into anything. It's just… my ex is going to be there.'

'Em's going to be there?' Kate had been confused. She'd turned back to Em who looked similarly confused.

'No, no. The woman I was dating before Emily. I hate weddings. They're like Christmas, aren't they? They remind me of what I'm missing out on. You know, since the split with Em.'

Em had pouted, clutching her hands to her heart, and cocking her head on one side like a Labrador pleading for more food. 'Say yes,' she'd mouthed again.

Kate's heart had gone out to Peter. Weddings were difficult – even more so if an ex was one of the other guests – and she'd found herself agreeing. So now here she was, sitting on a hard pew in a chilly chapel with a load of people she'd never seen before in her life.

'Are you okay?' whispered Peter.

She nodded. 'I'm a bit cold.'

He stood up and removed his cashmere overcoat, draping it round her shoulders.

'No, really, Peter, you'll freeze,' she said.

'I'm fine,' he said. He took her hands in his, and began to rub them together in an attempt to warm them up. 'Hopefully it won't be too long a ceremony and there'll be a huge log fire at the reception venue.'

'Hopefully,' said Kate. She glanced around, scanning the sea of faces. 'Which one's your ex?'

Peter smiled, still holding her hands. 'She's not here yet.'

The vicar indicated that the congregation should stand for the entrance of the bride. A piano version of 'Somewhere Only We Know' began to play; Kate vaguely remembered that the song had been used as the music for the John Lewis Christmas ad a few years back and cringed, remembering how much she hated those festive television adverts.

'She must be freezing too,' she hissed to Peter as the bride and her father began to walk up the aisle. But the bride looked anything but cold; she radiated warmth, giving shy little smiles and waves to the watching friends and family as she made her way towards her groom. She looked like she'd stepped straight out of Narnia, in a simple, dazzlingly white gown – no frills, lace or flounces, just an understated elegance that Kate couldn't help but admire – with a mass of blonde, curly hair, a silver tiara and a midnight blue velvet cape.

'That,' whispered Peter, as the bride gave him a little wave, 'is my ex.'

Kate squeezed his hand. She'd never been to the wedding of an ex-boyfriend, but this couldn't be easy for Peter. It hadn't worked out with... she didn't even know the bride's name. Then he'd got together with Em, and it hadn't worked out with her either. If you'd told her a few weeks ago that she'd be standing here in a chapel feeling – well, what was she feeling exactly? Pity? Empathy? – for Peter Ridley *and* holding his hand, for heaven's sake, she wouldn't have believed it. Yet here she was. She looked at Peter's face, at the forced smile behind which she could see the disappointment. He'd cared about and lost this woman, and was about to watch her marry another man.

She sighed, her heart full of longing. Not because of the picture-perfect chapel where the ceremony was taking place nor the delicate little posies that adorned the end of every pew, but because she wanted someone to look at her the way the groom was looking at the bride now as she reached the top of the aisle.

The last chord of the piano music rippled through the air.

'You look incredible,' the groom said softly to his bride. He couldn't take his eyes off her.

The bride blushed as she handed her flowers to her bridesmaid.

'So do you,' Peter whispered in Kate's ear.

'Thank you,' she said.

The vicar indicated that everyone should be seated, and Kate stole a glance at the man beside her. She remembered when Em had first met Peter. She'd been buzzing about him, unable to believe her luck. 'He's so handsome,' she had said. 'Brooding dark eyes. Hair is so perfect that it looks like the plastic hair on an action figure.'

Kate wasn't sure that hair that looked plastic was a plus point in a man, but she did like the way that Peter was always immaculately groomed. And always in the right clothes for the occasion too. The man did 'smart' exceedingly well, but he could pull off casual too, whether it was 'country walk' or 'city break' or 'relaxed evening with friends' kind of casual.

He wasn't Em's usual kind of man; she'd always gone for quirky guys before, and had reverted to type when she met Ludek. Em and Peter had always seemed like a mismatch. In fact, Kate thought now, she herself was a much better fit for him. She'd never considered Peter before – he'd always been out of bounds – but now realised that the two of them looked good together. They'd attracted a few admiring glances from other guests as they'd walked up the path to the chapel a little earlier.

They both wanted a family.

And liked a tidy house.

And they both loved Emily.

Did Peter *still* love Em? Kate wondered, as she mouthed the words to the first hymn. She never sang, because she wasn't ever sure that she was in tune, and if she couldn't do something perfectly, well, she simply didn't do it at all.

Peter, on the other hand, was belting out 'O Little Town of Bethlehem' in a hearty baritone.

Carols already. It was still November.

The music ended and the congregation sat down again.

'She always wanted a Christmas wedding,' whispered Peter, 'but she couldn't get a Saturday in December.'

The vicar began the business of marrying Clare in her Narnia dress to David in his pinstripe grey suit, asking if anyone had any objections to the proposed union.

'Thank you for coming with me,' whispered Peter.

'No problem.'

'Who gives this woman to be joined to this man?' said the vicar.

As the bride's father stepped forwards, Kate's mind began to drift. What, she wondered, could be done to attract more people to the valley over the winter? To ensure that more shops didn't close as Alessandra's had? The holiday lets were here to stay – there was no turning the clock back – but what they needed was for the visitors to continue coming, even when the nights grew longer and the weather colder. A few social media posts weren't going to be enough. They needed to do something to create a bigger splash.

The best man was proffering the rings now. Kate glanced at Peter; he was welling up. She'd never had him down as a romantic. She opened her handbag, pulled out her pocket-sized packet of Kleenex and handed them to him. He dabbed at his cheek, then blew his nose so loudly that the bride's mother turned round and gave him a hard stare. Kate stifled a giggle. Peter's eyes met hers and he gave a fake grimace.

'Whoops,' he said softly.

After more Christmas carols and prayers and the signing of the register, the ceremony was over and the congregation began to follow the bride and groom out of the chapel. Peter offered Kate his arm. 'Shall we?'

She hesitated before taking it. They walked out into the November sunshine, where the photographer was calling for the bride's family to get in position for a photo.

Kate stood beside Peter, feeling like a spare part.

The photographer called, 'Friends of the bride.'

'Do you think that's us?' said Peter. 'Or is there a special category? Exes of the happy couple? The ones they dumped along the way to true love?'

Kate laughed. 'If she didn't still see you as a friend, she wouldn't have invited you.'

'Good point.' He put a hand in the small of her back and steered her towards the happy couple.

He introduced her briefly, then she watched him kiss the bride on both cheeks, and shake the groom's hand, saying, 'You're a lucky man. I wish you both every happiness.'

Gracious, she thought. Even in defeat.

When the photographs were finally over and Kate's jaw was aching from smiling so much, they climbed into Peter's BMW and formed part of a convoy of cars from the tiny chapel to the country house hotel where the reception was taking place.

The guests were gathering in a large room. Waiters circulated with trays of drinks and canapés: mini-Yorkshire puddings filled with turkey and cranberry and smoked salmon blinis. A large flat-screen television stood in one corner of the room, already displaying a selection of pictures from the wedding ceremony. The wonders of digital photography, Kate thought, and steered Peter over to get a closer look. The chapel looked even more magical in the photos than it had in real life, the bride even more radiant.

Suddenly there was a photo of herself and Peter on the screen. They were standing arm in arm outside, chatting to each other, and it struck Kate how perfect the two of them looked together.

'We make a good couple.' Peter was clearly thinking along the same lines that she was. 'Shall I go and get us another drink?'

Kate stayed where she was, staring at the screen. The

pictures had moved on now, to photos of other guests, group shots of friends and family, a candid photo of the bride touching the groom's cheek, yet in her mind's eye, Kate still saw herself with Peter, saw how well-matched they were.

And then suddenly she pictured herself with Xander. She had always tried not to think about him, to put him to the back of her mind, but she couldn't help herself now, perhaps because of that guy she'd seen in Essendale who had looked so similar. She and Xander didn't look nearly as good together – they didn't fit: her in her smart clothes, him in his scruffy jeans – yet there'd been enormous chemistry with Xander. That undefinable something that you couldn't create. If it was there, it was there. And with Xander, it had definitely been there, but then she'd gone and blown it with him.

Still, what did it matter? She was with Peter. Now where was he and where were those drinks?

The wedding breakfast was held in another large room, dominated by an enormous Christmas tree. The meal itself was a Christmas dinner, complete with all the trimmings. As most of the guests oohed over the roast potatoes and pigs in blankets, Kate seized on the opportunity to eat four of her ten a day, and piled her plate with carrots, parsnips, cauliflower in a rather tasty cheese sauce, and sprouts cooked with bacon and maple syrup. The speeches were interminable, and she found her mind drifting again to the tricky problem of how to attract more visitors to Essendale and Hebbleswick over the winter months.

There was plenty of inspiration right here in this room, she thought, as the best man began to reel off a whole string of clichéd jokes he'd clearly grabbed from the internet. The tables oozed with Christmassy-ness. In the centre of each one was a group of three white candles surrounded by sprigs of fir, white roses and mistletoe. In each place was a wedding favour, a small wrapped-up gift, with the recipient's name and a tiny silver bauble tied on with a white ribbon. Snowflake-shaped confetti was strewn across the table.

When the meal was over and the Christmas-themed wedding cake had been cut, the guests had followed the bride and groom outside, and the women had crowded together to try to catch the bouquet. And Kate hadn't intended to catch it – didn't mean to try – but all those years at school of trying to be the best netball player she could possibly be, to make her mum proud of her, meant it was almost a reflex to stretch her arm up and grab it before anyone else could.

Then they'd piled back inside, with everyone laughing and saying to her, 'It'll be you next!' and Peter had looked at her coyly, and said, 'Good catch, Kate.'

The room had been cleared of tables and 'All I Want for Christmas' began to play. The bride and groom took to the floor for their first dance – a nauseatingly choreographed number – then Peter took Kate's hand and led her to the dance floor, slipping his hands around her waist. She nestled into him, enjoying the proximity of another human body.

And a little later, as they walked down the hotel corridor to their respective rooms, she paused for that fraction of a second too long outside Peter's room when he said, 'Well, this is me.' Paused, in fact, for long enough for his lips to brush her cheek, then make their way to her lips. And before she knew it, she was inside his room and the door was closing behind them, with that satisfying clunk that only hotel room doors make.

# 8

Kate opened her eyes and stared at the unfamiliar ceiling. The all-too-familiar figure of her best friend's ex-fiancé lay in bed beside her.

She had slept with Peter.

Again.

Although admittedly, not much sleeping had taken place this time.

She hadn't intended to rush into things like that, but the mood had overtaken her, the romance of that silvery-white wedding. And there was nothing stopping them now, not since Em had given her blessing. Not only her blessing either; she was positively encouraging them to get together. Finding herself once again in a bedroom with Peter, one thing had quite naturally led to another. He was a dark horse, that Peter. She wouldn't have thought he had it in him to be so adventurous. All those years with Em, her friend had never let on. He'd put on quite a performance.

But that's what it had felt like: a performance. In fact,

looking back, all of yesterday had been a performance, hadn't it? Showing up looking like the perfect couple. Peter and his perfect baritone in the chapel. Posing for photos. The relaxed conversations with other guests as if he hadn't a care in the world, when she knew he was finding the whole watching-an-ex-get-married-to-someone-else thing difficult, even though he claimed to be pleased for her. And had he been thinking, *This should have been me and Emily?* Kate wasn't sure.

And then the pair of them on the dance floor... that hadn't felt quite real somehow. As if Peter was dancing with her not for his own benefit or enjoyment, nor for hers, but to put on a show. She couldn't have explained it properly, why she thought this. It was just a feeling.

Perhaps she was being silly. Paranoid.

Kate stole a glance at him. Even asleep, he was a beautiful man. So many people slept with their mouths open. Not Peter. He looked so perfect as he slept, an expression of complete contentment on his face, and not a hair out of place, even after all of their antics a few hours earlier. She smiled to herself, remembering Em's comment about Peter's 'plastic' hair.

She glanced at her phone. Quarter to eight. It felt earlier than that, but then it had been after six when they'd finally fallen asleep. Her mouth felt dry. She could murder a green tea. Or better still, a coffee. The dining room would be open by now. She was loath to wake Peter when he was sleeping so peacefully, so decided she'd go back to her own room, have a shower, then go downstairs in search of breakfast.

She slid out of bed, retrieved her dress from where it lay draped across a chair – Peter's doing presumably – and pulled it over her head. She glanced at the bridal bouquet, sitting on the dressing table; she should probably have put that in water. Bit late now. Then clutching her shoes, bag, knickers and bra, she opened the door and stuck her head out into the hallway, checking that no-one else was about. The coast was clear. She closed the door behind her as quietly as she could, then ran the few metres to her own room in her bare feet.

She texted Peter, explaining where she was, then showered, and dressed in a pair of tight jeans with a long cashmere sweater. She looked pretty good for someone who'd had barely any sleep, she thought, putting on a touch of mascara then running a comb through her hair. Since Peter hadn't replied – still asleep presumably – she headed downstairs in search of caffeine.

The hotel dining room was crowded, full of people Kate vaguely recognised from the previous day. She was scanning the room for an empty table, when a few heads turned in her direction. A buzz ran through the dining room and suddenly the entire room seemed to be staring at her, and then they began to applaud, some even getting to their feet. Someone whistled, and Kate wondered what on earth was going on. She and Peter had cut quite a dash on the dance floor the previous evening, but it had hardly been *Strictly Come Dancing*.

And then the bride and groom swept past her and she realised that they hadn't been applauding her at all, but the happy couple's appearance. She watched as they made their way to a table by the window, shaking hands and greeting their guests as they went, and suddenly she felt out of place.

'Can I help you, madam?'

A waiter was beside her now.

'Is there somewhere quieter I could have a coffee?' she said. 'And perhaps a spot of breakfast?'

'Come this way.'

She followed him through the oak-panelled hallway of the hotel, through a doorway, and into an old-fashioned library, with floor-to-ceiling bookcases and a pair of sofas in the middle on either side of a coffee table.

'This is perfect,' Kate said.

'What can I get for you?'

'Coffee and perhaps some scrambled eggs, please?'

'Certainly, madam. Anything with the eggs? Some toast perhaps? Bacon?'

Kate shook her head, but he continued making suggestions. 'Mushrooms? Tomatoes? Rosti? The chef is from Switzerland and he's renowned for his rosti.'

'Actually, that does sound delicious. Scrambled eggs, with mushrooms, tomatoes and rosti would be lovely. Thank you.'

As she waited for her breakfast, she wondered if Peter was awake yet, and sent him another text to let him know she was in the library, then she picked up one of the glossy magazines that lay on the coffee table and began to leaf through it.

It was full of the usual stuff you got in magazines at this time of year: party dresses, recipes for Christmas dinner, top gifts for him, top gifts for her. Nothing to write home about. There was a feature on making your own Christmas tree decorations, but Kate never bothered with a tree.

And then a picture caught her eye. A photo of a town square, its buildings softly lit against the night sky. Judging from the style of architecture, this was in Austria perhaps. Or Germany. The most impressive building had a colonnade, and above it, two rows of windows, all lit up in different colours. Where was this magical place?

Gengenbach in the Black Forest, according to the caption.

'Madam.' The waiter placed a tray in front of her on the low table. 'Can I get you anything else?'

'No, that's fine, thank you,' Kate said automatically. Her mind was elsewhere; the cogs were beginning to turn.

She forked some scrambled eggs into her mouth, barely tasting them as she read about the town in Germany. According to the article, around a hundred thousand visitors descended each year over the festive season. The building in the picture was the town hall; during December, it was transformed into an enormous Advent calendar. Each of those coloured windows was a display. Kate squinted at the photo, trying to get a closer look. Every evening in December in the run-up to Christmas, a new window display was revealed.

What if they did the same in Essendale?

Okay, so they wouldn't get a hundred thousand visitors, but it might draw a few people in.

Only they didn't have an impressive town hall.

In fact, Kate couldn't think of a single building in the valley that had twenty-four big windows, but she could think of twenty-four buildings that had large windows where you could set up Christmas displays. What if they created some kind of trail, with a map, so that visitors could walk between the windows, thereby seeing more of what Hebbleswick and Essendale had to offer? Each display might be specific to the building. The board game café could fill its windows with Christmas board games, the florist with Christmas wreaths. Perhaps the two primary schools would join in.

She absent-mindedly forked a piece of rosti into her mouth, still mulling over her windows idea. God, that rosti was good. Crispy, yet buttery.

The secret to a good rosti was clarified butter apparently. For a second, she couldn't remember how she knew that, but then she remembered. Xander. They'd once had a conversation about rosti; they were one of his favourite foods, and he'd prided himself on being able to make them. She had to stop thinking about him. He was two hundred miles away in London and had probably forgotten all about her, whilst upstairs in this very hotel was a man with whom she potentially had a future.

She put Xander and his culinary expertise to the back of her mind, and focused on her Christmas windows idea. It would be like a giant, walking Advent calendar, she decided. She laid her fork down and googled 'walking Advent calendar'. It seemed she wasn't the first with this idea. Other towns – including some in West Yorkshire – had had a version of her windows trail in previous years. They were known as 'living Advent calendars', rather than 'walking'. She flicked through the pictures; there were some absolutely gorgeous displays: reindeer, angels, wintry forests and fairy lights, lots and lots of fairy lights. It didn't matter that it had been done before; in fact, it might help her persuade the shopkeepers and residents of the valley that it was worthwhile. And they wouldn't only put up fairy lights and pictures; they'd create a variety of 3D displays.

Kate normally had a notebook where she jotted down

ideas, but she hadn't brought it this weekend; you could hardly carry an enormous handbag at a wedding. She pulled out her purse and dug out a small bundle of scrunched-up receipts, flattening them out.

'Is everything okay with your breakfast, madam?'

She looked up to see the waiter beside her, concern on his face as he looked at her practically untouched plate.

'Sorry, it's delicious, yes,' she said. 'I don't suppose I could borrow a pen, could I please?'

When Peter entered the library a few minutes later, he found Kate frantically scribbling on bits of paper, her eggs and rosti still only half eaten on the table in front of her.

'What do you think?' she said to him an hour later, as they set off towards Essendale in Peter's BMW. He hadn't said a word as she'd outlined her living Advent calendar idea.

'Would you organise it?'

'Me? No. It needs someone who's good at organising *and* likes Christmas. Jo is the obvious candidate. I'd just do the marketing. Is it a mad idea?'

He took his hand off the steering wheel and squeezed her hand. 'It's a great idea.' Replacing his hand on the wheel, he glanced in the rear-view mirror then said, 'Actually I've had an idea myself.'

'To attract more visitors to Essendale?'

'No.' He paused for a moment, focusing on the traffic, as he turned right onto a busy A road. 'No, not about that. I was wondering… I think you and I would be good together, Kate. I'd like to date you properly. Is that a mad idea?'

When she'd left Essendale on Saturday morning, Kate hadn't had a clue how she was going to go about transforming the valley's fortunes and attracting more visitors to their two towns. By the time Peter's Beamer drew up outside her little terraced house, she had a mission. And not only that, she'd agreed to date Peter.

# 9

There were two people you probably didn't want to see the day after a night of passion with a man you'd recently started dating. One was that new man's ex – even if she did approve – but Kate was dying to tell Em about the living Advent calendar idea, so had arranged to meet her and Jo in the board game café. The other person was *your* ex, the one you'd never been quite able to get out of your head even though the two of you had only ever had a handful of dates – not enough really to even call him an ex – and you knew you weren't suited to each other so it would never have worked out anyway.

And yet there he was again, heading towards Costa Coffee: the guy who looked like Xander. He had his hands in his pockets, the way Xander always did; she'd never known him wear gloves. That same bouncing step. And the scarf. It was the scarf more than anything that made her think this was Xander.

But then lots of people wore a scarf in the winter. And he

was too far away and the day was far too gloomy for her to see what sort of scarf it was. It could have been anything. But then again, it could have been Xander's university scarf, the one he always wore.

Always wore in the winter anyway.

She pushed open the door of the board game café, still thinking about Xander, realising now that she didn't know what he looked like on a summer's day. They'd met at the beginning of November and by mid-December, it was all over. Did he walk with his hands out of his pockets in the warmer months? Was the scarf consigned to the wardrobe? Did he get his knees out and wear shorts? For all she knew, he wore socks under his sandals. She smiled to herself; now that *would* be a deal-breaker.

Em looked up from the till. 'Someone's happy.'

'Yeah, yeah, I am,' said Kate.

'You're positively glowing. More than Taylor and she's pregnant. I'm guessing things went well with Peter at the wedding.'

'Yeah, they did.'

'I knew you'd be a good match – I knew it,' said Em gleefully. 'Look at you, Kate. You look smitten *already*.'

'Don't be daft.'

Things *were* going well with Peter. She had had a lovely time at the wedding and a lovely time afterwards in that hotel room too. But smitten? No. Not yet, anyway. The glowing cheeks were because she'd stepped from a frosty street into a cosy, warm café. Or because she was bursting with excitement about her living Advent calendar idea.

Or because she'd seen Xander.

No. That wasn't Xander. And even if it were, what did

it matter? Their brief rel... no, she couldn't even call it a relationship. Their brief dalliance had been over years ago. He wasn't right for her.

'Have you time for a tea break, Em?'

Em gestured at the almost empty café. 'Unless we get a sudden rush of people, yes, I have time for a tea break.' She turned away, poking her head through the serving hatch into the kitchen. 'Lud, any chance you could serve for me please? So I can have a break and chat to Kate?'

'Sure,' came the reply. He emerged from the kitchen seconds later. 'You two sit down; I'll make the drinks. One normal tea and one green tea coming right up. Now Kate, I don't suppose I can tempt you with a slice of *makowiec*. Fresh from the oven.'

She shook her head. 'Thanks for the offer, but I think I'll pass.'

'I'll try it,' said Em.

They walked past the only two occupied tables, where games of Wingspan and Ticket to Ride were in full swing, and took a seat in the window.

Like many November days in Essendale, it was grey and drizzly. The rain streaked down the window of the café. Few people had ventured out of their homes, but those who had wore anoraks and carried umbrellas. The geese were huddled together, sheltering in the doorway of the Costa across the road. But nothing could dampen Kate's mood as she sat opposite her friend.

'So tell me all,' said Em. 'How was the wedding? Are you and Peter...?' She stopped as Ludek arrived at their table, bearing a tray with two steaming mugs and a slab of cake. 'Thanks, Lud.'

'Yeah, thanks,' said Kate. She waited till he was heading back towards the counter, the empty tray tucked under his arm before she continued. 'The wedding was lovely, and yes, I think Peter and I are... well, we're dating. But we can chat about that later. Or not. I don't know how much detail you want given that you and he were...'

Really, this whole situation with Peter was odd. Dating your best mate's ex. But she supposed she'd get used to it. Anyway, she wasn't here to talk about him. She was here to talk about the living Advent calendar, to get Em – and Jo when she arrived – on board.

She glanced out of the window, trying to picture how the high street would look if the project went ahead. Perhaps there would be Christmas books in the library's big window and something creative in the Oxfam shop. And lights – there *had* to be more lights. Lots of them. The town had to sparkle.

And then there he was again, coming out of Costa, with a takeaway cup in his hand. He reached down and ruffled the feathers on the top of one of the geese's heads, and it didn't attempt to peck him. What was he? Some kind of goose whisperer?

'What's that smile for?' said Em. 'Are you thinking of Peter?'

'I thought I saw someone I knew.'

Em looked puzzled. 'This is Essendale. You know everyone.'

For some reason, Kate had never told Em about Xander. Every other man she'd ever dated, but not him. It had happened two hundred miles away, for a start, when she'd been on that secondment in London. And it had been so brief. And nothing had really happened; they'd barely kissed. She'd realised he wasn't suitable, wasn't what she was looking for, so what was there to tell?

*I went on a few dates with a gorgeous man who was great company, but we didn't have much in common. And then the deal-breaker. The inevitable deal-breaker. And then it was over. The End.*

She and Xander didn't have much of a story.

And yet...

And yet here he was now – or at least, here was a man who *looked* like Xander – and she felt completely discombobulated.

And Em knew something was up, and was staring at her questioningly.

'A blast from the past,' Kate said, trying to keep her tone light. 'Not someone I expected to see round here, but it probably wasn't him anyway. Just someone who bears a bit of a resemblance.'

'Who are we talking about, Kate? A bit of a resemblance to who exactly?'

Kate shrugged. 'A guy off a dating app from years ago. We had a few dates. It didn't go anywhere. It was when I was in London.'

'You never mentioned dating anyone in London.'

'Like I said, it was only a few dates. We had nothing in common. He took me to an exhibition about the Cold War on our first date.'

*A guy off a dating app. Only a few dates. Nothing in common.*

And yet she'd never quite got him out of her system. It was the way he'd laughed at her jokes. The enthusiasm, the passion, as he'd talked her through that exhibition. The easy conversation, so different from most first dates where both parties were trying to impress the other. Being with Xander was like going to the world's best yoga class and feeling every muscle – no, every cell – in your body relaxing.

'A Cold War exhibition!' Em said. 'And I thought Lud was geeky. He's got a game about the Cold War. It's over there somewhere.' She gestured towards the shelves of board games. 'Don't think anyone's ever played it. You could invite your chap in for a game. If it was him.'

'It wasn't him.' Kate looked out of the window again. The man was nowhere to be seen, but Jo was hurrying across the road towards the café, giving them a cheery wave.

The door swung open. 'Sorry, I'm late,' Jo called, rushing over to the table and peeling off her coat.

Greetings were exchanged and an extra mug of tea and slice of cake brought for Jo, and then Kate finally began to explain the reason why she'd wanted to talk to them both.

'You know how we talked about how trade isn't great,' she said, 'and the shops are struggling. Including the café.'

Em glanced round. 'Certainly do. I'm worried, Kate. Seriously worried. This is my dream. I can't lose this. I've already started again once. If this one fails, I'm going to get a normal job.'

Jo looked up from the hot mug of tea she was cradling in her hands. 'Things are really that bad?'

'For two weeks running, I've made a loss.' Em bit her lip. 'Not a big one, but still, a loss is a loss. I do well in the spring and summer, and the first couple of months in the autumn, but then people don't venture out in the evenings when the weather is cold. They stay at home and watch telly instead of coming here to play board games. I'm not expecting to make massive profits over the winter, but I do need to break even.'

Kate reached over and took Em's hand, giving it a gentle rub. She didn't know if her idea would be enough, if it would really draw people out of their homes in the cold weather, and attract more visitors to their valley, but it was surely worth a try. 'Okay, so I had an idea.' She paused, torn between wanting to sell her idea to Em, to get her on board, and not wanting to raise her hopes too much. 'It mightn't work, but we could give it a go. It'd be fun too.'

'Well, tell us then,' said Em. 'We're all ears.'

Kate took a sip of her green tea, scalding her tongue. She was excited about the idea of the living Advent calendar, but anxious now too, conscious of how much was riding on it. The café's future. Em's future. The future of Essendale's other small businesses. It was ridiculous to think that a few festive window displays could transform things for the small town, wasn't it? But then it was better than nothing.

'My idea,' she said slowly, 'is to turn Essendale and Hebbleswick into a living Advent calendar.'

She outlined the concept, scrutinising her friends' faces for their reaction.

'It's brilliant,' said Em. 'I love it. Like you said, it might work. It might not. But it should be fun. And given that this year's festive lights are a bit pathetic, it might brighten up the towns too. Give them more of a Christmassy feel. What do we need to do?'

'Well, the first thing is obviously to find someone who'd organise it. And Jo, I thought you'd be the obvious candidate. You love Christmas and you're brilliant at organising, and I'll do all your publicity obviously and—'

'No, Kate. Stop,' said Jo. 'I couldn't possibly. Sorry.'

'Oh.' Kate didn't know what to say. She'd been counting on Jo saying yes.

'If it wasn't December,' said Jo, 'then of course, I'd love to help.'

'We can hardly do an Advent calendar in March, can we?' Kate tried but failed to keep the disappointment out of her voice.

'I really am sorry, but Christmas is one of the busiest times of year at school. I'm rushed off my feet. I can't take anything else on. And there's not much time either. People usually spend months organising things like this.' She stopped for a moment, then put down her tea and added, 'I don't mean that to sound so discouraging. Why don't you do it yourself? You're every bit as capable as me.'

Kate sighed. 'I'm not sure. The organising *and* the publicity? And I hate Christmas. Hardly the person to be organising a Christmas event. Maybe we should forget the whole thing.'

'No,' cried Em, a little too loudly. The players at the neighbouring table looked up from their game of Wingspan. Em leaned across the table towards Kate and Jo, and lowered her voice. 'We can't forget it. The town is so dreary with those pathetic lights the council have put up. This would cheer everyone up. We could do the first window in the board game café, and make a bit of an event of it. Have mulled wine and mince pies afterwards. I'd have to get a temporary licence to serve alcohol, but I can look into that. And if not, Yorkshire tea and mince pies. Almost as good.'

'Sounds wonderful, doesn't it, Kate?' said Jo.

Kate nodded absent-mindedly. In her mind, she was picturing the café full of people, Em wearing a silly Christmas outfit and smiling as she handed round the mince pies. Kate could almost smell the mulled wine.

'And even though I can't organise it, you know I'll support it,' Jo continued. 'Perhaps Hebbleswick Primary could do a window?'

Kate nodded. 'I've already drawn up a list of places with big windows that might work, and the school's on that list. Essendale Primary too.'

'Ooh, window wars. We'll have to make sure ours is better.' Jo laughed. 'Kate, it sounds like you're *already* organising this. You've got the list. What other places are on there?'

'Mostly shops. The library. And maybe a couple of private homes if people were willing.'

'The health centre's got a big window,' said Em. 'We could ask Lud and Razz, couldn't we, Jo?'

Jo nodded. 'Good idea. Kate, why don't you arrange a meeting and invite everyone along and see how many people want to participate?'

'You can use the upstairs of the board game café,' said Em through a mouthful of makowiec.

'Great,' said Jo. 'You'll need to crack on with it as it's mid-November now. Two weeks for the first venues to create their displays and for you to kick the publicity machine into motion. It's not much time, but it's doable.'

'If anyone can pull it off, it's you, Kate,' said Em. 'I have every confidence in you. Kompleet Marketing's employee of the year not once, but three times.'

Kate laughed. 'Oh, Em, I don't know.'

There were so many reasons to forget about the whole thing. The whole Christmas vibe – she didn't feel it. There wasn't much time; not only would she have to get everyone on board and make sure there would be a wide variety of different windows, but she'd have to organise a trail map and get that printed too, and there was all the marketing. And would it even work? If it didn't bring in the tourists, there was little point in going to all that effort.

'I know *exactly* what our window is going to look like already,' said Em. 'I'm going to put a Christmas tree in the window, and put loads of presents underneath it. Some will be wrapped, some will look as if they've just been unwrapped. And of course, all of the presents will be board games. I'll decorate the tree obviously, and there'll be loads of fairy lights, and stockings hanging up, and oooh, how about this?' Her eyes were bright with excitement. 'How about I put a tray there too, with a half-eaten carrot, a half-eaten mince pie, an empty sherry glass and a bottle of sherry, as if Santa has been?'

Kate looked at her friend's face; Em looked like a child herself on Christmas morning, discovering that Santa had indeed been. She had no idea if her idea really would persuade more visitors to brave the cold and visit the valley in December, but she had to try, didn't she? She and Em had always stuck together through thick and thin, and this was thin – Em had said the business was really struggling. If it got a few more feet through the door, it was worth it, wasn't it?

'Your window sounds lovely, Em,' she said. 'Go on then. I'll organise it. Let's turn this valley into a winter wonderland and hope people flock from miles around to see it.'

## IO

First dates were always exciting. The wardrobe doors would be open, there'd be a selection of outfits laid out on the bed, and Kate would be in a quandary about which one to wear. Hair would be washed, blow-dried and straightened into her characteristic sleek bob. The usually immaculate bathroom would be in disarray, with hair products and make-up everywhere – she would tidy up later. Her stomach would be turning somersaults, wondering if tonight would be the night, if this man would be The One. Because you never knew, did you, when life would take an unexpected turn, and something you'd spent years longing for – and had almost given up hope of ever finding – would finally come your way.

This evening, Kate looked at her hair in the bathroom mirror and decided that since she was running slightly late, she didn't really need to wash it. A bit of product and the straighteners and it would be absolutely fine. She opened the wardrobe doors and knew exactly what she'd wear for her first date with Peter: her navy cashmere sweater dress. Strangely enough, her stomach was not turning somersaults; it wasn't even doing a forward roll.

Where was that first-date excitement?

But then this wasn't *really* a first date. It wasn't like a date with a *new* man. She'd known Peter for years. He knew what she looked like. He knew what she looked like *naked*, for heaven's sake. They'd been to that wedding together, and before that, there'd been that evening in the pub in Leeds, so this was really a third date, not a first.

And there was the rub. She didn't have third-date excitement either.

Third-date excitement was usually even better than first-date excitement. By a third date, you knew you liked someone, and were pretty sure they liked you too; they'd hardly be on a third date with you otherwise. She usually didn't kiss a guy on a first or a second date, so on date three, there'd be the anticipation of that first kiss. If her stomach turned somersaults on a first date, by the third, it was doing a whole gymnastic routine.

But this evening: nothing. Not even a flutter.

Perhaps it was because they'd already spent the night together. That will-he-kiss-me-won't-he-kiss-me excitement wasn't there.

'It doesn't matter,' she said to herself in the mirror. 'It's only because you know Peter already. It doesn't mean it isn't right or that it won't work out.'

She applied a second coat of mascara to her upper lashes.

'Em thinks you and Peter make a good couple. Em knows you better than anyone. She probably knows Peter better than anyone, with the exception of his mother.' She shuddered, thinking of Mrs Ridley, wondering if she'd one day make her life as difficult as she used to make Em's. 'If Em thinks he might be right for you, you've got to give it a proper chance, Kate. You're not getting any younger.'

Perhaps she'd been putting too much emphasis on finding someone with whom she felt the spark. If she had a pound for all the times she'd said to Em during their post-date analysis sessions, 'He was nice, Em, but there was no spark', well, she'd have a tenner at least. She'd bought into that Hollywood version of romance, was expecting one day to have her meet-cute moment, for the thunderbolt to strike, for her stomach not only to do a whole gymnastic routine but one worthy of Olympic gold. She'd read all those dating self-help books with that goal in mind, but what if it was nonsense? Surely it was lust, pure and simple, that led to that initial stomach-flipping moment with another human being. Chemicals in the brain going crazy. The stuff of a teenage crush, rather than a proper grown-up relationship. You needed a more solid foundation to build something long-lasting, and Peter ticked so many boxes.

He was an attractive man, there was no denying that.

Financially secure with his own house.

Trustworthy.

Kind. Look at how supportive he'd been when Em was struggling with her first café, even though they'd split up by that point.

Well respected. A real pillar of the community here in Essendale.

He had so much going for him.

There was a knock at the door. That'd be him now. Some men she'd dated in the past would have sat in their car and tooted their horn. Not Peter. He'd made an effort to find a parking space – not always easy in Essendale's narrow streets, constructed at a time before cars existed, let alone before most households owned one. Or two, as her neighbours did.

She checked her appearance one last time and went downstairs to greet him, still trying to convince herself that this was what a grown-up relationship felt like and all those times in the past when she'd been beside herself with excitement about a first date were just silly teenage crushes.

Peter was standing on the doorstep, impeccably dressed in chinos, a casual shirt under a cable knit jumper, and a long woollen overcoat, which wasn't buttoned up.

She grabbed her coat and bag, and followed him to the spot where his shiny BMW was parked. The car chirruped as he clicked his key fob, and he opened the passenger door for her to step in, then closed it afterwards. The gesture was perhaps a little old-fashioned, but Kate rather liked it. It was gentlemanly. Chivalrous. It was Peter down to a tee.

It was only a short distance to Hebbleswick. They could have walked to the Red Lion for a drink, but Peter wasn't really a pub sort of guy. Gastropub maybe, but Kate had never once seen him in Essendale's nice but ordinary boozer. Hebbleswick had a wine bar, which was much more Peter's style. Hers too, really, but she liked the Lion, because she invariably knew everyone in there.

Peter ordered the drinks. Sparkling water for him. A Shiraz for her. He'd reserved a table in the corner; unnecessary as like everywhere else, the bar was unusually quiet.

'How are you, Kate?' he asked.

He had only seen her a few hours earlier when he'd dropped her off after the wedding.

'I'm good, thanks. How are you?'

It felt awkward again, as it had that first evening in Leeds. After the passion of the previous night, she'd expected they would slip more naturally into conversation with each other.

'Good, thank you. Did you do anything this afternoon?'

'I had a cuppa with Em in the café.'

'Oh? Did you talk about us?'

'A little.' Kate saw the disappointment on Peter's face. 'It's a bit odd. You know. With her being your ex. I mean, she's fine with it, but I wouldn't feel right telling her all the details. In any case, I was sounding her and Jo out about the living Advent calendar.'

'And what did they think?'

'They both thought it was a good idea, but I was hoping Jo would be the organiser and I'd do the publicity. Only Jo said no. Said she hasn't got time. So I've decided to do it myself.'

'Wow, Kate, that's brilliant.'

'Do you really think so? I know it's going to be quite time-consuming and it's not ideal timing with us starting seeing each other. I'm going to be tied up every evening in December for a start.'

If she were in his shoes, she thought, it would definitely put her off.

But Peter, to her surprise, seemed undeterred. 'It's one of the things I admire about you, Kate. The way you get stuck into these community projects. The Scrabble festival. The upcycling fashion show. I'll support you in any way I can. What's the first step?'

She took a sip of her wine. 'There'll be a meeting on Wednesday evening. I'll invite everyone along and we can pool ideas. And I need to do a recce – go for a walk round Essendale and Hebbleswick and suss out the best windows to make sure those people come along on Wednesday. There's so little time. In two weeks, we'll be unveiling the first window.'

'If anyone can pull it off, you can,' said Peter.

'That's what Em said.' Kate smiled. 'I know I can do the marketing. I *think* I can probably get everyone organised, allocate dates and so on and get a trail map printed. But it feels a little odd, that's all, organising a Christmas-themed event when I don't even like Christmas. I'm not sure I'm the right person to inspire people to create the kind of breathtaking festive windows I need them to make if we're really going to pull the crowds in. And it's so last-minute. I need to hit the ground running.'

Peter ducked down, looking under the table.

'What are you doing?' Kate was baffled. He was looking at her shoes. Did Peter have some foot fetish that Em had failed to mention?

'Checking you aren't wearing heels. Drink up, there's no time like the present.'

'What?'

'Let's hit the ground running. Or rather walking. Let's go and check out all your locations.'

'But it's dark,' she said, although she hadn't quite managed her ten thousand steps today, so the idea was quite appealing.

'Exactly,' said Peter. 'You can picture what all the windows will look like lit up by beautiful Christmas displays.'

'You really want to venture into the cold, rather than sitting in a cosy wine bar?'

'I do. If it'd help. And two pairs of eyes are better than one, surely?'

'Definitely.'

She drained her wine and stood up. Peter held her coat up for her, and she slid her arms into the sleeves. Another old-fashioned but rather lovely gesture. He opened the door of the bar, stepping aside for her to go through, then took her hand and said, 'Where should we start?'

They began on a back street at the far end of Hebbleswick. It was a row of stone terraced houses like any other, except for one building: the old co-operative where Taylor had once lived and worked. It had had some building work since Taylor had left – or rather been forced to leave – and was a home again now, and no longer a shop, but still had its enormous front window.

'What d'you reckon?' said Peter.

'It'd be brilliant if the new tenants agree. Let's call it a possible.'

It was Sunday evening, so most of Hebbleswick's residents were inside, sitting by the fire, watching *Call the Midwife* and drinking cocoa. Like its neighbour Essendale, Hebbleswick had the most pathetic display of Christmas lights; so pathetic that Kate wondered again why the council had bothered. They reached the main street where some of the shop windows were already dressed with fairy lights and decorated with sprayed-on snowflakes to reflect the season. The jewellers must have bought a job lot of gold baubles; there were dozens of them, hanging behind their usual display of rings and necklaces. The staff and volunteers of the hospice shop had gone to considerable effort with a fully decorated Christmas tree and some books and toys that might make good gifts.

'They already have festive displays,' she said to Peter. 'I should have thought of that.'

'They do. But they're like the displays on any other high street in any other town in the country. They're nice, but not particularly special.'

Would all these shops agree to remove the displays they already had, only to create another one for her living Advent calendar? She should have been planning this back in August, not at the middle of November.

''Spose you're right. We need people to create windows that people will talk about. That they'll take photos of. Perhaps put those photos on Instagram and videos on TikTok.'

'Exactly.'

They pressed their noses up against the grocer's. There were a few concessions to Christmas – some puddings, mince pies and jars of cranberry jelly on display – but it wasn't particularly festive.

'This could be so much more,' said Peter. 'With a little encouragement.'

'You really think it'll work?' Right now, Kate felt she was the one who needed encouragement.

'Yes, I do. It's a fabulous idea.'

They walked on round the town, with Peter making notes on his phone about potential windows to use, and

Kate taking photos to look through later. Then they jumped back in the car and did the same thing all over again in Essendale.

As first dates went, Kate thought as they stood outside the board game café, looking at the high street and working out which would be the best locations for the displays, it was certainly one of her more noteworthy ones. Not quite as unusual as a Cold War exhibition, but still different. Once they'd left the wine bar, the conversation had become less stilted, less awkward. Kate had expected to do all this by herself; it was lovely to have someone by her side, supporting and helping her.

'It's a shame about Alessandra's,' Peter said.

'Yeah, the clothes weren't to my tastes, but she poured heart and soul into that business. I know she was coming up to retirement age, but I don't think she wanted to sell up this early.'

'No, she didn't. But I didn't mean that. I meant from the point of view of the living Advent calendar. It looks terrible, Kate. A boarded-up shop in one of the towns we're trying to promote.'

She hadn't noticed until now that the huge empty window of the shop had been covered over with large sheets of cardboard. It did indeed look dreadful, and was not at all what you'd want any visitors to see.

'Can't do much about it though, can I?' she said. 'We don't even know who's bought that shop.'

'I've already asked around,' said Peter, 'but none of my business contacts know who it is. It certainly isn't one of them.'

'Let's pop a note through the letter box. Then if the new owner visits, or moves into the flat upstairs, they'll see it and get in touch.'

'Good plan,' said Peter.

She reached into her handbag, found the notebook she always carried and tore out a page. Peter took a fancy silver pen from the top pocket of his jacket, and clicked the top so it was ready to write.

*Hello! And welcome to Essendale. I'm Kate and I'm organising a community project here in the town during December. I would love to talk to you about it. Please could you contact me asap?*

She added her number, then they walked across the road and posted it through the letter box in the door of the shop.

'Do you think it'll work?' she said, as he took her hand in his. She couldn't get over how supportive he was being, how willing he'd been to venture out into the cold and traipse round the two towns looking at windows.

'Who knows?' said Peter. 'If it doesn't, you could always phone the estate agents. Ask them to pass on a message.'

Kate glanced up at the '*for sale*' board, now covered over with a big, red '*SOLD*' sign. She recognised the name of the estate agent, and shuddered at the thought of having to make that call, but if needs must, she would.

## 11

K ate was sitting opposite the most odious man.
Tarquin.

She'd never had dealings with him herself, but Jo had
dated this guy, and he'd tried to force himself on her.
Later he'd tried to blackmail her into sleeping with him,
and he'd done the same with Taylor. He was also behind
the demise of Em's original Little Board Game Café; he'd
sold the building from under her, and in its place was now
a rather ordinary block of flats. Kate had good reason to
hate Tarquin.

But she was charm personified now as she sat in his
office in Huddersfield, trying to find out who the mystery
buyer of Alessandra's was. Peter was right; the boarded-up
window of the former dress shop was an eyesore. However
lovely the rest of the town looked, it would hardly create
a good impression on the visitors she hoped to attract if
one of the shops was obviously standing empty, but there'd
been no response to her note. There was nothing for it,

but to leave work early and traipse to Huddersfield in the hope of enlisting Tarquin's help with contacting the buyer. Thankfully Jeroen, her boss, was understanding – mindful no doubt of all the extra hours Kate had put in over the years with never a word of complaint. Nevertheless, she was beginning to realise that organising the living Advent calendar and doing a full-time job was going to be a bit of a juggling act.

If she didn't know what he was like as a person, Kate would have found Tarquin extremely attractive. Smartly dressed in a three-piece suit – yes, he really was wearing a waistcoat – with a bright yellow tie and matching handkerchief in the pocket. And was that a pocket watch chain she saw dangling under there? He had dark brown hair, a strong jawline and the longest eyelashes; what she wouldn't give for eyelashes like that. It was funny though how someone could be blessed with the most perfect physical features – Tarquin wouldn't have looked out of place modelling clothes in a magazine or in one of those Christmas perfume adverts that irritated her so much – but when you knew what a totally rotten person they were, they appeared ugly.

And the reverse was true too. Even if you weren't instantly attracted to someone, but they were a lovely person and you got to know them, the physical attraction could grow. That, she knew, was what had happened when Jo had met Razz.

'How can I help you, er… Miss…?' Tarquin began. 'Is there a particular property that you're interested in?'

'Ms Harker, but call me Kate,' she said. 'And no. I'm not looking to buy anywhere. I'm hoping you can help me with something. I live in Essendale.'

'Lovely area,' Tarquin interjected.

'Yes, yes, it is. But a lot of the homes there – and in nearby Hebbleswick – are now holiday lets,' she said. 'The tourists are great in the summer – they spend a lot of money in the two towns and we welcome them.'

'And you'll be welcoming even more of them soon.'

'I'm sorry? How d'you mean?'

'There's a plot of land coming up for sale between Hebbleswick and Essendale, and I happen to know that the council would be very amenable to granting planning permission.' He tapped his nose to indicate that he was privy to some massive secret. 'I'm acting for the vendor, of course. But I'm thinking holiday homes on there and I'm hoping I'll get to sell those too. Could be very lucrative. Very lucrative indeed. You know, I've always fancied a Ferrari. Or an Aston. Which has more sex appeal, do you think?'

Kate's jaw dropped. He was hitting on her, trying to impress her with his wealth. How very unprofessional. It had the opposite of the desired effect anyway; there was something very unattractive about a show-off. Peter was rich, but never made a song and dance about it.

And which plot of land was he talking about?

Anyway, none of that mattered now. Time to get back to the living Advent calendar and Alessandra's window, which was the reason for her visit.

'I know nothing about cars,' she said. 'But more holiday homes – interesting. Like I said, the tourists spend a lot of money in the two towns in the spring and summer, but they don't come over the winter months and the local businesses are struggling. As a community, we felt we needed to do something about that. We want to attract more people over the festive season.'

She outlined the concept of the living Advent calendar, trying to ignore the supercilious look on Tarquin's face. He looked even less attractive now.

'If you're hoping for sponsorship,' he sneered, 'you're rather late in the day. It's almost December now.'

Jeez, he hadn't listened to a word she'd said.

'No, I'm not looking for sponsors. This isn't directly a money-raising venture.'

She was sure she'd already made that clear.

'It's not a charity thing?' he said.

'No.' She tried to keep the impatience out of her voice; she'd told him this already. 'No, it's about revitalising the town centres of Hebbleswick and Essendale over the winter months. Attracting more visitors.' She felt like a stuck record.

'You think people will travel to your little town to look at shop windows? When they could go to Leeds or Manchester? Plenty of lovely festive displays there. Christmas markets too.'

She hated to admit it, but he had a point. Every window without exception had to be different. Had to scream Christmas, but in a unique way. They couldn't just repeat the kind of displays you'd see in every town centre at this time of year. She was reliant on the 'windowers', as she'd started to call them, to come up with quirky and original ideas. They had to be brilliantly executed too.

'Our windows will be special,' she said, trying to sound more confident than she felt. 'But it doesn't look good to have Alessandra's standing empty, not when it's in such a prominent position on the high street. Do you have any idea when the new owner might be opening up his or her shop? And how I might contact them? Ideally, I'd like them to do one of the displays.'

'I see,' said Tarquin. He frowned at his computer screen, and tapped away at the keyboard. 'I shouldn't tell you this, but I can't resist a pretty face. The sale has completed already, so he could be moving in any day now.'

'I don't suppose you could give me his number?' said Kate hopefully, ignoring his smarmy comment.

She knew full well that Tarquin shouldn't do this – it would breach data protection laws for one thing. She could have asked him to pass her number on, but she didn't trust him to do that. She also guessed that he was the kind of guy who bent rules when he saw fit, and she was hoping that he might do so on this occasion.

'I would really appreciate it,' she purred.

Tarquin glanced over his shoulder to where his colleague was sitting. She was busy on a phone call and typing up notes at the same time. He leaned towards Kate, close enough that she could smell his breath, and she felt glad that his desk was between them. 'How much would you appreciate it, Kate?'

Even if she hadn't known about Jo and Taylor's experiences with this man, Kate wasn't naïve; she knew exactly what he meant. In fact, she'd been expecting this, and on her phone she had a secret weapon that Tarquin didn't know about. When he'd tried to blackmail Jo into sleeping with him, she'd managed to record the conversation, and she'd kept it. When Kate had told Jo of her plan to find out who'd bought Alessandra's, she'd warned Kate to be careful – 'Tarquin is a really dodgy character, Kate! Don't be alone with him!' – and then she'd WhatsApped her the recording.

Kate slipped her hand into her handbag and took out her phone. One tap and he – and his colleague who'd now hung up her phone call – would hear that conversation with Jo, recorded here in this very office.

But she couldn't do it. She wouldn't stoop to his level. It wasn't right to force him to break client confidentiality, not to mention data protection laws. She slipped her phone back into her handbag, and said, 'I shouldn't have come here. I'm sorry. I should have known you couldn't hand out someone's number.' She stood up and smiled at him. 'Sorry to have wasted your time.'

Tarquin stood up too. 'Not at all,' he said. He was all smiles suddenly now. 'It was lovely meeting you, Kate. Perhaps you'd let me buy you a drink sometime? Are you free at all this week?'

'Thank you, but I'm seeing someone,' she said. 'And I don't have a spare minute anyway. The living Advent calendar is keeping me very busy.'

She'd be even busier now, she thought as she walked away, back towards the train station. Since putting a note through the letter box hadn't worked, she was going to have to add a surveillance operation at Alessandra's to her growing list of tasks. She smiled to herself as an image flashed into her mind of herself and Peter, sitting in his Beamer with a flask of coffee in the wee small hours, watching the former dress shop like detectives doing a stake-out in some nineties cop show. The slightest sign of life and they'd spring out of the car and race over to hammer on the door. Peter would do it too, she thought; he was so supportive. She'd definitely struck lucky there.

It was half past four when she reached Essendale, but it was already dark. She walked down the high street, thinking how sad it was that no-one was about.

'Not even five o'clock and everyone's already tucked up in their homes for the evening,' she said to herself, and was once again struck by the enormity of the situation. The living Advent calendar was a fun project – to her surprise, she was really enjoying it so far, even though she didn't like Christmas – but for the local businesses like the florist's and the board game café, it was much more than that. Hopes were pinned on it.

She was so wrapped up in her thoughts, that she didn't notice that there were lights on in the flat above Alessandra's.

## 12

Kate had been to Peter's house before, many times, because it used to be Em's house too. Somehow her friend had never quite fitted in there. The place was too modern for Em, not nearly quirky enough, but standing in the hallway now Kate could see herself living here. Whilst the exterior of her own house was completely different – Peter's house was a modern, detached place, whilst Kate lived in an old stone terraced cottage – the interiors were very similar. Clean and tidy, with nothing out of place. Even Marie Kondo herself would fit in here.

It was Tuesday evening, and Peter had invited her over for dinner.

'Something smells good,' she said. 'Really good.'

'Thank you. May I take your coat?'

She slipped it off and handed it to him.

'I'll pop it in the armoire.' Peter opened what was

essentially a large wardrobe that stood in his hallway to reveal a row of coats all hanging neatly inside.

The guy really was a neat freak. Tidy though she was, open any wardrobe or cupboard in her own house and the chances were that the contents would come tumbling out. No wonder he and Em hadn't lasted.

'Come through,' he said, opening the door into the lounge and stepping aside to let her go in first.

Kate looked around the room and gasped. A Christmas tree stood in one corner – a real one too judging by the delicious scent in the room. It was beautifully decorated with the palest blue glass baubles and ribbons. Underneath was a veritable mountain of gifts, all tastefully wrapped in different shades of blue paper, with silver and white ribbons. In the fireplace, Peter had lit a collection of candles, with more on the window ledges. The whole room screamed Christmas, but in the most tasteful way imaginable. Kate felt like she'd stepped into the pages of the John Lewis Christmas catalogue.

'Wow,' she said. And then: 'But I thought you weren't into Christmas?'

'I'm not.'

'This is you *not* being into it?' She looked at the collection of cards on the mantelpiece and the stockings hanging in a row underneath. 'And it's only November. That tree's going to shed a lot of needles into your plush carpet between now and Christmas.'

'That tree is going straight back to my mother's patio first thing tomorrow morning,' Peter said.

Kate looked again at the tree and saw that it was in a large pot. 'Your mother's patio?'

'This is all for your benefit,' he said. 'To get you in a Christmassy mood and help you feel inspired for organising your living Advent calendar.'

'You've done all this for me?'

'All this and more,' he said. 'Now, take a seat and I'll pour you a sherry.'

'Sherry?'

'It's *Chriiistmaaaaaas*,' he said, doing a poor imitation of Noddy Holder.

Kate didn't usually drink sherry, but the Croft Original was surprisingly enjoyable.

Peter served up a smoked salmon starter, followed by a traditional turkey dinner, with all the trimmings. All the trimmings except for roast potatoes. Peter didn't eat carbs, he told her, so had cleverly roasted Jerusalem artichokes instead. This suited Kate, as they counted towards her ten a day. He insisted they pulled their crackers, read out the corny jokes and wore their party hats.

'I can't believe you've gone to all this trouble,' she said.

'You're worth it.'

'How ever did you find the time to decorate the place *and* cook the meal?'

'I took the day off. The benefit of running your own company.'

That must be good. If only *she* could take a few days off. Or even the rest of the year. Jeroen was a very amenable boss, but she knew she couldn't push it too far.

'Are you feeling inspired yet?' he asked. 'Feeling in a Christmassy mood?'

'A little,' she admitted.

When they'd finished eating, Peter cleared the dishes

away, refusing Kate's offer of help, and then they settled on the sofa and he switched on the TV. A few clicks of the remote control, and one of the late Queen's Christmas speeches began to play.

'I'm not into Christmas, as you know,' he said, 'but you can't beat a Queen's speech. This is one of my favourites.'

'What year is it?' Kate asked.

'Twenty-twelve,' said Peter as if it were perfectly obvious. 'That's why she's mentioned her Diamond Jubilee.'

'Of course.'

Kate drifted off during the speech – no disrespect intended to Her Majesty; she was exhausted – and woke with a start when Peter clicked off the TV. If he'd noticed she'd been asleep, he made no reference to it, but went over to the tree and retrieved one of the parcels.

'Most of them are empty boxes,' he said. 'But this one… well, I bought you a little something.'

Kate wasn't sure what she was most surprised by: the fact that he'd wrapped a load of empty boxes for this Christmas charade, or that he'd bought her a gift so early in their relationship. 'I haven't bought you anything. I feel bad now, tipping up empty-handed.'

'But you didn't know we were doing Christmas,' he said. 'Go on, open it.'

The gift was small and rectangular-shaped. She knew immediately that it was jewellery of some description and hoped he hadn't spent too much. It was exquisitely wrapped in dark blue wrapping paper, with a large silver bow. She pulled the Sellotape off gingerly, not wanting to spoil the paper.

Inside, as she suspected, was a box, that had clearly

come from a jeweller's. She flipped open the lid; sitting on a bed of red velvet inside was a silver heart-shaped pendant, containing a small black stone.

'Whitby jet,' said Peter.

She leaned over and kissed his cheek. 'It's beautiful. Thank you.'

He brushed a hair from her face, then kissed her back, on the lips now. 'You're welcome. Now, Christmas wouldn't be Christmas without a board game, so I've borrowed one from Emily.'

'You've borrowed a board game?'

'I have indeed.'

'But neither of us like board games,' Kate said.

'We're doing Christmas,' Peter said. 'Technically, it's a card game not a board game. And it's got cute animals.'

'Go on, then.'

The game was called Forest Shuffle and, as he'd promised, it did have cute animals, as well as birds, trees and a few creepy-crawlies too. Peter had done his homework and knew how it worked so he explained the rules; they'd each have a hand of up to ten cards. On their turn, they could either take two extra cards or play a card into their forest, by paying its cost. There were eight different types of trees. Bird and butterfly cards could be played on top of each tree, animals on either side, and some plants and insects were played underneath the tree. The cards all scored a variety of points, and some had bonus actions on them too.

'Complicated,' said Kate.

'Em said it's one of the simpler ones.'

'At least the cards are pretty.'

Kate began by playing a beech tree into her forest, which gained her an extra card, then Peter played some kind of fir.

'Did you have any luck finding out who bought Alessandra's?' Peter said.

'The estate agent wouldn't tell me. And there was no response to my note.' She played a chaffinch onto the top of her beech tree.

'Shame.' Peter took two more cards.

'I did find out something. There'll be more holiday homes soon. He said there's a piece of land for sale near Essendale, and he's confident that whoever buys it will get planning permission.'

'Interesting. It's your go, by the way.'

She looked at her cards. She had a wolf, but that would only score points if she also played some deer, and she had no deer in her hand. Not yet anyway. She decided to play another beech tree, since the beech trees would only score points if there were at least four of them in her forest.

Peter put a badger beside his fir tree. 'You know, I'm not into games, and I was quite taken aback when Emily turned her café into a board game café, but I'm rather enjoying this one. Maybe it's the company.'

'Maybe it is.'

He was right. Of the games she'd played since Em had set up the café, this was definitely her favourite so far. She picked up two cards, praying for more beech trees but got a linden tree and another wolf. Still no deer.

'Did the estate agent say where this piece of land was?' said Peter, frowning at his cards.

'Not exactly. Somewhere between Essendale and Hebbleswick. Why?'

'Just wondering. And he said it would be holiday homes?'

'Yeah.'

'What we really need are more homes for locals,' Peter said. 'Preferably affordable ones. It's hard to recruit staff these days as there's nowhere for anyone to live.' He played a red deer into his forest.

'I can imagine. I was really lucky to buy my house when I did. I mean, it's not exactly fancy – not like your place – but I do love it.' Kate played the linden tree into her forest, because it was a rather pretty shade of yellow.

Her game plan was flawed, she realised later. Whilst her forest was undoubtedly prettier than Peter's, he had paid attention to the scoring and the bonuses on the cards. Kate had opted for butterflies on the tops of her trees, since they were the most colourful cards in her hand. Peter had played three owls and a couple of hawks; they were brown and grey respectively and didn't look as good as the butterflies, but were worth more points.

'This is one of the loveliest Christmases I've ever had,' she said to Peter.

'And it's only November.' He laughed.

'My actual Christmas won't be a patch on this.' She felt suddenly deflated, thinking about the miserable day she'd no doubt have with her father. The cook-in-the-bag chicken. The frozen sprouts. The shop-bought Christmas pud. And the lack of conversation; she and her dad never had anything to talk about.

'Mine won't either,' said Peter. He stood up, leaving the forest cards where they were, and moved round to her side of the table, taking her hand and pulling her to her feet. 'You know what our forests are both missing?'

She glanced down at the table, then back at him. 'No. What are they missing?'

From behind his back, he pulled out a green twig with two perfect white berries, and dangled it above her head. 'Mistletoe.'

Where had he been hiding that?

She closed her eyes, tilting her face up towards his. His lips touched hers, lightly at first, then a little more urgently. She leaned into him. He lowered the hand that was holding the mistletoe, and she heard it drop onto the table behind her. Then he pulled her into him, enveloping her, slipping his tongue into her mouth.

He was an expert kisser; that was for sure. He'd put together this amazing Christmassy evening, especially for her. She couldn't quite believe the lengths he'd gone to. And that pendant wouldn't have been cheap; he could have bought her a token gift. So why, Kate wondered, as she kissed him back, didn't she feel over the moon that she was dating Essendale's most eligible bachelor?

# 13

It was standing room only in the upstairs room of the board game café the following night. Kate clapped her hands and everyone fell silent.

She glanced at the sea of faces, mentally ticking off who was there and who was not. Most of the people she'd invited had turned up: the librarians from both Hebbleswick and Essendale libraries, Jo representing Hebbleswick Primary School, and Mrs Saunders, the head teacher from Essendale Primary, the owners and managers of various shops in the two towns and Reverend Stone from the parish church in Hebbleswick. Razz and Ludek were there, on behalf of the health centre, and Harry too, who didn't have a business but was there in place of Taylor who did. 'In any case,' he'd said when he came in, 'I also have an idea for a window of my own.'

Peter was there too, of course. 'I'll be cheering you on,' he'd said, 'and I'll make notes too, if you want me to.'

Unfortunately, he'd brought his mother, the intimidating

Mrs Florence Ridley, soon to be Mrs Baranski, as she was engaged to be married. Stanisław Baranski – known as Mr B to most people – was a popular figure in Essendale. He was a quiet kind of chap in his late sixties – early seventies possibly – who'd been Em's first customer when she'd opened her café. To everyone's surprise he had proposed to Peter's mother, and the pair of them could often be seen in the board game café, brandishing an Oxford English Dictionary as they argued over a game of Scrabble.

The one person who was not there – not as far as she could tell anyway – was the new owner of Alessandra's. He hadn't yet responded to her note, but Kate had been hoping he might have got wind of the meeting and come along. No such luck.

She was no stranger to public speaking, but for some reason felt nervous this evening. She'd stood up here, in this very room, a while back when everyone had gathered for the clothes upcycling evenings. As she'd explained how that particular project would work and introduced Taylor, who'd acted as the tutor, she'd felt brimming with confidence, but tonight it was a different story. Her mouth was dry. Her legs were shaking. She could hear the tremble in her voice as she welcomed everyone. This was her baby, her project, and she desperately wanted them all to love it.

'Our little towns – like many towns in the UK – are changing,' she said. 'We get lots of visitors in the summer months, and many of the houses here are now Airbnbs, which is good on the one hand because the visitors need somewhere to stay, but it does mean that there are fewer permanent residents.'

A man sitting at the front shifted in his chair and took

out his mobile phone. Kate dug her fingernails into her palm. She was losing her audience, explaining things they were already well aware of, but she needed to present the full picture, to outline her plan. She looked at Peter for reassurance. He smiled and nodded. Harry, beside him, gave her a thumbs up.

'But the visitors don't come in the winter – not so much anyway,' she continued.

'Tell us something we don't know,' came a voice from the back.

Kate frowned. She hadn't expected such a tough crowd. 'I've heard that some local businesses are struggling. Alessandra's has closed recently.'

'Get on with the free marketing advice,' someone shouted. 'That's what we're all here for.'

Kate took a deep breath. 'I'm very happy to share some marketing tips on another occasion,' she said, 'but that's not what this evening is about.'

A man at the back stood up. Kate recognised him as the owner of the jeweller's in Hebbleswick. He headed for the stairs, mumbling, 'I've not got time for this.'

And then Mrs Ridley got to her feet too. She was a formidable woman, and Kate had always been a little wary of her, even more so now that she was dating Peter. Mother and son were co-owners of Ridley's Engineering, Essendale's biggest employer. When Em had been engaged to Peter, she'd been terrified of her future mother-in-law, always calling her Mrs Ridley, hardly ever Florence. Peter's mother criticised everything about Em, from the way she kept the house to the clothes she wore. Kate dreaded to think what this dragon of a woman was going to come out with now.

'For heaven's sake,' Mrs Ridley began, and Kate braced herself. 'Give the girl a chance.'

Kate closed her eyes for a second in relief. 'Thank you, Fl... Mrs Ridley. I'll try to keep this brief. We need the visitors to carry on visiting over the winter months. To spend money in our towns. To keep everyone afloat. We don't want to become one of those places where almost every property is an Airbnb, and everything shuts over the winter and the streets are completely empty.'

A few people shook their heads and a man called out, 'But what can we do about it?'

'We're going to put ourselves on the map. Our two towns are going to become one giant Advent calendar.'

A few jaws dropped at this.

'Twenty-four shops or businesses, the libraries and the schools too if they'd like to, will each create a special Christmas display in their windows. But – and this is the crucial part – they do it secretly. Perhaps obscure the window with Windolene or cardboard or curtains so it can't be seen. We'll have to work out what's best. One by one, beginning on the first of December, we have a big reveal of each window. An unveiling. I was thinking this might be at six o'clock. For the first one, our launch evening, we'll make it a bit special – perhaps serve mulled wine and mince pies.'

'So one window is opened every evening?' Peter said. 'Like in a real Advent calendar?'

He knew this, of course, and was just helping her out, asking a question to make sure the plan was clear to everyone. She would thank him later. For now, she said, 'That's exactly it.'

'Genius,' said Harry. He'd heard the idea already and was also speaking up to be supportive.

Kate smiled at him to show her gratitude.

'And what would be in the windows?' someone standing at the back called. Kate wasn't sure who had spoken.

'Whatever you like, as long as it's Christmassy. If you run a shop, it might be something related to what you sell. The libraries might create Christmas displays with a bookish theme. Other towns have done this – if you google them, you'll get some ideas. But we need to think big. Think 3D displays rather than simply buying a can of snow spray and stencilling a few snowflakes onto the glass. We need more than that. Let your imaginations go wild.'

'Razz and I are planning one at the health centre,' said Ludek. 'It'll be Christmassy and health-related and highly informative.'

Kate nodded. 'That sounds brilliant; thanks, Ludek. You don't have to have a business to create a display. Private homes can participate too, as long as they have a big enough window.'

'Wonderful,' called Mr B. 'I can put my baubles on display.'

A titter went round the room, as Mrs Ridley said, 'Stanisław! Really!'

Kate ignored the double entendre and continued. 'Now what I suggest is that you all grab yourselves a drink downstairs in the café, and have a think about whether you'd like to participate. If you've already got an idea of what your window display might look like, brilliant, but if not, we can put our heads together. I'm going to stay up here and start compiling a list of who's going to take part, and then I can allocate dates. One final thing: keep your window secret. Don't breathe a word of what it's going to look like to anyone but me, so that it's a lovely surprise on the evening of the big reveal. Now if you'd like to, make your way downstairs to the café.'

They all trooped off down the stairs, returning one by one to whisper their suggestions to Kate. Only they didn't simply outline their suggestions; they told her of their worries and their struggles, of how difficult times had been recently, of their frustration at the way their little towns were changing, and how they'd felt powerless to do anything about it until now. She felt like a priest in a confessional box.

All the while, Peter sat beside her, not saying anything but frantically scribbling down all the many suggestions for different displays. She had worried that she wouldn't get enough takers to fill the twenty-four evenings of Advent, but she had almost thirty prospective 'windowers', and would have to disappoint some people. At least seven people wanted to create a nativity scene. A local farm shop wanted to carve one out of root vegetables, and a narrowboat that doubled as a wool shop offered to make a knitted version.

'Lovely ideas,' she said. 'I will write them down for consideration, but we don't want too many nativity scenes. We've got to have a bit of variety, or the visitors will get bored.'

It was agreed that the board game café would be the first window, and that Em and Ludek would put on a display of games to enjoy with your family after lunch on Christmas Day. The café was the ideal place, given that Em would be able to serve mulled wine, mince pies and other refreshments after the window was unveiled.

Harry said that whilst he wasn't a business, he would like to offer up his garden shed, which happened to have a large window – well, larger than your average garden shed window at any rate.

'I'll transform my model railway landscape into a winter wonderland,' he said. 'Snow on the hills. Tiny Christmas trees in front of the buildings. Santa on a chimney. That kind of thing.'

'It sounds wonderful, Harry,' Kate said, because it did.

Her list of potential windows grew as the evening progressed. A steady stream of shopkeepers and business owners traipsed up the stairs to make their suggestions. Jo wanted to create a Scrabble-themed Christmas window at Hebbleswick Primary, though she wasn't yet sure how that would work. Her nemesis, Mrs Saunders, the head teacher of Essendale Primary was hot on her heels.

'What are Hebbleswick Primary planning?' she asked as soon as she sat down.

Kate hoped this whole thing wasn't going to create any rivalry between the towns. This was about community and co-operation, not competition.

To her relief, the managers of the two local charity shops arrived together, keen to ensure that they didn't both come up with the same idea. They not only offered their windows, but said they would search through their stocks of donated items for large curtains, bedsheets and duvet covers to make the drapes to cover each window until the big reveal.

This was really happening, Kate thought, watching the two women disappearing back down the stairs, still chatting about their windows. She felt an enormous burden on her shoulders. So many people's hopes were pinned on this daft little idea of hers and she hadn't a clue if it would actually work.

# 14

'Carrot cake,' Em said, placing a tray in front of them. There was a mug of green tea for Kate, a black coffee for Peter, and two thick slabs of cake. 'One of your five a day.'

'Thanks,' said Kate. 'How many people are still waiting to see us?'

'Only the vicar,' Em said. 'Shall I send him up?'

Kate nodded. She was relieved that the evening was almost over – she was conscious that she had work the following day – but was disappointed that the new owner of Alessandra's hadn't put in an appearance.

'Knock, knock,' said Reverend Stone, tapping against the wall as he made his way into the room. 'Good evening, Kate. Peter.'

'Reverend,' said Peter, holding out his hand. 'How are you?'

The vicar sat down opposite them with his hands in front

of him, almost in a prayer-like pose. 'I'll keep this brief. It's obvious that the church will be the final window…' he held up his fingers to indicate inverted commas as he said the word 'window' then replaced them in their prayer-like pose '…although it won't be a window as such.'

Hang on a minute. Obvious? It wasn't obvious at all.

'How do you mean, it won't be a window as such?' Kate said.

'I mean, the final window will obviously be our nativity scene outside the church.'

'But it's not a window. This is about window displays.' She knew she sounded irritated, but she was tired.

'But it *is* a display,' said Reverend Stone firmly. 'Christmas Eve is our Lord's birthday. Clearly our final *display* should mark that occasion and convey the true meaning of Christmas. What better way than by unveiling our own nativity scene?'

She looked at the man sitting opposite her now, and hadn't the heart or the energy to tell him that his nativity figures weren't what she had in mind, particularly not for Christmas Eve. Instead she said, 'Vicar, we couldn't possibly ask you to break with tradition, and keep your beautiful nativity scene under wraps until the twenty-fourth.'

It would look totally ridiculous, she thought, if the church put the figures outside the church, then covered them with drapes for almost the entire month. Everyone would know exactly what was underneath. She stifled a giggle at the thought.

'Honestly Kate, it would be fine. I'd be glad to—'

'But what about all the worshippers coming to Sunday service during Advent? Won't they be expecting to see the nativity scene?' This, she felt, was her trump card.

'I'm sure they'll understand,' said Reverend Stone.

Kate sighed. 'I'm going to say to you the same as I've said to everyone; I'll get back to you within the next few days when I've been through all the ideas and check that we don't have two displays that are too similar. I'll be drawing up the dates, too, of which window is being revealed on each evening.'

'Yes, with the nativity scene being unveiled outside the church on Christmas Eve,' said the vicar, as if he hadn't heard her. 'I'm glad that's settled.'

Before she could argue any further, he stood up and headed back down the stairs.

'Bugger,' said Kate, when she was sure he was out of earshot.

She thought of the tired, life-sized Mary and Joseph that the church trotted out every year. The paint was flaking on several of the figures. The shepherds' lambs had been stolen three years ago, and they hadn't been replaced. One of the wise men was pointing up – at the star presumably – but his finger was missing, so he was effectively holding a fist up at the sky, as if challenging God himself to a punch-up. There had been several baby Jesuses over the years, the original one having gone missing years ago. Last year's baby Jesus had, Kate recalled, been a rather scruffy Cabbage Patch kid.

The most important windows were the first and the last – Christmas Eve itself – and she wanted that final one to be something incredible, something that would get everyone talking. As they ate their turkey and their stuffing, their roasties and their sprouts, she wanted all of Essendale and Hebbleswick to be saying, 'Well, what about that display last night? Wasn't that amazing?'

'The Christmas Eve window has to have the wow factor,' she said to Peter. 'To have impact. I'm absolutely determined that it isn't going to be the same-old, same-old nativity scene at the church.'

'Well, good luck with that.' He handed her a notebook, in which he'd taken copious notes. 'Reverend Stone isn't going to change his mind in a hurry.'

She ignored his comment about the vicar, and flicked through the notebook. 'This is great, thanks. You'd make someone a brilliant PA.'

'I'll bear that in mind if Ridley Engineering ever goes under.'

'Oh, that's not likely, is it? I mean, I know you went through a rough patch a while back, when you had to lay people off…'

Her voice trailed away. He had laid Em off in that rough patch. She'd been his fiancée at the time and it was, in Kate's opinion anyway, the beginning of the end of that relationship. Her eyes met Peter's and she guessed he was thinking the same thing. Was that regret in his eyes?

Peter cleared his throat. 'Things are going well at the moment. Very well. Thankfully Ridley's doesn't rely on visitor numbers. Although please don't broadcast that, Kate. I'd hate to look like I'm bragging when other people are struggling.' He sighed. 'We need to make sure this project of yours is a success and we get lots of new visitors supporting our local businesses.'

'Let's hope so.'

'It'll be great, Kate. You'll see.'

'And then it'll fizzle out at the end when, on Christmas Eve, the vicar unveils the same nativity scene that has stood outside St Cuthbert's every December for donkey's years. I either let him go ahead with that, or risk creating an almighty row. No pun intended. Upsetting the local clergy isn't going to be good PR.'

'You'll have to use all your powers of persuasion to convince him to let someone else have the Christmas Eve spot.'

Kate shook her head. 'He was adamant. Like you said, he's not going to change his mind in a hurry. I'll have to think of something to convince him.'

She stood up and tucked the notebook into her bag.'

'I'll run you home. Unless you'd like to stay at mine?'

It was tempting, but Kate was exhausted. 'Would you mind if I don't? I need my beauty sleep tonight.'

'Of course I don't mind. Come on.'

They went down the stairs and thanked Em and Ludek for allowing the meeting to be held in the upstairs room. There were only two tables occupied in the board game café.

'Hope your plan works,' said Em. 'It's hardly worth opening some evenings these days. Though we've done a roaring trade tonight with everyone coming to the meeting.'

'So if nothing else, it was worth it for that.' Kate smiled. The enormity of the task in hand was beginning to hit home now, after an evening of listening to so many of the local business people explaining how tough things had been recently.

It was only a two-minute drive to Kate's house, barely time to relax into the heated leather seats of Peter's BMW. There was nowhere to park, so he gave her a quick kiss on the lips to say goodnight. She watched him drive away, then unlocked her front door and stepped inside, pulling off her coat and hanging it up on the coat rack.

He'd been so incredibly supportive this evening, sitting beside her, never interfering, listening quietly and taking notes. The town's biggest employer and he'd acted as her secretary! She would text him and thank him again, she decided, and reached into her bag for her phone. But it wasn't there. She must have left it on the table upstairs in the board game café. She pulled her coat back on and stepped back out into the night air. With any luck, the two tables in the board game café would still be playing – perhaps Terraforming Mars or one of the other longer games – and Em wouldn't have closed up yet. She hurried down the street, back towards the town centre, hoping she wouldn't be too late. She wasn't wearing a watch and, without her phone, had no way of checking the time.

As she walked, she thought about all the ideas people had come up with for their windows. Did they have that wow factor that was so necessary to get people talking and ensure that more visitors came to their towns? And how on earth was she going to persuade the vicar that his nativity scene wasn't going to take centre stage on Christmas Eve? If she couldn't convince him, they'd have twenty-three fabulous displays, only for the project to finish like a damp squib. And one way or another, she wasn't prepared to let that happen.

She turned onto the high street and saw immediately that the board game café was already in darkness. She'd have to come back in the morning; a night without her mobile wouldn't kill her. Might even do her good. A short technology detox. She'd been intending to do one of those for ages. She was about to head home, when she realised the café might be in darkness but the flat above Alessandra's wasn't. There was a light on, and through the curtains, she could see the silhouette of someone moving around inside.

Was it too late to be knocking on a stranger's door? They clearly weren't in bed already. And they hadn't responded to her note. She wanted that window; it looked terrible covered in cardboard and would make such a fantastic display space. Besides, the new owner would surely be pleased to be part of her event; what a fantastic way to launch their new shop.

She crossed over the road and hurried towards Alessandra's, praying that the lights didn't go off before she could get there. In her head, she ran over the conversation she would have with the mystery new owner.

'Hi, my name's Kate. I'm sorry to bother you when it's so late, but I saw the lights on and I wanted to talk to you about Essendale's living Advent calendar.'

She'd never been to the flat above the shop, but knew that the entrance was through a small door to the right of the big shop window. She paused outside, her heart beating.

It must have been fate that she'd left her phone inside the café tonight.

She pressed the bell and waited. She heard footsteps coming down the stairs, then the door opened a few inches and a very familiar face peered out.

# 15

'Xander?'

Her brain was struggling to compute this. What was he doing here? And those times recently when she'd seen a man who *looked* like him, well, it was obvious now. That man *was* Xander.

'Kate.' He seemed as surprised as she was. 'How are you? Come in. Long time, no see. It's been…'

'Four years,' she said, and managed to stop herself from adding, 'Minus eleven days.'

'Four years. Who'd have thought? It doesn't seem that long.'

That chocolatey voice. Those kind eyes. Xander. Here in Essendale. In the flat above Alessandra's, of all places.

He stepped aside and gestured for her to go up the narrow stairway that led, presumably, to the flat above the shop.

Her heart seemed to thud heavier with every step and not with exertion; she was fighting fit.

'May I?' she said when she reached the tiny landing and the door to the flat.

'Yes, of course.'

She pushed open the door and stepped into what was clearly the lounge. As someone who'd seen the kinds of clothes that Alessandra's used to sell, Kate wasn't at all surprised by the décor in this room. The frills and flounces of the dresses were echoed by the frills and flounces of the curtains that hung across the enormous window. The floral sofa was also reminiscent of the fabrics of the garments that had once been on sale in the shop. The kinds of clothes Peter's mother often wore. At least the walls and carpet were plain. It wasn't a bad room; it just wasn't to her taste. Or, she imagined, to anyone's under forty.

Although Xander must be *over* forty by now, she realised. He was nine years older than her.

'The previous owner left the sofa,' said Xander.

'Do you… are you…' she began, then took a deep breath and started again. 'And are you the new owner?'

'Yes, I am.'

'Oh.' She needed a moment for this to sink in. 'You've bought a dress shop?'

'Yes, I've been looking for one for a while. And this is ideal. I only need to change a couple of letters on the sign – Alessandra's to Alexander's. Shouldn't cost more than a couple of quid and I'll be all set to go. I hope you'll be coming here for all your wardrobe needs.'

His eyes were twinkling at her, but nevertheless, she was tired and it took a second for her to realise he was joking. 'Seriously, Xander, why on earth have you bought a shop? Has the university given you the heave-ho?'

'Au contraire. I've got a new post. A promotion. A chair in Leeds.'

'Do you get a table with that?'

He laughed. 'It means, I've become a professor.'

'Yeah, I know. Congratulations. So why've you bought this place? Are you going to live here?'

'Certainly am.'

Which meant she'd bump into him. Probably quite frequently. Her home was less than a mile from his. Her best friend owned the café across the road.

'Why here?' she said, longing for him to say, *Because of you.*

'I didn't want to live in the city centre. I literally drew a circle on a map and picked out a few towns within commuter distance. And Essendale was one of them. I remembered you saying you'd lived here, and that you liked it. I didn't realise you'd come back.'

'My London job was a secondment.' She tried to keep the disappointment out of her voice.

'Yes, I remember now. Anyway, I came for a look round one day.' He paused. 'I rather fell in love…'

Kate's heart seemed to stop for a moment.

'…with this little town of yours.'

And then it plummeted.

As if he'd really been about to tell her he'd fallen in love with her! Not after she'd so unceremoniously walked out on him. And it had been four years ago. He'd hardly have been holding a torch for her all this time.

'The whole area is rather fascinating,' he was saying now. 'Lots of history.'

'It really is a lovely place,' said Kate. 'I missed it when I was in London.'

*Although I enjoyed my time with you*, she wanted to add.

He smiled. 'I can imagine.'

She hesitated. What was the etiquette when you bumped into someone you'd dated years earlier? Someone you'd walked out on? Was it all water under the bridge as far as he was concerned, just a few dates, long forgotten, or ought she to apologise? She *wanted* to apologise – she'd been in the wrong – but wasn't sure where to start or how to explain her actions. Not without telling him of her parents' troubled marriage and the profound impact that had had on her life and the choices she'd made.

So instead she said, 'Why have you bought a shop if you're still working in academia?'

'I was buying a house in Hebbleswick,' he said. 'Only I got gazumped. By a second-home owner, which makes it worse somehow. They've got two houses, when I can't even get one. This was the only thing on the market in my price range. I wasn't sure at first, but I reckon if I can find a tenant for the shop, it'll be a bit of extra income. I might have been promoted, but university salaries…' He grimaced. 'Look, shall I make some tea? There's only one mug, but I'm sure I can find another in one of the boxes.'

He gestured towards a small stack of boxes in one corner of the room. Kate suspected that somewhere in those boxes, alongside the mugs, was the reason that she wasn't with Xander.

'Don't worry about the tea,' she said. 'This isn't really a social call.'

'Oh?' said Xander. 'I thought you might have come round with a casserole or a cake or something. To welcome the new arrival in the neighbourhood. Isn't that what happens in places like this?'

Kate opened her coat and pretended to look inside. 'As you can see, I don't have a casserole secreted about my person. I'm empty-handed, I'm afraid. Sorry about that.'

'No problem. So if this isn't a social call, why are you here?'

'It's a bit of a long story,' she said.

'In that case, why don't we head over to the pub?'

Kate hesitated. She'd told Peter she was tired but was now considering going to the pub with a guy she used to date. She ought to say no, but she wanted to get Xander on board with the living Advent calendar – Alessandra's had such a great window – and what better way to persuade him than over a drink?

The Red Lion was unusually quiet. Once again, Kate was struck by how many businesses – how many people – would benefit if her project did what she intended and attracted the crowds. She was also struck by how many would suffer if it didn't. Xander got the drinks in, whilst she grabbed a table in the corner, watching his rear view as he chatted to the landlord about the best locally brewed beers, and marvelling at how strange it was that he'd turned up in her life again after all this time.

Finally he arrived at the table, having tasted at least three tiny samples of local beers. He put down his pint and her glass of Merlot and sat opposite her on a tiny stool, rather than beside her on the bench.

'Cheers,' he said.

'Cheers. Here's to your new life in Essendale and your new job in Leeds.' She clinked her glass against his, still struggling to believe this. She never thought she'd see the day when she was sitting in her local with this man.

'Thanks, Kate. Now are you going to put me out of my misery and explain why you happened to be knocking on my door at…' he glanced at his watch '…at nearly ten p.m.?'

'It's about the window of the shop,' she said. 'I'd better start at the beginning.'

She outlined the problem. The words were all too familiar to her now. 'There are more and more tourists every summer and more homes here are becoming holiday lets…'

'Or second homes,' he interjected.

'Or second homes, which means fewer local residents. And since the tourists stay away in the winter when the weather isn't so good, the businesses are starting to struggle.' She could have recited this in her sleep. 'That's why Alessandra's closed. Not enough trade.'

Xander looked surprised at this. 'I thought she was retiring?'

'Yeah, well possibly. But earlier than she wanted to. Or so I heard on the town grapevine.'

'I picked a bad time to buy a shop then,' said Xander. 'Will I even find a tenant?'

'Well,' she said, 'that brings me rather neatly to the reason for my visit.' Suddenly she was filled with a desire to impress him. 'I've come up with a plan to attract more visitors in the winter. A living Advent calendar.'

She told him her plan; again, she could have done this in her sleep.

'The thing is, Xander,' she said, 'your boarded-up window isn't a good look. It creates the wrong impression, so I was wondering if we might use it for one of our displays. You don't have to do anything; I'll find someone to create the actual display.'

'It sounds interesting,' he said. 'Let me have a think about it.'

'Oh,' she said, suddenly deflated, surprised he hadn't immediately agreed. 'A Christmas display in the window might make the place more appealing to any prospective tenants. It would certainly look a lot better than the cardboard that's there now.'

'Like I said, I'll have a think about it. Give me your number and I'll let you know.'

She felt a pang of disappointment that he hadn't kept her number. She had his. She'd been on a lot of dates over the years from those dating apps, but made a point of deleting the guys' numbers when it didn't work out. But for some reason, she hadn't deleted Xander's.

'I'll call you now so you've got my number,' she said.

'You've still got mine?' He sounded surprised.

'I think so.' She reached in her handbag for her phone, but it wasn't there. Of course! It was still in the board game café. She was so flustered at seeing Xander again after all this time that she'd forgotten the reason she'd ventured back out again. 'Oh, I don't seem to have my phone on me.'

He took a pen from his pocket and scribbled a phone number on a beer mat, before handing it to her. 'In case you haven't.' He paused. 'Listen, Kate. I know things didn't work out between us, but I hope we can be friends. For one thing, you're the only person I know here.'

'Of course we can,' she said. 'And you'll have to get involved in the local community. Meet a few more people. There are allotments. And a Scrabble club in Hebbleswick. I think there's a knitting group there too, but I'm guessing that wouldn't be your thing.'

'No, I'm not much good with the old knitting needles. Anything else?'

'Well, we've no battle re-enactment society, if that's what you're wondering.'

He laughed. 'Perhaps I could start one.'

At that moment, the landlord walked past their table, carrying two bowls of hot chips.

'Hmmm. They smell good. Is this place okay for food?' said Xander. 'Or have you any other recommendations for local eating establishments?'

'There's the board game café,' she said. 'My best mate owns that. Or are you meaning more gastropubs and cordon bleu dining?'

'You may remember that's not really my style.'

Her eyes met his and she knew exactly what he was thinking.

Because she was thinking it too.

# 16

Four years earlier

The waiter stood at their table, pen poised. 'Are you ready to order?'

'I'll have the chicken Caesar salad, please,' Kate said. 'No croutons and not too much dressing. In fact, if you could bring the dressing in a little jug on the side, that would be much appreciated.'

'Blimey,' said Xander. 'It's like that scene from *When Harry Met Sally*.'

Kate laughed. 'Well, if you think I'm going to have an orgasm at the table, you're going to be very disappointed.'

She almost added, *But I'd be up for one later*, but realised in the nick of time that the waiter was still standing there, red-faced, waiting to take the rest of their order. And besides, she hadn't known Xander long. They weren't sleeping together yet.

When they were alone at the table again, Xander said, 'Honestly, Kate, that poor lad. He looked barely out of school. Bet he hasn't even heard of Meg Ryan.'

'Surely *everyone's* heard of *When Harry Met Sally*. I wasn't even born when it first came out, but I must have seen it at least six times.'

'Are you a bit of a cinema buff as well as a history enthusiast?'

Kate hesitated. The truth was, she was neither, but she *still* hadn't confessed to Xander that she'd lied on her dating profile. She should have told him at the start – it would have been far easier – but he'd gone to the trouble of buying tickets for that Cold War exhibition so she didn't feel she could admit the truth.

As time went on, it had become more and more difficult – partly because the more she got to know him, the more she liked him, and partly because he had taken her on a series of history-related dates.

On their second one, he'd picked her up in a dilapidated old Citroën. As she'd climbed into the passenger seat, Kate had glanced behind her, and seen a collection of yellow parking tickets, along with several empty crisp packets, an old towel, two carrier bags containing heaven only knew what, and a pile of books. University library books, by the look of them.

'I didn't think anyone in London owned a car,' she said.

'This isn't just a car. This is my office.'

He'd driven her to what appeared to be an ordinary bungalow in Essex, but was actually the hidden entrance of a secret nuclear bunker. Not so secret these days, as there were big brown signs on all the surrounding roads, directing tourists to the site.

On their third date, he'd taken her to Wapping, an area that had suffered greatly during the Second World War.

He'd told her a little of the history of the docks, showed her where pirates had been executed centuries earlier, and then led her to the statue of the boy and the tiger in Tobacco Dock. The tiger had escaped upon its arrival from Bengal in 1857, and clamped its jaws around a nine-year old boy.

'Cheerful, these dates we keep going on,' she'd said. 'Nuclear war. Executions. And a child being eaten alive by a tiger.'

'He wasn't eaten,' Xander had said. 'Someone saved him using a crowbar.'

'Oh, that's all right then.' Kate slapped his arm playfully, and as she withdrew her hand, he caught it suddenly, pulling her towards him, so their faces were only millimetres apart. She held her breath. Closed her eyes. Felt his lips brush fleetingly against hers. Parted her lips, anticipating a longer, more passionate kiss, but he moved away. She opened her eyes to see a group of tourists, mobile phones poised, trying to take a photo of the famous statue. Xander pulled her hastily out of their way.

She had to wait for their fourth date for him to kiss her properly. They shared a chilly picnic in the garden of St Dunstan in the East, a church designed by Christopher Wren, which had been damaged during the Blitz and was never rebuilt. It was chilly. In the atmospheric setting of the ruins, Kate had snuggled into Xander for warmth. Or at least she'd pretended it was for warmth, but, in reality, she was deliberately giving him an opportunity to kiss her again, and he'd obliged.

If she'd had to describe that kiss afterwards, the word she'd have used would have been tender. Xander had smooth, soft lips and a gentle, probing tongue, which he ran slowly along her lips, causing a shiver to run down her spine as she allowed herself to imagine what it might feel like for that tongue to explore other parts of her. But they hadn't quite got to that stage of their relationship. He too liked to take things slowly, he'd told her as they said goodbye a short while later on the Tube station.

Perhaps tonight would be the night, Kate thought now, as she sat opposite him in the restaurant on this, their fifth date, and the most conventional one yet.

'So are you?' he said.

'Am I...?' She'd been so lost in her own thoughts that she'd forgotten his question.

'A cinema buff as well as a history enthusiast?'

She paused again. She couldn't carry on pretending; it wasn't fair. 'Not really,' she said, 'but then I'm not much into history either. My profile wasn't one hundred per cent... I wanted to make myself sound more interesting. I'm so sorry, Xander.'

'So all those dates...? You were pretending?'

'Well, yes and no.' She scrutinised his face, trying to discern if he was disappointed or angry, but he looked more surprised than anything. 'I should have told you sooner, but you went to all that effort with those exhibition tickets. And actually, I *did* find it interesting. You've a real gift for bringing the past to life.'

'Thank you,' he said. 'I can't believe you lied like that.'

'More of a fib than a lie. An exaggeration. History *was* one of my favourite subjects at school,' she said defensively. 'Well, it was one of the ones I disliked least. Though admittedly that was largely because the history teacher was pretty gorgeous. We all had a crush.'

'Are you just into history teachers? Or history lecturers too?'

'Lecturers are even better,' she assured him.

'Good to know. So what about design? Was that a fib too?' he said, one eyebrow raised.

'Design-*er* handbags. Though I don't actually own one. Can't afford it. But I like window shopping. Are you cross?'

'Not cross. But I'm afraid an interest in history is a non-negotiable as far as I'm concerned. I'll be asking all my future dates to produce their National Trust membership card.'

It took her a second to realise that his eyes were twinkling again and he was joking.

He was always so chilled, so laid-back. She should have known he wouldn't be angry about her little white lie. Should have told him from the start really.

'And there I was,' he continued, 'trying to take you to places you'd find really interesting.'

'Honestly, Xander, I *did* find them interesting. And...' she paused for a moment, wondering whether to ignore the dating advice in her self-help books and lay her cards on the table '...and I find *you* really interesting.'

He held her gaze for a moment. 'I find you...' he began, but then the waiter was back at their table, and plates of food were placed in front of them with a flourish.

When Xander had said that no, they didn't require anything else, thank you, they stared down at their food. The portions were pathetically small, but that was what you expected in a place like this. The more expensive the menu, the less food they put on the plate.

'Is that it?' Xander said. 'Did we accidentally order off the children's menu?'

It took him all of six mouthfuls to devour his food; Kate took a little longer, as she'd read somewhere that chewing food for longer was good for her gut bacteria. Practically as soon as she had laid down her knife and fork, Xander summoned the waiter and asked for the bill.

'You don't mind, do you?' he said. 'I thought I might take you to another of my favourite places.'

The Citroën was parked a couple of streets from the restaurant with yet another yellow parking ticket under the windscreen wipers. Xander pulled it off, flinging it onto the back seat with the others.

Kate had always felt there was something exciting about getting into a car with a man. Perhaps it was sitting in such close proximity or the phallic shape of the gearstick between her and the driver, or the potential for him to reach over and place a hand on her thigh. She longed to reach over and stroke Xander's hair, but instead fiddled with a loose thread on her coat as he cut through the rabbit maze of side roads that criss-crossed the outskirts of the city. He weaved around parked cars and oncoming traffic like a Formula One driver negotiating a chicane, and finally pulling up on a street of terraced houses, alongside a small row of shops – a newsagents, betting shop and a fish and chip shop – and a bus stop, where a group of youths were sitting drinking cans of cheap lager. She assumed Xander lived here somewhere, but he took her hand and led her, not towards the front door of one of the houses, but into the chip shop.

Kate hadn't been inside a chippy for years. She inhaled

deeply, relishing the smell of frying food, something she never allowed herself to touch.

'This is more like it,' Xander said with a grin. 'What d'you fancy? Shall we share a portion or would you like one each?'

'Let's share.'

She watched him order, watched the man behind the counter shovelling what seemed like a mountain of hot, golden chips onto a big square of paper.

'Salt and vinegar?' the man asked.

Xander looked at her questioningly.

As a child, she'd loved chips with lashings of salt and vinegar, but as an adult, she never added salt to her food, and the only vinegar she ever consumed these days was of the apple cider variety.

'I don't mind. Have what you normally have.'

Xander asked for both. The man shook salt all over the chips, then added a liberal sprinkling of vinegar too.

'Never let it be said that I don't know how to treat a woman,' Xander said when they were back in the car. He'd unwrapped the bundle of chips and offered it to her.

Kate hesitated, then picked out one of the smallest chips, and blew on it, stalling the moment of actually eating it. She normally avoided fried foods, and potatoes didn't count as one of her ten a day. The windows were beginning to steam up now, obscuring the view of the row of terraced houses in front of them. She took the tiniest bite, but once she'd started, she found she couldn't stop. She took another chip. And then another. And another.

'Steady on, there.' Xander laughed. 'Leave some for me.'

When the chips were finished, Xander scrunched up the greasy paper they'd come in, throwing it into the back of the car with the other detritus.

Kate turned round and looked at it, then looked back at him and said, 'This is the messiest car I've ever been in.'

'I'm probably the messiest person you've ever met. I'm guessing you're one of those tidy people.'

'I taught Marie Kondo everything she knows,' Kate said.

'Marie who?'

'Never mind. So is your house terribly untidy too?'

'Would you like to find out?' he said. 'Come back for coffee?'

They both knew what that might mean – taking their fledgling relationship to the next level.

'I would *love* to come back for coffee,' she said.

Coffee and…?

Xander turned the key in the ignition and after a couple of false starts, the Citroën sprang into life. Humming softly to himself, he negotiated the narrow streets of west London. Kate's heart was full of optimism. There were all sorts of reasons why she *shouldn't* be with this man: he was older than her; messy whereas she was tidy; obsessed with history, a subject she knew little about; and he lived in London, whilst she was only here on a short secondment and would be returning to Yorkshire at the end of January.

But there was one reason – one big reason – why she *should* be with him: she was beginning to fall head over heels.

She smiled to herself. She loved this heady feeling, this first flush of love and lust. The anticipation of his lips on hers, his fingers teasing and caressing her skin, his naked body pressed up against hers. In these minutes as they drove through west London, Kate felt blissfully happy. Blissfully unaware too that within the next half hour, everything would have changed.

## 17

It was perhaps one of the most unusual requests that the little towns of Essendale and Hebbleswick had ever had. In the past, there had been calls for flood wardens, litter pickers and neighbourhood watch volunteers, and now Kate was scurrying around for fairy lights and unwanted curtains. Old duvet covers and sheets would also suffice. The two charity shops had some, but not nearly enough, so could everyone please search the backs of their cupboards, their lofts and their garden sheds?

Various collection points were set up around both towns, but more often than not, people would knock on Kate's door of an evening and hand over their findings. Or they'd ask Emily in the board game café if she could pop their unwanted curtains behind the counter for when Kate was next in. And many stopped Kate when they saw her in the street, and handed over plastic bags. Kate would find herself struggling to walk home as she laboured under a mountain of Essendale's unwanted fabrics.

A friendly electrician, with whom she'd once had what she referred to as a 'dalliance', had agreed to check all the lights were safe. She suspected he wanted to rekindle their romance, but she was dating Peter now, and besides, she remembered why it had been a dalliance and not a relationship; the man was a keen golfer, and spent all of his weekends up at the club. She didn't fancy being a golf widow.

The fairy lights that he deemed unsafe were taken to the local refuse centre, along with a few bedsheets that had questionable stains and couldn't possibly be used for the project. Even so, her previously immaculate and clutter-free house was now unrecognisable. There was something quite claustrophobic about being surrounded by this much stuff.

It wasn't only the clutter in her home that was getting her down, but the clutter in her mind too. There was so much to remember. Organising the living Advent calendar was becoming a full-time job, but Kate still had an *actual* full-time job to contend with, and that actual full-time job entailed schlepping to and from Leeds every weekday on trains that seldom ran on time.

It was understandable, given how much she had on her mind, that Kate made a slip-up at work. In the grand scheme of things, it was only a tiny error – a typo in the proof copy of a brochure that she'd sent out to clients for their approval – but for the woman who'd repeatedly won Employee of the Year, had three Little Miss Perfect mugs, all gifted by colleagues, and who *never* made careless mistakes, it was a big deal. Jeroen had told her not to worry about it, but Kate couldn't help herself.

She reached Leeds station that evening feeling hungry – there hadn't been time for lunch – and exhausted and upset with herself. She sat on the furthest bench on the platform at Leeds station to wait for the train. She'd chosen this seat deliberately, so no-one would see the tears streaming down her face; she never cried, and certainly not in public. Her mascara had probably run, and the wind at this end of the platform was playing havoc with her usually perfect bob. She glanced at her phone; the train to Essendale should be here in five minutes, so she needed to pull herself together, as the chances of getting a carriage to herself at this time in an evening were slim, and she couldn't let anyone see her in this state.

She dabbed her cheeks with a tissue then ran a brush through her hair, checking her appearance using her phone screen. She didn't look her usual immaculate self, but she would have to do. Then, as the train arrived, she stood up, patted down her skirt and strode to the nearest door. She found herself a seat, angling her entire body towards the window to avoid making eye contact with any fellow passengers. She definitely didn't want to engage in small talk tonight.

'Excuse me, is this seat taken?'

Kate looked up to see Xander towering over her. Without waiting for her reply, he sat down beside her, saying, 'Budge up, lass,' in a fake northern accent.

The train doors closed, and he added, 'A minute later and I'd have missed it.'

*I wish you had*, Kate thought. Uncharitable of her, but she didn't want him seeing her like this.

His face was full of concern. 'You okay? You don't seem your usual unruffled self.'

'Fine, thanks,' she said automatically, forcing her mouth into a smile.

'You're clearly not. Why don't you tell Uncle Xander all about it?'

Kate managed a small smile, this one genuine. 'It's nothing. I made a stupid mistake at work.'

'We all do that from time to time.'

'I don't. My colleagues have nicknamed me Little Miss Perfect. I've got three mugs with it on.'

'Three?'

'Office Secret Santa.'

Xander harrumphed. 'Wonder what you'll get this year then. Now you're no longer Miss Perfect.'

'It was one slip-up,' she said indignantly. 'One *tiny* slip-up'

'Exactly. No need to relinquish your nickname yet, and no reason for tears either.' He smiled at her gently.

Now he'd put it like that, she knew he was right. She'd overreacted; everyone made mistakes now and again.

'I know. I'm making a mountain out of a molehill. Probably cos I'm tired and hungry.'

They made idle chit-chat for the rest of the journey – how his new job was going, whether he'd unpacked yet – but as the train pulled into Hebbleswick Station, Xander stood up.

'Come on.'

'One more stop,' she said, assuming that in the dark he was confused about where they were. The two stations looked pretty similar, and he had only recently moved to the area.

'I know. Let's get off here. I know exactly what you need.'

Without waiting for an answer, he took hold of her hand,

pulling her to her feet, and steering her off the train and onto the platform.

'Where are we going?' she said.

'You'll see.'

He let go of her hand, and she followed him into the car park. One corner had been cordoned off for a mobile food van. Kate had never noticed it before, but it must be a permanent fixture as there were three wooden picnic tables in front of it, crowded with people.

'Chips,' said Xander. 'The perfect comfort food on a cold, damp evening.'

She was too tired to protest, to tell him that she didn't eat deep-fried food. Besides, they did smell incredible. She remembered those hot, golden morsels of deliciousness that they'd shared in his car four years ago, back before she'd seen what she'd seen and had then ruined everything.

It was immaterial now anyway. She was dating Peter. A wonderful, supportive man. A man she'd barely spoken to since the previous week's meeting about the living Advent calendar as she'd been so busy. She felt a little guilty now, standing here with Xander. She ought to get home to Essendale and text Peter to see if he was free.

On the other hand, she was hungry. And it was just a bag of chips, not a date. She joined the back of the queue, rubbing her hands together to warm them up, and Xander slotted in behind her.

'You cold?' he said. He didn't wait for her answer, but took off his scarf and wrapped it around her neck. 'I'd give you my gloves too, but I don't actually have any. I'm always losing them.'

She smiled. 'Thanks for the scarf.'

'You're welcome. Now what will you have? I fancy a meat and potato pie with chips.'

'Just a portion of chips, please.'

Food purchased, they went to find a seat. There were no empty tables, but a family shuffled along the benches so that Kate and Xander could perch at the end of theirs.

Xander was right, Kate thought, taking a delicate bite of one of the chips. They *were* exactly what she needed – the perfect comfort food. But it wasn't only the chips that she found comforting, but Xander's presence too. He was such easy-going company and she always felt more relaxed around him. She wondered again if she oughtn't to apologise for the way things had ended between them four years ago, and had opened her mouth to say something when he suddenly spoke.

'I've been thinking about your Christmas windows project. And the answer is yes, there can be a display in Alessandra's – Alexander's – but I'd like to do it myself. What d'you reckon?'

Kate thought for a moment. She hadn't yet finalised the list of windows or worked out which order they'd be unveiled in; she'd been waiting to see if Xander would say yes to Alessandra's being used.

'It depends. How are you with fairy lights?' She blew on a hot chip before popping it into her mouth.

'I'm a dab hand as it happens. Got a PhD in them. Wrote my dissertation on the energy consumption of low-wattage LED bulbs.'

'You did not.' She smiled. 'You probably did it on something related to the Cold War.'

'Yeah, the use of LED bulbs in communist Poland.'

'Hmmm.' A likely story. Kate was pretty sure LED bulbs hadn't been invented back then.

'Actually, I'd like to do the Christmas Eve window,' he said.

'No chance. I'm afraid that honour goes to the vicar. Even though he's not actually doing a window display. He wants to unveil the church's nativity scene. Same old, same old. Bit of a shame really. Christmas Eve is the final window and it ought to be one of the highlights – if not *the* highlight – of the whole project. Something that will get people talking. But the vicar says it has to be the nativity because that's the true meaning of Christmas.'

'Sounds like you're in a bit of a pickle.' Xander stabbed another chip with his wooden fork.

'Yeah, I am.'

'So let me do it. I'll create something with a wow factor, something that will leave a lasting impression on people *and* convey the true meaning of Christmas.'

'The vicar will never agree.'

'I bet I can persuade him.'

'Well, I couldn't, so I don't see how—'

'Trust me. I'll talk him round.'

'And what would your display be, exactly?'

Xander thought for a moment, then said, 'You know, I'd rather keep that a surprise.'

Kate sighed. She'd tried and failed to persuade the vicar to relinquish Christmas Eve. If Xander managed to convince him, could she trust Xander with the most important display of the entire project? Admittedly it would be fun if the final window was a mystery, even to her. She could then enjoy the big reveal along with the rest of the crowd. (Assuming there was going to be a crowd, and not just one man with a couple of whippets who happened to be walking past. She needed to get her finger out and generate some more publicity.)

It was either Xander's mystery window or the vicar's boring nativity scene.

'Okay,' she said slowly. 'If you can persuade the vicar, the Christmas Eve slot is all yours.'

It was a gamble. Was Xander creative? Did he have the skills and imagination to do as he'd promised, and make a window that would have that wow factor *and* convey the true message of Christmas?

It didn't matter anyway, she thought. One thing she was certain of: he'd never persuade the vicar to give up Christmas Eve.

# 18

She was on the train to work the following morning when Xander's text arrived. It was brief and to the point.

The vicar said yes.

She phoned him immediately. 'Are you sure?'

'Yes. You can put Alexander's on your schedule for Christmas Eve.'

She heard him through her phone, then realised she could hear his actual voice too. She stood up and glanced round the carriage. Sure enough, he was sitting two rows behind her. He hung up the call when he saw her and patted the empty seat beside him.

She walked over and sat down. 'I didn't see you at the station.'

'I was late. Jumped on in the nick of time.'

'Did he really agree to the window?' Kate said.

'He did. I phoned him first thing.'

'How on earth did you persuade him?'

'He liked my idea.' Xander smiled.

'Which is…?'

'I told you, Kate. Top secret.'


With Christmas Eve agreed upon, Kate drew up the schedule, and let all the windowers know when their displays would be. It was full steam ahead then, until the first of December, when the board game café window would be the first to be unveiled.

She'd never known the days to pass so quickly. Every evening after work she worked on the publicity campaign, sending out press releases to various local newspapers and radio stations, and posting on every social media platform she could think of. Sometimes she had a meeting or two as well, encouraging the windowers to think big, to be ambitious, to go beyond a few fairy lights draped around the stuff they normally had on display.

She barely saw Peter, but he was busy too, working late each evening, perfecting a contraption that could be quickly installed – and uninstalled again – in each location and would lift the drapes, revealing the displays.

There was only one thing left to be done: to prepare the first window itself. Kate had wanted to do this several days in advance, but Em didn't want the café window to be covered with drapes for longer than necessary.

'It'd build the suspense,' Kate had said. She remembered saying much the same thing to Em when she'd transformed her first business venture from an ordinary back street caff into a board game café. Cover the window. Create excitement. Let people wonder about what's happening inside.

Em had agreed back then, but this time she'd been adamant. They all saw precious little daylight at this time of year, she said. Customers wanted to be able to look out as they drank their morning coffee or ate their lunch. The window could be covered up, but only for one day. They would prepare the display the previous evening, beavering away late into the night if necessary to create the most magical Christmassy scene in the front of the board game café. Like the elves in the elves and the shoemaker story, Kate thought, as she tapped on the door of the café on the last evening in November. Working as Essendale slept.

Em opened the door just enough to let her squeeze in.

Peter was already there, halfway up a ladder with a drill in his hand. When he saw her, he descended, planting a kiss on her lips. Kate felt awkward kissing him in front of Em, but her friend seemed completely oblivious. She was head over heels with Ludek, Kate reminded herself. There was nothing between Em and Peter now.

'Right, what can I do?' Kate said.

Em gestured towards a table that was stacked high with games, along with several rolls of Christmas wrapping paper, Sellotape and scissors. 'You can start wrapping all that lot.'

'All of them?' Kate was sure they'd agreed that some of the parcels would be left open.

'All of them,' Em confirmed. 'Then we'll unwrap some of them again.'

'What's the point of that?'

'To make sure the paper is creased – otherwise it won't look genuine.'

Kate laughed. 'And I thought I was the perfectionist around here!'

She set to work with the Sellotape and scissors, wrapping the first of the selection of games that Em had laid out: Azul, Wingspan, Clank and Alhambra.

'Let's hope no-one wants to play these until the New Year,' she said.

'There are plenty of others,' Em said, gesturing at the shelves. 'And more at home if we need them.

'There was another knock at the door and Mr B appeared. 'Evening,' he said. 'Isn't this exciting? Ludek, *czy możesz mi pomóc wyjąć choinkę z samochodu?*'

Ludek and Mr B went outside. Kate looked questioningly at Em who said, 'Nope. I still haven't learned Polish. Well, I can say hello, please, thank you and doughnuts, but that's my limit.'

'Doughnuts?'

'*Pączki*,' said Em proudly. 'I think that might be my favourite Polish word. I love Ludek's *pączki*.'

The men returned a few minutes later with a huge Christmas tree, which they positioned on the right-hand side of the café window.

'I can translate now,' said Em. 'That was the Polish for, *Can you help me get an enormous tree out of the car?*'

'Yeah, even I could have worked that out.'

Kate resumed her gift-wrapping duties, as Em directed the three men to move the tree a little to the right, then the left, then back a bit – 'no, not that much' – until she was finally happy with its position. Peter went back up the ladder, fiddling with the contraption he'd rigged up, and Em and Ludek began to decorate the tree.

No-one passing by on the pavement would have any idea of the hive of activity inside, Kate thought. Mr B was stuffing stockings now. Em and Ludek were having a gentle argument about whether to use tinsel or whether it looked tacky. Was this what it would feel like to be a parent on Christmas Eve? Kate wondered. Secretly wrapping up gifts, filling stockings and putting up a few last-minute decorations, all ready for the children to descend the stairs the next morning with eyes as big as saucers.

One day, she thought. One day.

She glanced up at Peter on the ladder, at the frown of concentration on his face. Might he be the one? Every time she saw him, she liked him more and more. He was nothing like the stuffy businessman she'd always assumed him to be when he was dating Em. He was far more thoughtful for a start. Although when she'd mentioned this to him, he insisted he'd changed. 'I learned a lot about myself when Em left me,' he'd said. 'Had to face a few uncomfortable home truths. I didn't treat her as well as I should have and that will always be one of my biggest regrets. I've resolved to be a better man. A better human being.'

She was certainly reaping the benefits of those changes now. Look at him, fixing the drapes above the window. He was giving up every evening between now and Christmas Eve to do this. Well, except for three, which were a little bit different and wouldn't need Peter's rigging.

'This is my community too,' he'd said. 'I'm friends with many of the business owners around here. Although even if I wasn't, I'd do it for you.'

Mr B had finished the stockings – they were hanging up in the window, beside the Christmas tree – and had moved on to Santa's tray. He'd already placed a mince pie on a plate and had poured a glass of sherry. He emerged from the kitchen now with a large carrot in his hand. He bit off the bottom and began to chew it, placing the remaining carrot on the tray.

'I've made it look as though one of Santa's reindeer has taken a bite,' he said. 'Perhaps I ought to do the same with the mince pie.'

He swallowed the carrot, and picked up the pie.

'I think you should drink at least half of the sherry,' said Kate. 'We all know that Father Christmas enjoys a tipple.'

'Good point,' said Mr B, picking up the glass and downing almost all of it. 'Well done, Kate. You think of everything.'

They were all working so hard, she thought, taking one of the game boxes – Ticket to Ride: Nederland – and selecting a piece of shiny red paper to wrap it in. This time tomorrow, the first reveal would be over. Would people come to see it? Would the café be full afterwards with people enjoying Em's non-alcoholic mulled wine? (Em had forgotten to apply for a temporary licence so no alcohol could be served.) Or would they all be sitting here in front of a mountain of mince pies, lamenting the fact that no-one had bothered to turn up?

## 19

Underneath her calm, professional exterior, Kate had been a bag of nerves all day. She knew that the board game café window looked amazing, that Em and Ludek had a fun evening planned for after the big reveal, and that she herself couldn't have done more to publicise the event. There were posters all over Hebbleswick and Essendale, and they'd been distributed widely to other Yorkshire towns. Her social media posts were already getting lots of shares and comments. They'd had a mention in at least two local newspapers and a shout-out on local radio too. Now it was a waiting game to see if all her marketing had done the trick and people actually showed up.

Kate had arranged to work from home, although in truth, her mind wasn't on the job. She phoned Em twice, and texted her three times to ask the same question: Is everything ready?

The answer was the same each time: Yes, stop fretting.

At half past four, she couldn't stand it any longer and

decided to go and see for herself. It was dark already. With the paltry Christmas lights that the council had put up, the town looked anything but festive. Only one bulb was working on Rudolf who was suspended from a lamp post; it happened to be the red one of his bright, shiny nose, and it was reflected in the window of the flat above the florist's, making it appear as if nefarious activities took place up there.

'Pathetic,' Kate said out loud as she walked down the high street. If nothing else, the living Advent calendar would bring some Christmassy-ness to their lovely high street.

She pushed open the door to the café. Em looked up from the till where she was punching in numbers and raised her eyebrows in a 'What now?' kind of way.

'Suppose you've come to ask if everything is ready?' she said to Kate as she handed a customer their change.

'Yep. Sorry.'

'It *is* ready, Kate. This evening's going to be great. Stop worrying.'

'Can I check the window?'

Em nodded. Kate weaved her way between the tables to the front of the café. Peter had rigged up the drapes so they concealed the window display from both the outside and the inside. She unfastened one of the clothes pegs that held them in place, and poked her head through.

It was dark between the huge swathes of fabric. The lights hadn't been switched on yet, so Kate used the torch on her phone to check that everything was exactly as they'd left it the night before. The tree, beautifully decorated by Em and Lud; they had used the tinsel in the end and it didn't look tacky at all. The bulging stockings all hanging in a row, full of promise, though Kate knew they contained only scrunched-up old newspaper. Mr B's tray for Santa with its half-eaten carrot, mince pie and almost-empty sherry glass. And the presents, some wrapped up, the rest in various states of *un*wrap to make it look as if the recipients had already made a start on their gifts.

She felt a surge of pride in what they'd achieved. Even without the fairy lights, their first display was magical. Now all they needed was for the crowds to come and see it.

At ten to six, Peter arrived, and Em turned the sign to '*CLOSED*' and locked the door.

'There's quite a crowd out there,' Peter said to Kate. 'You needn't have worried. Right, flick the fairy lights on, and I'll take the inside drapes down.'

Kate dutifully flicked the switches on the sockets that powered the lights in the window. She couldn't remember the last time she'd felt that buzz of excitement about Christmas – she'd experienced it as a child but never as an adult – but she had it now, as Peter removed the fabric that separated the Christmas window from the inside of the café. She took a deep breath, enjoying the heady, fragrant mix of pine needles emanating from the tree in the window, and the mulled wine and mince pies coming from the board game café's kitchen.

They'd asked the mayor to make the opening speech, but she'd had a prior commitment, so, as a respected local GP and well-liked figure in the community, Ludek had agreed to do the honours.

At one minute to six, Em turned off all the lights in the café. With the serving hatch from the kitchen closed, the café was in darkness, save for the twinkle of the fairy lights in the window. Em, Peter and Ludek said nothing, and Kate wondered if they, like her, were all saying a silent prayer that the evening would go well.

'It's time,' she said.

She and Ludek went outside, standing in the doorway, leaving the door open a crack so that those remaining inside could hear his speech.

He cleared his throat. 'Welcome, everyone, to the first night of our Christmas windows project. We've turned Hebbleswick and Essendale into one giant Advent calendar in the run-up to Christmas, and every evening at six p.m. we'll be revealing one of our windows. There are maps available in most of the shops and in the library, which show you where all the windows are and when each will be unveiled, so we hope you'll visit all the others too. This was the lovely Kate's idea—' he gestured at Kate '—to bring more visitors to our glorious valley over the winter months, so we do hope you'll spread the word to encourage more people to come along and see it.'

As Ludek spoke, Kate scanned the sea of faces. So many faces. Her friends were all there: Jo and Razz, Taylor, Harry and little Max. Andrea the florist. Reverend Stone. Hilary, the local librarian. Several of the shop owners from Hebbleswick had made the journey too. She knew everyone, she realised, if not by name, at least by sight.

'Since this is the opening night of the project,' Ludek continued, 'we'll be celebrating afterwards with mince pies and mulled wine in the board game café. Non-alcoholic mulled wine, I'm afraid, but still delicious. Other refreshments are available too. At seven p.m., I'll be running a little board game session, featuring games you might enjoy playing after your Christmas dinner if you're tired of the usual Monopoly, Cluedo and Scrabble.'

'As if anyone could ever get tired of Scrabble,' came Jo's voice from the crowd.

'Now, without further ado,' said Ludek, 'I hereby declare the first Christmas window open.'

'Drum roll, please,' said Kate.

She began to slap her own thighs with the palms of her hands, and the crowd obligingly followed suit. The drapes began to lift revealing the bottom of the window, the gifts on the floor beside the tree, then the tree itself. The stockings lined up, bulging with gifts. Peter's mechanism worked flawlessly, as Kate had known it would. She looked in amazement; she'd seen the display from the inside, of course, but never from this perspective, and it was spectacular. Magical. There were gasps from the onlookers, umms and ahhs, and a little friendly jostling as the people standing behind tried to get a better view.

'Gorgeous,' she heard someone say.

'Well, isn't that lovely?' said another.

Ludek slipped an arm around her, hugging her and whispering, 'Well done, you. I'm going inside to help Em with the mince pies.'

And then he was gone, and Kate remained alone in the doorway, fascinated by everyone's reactions.

Slowly, the people at the front moved aside, some heading past her into the board game café, and more taking their place. Children pressed their noses up against the glass.

'Look, Mum, Santa's been,' said one. 'He's eaten half a mince pie.'

'But he's managed most of the sherry,' said another.

'And his reindeer has had some carrot!'

They'd done it, Kate thought. One down, twenty-three to go. And if they all got as good a reaction as this window had, she'd be very happy indeed. She felt an enormous sense of satisfaction that the first big reveal had gone so well, and then warmth and fuzziness at how she was a part of a fabulous community and had lovely friends and a wonderful new man now too. She looked round for Peter, but he was still inside the café. She went inside to fetch him; he really ought to see how good the display looked from the street.

The café hadn't been this busy since the school summer holidays. Em and Ludek were bustling around behind the counter, already doing a roaring trade. Em looked dazzling, her face glowing with pleasure. When the café was full like this, when she was rushed off her feet, Em thrived. She beamed at the customers as she took orders and handed over drinks. Kate had seen this before, though sadly not so often in recent weeks, but hopefully that was about to change.

And there was Peter in the corner, watching proceedings, a proud look on his face. Only his pride wasn't directed towards Kate. He was looking at Em, and Kate realised with sudden clarity something that she should probably have realised before: Em was over Peter, but he was still in love with her.

The joy, the triumph that she'd felt a few moments earlier at seeing the café so full, at seeing her living Advent calendar was beginning to work, left her like the air going out of a balloon. Kate felt literally deflated.

There wasn't a spark with Peter; that was true. He didn't make her heart pound or her palms clammy or her stomach turn somersaults, but she *liked* him. Respected him. Enjoyed his company. They wanted the same things out of life, had shared values. She found him attractive – not to the extent that she 'fancied the pants off him' as she and Em used to say about boys in their teenage years, but the time they spent in bed together was definitely pleasurable. This, she had thought, was what a grown-up relationship was like, and she had wanted it to work out.

And then another realisation, as sudden as the first: she *still* wanted it to work out.

Em wasn't in love with Peter. Hadn't been for years. She was crazy about Ludek, would never leave him. Peter's love for her was completely unrequited.

Ludek was clapping his hands now, asking everyone to grab a seat. Chairs had been carried down from upstairs, and people were jostling for a space around one of the tables. When they'd all settled, Ludek began to speak.

'Now, hands up if you only ever play a board game on Christmas Day?'

Most people glanced around the room before tentatively putting up a hand, as if they were confessing to something truly terrible.

'I thought so. Tell me some of the games you enjoy playing,' Ludek said.

'I wouldn't go as far as to say *enjoy*,' someone at the back quipped.

Ludek laughed good-naturedly.

'Scrabble,' called Jo.

'Brilliant. I was hoping you'd say that. If you enjoy Scrabble – or perhaps its online version, WordPals or online word puzzles like Wordle – we have an excellent selection

of alternative word games for you to try. This is Hardback.'
He held up a box. 'It's a card game. Each card has a letter
on and you use the cards in your hand each turn to make a
word. Some letters will score you points. Like in Scrabble,
the number of points varies, and the harder-to-use letters
like X and Z will generally be worth more. Other letter
cards are worth money, which allows you to purchase
better cards – ones that score you more points or gain you
more money.'

'Sounds great,' called Razz.

Ludek went on to describe the word games Just One and
Codenames – both ideal for bigger groups – along with
three others: So Clover!, Bananagrams and Boggle.

'Any games for people who like Cluedo?' someone
shouted.

'Funnily enough, I have.'

He recommended Awkward Guests for the Cluedo lovers
in the room and Acquire for the Monopoly fans. Kate
looked towards the window and saw Xander with his nose
pressed up against the glass, peering in.

She gestured to the door, indicating for him to come
inside.

'Sorry,' he mouthed to Kate as he did so. There wasn't an
empty chair so he leaned against the door, listening to the
end of Ludek's talk.

When the speech was over, a few people went up to
chat to Ludek and a few took some of the games he'd
showed them and found themselves a table, but most drifted
off into the night.

'Hey, you made it,' Kate said to Xander, as he stood at
the counter.

Em handed Xander a glass of wine and a mince pie, and he handed her a scrunched-up note and moved away from the counter without waiting for his change.

'Kate, I really am sorry that I missed the first big reveal,' he said. 'It was a student with problems. Floods of tears. Thinking of quitting uni altogether. I couldn't leave.'

'That's okay. This display's going to be up for over a month. Plenty of time to admire it.'

'I already have. It looks fabulous. You've done an amazing job.'

'Yeah, well. It was mostly Ludek and Em.'

She felt someone watching her and turned to see Peter standing beside her.

'Oh, Peter,' she said. 'Peter, this is Xander. Xander, Peter, my er…' It was a little too early to call him her boyfriend.

Peter slipped a proprietorial arm around her waist. 'I set up the drapes for the big reveal this evening. I'll be doing that every night actually.'

Xander turned, glancing up at the mechanism suspended from the café ceiling above the window. 'That's quite a contraption,' he said. 'Design it yourself?'

'Yes, I'm an engineer by trade, though more hands off these days. I own Peter Ridley Engineering Limited.'

'Oh, in the big building? Yeah, I've noticed that. Impressive.'

'Thank you.'

Kate noticed that Peter sounded a little stiff. Feeling decidedly awkward, she feigned a yawn, and said, 'I'm really tired. You'll both have to excuse me – I think I might head home.'

'I'll drive you,' said Peter quickly.

'Actually, I could do with the walk. I need some air. And I haven't done my ten thousand steps today.'

She kissed him lightly on the lips, gave Xander a little wave and headed outside.

The first evening had gone well, but Kate felt uneasy. She couldn't quite put her finger on why. It wasn't the awkwardness between Xander and Peter, nor the way Peter had been looking at Em. She ought to be feeling happy at the way the evening had gone; far more people than she'd expected had braved the cold to see the first window being unveiled.

The problem was, she had *known* all of those people. Every single one. Not all their names, granted, but she knew their faces; they were residents of the valley. There hadn't been a single person – not that she'd spotted anyway – from out of town. Not one person had even ventured from nearby Halifax.

So yes, the first evening of the living Advent calendar had generated business tonight for the board game café, but in terms of its actual goal of attracting more visitors to the two towns, it clearly had a way to go.

## 20

'Last night was brilliant, Kate! Well done!'
Kate had barely stepped outside her front door on the second of December when congratulations began to roll in.

It was Saturday. She'd had a long lie-in to recover from the launch of the living Advent calendar, and then spent a while on social media, uploading the best photos from the previous evening and a short 'reel' that she'd made, and checking to see what other people had posted about the event, all the while feeling despondent about the whole thing. The occupants of the two towns had turned out in force, and that was wonderful and she was grateful to live in a place with such community spirit, but they needed new people to come too; that was the whole point of all this hard work.

She went over to Peter's for a quick brunch of scrambled eggs, spinach and baked mushrooms, and they were now on their way to the florist to get everything ready for the second big reveal.

Everyone she passed seemed to have something to say about the board game café window.

'Loved the half-eaten carrot, Kate!'

'Christmas windows! Genius idea!'

'Kate, you're a marvel. Don't know what this town would do without you!'

She smiled and said yes, hadn't it been lovely, and she hoped they'd come along every evening. No-one else – not even Peter – seemed to have realised that the event hadn't attracted even *one* out-of-town visitor.

And that wasn't the only reason she felt disappointed. The man walking beside her now, a ladder tucked under one arm and a toolbox in his hand, was still in love with Em.

Over the years, Em, Jo and Harry had all turned to Kate for dating advice. Other friends too, and a couple of colleagues. If any one of them had said to her, 'I've realised that the person I'm dating is in love with someone else, what should I do?' she knew full well what her answer would have been. End the relationship.

Yet she didn't want to end things with Peter. For one thing, there were so many positives to this relationship and they'd barely given it a chance, with her being so busy with the living Advent calendar. For another, she didn't relish the thought of going back on those wretched apps and spending even another minute gazing across a table at a random man, trying to make conversation to get some sense of who this stranger was.

So what if Peter was in love with Em? She couldn't blame him. Em was the loveliest person. Quirky. Kind. Funny. Kate loved Em herself, though obviously not in the same way.

And it wasn't as if his feelings for Em were a threat to her relationship with Peter; Em would never leave Ludek. There wasn't a cat in hell's chance of that happening. Em and Peter had had their time and he had blown it – his words, not hers.

*It's not as if you're in love with him.*

This thought surprised her. She'd known it deep down, but hadn't acknowledged it before. She wasn't in love with him, and wasn't in danger of falling anytime soon. Her mind didn't wander off at work, wondering what he was doing. She didn't lie awake thinking about him either, but had put this down to tiredness; she was doing so much at the moment that she fell asleep every night the moment her head hit the pillow. But maybe this would all come in time. Maybe when she was more relaxed, when Christmas and New Year were over and she and Peter could spend some proper time together, maybe it would come.

She glanced up at Alessandra's. The curtains were still closed. That was another thing that wasn't helping: the proximity of Xander, the one man she never had been quite able to get out of her system, even though she knew a relationship with him wouldn't work and wasn't what she wanted. The attraction was still there though – at least on her part. That was undeniable.

They headed into the florist's shop. The previous evening,

Peter had taken down the drapes and his rig from the board game café window, and transferred them here.

They exchanged a few pleasantries with Andrea, the owner, then Peter put up his stepladders and began to attach the rig above the window, with Kate supporting the opposite end to make it easier. She watched him as he worked; she liked the look of concentration on his face. Bless him, he was so kind to be giving up his time to fix this up for her project. Although...

Was he doing it for her? Or was he doing it for Em? Was all this because he knew the board game café was struggling and he wanted to do his bit to help his ex?

He spotted her watching, and gave a little wave with the hand that wasn't holding the drill. Then he made as if he was going to fall from the ladder. Kate laughed, pushing the thought of how he'd looked at Em out of her mind and resolving that she was going to do everything she could to make this relationship work. He was a good man. The right kind of man to have a family with.

Peter had designed the mechanism well; it was soon in place, and the two of them unfolded the fabric, hanging it over the rig. He checked that the whole drapes went up and down smoothly, before declaring that Andrea could assemble her window.

'Now if you ladies don't mind,' he said, 'I've been summoned for afternoon tea with my mother.' He leaned into Kate and kissed her cheek, then whispered, 'I'm going to tell her about us.'

Kate's stomach churned at the thought. She was sure the formidable Florence wouldn't consider her suitable for

Peter. It was bad enough that he was still in love with Em; she didn't need parental disapproval on top of that.

Although looking on the bright side, it was surely a good sign that he was telling his mother. He'd hardly announce that he and Kate were dating if he didn't think their relationship had some longevity.

When Peter had gone, Andrea said she was intending to close the shop at four o'clock and would arrange her Christmas display then. 'I don't want to do it with customers coming in and out,' she said.

Not a single customer had come in in the entire time she'd been here, but Kate didn't argue. Andrea said she didn't need any further help – all the Christmas wreaths, the bouquets and centrepieces were ready in the back room, and just needed popping in place – so Kate decided to head for the board game café.

She was delighted to find the place busy. Or at least, busier than she'd seen it recently, with the exception of the previous evening. And busy enough that Em couldn't sit down for a chat, so Kate slipped behind the counter, making herself a mug of green tea and fixing a mug of Yorkshire tea for Em.

'Happy with last night?' asked Em, when the queue for cakes and hot drinks had died down.

'Yeah.' Kate was cautious with her response.

'You don't sound too sure.'

That was the trouble with knowing someone for most of your life: you couldn't get anything past them.

'No, well…' Kate hesitated, but then she didn't like keeping secrets from Em. 'Look, please keep this to yourself, but although there were loads of people here last night, which was great, none of them were new in town, were they? And the whole point of the living Advent calendar was to attract visitors to the valley.'

'It was only the first evening. And if everyone who came tells their friends about it, or shares a post on Instagram, then maybe more people *will* come. Look at the café – it's not full, but it's definitely busier today than it has been in recent weeks. Miles busier than last Saturday. Whether that's the result of last night, I can't say, but it could be. You're doing your best, Kate. No-one expects you to single-handedly turn things around for the town, and they certainly don't expect you to do it overnight.'

'Hmmm.' Em had a point. Maybe in time, word would spread. 'I think what I really need is some proper coverage in the press, but I've tried the usual places. The local TV news weren't in the least bit interested. We've had the briefest of mentions in local papers and on local radio. We need more.'

'Give them another try perhaps?'

Kate shook her head. 'The thing is, if they were going to come, they'd have come for the opening evening. That's the important one.' She lowered her voice. 'That's partly why I wanted the first evening to be the board game café, but don't tell anyone. I don't want to be accused of favouritism.'

Em laughed. 'Is this your favourite café, Kate?'

'Course it is. You know that.'

'Even though it's full of board games? And you don't like board games?'

'Even though it's full of board games.' Kate took a sip

of her green tea. 'It's disheartening though, Em. Marketing is what I do for a living – I thought I was good at it. But I don't feel I've done a good enough job of marketing the Advent calendar.'

'I bet more people will come along tonight. And wait till you see what Ludek and Razz have planned for tomorrow. On Monday morning, everyone will be talking about it at work, and their colleagues will all want to come along.'

Kate sighed. She hoped Em was right.

## 21

It was late morning, and after a brief but rather lovely Sunday lie-in with Peter, Kate had hurried along to the health centre and was now standing in the deserted waiting room staring at the strangest collection of objects she'd ever seen in her life.

During the week, this was the building where Razz and Ludek listened to lists of symptoms, soothed anxieties and dispensed potent drugs. Saved lives even. Consummate professionals who'd undergone years and years of training. But now the pair of them reminded Kate of naughty schoolboys as they proudly showed her the things they'd gathered for their Christmas window display.

There were four stuffed toys: a somewhat battered owl; a rabbit with what appeared to be a collection of little pellets – its poo presumably; a dog with a rather ludicrous wig skew-whiff on its head; and a sheep that appeared to be missing an eye, but Ludek produced a joke eyeball from his pocket and placed it next to the sheep.

'We raided the Oxfam shop,' he said.

'I hope that isn't real.' Kate pointed to a human skull. 'It's not, is it?'

The men flashed each other a look that left her question unanswered.

Beside the skull, was a small pile of moss, the kind you could buy in the garden centre if you were making a hanging basket. This was all very intriguing.

Kate had insisted that the windowers told her what they were planning for their displays before she'd allocated the dates. She'd wanted to avoid duplication; it wouldn't do if two displays were similar, especially if they were on consecutive evenings. Xander had refused point-blank; if she wanted the cardboard removed from the window of Alessandra's and a wonderful display in its place, he had made it quite clear that the contents of that display would be kept top secret. The health centre window was the only other mystery; Ludek and Razz had been a bit vague about the actual theme of their display when she'd been allocating the windows.

'We'll do something related to health over the festive season,' Ludek had said. 'Fun but informative.'

Kate had trusted him. Why wouldn't she? Not only was he a doctor and a well-respected figure in Essendale, but he was her oldest friend's partner.

Now looking at the mischievous expressions on Razz and Ludek's faces, she wondered if she'd been a bit too hasty. She glanced at the table again, unable to figure out how these seemingly random items could relate to health over the festive season. Alongside the toys and the skull, there was a model of the Eiffel Tower, a large bottle of water and a frying pan, which contained bacon, eggs and mushrooms, all fashioned out of what appeared to be plasticine.

'I made those,' said Ludek.

His eyes were shining and he looked so childlike, so pleased with his efforts that Kate wanted to pat him on the head. Instead, she said simply, 'Well done.'

She looked at the table again, trying to join the dots to see what the finished picture was, but she couldn't fathom it.

A jar of instant coffee with a mug of black coffee beside it. A packet of paracetamol. A bottle of vodka.

'It's water inside,' said Razz. 'For safety reasons, we drank the vodka.'

A bird cage with a model canary, sunshine yellow and sitting at a quirky angle, as if it were about to fall off its perch.

'That bird looks like it's the one who had the vodka,' said Kate.

Razz and Ludek exchanged glances again.

'Ironic,' said Razz.

Kate couldn't see the irony herself, but moved on to checking out a book. Ernest Hemingway's *The Old Man and the Sea*. How on earth did that relate to all this other stuff?

A bottle of beer.

'Again, empty,' said Razz, following her gaze.

'You two reprobates must have had a fun week.' Kate smiled.

A carton of tomato juice.

'That one's full,' he said helpfully.

A box of eggs. Bottles of Worcestershire and Tabasco sauce. Salt and pepper pots.

'I don't get it,' said Kate. 'How on earth does all this stuff link together? And what's it got to do with health?'

'You'll see,' said Ludek, tapping the side of his nose.

She had the sneaking suspicion that this pair were up to something so said firmly, 'I'm staying to help. To make sure the window is perfect before it goes on display.'

Although she wasn't sure why she was bothered; so few people had turned up at the florist's window reveal the previous evening that she was beginning to wonder if they shouldn't just abandon the whole thing.

Ludek smiled. Not his usual smile when he was jesting with customers in the café, or teasing Em or winning a board game, but the smile she'd seen him use at work on the odd occasion she'd had to consult him as a patient.

'Kate, this perfectionist streak in you,' he said, 'I worry sometimes… well, it's not good for your mental health. You need to let go a little. Relax. Stop worrying.'

Razz nodded. 'You can trust us. We're doctors.'

'I dunno,' she said warily.

There was an air of gleefulness about them and Kate felt quite certain that their 'health over the festive season' window wasn't going to be the informative display she'd envisaged. And was it even going to be festive? There was nothing Christmassy about all these weird objects.

'We have fairy lights,' said Ludek, as if he'd read her mind.

'Lots of them,' said Razz, indicating a stack of boxes under the table that she hadn't noticed before. There was also a pile of laminated sheets of card that appeared to be printed with text. The vital information, Kate assumed, that would make sense of this strange cornucopia of stuff.

'Leave us to it,' said Razz. 'Go and put your feet up for a few hours. We'll do a good job, we promise.'

They put on mock-serious faces and in perfect synchronicity mimed crossing their hearts. Then, before she could argue any further, they bundled her back into her coat and practically shoved her out of the door.

'Don't make me regret this,' she called over her shoulder to the guys, who were standing in the health centre doorway, as if waiting until she had definitely gone before they set to work.

At ten to six, she was back at the health centre, standing outside in prime position in front of the window, with a small crowd beginning to gather around her.

Razz and Ludek were obviously still putting the finishing touches to the display, because occasionally the drapes would move slightly.

'This had better be good, you two,' Kate mumbled under her breath.

She glanced around, trying to do a head count, which wasn't easy because a) it was dark and b) more people kept joining. It was a good turnout though; the best so far, in fact. The doctors were both popular figures in this town, so it was unsurprising that many locals had come along, but there were a couple of out-of-towners too, brandishing the official trail maps for the living Advent calendar.

She checked the time on her phone for the umpteenth

time. It was 17.59. As the display changed to 18.00, she shouted, 'Drum roll, please,' and everyone began to slap their thighs. The drapes covering the window began to lift, revealing the frying pan with the plasticine full English, the bottle of vodka, and the stuffed toy owl with an egg beside it.

The birdcage with the tipsy canary was suspended on the left of the window, and the other random objects were all displayed on boxes of various heights. The entire thing was illuminated by several sets of twinkling fairy lights.

But it wasn't the objects or the fairy lights that interested Kate; it was the large sign over the entire thing.

'A history of hangover cures!' she said aloud.

'I know, hilarious, isn't it? I saw it from inside.' Peter was beside her now; she hadn't noticed him slipping out of the health centre, after he'd raised the drapes.

Each of the objects had one of Razz and Ludek's laminated signs beside it, with information in bold, black text.

Do a few bars of Slade have you reaching for the sherry, the Baileys or even the eggnog? If you overdo the booze over the festive season and wake up feeling a little worse for wear, what can you do?

Over the centuries, people have tried many different cures for hangovers. The ancient Romans advocated a raw owl's egg or a fried canary. The Outer Mongolians opted for a pickled sheep's eyeball. Apparently, eyeballs are high in antioxidants, but we don't recommend them. The cowboys of the Wild West drank tea made from rabbit poo. Personally, we prefer a mug of good old Yorkshire tea.

'I wouldn't fancy rabbit poo tea or an eyeball,' Peter said, 'even if it was pickled. Good job I only drink in moderation.'

Kate looked around, trying to gauge the reaction of the crowd. This was nothing like the kind of thing she'd envisaged when she suggested the living Advent calendar, but it was witty and original, and she loved it. And so did other people, judging by the pointing and the nudging and the giggling.

'Thank you, Razz and Ludek,' she whispered quietly to herself.

'Hair of the dog.' Peter snorted, pointing at the dog in the skew-whiff wig alongside the bottle of vodka.

According to the two GPs, treating fire with fire was advocated by Hippocrates himself, after whom the famous Hippocratic oath was named. One of the laminated sheets explained that whilst consuming more alcohol might bring some temporary relief from the symptoms of a hangover, it wasn't advisable.

*Think of your liver*, the doctors warned.

The Ernest Hemingway novel had been placed beside the carton of tomato juice and the (empty) bottle of beer, representing the author's favoured hangover cure. The doctors had positioned a bundle of the moss next to the skull, along with a sign that read:

In days gone by, Europeans would dry moss inside a skull, grind it to a powder and snort it. Not sure it had to be a human skull, but since we had this one at our disposal... (And no, it's not a real one, in case you're wondering!)

'I was convinced that was a real skull,' Kate said to Peter.

'Me too.'

Whilst there's no scientific evidence whatsoever that most of these hangover cures work, read the sign beside the bottle of water, water can definitely help because people often suffer from dehydration after they've been on the lash. Alcohol is a diuretic – it makes you pee more often. Just 4 drinks can cause you to lose up to a litre of water.

Coffee may also help, since alcohol has a detrimental effect on sleep, and the caffeine in a mug of coffee may perk you up. A wide range of excellent coffees are served at the local board game café.

Kate laughed when she read this. 'The cheek of him,' she said. 'Advertising the café!'

'Em does do exceptional coffee though,' Peter said. 'She's very selective about the beans.'

Many people swear by a fry-up. Again, there's scant evidence for this, although both bacon and eggs contain an amino acid called cysteine, which can possibly help. If you'd like to put this to the test, the local board game café serves an excellent full English!

She spotted the Eiffel Tower beside the bottles of Tabasco and Worcestershire sauce, along with another egg, and the salt and pepper.

'Of course! A prairie oyster!' she said. 'I was wondering earlier what that was about.'

According to Razz and Ludek, prairie oysters had been

introduced at the 1878 Paris World Exposition, and had been named so because you had to swallow the concoction of Tabasco, Worcestershire sauce and a raw egg in one gulp, with the yolk whole, which was reminiscent of downing an oyster.

On the next display box was a bunch of asparagus, a banana, a pear and a kiwi fruit, which were, the sign announced, all healthy foods that were said to help, although again, there was very little scientific evidence.

A final piece of text on the right side of the window, in bigger letters than all the rest said:

We hope you've had fun reading about all these hangover cures. On a more serious note, the best 'cure' is not to get a hangover at all! As your local GPs, we'd advise you to drink moderately this Christmas! Drs Razz and Ulanicki.

'It's a great window, isn't it?' Peter squeezed her hand.

'Yeah, it really is. Fun, but with a serious message that's so appropriate for the season. I couldn't have asked for more.'

## 22

After the unveiling of the hangover cures window, Kate and Peter walked hand in hand down the street away from the health centre and towards the middle of the town. She'd been preoccupied earlier, so hadn't noticed until now that almost every other house had something in their window. Some had a Christmas tree, others had fairy lights and a few had created little festive displays of their own: children's drawings of Santa and reindeer adorned one window, a collection of beautiful coloured baubles suspended on coloured ribbons of different lengths in the next and in another, the branch of a tree, sprayed with fake snow, with a little robin redbreast sitting at the top.

A few weeks ago, Kate would have inwardly groaned at the sight of all this festivity, but now she positively loved it. The windows weren't attracting hordes of visitors from out of town – not yet anyway – but they were definitely inspiring the locals.

'People are really getting into the spirit of it,' she said. 'This street looks so lovely, doesn't it?'

'It's all your doing. I'm so proud of you.' Peter had his arm round her shoulders, and he pulled her closer into him. 'So proud.'

She smiled, but couldn't help remembering that on Friday evening, he'd looked proud of Em, as she handed out mulled wine and perfectly baked mince pies in the board game café. But no, she wouldn't think about that. Peter was with her now. Three windows had been unveiled, each unique and beautiful in its own way, and the residents of Essendale were creating their own unofficial window displays too. The town was looking splendid, so much more festive, so much more inviting, than it had a week ago.

'This could become an annual thing,' said Peter.

'Yeah, maybe,' said Kate. 'Who'd have thought it when we met in that pub in Leeds and discussed how much we were dreading Christmas that we'd end up doing a living Advent calendar project together?'

'It's all down to you. All I've done is rig up the mechanism for the big reveals.'

'But that's a vital part of it. And you've made me feel supported, every step of the way.'

'You're lovely, Kate.'

She thought she felt a 'but' in the air. Was there something missing for him? Other than the fact that she wasn't Emily.

No, she wasn't going to think like that. She was going to count her blessings. The living Advent calendar might have got off to a slow start in terms of attracting new visitors to the town, but the residents were certainly enjoying it.

On Monday evening, it was Essendale Library's turn to host the Advent window.

The librarians had created a giant-sized book, opened to reveal two pages from one of the most famous Christmas books of all time: *A Christmas Carol* by Charles Dickens. The book formed the backdrop of their display, which featured several scenes from the book, cleverly recreated with silhouettes of cardboard figures: the hunched figure of Ebenezer Scrooge, complete with nightcap and candle, his ghostly visitors and a rather emaciated Tiny Tim. Some model Victorian streetlamps added to the overall effect.

The following evening, it would be the Oxfam's shop turn to host the window, and then on the sixth of December, Mr B's 'Christmas in Poland' display would be revealed at the house he shared with the formidable Florence. (Although she seemed slightly less formidable since Peter had told Kate that his mother was delighted that the two of them were 'courting'.) After that, there would be two weeks of displays in neighbouring Hebbleswick, before the final four windows were revealed in Essendale.

And then it would be Christmas Day, she thought gloomily, and she'd be spending the day with her dad. She wondered if she could make her excuses to him, and have Christmas lunch with Peter instead, but however much she resented her father, however much she blamed him and his obsessive hobby for her mother's absence, she wasn't hard-hearted enough to leave him on his own on Christmas Day.

After the unveiling of the library's window, Peter and

Kate, along with many other residents, headed to the Red Lion.

Like many of the local business, the pub had been struggling in recent weeks and the landlord had had his own idea for boosting trade: a quiz night. Jo had insisted that they made up a team. Kate tried to argue that pub quizzes weren't really her thing, but since she'd once dragged Jo along to one – it was a quiz with a difference; a speed-dating quiz – she didn't really have a leg to stand on. Besides, she felt she should support local initiatives since she wanted people to support hers.

Bring Peter, Jo had texted.

Kate had felt sure Peter wouldn't be up for the quiz – pubs weren't really his thing – but to her surprise he had readily agreed.

'Mother's going,' he'd said. 'Stan's agreed to be the quizmaster.'

Teams were limited to five players, so that evening, Kate, Jo and Razz and Harry – Taylor was at home looking after Max – found themselves a corner table and grabbed a pen and answer sheet, and Peter went to get the drinks in. He was quite some time; the landlord hadn't expected his plan to work quite so well. There wasn't an empty table in the place, resulting in a long queue at the bar.

'How's it going with Peter?' whispered Jo.

Kate wasn't quite sure why she was whispering; Peter was too far away to hear over the buzz of excitement in the pub. 'He's lovely. Kind. Supportive. I like him.'

'I'm sensing a but,' said Jo.

Kate hesitated, reluctant to admit that her new relationship wasn't perfect, but also keen to hear her friend's perspective on that. 'There wasn't that initial spark, you know.' She looked from Jo to Razz and then to Harry.

Jo placed her hand over Razz's hand and said, 'I didn't have that initial spark with Razz, to be honest. When I first saw him, it wasn't love at first sight or anything. He kind of grew on me over time. And I'm blissfully happy now.'

'We both are,' added Razz.

'I had the spark with Taylor,' said Harry, 'but she didn't with me. And I think – I hope – she'd say that she's blissfully happy too. Now the morning sickness has worn off.'

'It's different for everyone,' said Razz. 'The spark is simply a biological reaction, chemicals in your brain, designed over millennia of evolution to ensure the survival of the species. It doesn't guarantee whether a relationship will work out or not.'

'It's not only that.' Kate was on the cusp of telling her friends that she suspected that Peter was still in love with Em, but she stopped speaking as she saw him approaching, five drinks precariously gripped between his hands as he negotiated his way through the busy pub. She sprung up to help him, just as Mr B tapped on the microphone.

'Testing, one, two, three, testing. Can everyone hear me?' His voice boomed through the pub, accompanied by ear-piercing squeaks of feedback from the mic.

A few people called back, 'Yes' and 'Loud and clear' and one joker shouted, 'Did someone say something?'

'Our first round,' said Mr B at a lower volume, 'is a picture round. You'll find the pictures on the back of the answer sheet, and I'll give you a few minutes to complete it whilst everyone finishes getting their drinks. Twenty points at stake in this one.'

Kate turned over the answer sheet to find ten small images of paintings.

'Art!' said Jo. 'Isn't it normally celebrities at this kind of quiz? The eyes and nose of one, with the jaw of another and you have to identify them both. I haven't a clue about these.'

Harry slid the sheet across the table and leaned over, studying it in great detail. 'I know one. The train one.'

Kate laughed. 'You *would* know that.'

'It's Turner's *Rain, Steam and Speed*. We've got it on our bedroom wall at home.'

'It's a pub quiz,' said Jo. 'Not University Challenge. You'd think he'd have picked easier ones, like *The Scream* and Van Gogh's *Sunflowers*.'

Peter was peering at the sheet now. 'I think this one's by Mondrian.' He pointed at one that was black lines and coloured squares. 'No idea what it's called though.'

'We're not the only people who are struggling. Take a look around,' said Razz.

Kate turned around. Razz was right. Mr B had clearly misjudged things, making the round far too difficult; she saw face after baffled face. Except for one team. One team were confidently scribbling down their answers, and looking rather pleased with themselves. And sitting on that team, with his back to her, was the unmistakable figure of Xander.

She turned back to her own team then, and frowned at the sheet of pictures.

'You okay, Kate?' said Jo.

'Yeah, fine thanks. Do you think the third one might be a Van Gogh? The swirly brushwork makes me think it is.'

'I didn't know you were an art expert,' said Peter.

'And now,' Mr B's voice boomed out, 'the music round. Is everyone ready?'

'Ready as we'll ever be,' someone shouted.

'It'll be all Bach, Brahms and Beethoven,' said Razz, 'if the art round was anything to go by.'

But it was Boyzone, not Brahms, which blared out from the speakers.

'Keith Duffy, Stephen Gately, Ronan Keating, and Shane Lynch, but which of them wasn't an original member?' said Mr B. 'Which of the following people was *not* an original member of Boyzone...'

'Shane Lynch,' said Peter, reaching across the table and taking the answer sheet.

Kate glanced over at Xander's table. She didn't recognise the three people he was sitting with; they weren't locals, that was for sure. On the empty chair beside him was a padded anorak and the old uni scarf. He was leaning over the answer sheet now, conferring with his friends.

Another song began to play, and Kate reluctantly turned her attention from Xander back to the quiz.

'That was "Father and Son" by Boyzone,' said Mr B, 'but who wrote and sang the original version?'

The entire music round was focused on boy bands. Between them, they knew that Lulu had featured on Take That's 'Relight My Fire', and that Craig Logan was the third member of Bros, alongside Matt and Luke Goss, but the other questions were far too obscure.

The current affairs and general knowledge rounds proved no easier. You practically needed a PhD in nuclear physics to stand a chance in the science round, and one team was caught using the calculators on their phones for the maths section. Xander's team, Kate noticed, were looking rather pleased with themselves.

At the halfway point, Kate went up to the bar to buy another round of drinks, giving Xander a little wave as she passed his table.

'What were you thinking,' she said to George, the landlord, 'appointing Mr B as quizmaster?'

George shrugged. 'He offered.'

(She would later learn that Mr B was secretly addicted to TV quiz shows such as *Mastermind*, *Eggheads*, and *University Challenge*. He'd clearly never been to a pub quiz before, and had misjudged the intellectual level of the entire event.)

As soon as the break was over, Mr B announced that the history round would be next. 'Twentieth-century questions,' he said. 'To make it easier.'

'Well, we've no chance now,' said Kate. 'I happen to know that Xander over there is a university professor specialising in twentieth-century history.'

'Oh?' said Jo. 'How do you know that already? I thought he was new in town.'

'We go way back.' Kate took a sip of her vodka, deliberately ignoring the quizzical look that Jo was giving her now.

'Which British monarch died in 1936?' said Mr B, and immediately repeated the question with slightly different intonation. 'Which British monarch died in 1936?'

'Well, that's easy.' Peter took control of the pen and answer sheet again. 'George V.'

'Keep your voice down, Peter,' said Jo. 'We don't want the other teams to hear our answers.'

'Whose tomb was discovered in Egypt in 1922?'

'Even I know this one,' said Jo, but Peter had already written 'Tutankhamun' on the answer sheet. Harry and Razz nodded their assent.

'Who was the ex-peanut farmer who became a US President?'

'Flippin' heck,' said Jo. 'Right when I thought it was getting easier.'

After a lot of whispered conferring, they decided to have a wild guess and put Jimmy Carter.

'Benjy and Laska went into space in 1958, but what were they?' Mr B said. 'Benjy and Laska.'

'Dogs?' Harry didn't seem too sure.

'The dog was called Laika, not Laska,' said Razz. 'Monkeys maybe? Or mice?'

They settled on monkeys.

'Finally, bit of a tricky one now, which Cold War leader's tantrums once left him with cold feet?'

'I haven't a clue,' said Peter.

Jo shrugged.

Razz and Harry looked at each other and shook their heads.

Kate looked over at Xander and inadvertently caught his eye. He raised his eyebrows, and she wondered if he was thinking the same as she was, if he was casting his mind back to their first date at that Cold War exhibition. All those years earlier. All those miles away. Apart from his smile, his gorgeous eyes and his gentle way of explaining everything, the thing that had stuck in her head most was the photo of Nixon and Khrushchev looking at a kitchen, the one that had reminded her of IKEA.

'Khrushchev,' she whispered to Peter. She wasn't sure if it was the right answer, but since none of the others had a clue, there was nothing to lose. 'I think it's K-H-R-U.'

'Wow.' Peter squeezed her knee under the table. 'I'm impressed.'

After two more fiendish rounds, Mr B declared that the quiz was over and told the teams to swap papers for marking. Xander stood up immediately. Kate turned to talk to Jo, but out of the corner of her eye she could see him making a beeline for their table, even though they weren't the closest.

'Shall we swap?' he said, holding out his team's answer sheet.

'Sure,' said Peter, taking the sheet and offering theirs in exchange. Kate watched as Xander's eyes flicked down their list of answers.

'Khrushchev,' he said, looking straight at Kate. 'You remembered.'

# 23

Kate could feel her teammates looking at her as Xander walked back to his own table.

'What did he mean by that?' said Peter eventually.

'Oh, nothing really.'

'They're all academics,' said Razz.

'How d'you know?' said Kate.

Razz pointed at the team name written at the top of Xander's answer sheet: *The Professors*. Kate glanced over at Xander and his teammates; they must be his university colleagues. That would explain why they were the only team in the pub who *hadn't* appeared to find the questions too difficult.

At a painstakingly slow speed, Mr B began to go through the art round, asking for suggestions from the participants, before revealing the correct answers.

Harry took control of the pen and began to mark The Professors' answers. 'Gosh, they *are* doing well. They've got loads more than us.'

'Well, they spend all day reading books.' There was a note of bitterness in Peter's voice that Kate hadn't heard before, not even back when it had been obvious that things weren't going to work out between him and Em.

Jo flashed him a look. 'And educating future generations. Very important job.'

The Professors didn't do so well on the music round, which Peter looked rather happy about, but they excelled on the next two.

Then Mr B announced that Khrushchev was indeed the Cold War leader whose tantrums had left him with cold feet, and went on to explain that the leader was said to have brandished his shoe at the United Nations General Assembly. 'According to some accounts,' said Mr B, 'he even banged it on the rostrum.'

'How *did* you know?' said Peter softly to Kate. 'And how did he know that you'd know?'

He nodded towards Xander who was engrossed in a discussion with his teammates.

'He took me to an exhibition once,' she said. 'About the Cold War. It was years ago. It's not important.'

'Okay,' he said, but there was something in his tone that told her that he didn't believe her, that he knew that it *was* important.

'My round,' said Harry, standing up when the marking was over and answer sheets had been swapped back. 'Same again? Lend us a hand, Kate?'

'Thanks for rescuing me,' she whispered to Harry as they walked up to the bar. 'It really was only a few dates. I don't know why Peter's acting all jealous.'

'He must be smitten,' said Harry.

Yeah, he is smitten, Kate thought. He's smitten with Em. But she said nothing. She stood behind as Harry placed the drinks order, and then suddenly Xander was beside her.

'Well done,' he said. 'It was a tough quiz. Fourth isn't bad.'

Kate smiled. 'First is even better. Well done you.'

'That's what you get if you put a team of academics together. They're all colleagues.'

'I guessed they might be. Listen, I...' she said at the same time as he said, 'Kate, I wanted to...'

'You go,' she said.

'No, please.'

'Since you moved here,' she said, 'I've been wanting to apologise. For leaving so abruptly. It was just...'

'It was years ago, Kate,' he said. 'All forgiven and forgotten.'

'Forgotten?' She found she didn't like the thought that he'd forgotten. Not when she hadn't forgotten him.

'You weren't the first woman to be put off by me being a geek,' he said. 'And I'm sure you won't be the last.'

She wouldn't be the last; he was still single then, presumably.

'It wasn't the geekiness. Look at my friends.' She gestured at the table. 'All geeks. Jo and Razz are complete Scrabble nerds, and Harry's a trainspotter. You can't get much geekier than that. Besides, I already knew you were geeky. I mean, who takes a woman to an exhibition about the Cold War on a first date?'

He laughed. 'A man who thinks that the woman concerned is into history and design. I thought you'd love it.'

'You know what? I *did* love it. Although I hope your window display isn't going to be geeky.'

'Now that would be telling.' His eyes were twinkling at her now.

'You're not going to give me a clue?'

'You're right. I'm *not* going to give you a clue. I'm a man of mystery.'

She laughed.

'Anyway,' he said slowly, drawing out the syllables. 'Anyway, Kate, it's lovely seeing you again, but I'd better get a round in for my friends. They'll be parched. Winning quizzes is thirsty work.'

'Sure, see you around, Xander.'

She looked round for Harry, suddenly remembering that she was supposed to be helping him to carry the drinks, but he was back at the table already. In fact, Razz was one-third of the way through his pint. And Peter was nowhere to be seen.


She caught up with Peter before the florist's, and began to walk alongside him, struggling to keep up as he was going at quite a pace.

'I don't want to come over as possessive,' Peter said. 'I'm not the jealous type. But I couldn't help noticing the way the two of you looked at each other.'

'Me and Xander?'

This was a bit rich given the way Peter still looked at Em.

He stopped dead in his tracks and turned to face her. 'Is there anything going on between the two of you, Kate?'

Kate hesitated. 'There *was*. There isn't now. I'm with you, Peter. And anyway, it was years ago and we only had a few dates.'

'But the way you looked at him...' Peter began walking again.

'What about the way you look at Em?' she called out after him.

He stopped again. He was outside the board game café now, with Kate a couple of metres behind him. She caught him up, took a deep breath, and said, as calmly as she could, 'I've seen the way you look at her. You're going out with me, but you're still in love with her. Maybe there's a little spark between Xander and me, but we had five dates *years* ago and it didn't work out. You were *engaged* to Em, and you're quite clearly still carrying a torch for her. And I don't blame you. She's lovely.'

'Do you think she knows?'

And there it was. His first concern was not for her, but for Em.

They both glanced into the board game café, and watched Em as she walked round the café, collecting a couple of empty mugs. She saw them looking in, and gestured for them to come inside, but they shook their heads. Em looked puzzled, but shrugged as if to say, 'Suit yourselves.'

'No, Peter, I don't think she does,' said Kate. 'And she won't hear it from me.' There were a few seconds of silence as they both continued to stare into the window of the café.

Then Kate looked back at Peter. 'I'm not cheating on you, if that's what you think. I wouldn't cheat.'

'That's not what I'm implying at all.' He took her hands in his, then looked into her eyes. His expression was soft and kind, not angry or jealous as she'd expected. 'Kate, you're right. I hold my hands up.' He released her hands for a moment, held his hands up, then took her hands again, and began stroking them with his thumbs. 'I'm still in love with Emily.'

'I knew I was second best,' Kate said. 'But that's okay, Peter.'

'No. No, it's not okay. You're an amazing person. You shouldn't be with a man who's still hankering after his ex. I should never have asked you out, and I'm sorry. I thought I was over her, but you're right. I'm not. Perhaps I need counselling or something before I date anyone again. It was never my intention to mess you about. But you're a very attractive woman, and when I saw you walking into that pub in Leeds that evening...'

'You saw me walk in?'

So it wasn't coincidence? He hadn't just happened to go for a drink in the same pub as she had? That made sense now. Peter wasn't a pub kind of person. Looking back, it had struck her as odd that he'd be there on a Friday night by himself.

He held his hands up again. 'Okay, confession time. It was true that I was out with a client, and they had to go home early. But then I saw you go into the pub and I followed you. I've always admired you and I thought we might make a good couple.'

'We *do* make a good couple,' said Kate. The tears were streaming down her face now.

'Yes, we do. Except for the fact that both of us are in love with other people.'

'I'm not in love with Xander.'

'Maybe not yet, but there's something between the two of you. And the thing is, there can never be an Emily and Peter, but there could still be a Kate and Xander. You could make it work with him. I don't want to be the person standing in your way.'

She looked into Peter's eyes again. 'You're not. There's a reason – a good reason – why I'm not with him. You know, I really misjudged you when you were with Em.' She sniffed. She wanted to wipe her eyes and was worried her nose was running, but Peter was holding her hands again, stroking them with his thumbs, and it felt rather lovely. 'I didn't think you were good enough for her. And then when you fired her from Ridley Engineering I was furious with you.'

'Rightly so. I had to let her go – it was a business decision – but I went about it in entirely the wrong way. And you were right. I wasn't good enough for Em. I didn't support her dream of running a café. I moaned about how messy she was. I let my mother talk down to her. And I'll probably spend my entire life regretting all of those things, because I lost her and I deserved to.'

'Oh, Peter.' Kate leaned into him, and he wrapped his arms around her. She buried her face in his neck, holding him close. She was crying properly now, partly for him, partly for herself. He was a gorgeous man, and a part of her didn't want to let him go. Wanted to convince him that they could make this work. He'd make a wonderful husband and father – she knew that. So what if they were both in love with other people? You could love someone, couldn't you, even if you weren't *in* love with them? She so wanted to settle down, and had thought that maybe this time…

But no. She knew – or at least a part of her knew – that he was right. Given more time, Peter's wounds would heal. He would get over Em and then he'd be in a position to fall head over heels with someone again, and Kate knew it wouldn't be her.

She pulled away from him, glancing into the board game café. Em was gawping at them from behind the counter, but she turned around when she saw Kate looking, busying herself with the coffee machine.

'So this is it?' Kate mumbled to Peter.

'This is it. I care about you. I want you to be happy. And I want me to be happy. I'll still be there every evening, sorting out the drapes for the windows – you don't need to worry about that.'

That was one good thing anyway. Though it was always awkward seeing someone after a split, even after a short period of dating like this one. She hoped it wouldn't be difficult as they prepared for each evening's big reveal.

'And I'll still be your friend, if you'll have me,' Peter added.

She slapped his arm. 'Course I'll have you, Peter. Course I will. And Peter…'

'Yes?'

'If you ever need any dating advice, I'm your woman.'

He gave her a faint smile. 'I'll bear that in mind. Can I give *you* some dating advice? Give Xander a second chance, Kate.'

She sighed. 'I can't, Peter. No matter how lonely it can get being single, it's even lonelier being in the wrong relationship. And I know it'd never work between me and Xander. He reminds me too much of my dad.'

# 24

Four years earlier

The car still smelled of chips as they pulled up outside a bay-fronted end-of-terrace house. Kate followed Xander up the path to a racing-green front door, the paintwork chipped in a number of places.

'After you,' he said.

She stepped into the hallway and looked around. She had thought his car was cluttered; his house was even worse. Coats and anoraks were dumped on top of a coat stand, rather than being hung from it, and a collection of shoes, some the wrong way up, were shoved up against the skirting board. Yet more coats were slung over the banister. A striped, green carpet led the way upstairs and she wondered if she might be climbing those stairs later tonight. What would his bedroom be like?

'Shall I take your coat?' he said.

'Thanks.'

She wrestled with the stiff buttons, feeling suddenly hot and awkward, but finally slipped it off and handed it to him. He dumped it over the banister with his own, then led the way to the lounge. The entire room was dominated by shelves, most of which were sagging under the weight of books. There were stacks of books too on the huge, battered leather sofa that was pushed up against one wall.

Xander hastily shifted some of them, making room for her to sit down. 'Coffee?'

Kate usually drank green tea, but a coffee sounded wonderful. She wondered if it would stop her sleeping, but maybe she wouldn't sleep much tonight anyway. Maybe they'd spend all night making love. She shivered, wondering what it would be like to lie in bed alongside this gorgeous man, to feel his bare skin against hers. He'd be a considerate lover, she decided, because he was a considerate man.

'I think I've got some decaf,' he said, 'if you'd prefer.'

See? Considerate.

'Or tea? Or there might some of that herbal stuff. My ex used to drink it.'

This was the first mention of an ex, but of course, by his age, there were bound to be exes. Kate wondered what she'd been like. How long had they been together? When had they split up? She wanted to ask, but didn't. It was one of her rules: don't talk about exes on a date.

'Yes, decaf please,' she said.

'Coming right up. Make yourself at home.'

He disappeared, presumably to the kitchen, and she sat down and pulled one of the cushions onto her lap, absent-mindedly stroking it as if it were a cat. She stood up again, checking her mascara hadn't smudged in the enormous mirror that hung over the fireplace, and touched up her lipstick. She looked good. A little tired, perhaps. Maybe she should have asked for normal coffee.

She glanced round the room again.

How long did it take to boil a kettle?

Curious to see a little more of the house, she shoved her phone in her pocket and went in search of the kitchen, treading as softly as she could because she wanted to surprise him. She had a brief fantasy of sneaking up behind him and putting her arms around him. Then he would turn and kiss her passionately up against the kitchen cupboards. Perhaps he'd lift her onto the worktops, and she'd wrap her legs around him…

In the hallway were two closed doors. She wasn't sure which led to the kitchen, but chose the first, turned the handle and stepped inside.

His dining room. It was dominated by yet more bookcases, all heaving with hardbacks and an enormous oak dining table.

A dining table that was covered, completely covered, with toy soldiers.

Not what she was expecting.

She peered at the soldiers. They were less than half the length of her little finger, yet every detail, every mouth, every eye, every button and epaulette had been carefully painted. Hand-painted probably. By Xander himself?

Her heart sank. More plummeted actually.

In her fantasies about meeting Mr Right, she'd never once envisaged falling in love with a man who played with toy soldiers. She'd known he was a bit geeky – after all, he'd taken her to a Cold War Exhibition on their first date – but toy soldiers?

He was such lovely company, and she fancied him something rotten, yet she saw those toy soldiers and she wanted to run.

There was a clatter from behind a second door. It must lead to the kitchen. She could hear him now, opening and closing cupboard doors. The sound of the kettle boiling, the clink of a teaspoon in a mug.

She took a step backwards towards the door behind her. A floorboard creaked. The door to the kitchen opened and Xander walked in.

He smiled; if he was surprised to find her in the dining room, rather than in the lounge where he'd left her, he didn't show it. She looked away. Was it possible to feel regret for what you were about to do and yet know you were going to do it anyway?

'So sorry,' he said. 'Can't find the biscuits. But I made you a coffee. Decaf as promised.'

He handed her a steaming mug. She looked around but there was nowhere to put it. Not a coaster in sight. Not one square inch of free space on that dining table.

'What do you think?' he said, picking up one of the soldiers and gazing at it rather too fondly. 'I painted each and every one myself.'

Just as she'd thought. 'It must take hours. And a steady hand.'

'I have a very steady hand.' He smiled.

There was a hint of innuendo in his tone. He was flirting with her. Five minutes earlier, she'd have been delighted at this, but now…

There was an awkward silence.

'Yeah, it does take hours,' he continued. 'I dread to think how much time I've spent doing this over the years.'

An image popped into her mind. An image of Xander, paintbrush in hand, surrounded by a collection of tiny pots of paint, working away into the wee small hours by the light of an angle-poise lamp.

Another image, from her childhood. She'd wandered downstairs, unable to sleep, in search of a glass of milk. And there was her mum. Waiting. Watching through the kitchen window. Desperate for some adult company. The back garden illuminated by the light from the shed, as her father spent yet another evening fiddling with his transistor radios.

It had been every evening. And every weekend. His days off too. The Sunday roast would grow cold on the table as her mum went to call him in for a third time. Their holidays were long weekends in North Wales rather than a fortnight in Lanzarote like some of her school friends. They were cut short, she'd always imagined, because her dad had different priorities.

Her mother's feelings of isolation were palpable; even as a small child, Kate had been aware of them. She had tried to be there for her mum as best she could. In primary school, she was always tired in class because she was allowed to stay up later than the other kids; her mum liked them to watch TV together. As a teenager, she went out less than her peers. Barely at all. No parties, no discos. No hanging out on the benches in the park or popping over to Em's house to do their homework together. She stayed home and kept her mum company. But Kate knew it was his company her mum craved. Not hers.

This was why she didn't date anglers. She didn't want a man who had such a solitary – and perhaps obsessive – hobby, who'd spend his weekends sitting by a river under an oversized umbrella whilst she sat home alone, as her mum had. It was why she didn't want to be a golf widow. Why she'd split up from Michael with his IT obsession and fitness fanatic Rob before him. She had no intention of ending up lonely in a relationship, as her mother had been.

And it was also the reason why she barely had any contact with her father. If he had only paid his wife some attention, things would have worked out differently, Kate felt sure of it.

'You know, I'm really tired,' she said now, jolting back to the present moment and glancing at the toy soldiers again. She shoved the mug back into Xander's hand and faked a yawn. 'I'm going to head home.'

His smile disappeared. His eyes searched her face, baffled. The mood had changed, and she knew he couldn't work out why. She could enlighten him, but what would she say? *I don't fancy you anymore because you play with toy soldiers.* It sounded so pathetic.

'Shall I run you home?' he said.

She shook her head. 'It's miles. I'll get the Tube.'

She wasn't sure how late the trains ran, but she could always get a night bus.

'At least let me give you a lift to the station.'

'I can walk.'

This didn't add up, of course. One minute she'd claimed to be tired; the next, she'd elected to walk to the station.

'Would you like me to walk with you? You don't know the way.'

'Thanks, there's no need.' She held up her phone. 'Google Maps.'

She turned and walked away, collecting her bag from the lounge and her coat from the banister. She glanced back as she stepped out of the front door into the night. He was watching her leave. His eyes looked sad. She closed the door gently behind her, feeling as if she'd kicked a puppy.

She'd reached his gate when it dawned on her that she was making a mistake. She loved Xander's company, and he was incredibly attractive. She'd been hoping that tonight would be the start of something.

Should she turn back?

She opened the latch of the gate, the hard metal cold against her fingers. And she remembered the cold metal latch of her father's shed. How he never even looked up when she took him a mug of tea. How he'd barely mumbled thanks.

She stepped onto the pavement, closed the gate behind her and walked away.

# 25

'Is everything all right?'

Kate pulled away from hugging Peter goodbye, and saw Em standing in the doorway of the board game café, curiosity finally having got the better of her.

'Why don't you both come in out of the cold?' Em said.

Peter handed Kate a clean handkerchief from his jacket pocket. 'You go and talk to Emily, and I'll head on home.'

She dabbed at her eyes with his hanky. 'You sure? Are you okay?'

He nodded. 'Goodnight, Kate. Goodnight, Emily.'

Kate stood on the pavement, watching him for a few seconds, then walked over to Em and wrapped her arms round her friend.

'Have you broken up?' Em said.

'Yeah.'

'Oh, Kate. Come and have a cuppa and tell me all about it.'

Of course, she couldn't tell her *all* about it, Kate thought as she sat opposite her friend in the warmth of the café a few minutes later, nursing a mug of steaming green tea. The fact that Peter was still in love with Em wasn't her secret to share.

'Someone I used to date showed up this evening,' she said. 'And Peter could see there was still a spark between us.'

'Oh, Kate!' Em sounded exasperated. 'Why go out with Peter if you have feelings for this other guy?'

'It's not like that, Em.' She resented having to defend herself given that this was only one half of the story, but she couldn't break Peter's trust. 'I didn't know Xander was in Essendale when I started dating Peter. And it wasn't my choice to end things anyway. I'm not going to date Xander. I know it won't work.'

'Because...?'

'It just wouldn't, okay? Xander and me... it was years ago. When I was in London doing that secondment. And it was five dates – that's all.'

'And you broke up because...?'

Kate sighed. She had briefly explained to Peter why she couldn't date Xander – not the whole story, only the bare bones – and now, for the second time in less than an hour, she found herself repeating it all again.

'Blimey, Kate,' said Em. 'And you never spoke to him again?'

'Not until I knocked on the door of Alessandra's hoping to persuade the new owner to let me use the window in the living Advent calendar and discovered that he *was* the new owner. And then he showed up at the pub quiz.'

She wasn't sure why she omitted about meeting Xander at Leeds station and going for chips with him; it wasn't as though anything had happened, but she felt it had been disloyal to Peter and was reluctant to mention it.

'Oh yeah, I heard there was a quiz. Couldn't go cos of this place,' said Em. 'How was it?'

'Fiendish,' Kate said. 'I don't think the landlord'll be asking Mr B to be the quizmaster again.'

Em laughed. 'Now back to this guy. Let me get this straight. The only reason you dumped him was his toy soldiers.'

'Yeah, I know it sounds trivial,' Kate said.

'It does.' Em shook her head. 'It does,' she repeated in a louder, more emphatic tone. She rolled her eyes. '*Really* trivial. There's nothing wrong with dating a geeky guy, Kate. Look at your circle of friends. You've got me, Jo and Taylor *all* dating the geekiest guys you could imagine, and we're happy. Yet Lud has his games, Razz has his Scrabble and Harry has his model railway.' She sat back in her chair, satisfied that she had made her point.

'Yes, I know. Window number twenty-three – Harry's model railway in his garden shed.'

Em sat up suddenly. 'Oh, I get it. I know what this is about. This is about your dad, isn't it? And his shed? And all those hours he spent playing with his transistor radios? You used to go on about it when your mum left.'

'Yeah, well, it was his fault. He completely neglected her. Never paid her the slightest bit of attention. It's no wonder she left.'

'Hmmm.' Em looked as if she was about to say more, but she didn't.

'I want a man who'll spend time with me,' said Kate. 'I mean, what's the point otherwise? I know some women are quite happy being golf widows, or staying home alone whilst their other half treks halfway round the world following the English cricket team on tour or what have you. But not me. I want someone by my side. A proper companion.'

'You know what I think you should do?'

Kate could guess what was coming. Em would suggest that she went on a few dates with Xander, that she should give him a chance.

'You should give him the opportunity to explain,' said Em, looking somewhat chuffed with herself; she clearly thought this was good advice.

'What's to explain? He likes toy soldiers.'

'Not Xander. Your dad. You never did talk to him properly about your mum leaving.'

On Tuesday morning, on the train on her way into work, Kate put her break-up with Peter and that conversation with Em firmly out of her mind, and looked through social media, checking the hashtag #EssendaleLivingAdvent to see if there were any new posts. Social media was vital to getting the word out about the project and attracting more visitors.

She liked and commented on everything she found, and shared the best ones too. The photos were sometimes a little blurry and sometimes the photographers had struggled to take a good photo of the window in question without getting a reflection, but they invariably said lovely things.

*A magical evening looking at the first Christmas windows in the Essendale living Advent calendar.*

*So imaginative. We loved it.*

*Well worth a visit. The health centre window was our favourite. Hilarious!*

She frowned as one post caught her eye. Someone calling themselves EcoEssendale had posted a picture of one of the windows with bright red text over the top of it, declaring in capital letters:

ESSENDALE SAYS SOD THE PLANET AS THE WHOLE TOWN GOES FAIRY LIGHTS CRAZY! #ESSENDALELIVINGADVENT

There was a link to a blog post too. With trembling fingers, Kate clicked the link, almost afraid to read.

The days are short. The nights are long. It's dark and it's dreary. Especially when you live in a valley in the shadow of the Pennines. There's not much daylight at this time of year so I can understand why many people feel the need to put up Christmas lights. I don't want to sound like the Grinch, but what about the environment?

The media is full of warnings about the irreversible damage that we're causing to the planet. We're constantly being told that we need to lower emissions. We all agree that we should buy less, eat local produce and cut down on our energy consumption. Yet come Christmas, and all of that flies out of the window. We buy massive amounts of gifts – many of which are unwanted by their recipients – and we forget about food miles. And, my biggest bugbear, we adorn our houses and gardens with festive lights, with scant regard for the amount of electricity they use.

At this time of year, known for its excessive consumption, more than ever we should be encouraging people to remember the planet. Yet one local woman is doing the complete opposite. Kate Harker has initiated a living Advent calendar in the towns of Essendale and Hebbleswick. Every evening, a window is unveiled revealing a Christmas display complete with masses of those electricity-hungry fairy lights. What's more, she's encouraging all the residents of both towns to light up their own windows, creating mini displays alongside the official ones.

Perhaps you're wondering if all these lights will have that big an impact on the planet. It's difficult to ascertain exactly how much electricity the Essendale and Hebbleswick lights will use. For one thing, it depends on the types of bulbs. Modern LED lights will use significantly less than older ones. For another, it will vary according to how long the lights are left on for. But I found one interesting statistic online: in the US, Christmas lights use over 3 billion kWh of energy each December, which means an extra 3.3 billion tons of $CO_2$. So for anyone thinking, don't be a Scrooge, it's only a few fairy lights, well, it might be just a few fairy lights, but those lights are completely unnecessary and have a detrimental impact. Because of this, I'd urge you all to unplug your festive lights and boycott the Essendale and Hebbleswick Living Advent Calendar.

## 26

By the time Kate reached the office, she was thoroughly wound up. The article had not only criticised her project, but had named her too. She felt as if she were being held responsible for the destruction of the entire planet, when all she'd tried to do was organise an event to help revitalise local shops and businesses.

She dumped her handbag on her desk and pulled off her coat. She was furious. How dare EcoEssendale, whoever they were, slag off her and her project?

'You okay, Kate?' said Jeroen, her boss.

'Yeah,' she said automatically. And then she paused for a moment, and said, 'No. No, actually, I'm *not* okay.'

'Want to talk about it?'

'It's not work-related.' She paused again. 'But yes, I *do* want to talk about it. If you have time.'

Jeroen already knew about the living Advent calendar; he'd very kindly agreed to her leaving early every day in December. He really was the best boss, though obviously she'd more than make up for the time. She plonked herself down on a chair in his office, and handed over her phone so he could read the blog post for himself.

'I don't know what to do,' she said.

'Oh, come on. You work in marketing. You've been employee of the year how many times is it now? If this was a client coming to you with this issue, what would you tell them to do?'

'Three times. I'd tell them to be proactive,' she said slowly. 'There's some truth in what this eco warrior person is saying. The festive lights *do* use electricity. Of course they do. But the whole point of the living Advent calendar is to encourage more visitors to come to Essendale and Hebbleswick because we need to keep our small businesses going. Shopping local *is* a very green thing to do, but the residents of our valley won't be able to do that if the shops all close.'

Jeroen nodded. 'Good point.'

'And we're talking a few fairy lights here. It's hardly Blackpool Illuminations. We're not talking those massive over-the-top displays on people's houses where they have illuminated reindeer on their lawn, and an inflatable, giant Santa lit up on their roof, and absolutely masses and masses of lights.' She shuddered at the thought.

'I rather like those displays,' he said. 'I take my elderly father on a tour of them each year.'

'Exactly,' Kate said. 'Christmas lights bring a lot of pleasure to a lot of people. Although admittedly the living Advent calendar hasn't drawn in as many people as I'd hoped – I didn't get the local media coverage I wanted – and there'll be even fewer now.'

'You could make this work in your favour. A bit of controversy might be the very thing to get the press interested.'

She pondered this for a second. 'You're right. I can use this blog post to my advantage. Do something that says yes, all these lights do use a bit of extra electricity, but it's for good reason.'

There was silence for a few moments as they both thought.

'If this was a client...' Jeroen said again.

'I'd say...' Kate began. She paused and closed her eyes for a second, before continuing. 'I'm thinking aloud here, but I'd say make one of the shop displays about how to have a green Christmas. About how to enjoy the big day without it costing the earth. Then I'd try and get the local paper to cover it. I was hoping they'd cover the opening evening, only they weren't interested, but like you said, now there's a bit of controversy...'

She looked at him, scrutinising his face for his reaction.

'That sounds like a good plan,' he said.

'The trouble is, all the windows are allocated. I'd have to ask someone to completely change their display.'

'You should do it tonight. Strike while the iron is hot. Which window is it?'

'The Oxfam shop in Essendale.'

'Bingo.' He punched the air. 'It couldn't be more perfect. Oxfam talk a lot about climate change, don't they? A display about how to have an environmentally friendly Christmas should be right up their street.'

'But it's this evening,' Kate said. 'Peter was rigging up the drapes first thing this morning so they could create the display. It'll be finished already. I can't possibly ask them to change it. There isn't time.'

'So here's what's going to happen,' he said. 'You're going to phone the manager now and explain the position. If she agrees, you can have the day off, and go and help her get the new display in place. Meanwhile, I'll get the new intern to research green Christmas ideas and to check the facts in EcoEssendale's blog.'

'You'd really let me have the day off?'

'Kate, you've been our employee of the year three times and what do we give you? A paltry certificate. Make that call. See if the manager will agree. And on the train home, start drafting a press release for the local paper. Newspapers love a spat.'

Kate rang the charity shop from the office, as Jeroen suggested. The manager didn't take much persuading. 'Wish we'd thought of it originally,' she said. 'It's a brilliant idea and fits right in with our ethos.'

They were chatting through the details as Kate reached Leeds station a few minutes later, her phone still pressed to her ear, and agreed that the display would be prepared in the back room. The shop would close half an hour early at half past four, which would give them only ninety minutes to remove the original display and install the new one. It would be tight, but achievable.

Even better, the manager not only agreed to change the display, but said they'd look into hosting some drop-in workshops on the green Christmas theme.

By the time her train reached Essendale, Kate had written

a press release and sent it off to three local newspapers, including a link to EcoEssendale's blog, and she'd begun to read through the research notes that the intern from Kompleet Marketing Solutions had already emailed over. Admittedly they were somewhat hastily cobbled together, but they were positively bursting with ideas.

I'll send more if I find them, the intern had written. Good luck x.

Another email came a few moments later, just as Kate walked into the Oxfam shop. BTW the bit about 3.5 billion tons of $CO_2$ appears to be wrong. I think I've found the website where they got that from, and it says pounds not tons. Still a lot, but an awful lot less.

And, Kate thought, it called EcoEssendale's credibility into question.

Before they began the display, the manager outlined some of her plans for the revised window, and Kate shared the ideas the intern had sent through.

They settled on a few areas to focus on, and as they talked, Kate typed up notes on her phone for some signs to print out for the display.

'Driving home for Christmas' might be a catchy song, but how much $CO_2$ does driving home emit? If you're travelling from London to Glasgow, making the journey using a petrol car will emit over 4 times more $CO_2$ per passenger than the equivalent journey by coach, or 3.3 times more $CO_2$ per passenger than an electric car. Obviously this will vary depending on the age and type of the car and the number of passengers, but it's better to use public transport if you can.

The manager had a small artificial Christmas tree and a real one – in a pot – of roughly the same size. Kate typed out a sign asking, 'Which do you think is greener?' And some information revealing the answer: it all depended on how many years you used your artificial tree.

They both agreed they should emphasise the positives when possible; rather than making people feel guilty about their festive consumption, they'd focus on the practical steps you could take to have a planet-friendly Christmas. There were ideas about how to have a low-impact Christmas dinner, along with the manager's favourite nut roast recipe, about using brown paper instead of shiny printed wrapping paper, to ensure it could be recycled, and about greener gifts.

'Ideal for the Oxfam shop,' said the manager. 'Buying pre-loved is an obvious way.'

Buying second-hand Christmas garments was another great way to cut back on those festive $CO_2$ emissions, and was obviously a perfect suggestion for the charity shop. Kate was very aware of the amount of clothing that ended up in landfill, having helped organise Taylor's upcycled fashion show a few months earlier, but she was nevertheless astonished to learn that two out of five Christmas jumpers were worn only once, and were thrown out after Christmas.

Come inside, Kate typed, and check out our pre-loved Christmas knitwear selection and our party dresses.

The volunteers at the shop had already removed the existing display from the window, and they all mucked in to help create the new one. They'd barely finished when there was a knock at the door, and Kate saw the reporter and photographer from the local paper standing outside. She and the manager both gave short interviews, with Kate taking care to say that she understood EcoEssendale's concerns, but that her whole reason for suggesting the living Advent calendar had been to give local shops a boost.

'And surely everyone would agree that buying local is a very environmentally friendly thing to do?' She smiled. 'If we don't do something to boost visitor numbers in this valley over the winter months, some of our local shops may go out of business. One has already closed recently here in Essendale.'

Peter arrived shortly after the interviews had finished, ready to ensure that the drapes lifted smoothly out of the way to reveal the newly created display.

'You okay?' he said.

She nodded. She hadn't given their break-up much thought, to be honest, as she'd been too busy fretting about that blog post. 'You?'

'Yes, a little sad, but I'm fine. Did you tell Em?'

'Yeah, but I didn't mention about your feelings for her.' Kate kept her voice low, so no-one would overhear.

'Thanks, Kate. I really appreciate that.'

At ten to six, she went outside with the photographer, to ensure he was in the best spot to get a good shot of the window. The reporter followed and began to interview people in the crowd, asking if they'd seen the other windows, and what they thought of the project.

Then it was time for the big reveal. Kate welcomed everyone as she had on the previous evenings, then called for the drum roll. The thigh slapping began, but also an impromptu countdown from ten.

When they reached zero, Kate watched the bottom of the drapes, waiting for them to rise. They didn't move for a moment, and then they seemed to stutter and judder, but finally they moved out of the way and the hastily arranged green Christmas display was revealed for the whole of Essendale to see.

They hadn't done a bad job, Kate thought, given the time constraint. Not a bad job at all. All she could do now was hope and pray that the newspaper article would be favourable and their environmentally friendly Christmas ideas would be well received.

# 27

Kate ought to have been pleased when her phone rang the following morning as she was waiting for the train into work, and a local TV journalist informed her that they would like to broadcast live from that evening's window unveiling. The controversy had done the trick; it had drawn the local newspaper into covering the event, and then the TV journalist had seen the resulting article online, before the newspaper was even printed, and had decided the event was worth featuring.

And in a way, she was pleased, but it wasn't great timing. For one thing, Mr B's 'Christmas in Poland' display wouldn't have been her first choice for the TV coverage; not because it wouldn't be excellent, but she'd have preferred it if the TV broadcast featured a window in a local shop rather than a private house, since the whole point of this living Advent calendar was to boost trade to local businesses. And it would have been a lot easier if that private house didn't happen to belong to Mr B's fiancée, Florence Ridley, who happened to be Peter's mother.

Why did it have to be now, so soon after they'd agreed to go their separate ways? There hadn't been any awkwardness between her and Peter at the previous evening's unveiling, but that was probably because she'd been so caught up in worrying about the negative publicity from the blog post and in creating the last-minute new display. But this evening, under the roof of Peter's mother, it might be a different story.

The train was late. Which was usually irritating but fortunate this morning, as Kate wasn't sure whether she was getting on it or not. She phoned Jeroen, who very kindly agreed that she could take the day off. Come January, she'd be putting a lot of extra hours in at work to make up for all of this. Then she made a second call, one she was really dreading. She rang Florence Ridley's landline.

Mrs Ridley was one of those people who still answered the phone by stating their own number.

'Hello, is that Mrs Ridley?' Kate said though she knew full well from the plummy tone that it was. She couldn't get used to calling her Florence. 'It's Kate here.'

'Oh, Kate, such a shame about you and Peter. I thought you were the perfect match. I can't understand for the life of me why you've split up.'

Ironic, Kate thought, that when she'd first started dating Peter, she'd assumed that Florence Ridley would disapprove of her the way she'd disapproved of Em.

She outlined the reason for her call and, to her surprise and relief, Mrs Ridley said that yes, she and Stanisław would be delighted to have the local news team there this evening. Kate said in that case, she would come over straight away to help put the finishing touches to his window. Thankfully, Florence Ridley thought that was a good idea; since this was the one that was going on local news to represent the entire project, it had to be perfect. It was their big chance to boost the visitor numbers and they couldn't afford to blow it.

Mrs Ridley and Mr B lived at the posher end of town, where the big, detached houses were. The kind of house Kate could have been living in one day if things had worked out with Peter. She sighed. It wasn't the thought of missing out on a big posh house that she was sighing for, but the fact that she was on her own again. Single at Christmas *again*.

She stood at the top of the driveway and took a deep breath. The gravel scrunched under her feet as she made her way to the shiny, jet-black front door. She hadn't even had time to press the bell when it opened and Peter stood there, in his suit trousers, a pin-striped blue shirt and a loosened tie.

'Mother told me,' he said, 'so I've taken the day off.'

'That's good of you,' Kate stepped into the wide hallway, onto an immaculate cream carpet. She felt hot suddenly. Rising energy prices were clearly not a worry in this house. 'Peter, I am really sorry, you know. About Xander. When you and I first got together, well, I thought he was history. I never imagined I'd see him again, let alone that he'd move…'

Florence appeared from a side door, kissed her on both cheeks then looked down at her shoes.

'Good morning, Kate,' she said. 'Come through.'

'You're honoured,' whispered Peter. 'She makes most people take their shoes off because of the carpets.'

They followed Florence through to the back of the house and into a lounge.

'This is the morning room,' Florence said.

The place was immaculate. More deep-pile cream carpets, enormous cream leather sofas and one wall that was entirely made of glass. Mr B had promised that the window was big – bigger than a lot of shop windows, he'd said – and it was. One huge pane from floor to ceiling offered sweeping views over the extensive garden, with its neat lines of shrubs, that appeared almost sculptural.

'Wow,' said Kate. 'This is gorgeous.'

As Mrs Ridley – Florence – made coffee, and Peter began to rig up the drapes, Mr B outlined his plans for the window. He'd wanted it to be unveiled on the sixth of December because that was the day of Saint Nicholas, which was a much more significant day in Poland than in the UK. Children would receive small gifts, if they'd been good.

Kate learned that Christmas in Polish was *Boże Narodzenie*, which translated to 'God's Birth', and the highlight was Christmas Eve, known as *Wigilia*.

'*Wigilia* begins with the appearance of the first star,' said Mr B. 'That reminds us of the Star of Bethlehem.'

He rummaged in a cardboard box and produced a star, a pretty star, made out of cardboard, painted silver with silver glitter on it; the sort of thing a child would make at primary school, though very neatly executed.

'Peter made that,' said Florence proudly. 'When he was six. Such a gifted child.'

Kate looked at Peter, who grimaced and mouthed, 'Sorry.'

'It's lovely,' she said. 'Very good for a six-year-old.'

'I had a gift for cutting out,' Peter joked.

'You were good at everything,' said Florence. She sighed.

Mr B coughed. 'Food is very important at *Wigilia*. We place hay beneath the tablecloth because Jesus Christ was born in a manger. We leave an empty place at the table, either for our Lord himself or for an unexpected guest – someone in need of food or shelter.'

Or someone who should be there, but isn't, Kate thought, thinking of her mum and wondering who she ate her Christmas dinner with these days.

'And the supper begins with breaking a Christmas wafer which we call *opłatek*. Twelve different dishes are eaten, symbolising the Twelve Apostles, but no meat. I've made a selection of dishes to put on display this evening. There's *barszcz* – that's beetroot soup – pierogi, carp and *makowiec* for dessert.'

'That's great, Mr B,' said Kate, ignoring the wave of sadness she felt about her absent mum, 'Shall we get cracking on with creating the window? You can tell me more as we work.'

'Of course. I have everything we need in the box, and Peter has printed out some labels by way of explanation.'

Kate watched as Mr B began to unpack the contents of his box onto the coffee table. There was a miniature sleigh complete with tiny passengers, pulled by a horse, which he had cleverly mounted onto a piece of wood sprayed with fake snow.

'*Kulig*. A horse-pulled sleigh ride. Another Christmas tradition. And this is *piernik* – Polish gingerbread – which we eat during Advent.' He pulled the lid off a biscuit tin, revealing a selection of ginger biscuits, some heart-shaped, others animal-shaped.

'He was baking all day yesterday,' explained Florence. 'We thought we'd hand them out after the unveiling.'

'Great idea,' said Kate. 'Shall we start putting things in place?'

Peter had finished rigging up the drapes, so helped Mr B manoeuvre an enormous Christmas tree into position at one side of the window. Beside it, they placed a small dining table with four chairs. Then Peter went out into the garden and returned with a bale of hay. Florence hastily laid out some old newspaper on the floor so he could put it down without messing up the fancy carpets. Mr B pulled out some hay from the bale, covered the table with it, then put a clean cloth over the top, leaving one corner tucked up so that the hay would be seen from outside.

They used two huge screens from Peter's office to section off the window from the rest of the room. They looked rather drab and corporate so Florence fetched some red velvet curtains from upstairs and Kate pinned them to the screens, making the whole thing look rather grand.

'It's a little too opulent,' said Mr B.

'It looks lovely,' Kate assured him.

'And now,' he said, 'for the baubles.'

He left the room, returning a few moments later with another cardboard box, which he placed carefully on one of the sofas, before sitting down beside it and opening the lid. He took out a round shape, wrapped in tissue paper, peeling off the layers then holding up the bauble so that it reflected the light. Kate stepped forwards to take a closer look.

It was exquisite.

'Hand-blown glass,' said Mr B proudly.

The bauble was a very pale gold colour, and had been

painted with a wintry scene depicting a snow-covered church and two trees.

'Here, Kate,' said Mr B. 'You hang the first one.'

She took the precious object from him, walked over to the tree and hung it from a branch halfway up on the side facing the window. Then Peter appeared beside her, brandishing a second bauble, the same colour as the first, but with two snow-covered cottages on. Soon the four of them were at work, peeling away the tissue paper from the decorations and positioning them on the tree. Each one had a different scene, but they were all similar, depicting simple houses in various different colours, churches, fences and a variety of trees, all covered with snow.

'Can you pull up the drapes please?' said Kate, when they had finally finished decorating the tree, and the crockery, cutlery and food had all been put in place on the table. 'I'd love to see the whole thing from outside.'

Peter obliged, lifting the drapes as she stood in the garden with Mr B on one side, and Florence on the other.

'Spectacular, isn't it?' said Florence. 'One of the best yet, I think you'll find. The visitors are bound to flock to our little valley once they see this on the television.'

Kate nodded, crossing her fingers behind her back. She hoped Florence was right.

# 28

It was mid-afternoon before the TV crew arrived. By that time, Kate had had several rehearsals with Mr B, priming him to talk about the living Advent calendar as a whole, and all the fantastic windows that would be unveiled in the run-up to Christmas in the effort to support local businesses. They'd tested the drapes several times, making sure that Peter's rig would work flawlessly.

'There seems to be a vehicle parked on my front lawn.' Florence came into the morning room, her face like thunder.

Kate followed her into the front room to see. A small, outside broadcast van was indeed parked in front of the window.

'I hope it doesn't damage the grass,' said Florence angrily.

'We can replant it easily enough, mother,' said Peter. 'A couple of ruts aren't worth making a fuss over.'

There was a knock at the door then, and Kate rushed to answer it first. She didn't want Florence giving the television crew an ear-bashing.

No sooner had the TV people finished setting up than the public started to arrive, following the signs that Kate had put up, which directed them to the back of the house. Florence peered out of the kitchen window, which also overlooked the back.

'There are *hordes* of people,' she said with dismay. 'I hope we aren't going to have this every night between now and Christmas.'

'But we want hordes of people,' Kate said.

Peter rolled his eyes at her, then turned to his mother, adopting a soothing tone of voice. 'We talked about this. There *will* be visitors every night – there may be anyway – but the window displays that are on private land are only "open" to people between four p.m. and eight thirty p.m. and during the day at the weekends.'

'And it's until Twelfth Night,' said Kate. 'You know, the sixth of January.'

'Thank you, I'm well aware of when Twelfth Night is. I just hadn't expected there to be so many.'

'Well, I think it's brilliant,' said Mr B.

The big reveal would be later than usual that evening, to coincide with the time of the broadcast. They were due to be 'live on air' at around a quarter to seven, but it was almost ten to, when the presenter held up her hand, indicating that the studio in Leeds was about to hand over to her and that everyone should be silent. She wore a strange expression on her face, as she listened to whatever was being said in her earpiece; Kate wondered if that was how she looked when she did her pelvic floor exercises on the train.

'Yes, thank you, John,' said the presenter, presumably addressing her colleague back in the studio. 'You're joining us right in time for this evening's big window reveal here in Essendale. Drum roll please.'

The thigh slapping began and the drapes began to lift. Then the presenter turned to Mr B and posed her first question. 'So Stanisław – or Mr B as I understand everyone calls you – most of the places taking part in the living Advent calendar are local shops, who are obviously hoping for a boost in trade, but this is your home. You don't run a business. What made you decide that you wanted to do this?'

Mr B hesitated.

Come on, Kate willed him on. Come on. If only telepathy worked. They had rehearsed this so many times. He missed his country, especially at special times of the year, and loved to remember the old traditions.

'Well,' he began, 'I wanted to put my baubles on display.'

There was a titter from the crowd. Kate's eyes widened. Not once had he come out with *that* line in rehearsal. She glanced at the presenter, who was biting her lip, clearly stifling a giggle.

And then, as Mr B began to explain how Poland made some of the finest Christmas hand-blown glass baubles in the world and how he'd been collecting them since he was a boy, when his grandmother gave him one as a gift, the presenter began to laugh. She tried to stop herself, covering her mouth with her hand, but to no avail.

'Sorry,' she said, managing to straighten her face for a second, before bursting out laughing again. 'Sorry.'

She was bending over now, turning away from the camera. She righted herself and tried to start again. 'And what...' Once more she erupted into giggles.

Kate glanced at the cameraman. He too appeared to be struggling to maintain his composure. Most of the people who'd been close enough to hear the interview were sniggering too. Mr B had stopped talking and was looking from the presenter to Kate, clearly not understanding what was going on.

The presenter cleared her throat and said, 'So sorry. Now, Mr B, tell me about some of the Polish traditions you've got in your window? Is that hay I can see under the tablecloth?'

When the interview was over; and the presenter had handed back to the studio, she couldn't apologise enough.

'I'm so sorry,' she said, as she sipped a mug of Yorkshire tea in Florence Ridley's kitchen. 'I wasn't laughing at you, Mr B. It was a silly double entendre. But it was most unprofessional of me.'

'No, I'm sorry,' said Mr B. 'And for Kate, especially. This was a golden opportunity for the living Advent calendar to get some decent publicity and I ruined it.'

'It's my fault,' said Florence, though she didn't actually apologise, Kate noticed. 'I should have explained it to you, Stan, after that meeting in the board game café. Your English is so perfect, darling, that it's easy to forget that it isn't your mother tongue.'

'That's nothing to do with it,' Mr B said primly. 'I just don't have that kind of prurient mind. Anyway, I really am sorry, Kate.'

'Don't worry about it,' said Kate. 'It's one of those things. And your baubles really are beautiful.'

The presenter gave an undignified snort, and soon they were all laughing, Mr B included, but deep down, Kate was gutted. She'd had her hopes pinned on this evening's broadcast, and didn't feel her living Advent calendar had got the airtime it deserved.

The crowd dispersed and the TV crew packed up and drove away, leaving two deep tyre tracks in Florence's previously immaculate lawn and only a few crumbs of gingerbread in their wake. Mr B was happy; his *piernik* had gone down a storm and several people had been keen to talk to him about Poland.

'Two people asked for my autograph,' he said. 'I enjoyed the evening immensely. I just wish I hadn't let you down, Kate. You work so hard.'

'You didn't,' she assured him.

'But you do work hard, Kate,' Peter smiled at her. 'Shall I run you home?'

'Thanks, but I'll walk,' she said. 'Clear my head. Raise my step count.'

She kissed Mrs Ridley on both cheeks, gave Peter and Mr B hugs, then stepped out into the night, scrunching her way down the drive.

She was bitterly disappointed. They'd had their big chance this evening to really make an impression on a wider audience and thereby attract the kind of visitor numbers that would really make a difference to the local businesses. Only that was never going to happen now, was it?

# 29

Kate could barely put one foot in front of the other as she walked home from Mr B's.

So many emotions in a single week. The build-up to the first window reveal. Everyone congratulating her saying what a great success it was – prematurely as it turned out. The anxiety each evening wondering whether anyone would show up and whether the latest display would be well received. The short-lived excitement when everyone loved the doctors' window, followed by fury when she read what EcoEssendale had written in that blog post. Then triumph and more excitement when the journalist from the local TV phoned, only for this evening to turn into a complete farce.

And if that wasn't enough for one person to be dealing with, she'd had the roller coaster of her love life to contend with at the same time. This time last week, she and Peter had been dating, and she'd been looking forward to the living Advent calendar's opening night, imagining them as the town's golden couple. Instead she'd had the disappointment of seeing how he looked at Em, and then, just as she was managing to put that from her mind, he had dumped her. She'd never been dumped in quite such a nice way before, but the end result was the same nonetheless.

And then there was Xander. Seeing him again after all this time. Longing for him, yet at the same time knowing full well that it wouldn't work out. There was no point in dating someone if they couldn't offer you the future that you wanted, and a long-term relationship with Xander was out of the question: she didn't want to end up like her mother, staring out of a kitchen window, longing for some attention and affection from a man who was more interested in his transistor radios or his little soldiers than he was in her.

'Kate.'

At first she thought the voice was in her head – one second she was thinking of Xander, and then she heard him say her name – but then she turned round and saw him standing on the pavement, thirty or forty metres behind her.

'Xander.'

'That was brilliant,' he said, running to catch up with her. 'I couldn't stop laughing.'

'I guess you mean the local news.' Her voice sounded flat. She *felt* flat.

'Yeah, Mr B and his baubles! Priceless!'

'Hmm.' She could see it must have been funny to watch, but from her perspective it hadn't been funny at all.

'Kate, are you okay? You don't look well.'

She bit her lip, blinking back tears, but no amount of blinking could stem the flow. 'I'm fine. It's… well, you've no idea how hard I've worked on this thing. Tonight was our big chance. In marketing terms, getting a slot on TV like this is like gold dust. I wanted everything to be perfect, and it turned into a complete farce.'

'A complete farce that's going viral,' said Xander.

'What?'

'Far be it from me to argue. You're the marketing expert, not me, but it couldn't have gone better. #MrBsBaubles is trending on Instagram and TikTok. Isn't that marketing gold dust?'

'They're not poking fun at him, are they?'

She couldn't bear that, not on top of everything else. Mr B was an absolute darling.

'Not at all.' He handed her his phone, and she saw that he was right. Mr B's baubles were all over social media. Initially people had been sharing the clip of the presenter getting the giggles, but now they were sharing photos of the baubles themselves, and they really did look stunning. Several people were wondering where the beautiful decorations could be purchased. In addition to the photos of Mr B's splendid window, there were dozens of posts on Instagram showing some of the other displays; loads of shots of the hangover cures, a couple of the green Christmas ideas in the Oxfam shop and several of the board game café too. Someone had already written a post entitled 'Ten Things To Do This Weekend In Yorkshire' and the Hebbleswick and Essendale Living Advent Calendar was number 3, after the latest exhibition at the Yorkshire Sculpture Park and the Christmas markets in York.

This was all thanks to Mr B, Kate thought. She couldn't wait to tell him.

'Thank you,' she said, handing the phone back to Xander.

'I can't believe this. And I can't wait to tell Mr B, but it's a bit late to phone him now.'

'Best tell him in the morning. You're very pale, Kate. Are you sure you're okay?'

She hesitated. 'I'll be fine. I need to get home and sit down. I haven't eaten all day.'

'Come back to mine and I'll cook us something,' he said. She hesitated.

'I've no idea where you live, but I'm guessing my place is closer.' He gestured up at the flat above Alessandra's, just across the road. 'I've some Lincolnshire sausages. Proper ones from the farm shop. Very high protein content. And I could whip up some of my special creamy mash and a jug of onion gravy. How does that sound?'

She had to admit it sounded good. She gave him a weak smile. 'You had me at high protein.'

'Come on then.' He hooked his arm through hers, in a mates kind of way, and guided her across the road, then fumbled in his pocket for what seemed like an age outside the shop. The huge window was still covered over, but with deep crimson fabric instead of the cardboard that had previously been there, and there was a large printed '24' in the left-hand corner, indicating the date when the unveiling would take place. Kate wondered if he had already begun creating his mystery Christmas Eve display behind that fabric.

'Have you made a start on the window?' she said.

Xander pulled out his front door key with a triumphant flourish, and tapped his nose. 'Maybe I have. Maybe I haven't.'

He unlocked the side door, and Kate followed him up the

narrow stairs to the flat. The small pile of boxes that had stood in the corner when she'd first visited him here had grown into a larger pile of boxes.

'My stuff's been in storage,' he said. 'I'm fetching it bit by bit. Now you make yourself comfy, and I'll start cooking. Glass of Merlot?'

'Please.'

She took him at his word, kicked off her shoes and put her feet up on the sofa. Then as Xander cooked, she sipped her wine, and flicked through social media. She was amazed at how popular the #MrBsBaubles clip was. She should have guessed that this might happen, that the presenter corpsing, as it was known in the trade, was exactly what they needed, but she'd been so focused on everything going perfectly to plan, that it hadn't crossed her mind that something going wrong might be a blessing in disguise.

Xander appeared with a steaming plate of food on a tray.

'Sorry, I don't have a table,' he said. 'Well, I do, but I haven't brought it over yet.'

The image of Xander's table, covered with little soldiers, popped into Kate's head. She looked up at him, and her eyes met his. Was he thinking about that evening too?

'Er, do you want to sit up a bit?' he said.

'Course.' She swung her legs back off the sofa and sat up, ready to receive the tray, which he placed on her lap. Four fat juicy sausages sat atop a mountain of mash.'

She gazed down at her food. It wasn't the kind of food she usually ate. Not a vegetable in sight, except for the potatoes, and sadly they didn't count towards her ten a day.

Xander went back to the kitchen and appeared a second later with his own tray, and a jug of gravy.

'I love cooking,' he said, 'but I never have anyone to cook for.'

'This looks delicious.' She took a sniff of her food. 'Smells heavenly too.'

And it *was* heavenly. Kate had never tasted such soft, buttery mash.

'Good?' asked Xander.

Kate closed her eyes and swallowed. 'Divine. Utterly divine.'

'You can't beat good old mash.'

She ate another forkful. And then another. And another.

'Love your spuds, don't you?' he said.

She laughed. 'I do. But I don't normally eat them.'

He almost choked on a piece of sausage. 'You don't eat spuds?'

She shook her head. 'Not usually. Sweet potatoes, yes. They count as one of your five a day. Only I aim for ten a day.'

'You can't beat potatoes. So versatile. The crispy skin on a baked potato – there's nothing better.'

Kate sighed. 'I know. As long as it's a not a microwaved one.'

'Who'd eat a microwaved one?' He flung up his hands in mock horror, almost knocking his tray and the jug of gravy off his knee. He adjusted the tray on his lap, using his finger to scoop up a drop of gravy that had dripped from the jug. He cut off a piece of sausage, but paused with it halfway to his mouth. 'Where's Paul tonight? Won't he mind you having dinner with me?'

'Paul?' Kate was puzzled for a minute. 'Oh, you mean,

Peter. That window this evening, that was his mother's house. Mr B is her fiancé. He stayed on there afterwards.'

'I see.'

She didn't answer his second question. It was her opportunity to tell him that Peter wouldn't mind where she had dinner because they were no longer seeing each other, but she didn't want to share that quite yet. She liked this newfound friendship with Xander and didn't want anything to complicate it. It wasn't as if she and Xander would get together. Yes, she liked him – had feelings for him even – but there was still a voice in her head that was warning her to stay away from him. It had been there for so long, saying, 'If you don't want to end up in a relationship like your parents' marriage, don't pick a man who's like your father.' And when a voice had been saying that to you for years and years, it was difficult – impossible even – to think, *Well, maybe it wouldn't be like that. Maybe I should give him a chance and see.* Far easier not to tell that man that you're single and available. Far easier to spend time with him as a friend – far safer too – and that was what Kate decided to do.

So there was no question of his arm slipping around her shoulder as they relaxed on the sofa after their meal, nor of an awkward moment on the doorstep when they wondered whether to share a goodnight kiss. Kate walked home with her stomach uncomfortably full, and her lips untouched.

# 30

Mr B and Florence were sitting in the board game café, arguing over the Scrabble board the following morning, when Kate went in to pick up a takeaway coffee.

She had phoned him first thing, to let him know that thanks to his double entendre, the living Advent calendar had more posts than ever on social media, and that she was optimistic that the visitors would be coming in their droves.

She went over to his table now, to thank him in person. 'You are okay with it all, Mr B? I mean, you're all over social media.'

'He loves it,' said Florence. 'Three people stopped us on the way here to tell him how much they love his display.'

'I *do* love it,' said Mr B. 'Sometimes, as an older person, I've felt quite invisible. But now, thanks to my baubles and your living Advent calendar, I feel people see me again!'

'He's been insufferable since you phoned,' said Florence. 'He keeps humming the theme tune of *Local Hero*.'

'Well, he is a local hero,' said Kate. 'In my eyes, anyway.'

'Would you like join us for a game?' Mr B said.

She shook her head. 'Board games aren't really my thing. In any case, I can't stop. I'm just grabbing a coffee on my way to check out tonight's display. Need to make sure it's one hundred per cent perfect, cos I've got a sneaky feeling there'll be even more people there tonight for the big reveal.'

Kate had never been on board a narrowboat before, let alone one that was also a shop. She wasn't quite sure of the etiquette so stepped onto the deck and, in the absence of any kind of doorbell or knocker, tapped on the top of the hatch.

Seconds later, it slid open, the little doors swung open, and she descended into the boat.

For some reason, she'd expected it to be dark, but the ceiling was dotted with bright spotlights and the walls were the palest shade of grey. Shelves, painted in the same colour as the walls, ran along both sides of the boat under the window, and were stuffed full of balls of wool, in a rainbow of colours. Large cardboard boxes, secured by heavy-duty tape, completely obscured the two windows that would ordinarily have looked out onto the towpath; Kate guessed that the Advent displays must be inside them. At the end of this section of the boat was a modern wood burner with a blazing fire. Kate pulled off the woollen felt hat she always wore on cold days like this – she wasn't really a beanie kind of person.

'What do you think?' said Mel proudly.

'It's gorgeous. I can't knit, but it makes me wish I could.'

'Anyone can learn,' said Mel.

Kate pictured herself, in thirty or so years' time, a lonely woman who'd never married, knitting booties and cardigans for Em, Jo and Taylor's grandchildren, because there was no prospect of her having any of her own. Mustering all the mindfulness skills she'd been practising for the last few years, she pushed the gloomy image from her brain, and tried to focus on the here and now: this beautiful boat, the lovely warmth emanating from the fire, and the prospect of not one, but two, woollen Christmas displays to thrill all their visitors.

Mel gestured towards a small armchair beside the wood burner. 'Take a seat,' she said. 'I'll make you a brew.'

Pulling off her coat, Kate did as she was told, gazing at the flames licking at the glass.

Mel went through a sliding door. Kate could hear the sound of running water and some kind of pump. Then gas being ignited. Somewhere outside, in the distance, a duck was quacking, but other than that, it was peaceful. You couldn't hear the traffic from the main road that ran nearby from Essendale to Hebbleswick.

Kate was itching to see what the rest of the boat was like. Hoping she wouldn't appear too nosy, she slid open the door, and poked her head round. Mel was standing beside the hob where a kettle was beginning to whistle.

'I hope you don't mind,' Kate said. 'I've never seen inside a boat before. I wanted to see your kitchen.'

'Galley,' said Mel. 'It's called a galley on a boat. Would you like the full guided tour?'

'If it's not intruding?'

'Not at all. Quite a few of my customers have asked to have a look over the years. The shop area doubles as my lounge or the saloon as it's called on a boat.'

'Sounds like something from the wild west,' said Kate.

'Yeah, knitting needles at dawn.' Mel laughed. 'And then this is the galley, as you can see.' She slid open another door, and gestured for Kate to walk through.

Beyond this door was a small bathroom with a toilet, sink and bath, probably three-quarters the length of a normal bath, with a shower above it.

'And through here is where I sleep.' Mel opened another door, revealing a cosy space at the end of the boat, almost completely taken up with a double bed, with cupboards along one side.

There would barely be room, Kate thought, for her shoe collection in those cupboards, let alone her clothes as well!

They returned to the galley, where Mel poured the now perfectly brewed tea, and then went through into the saloon.

'Might I take a look at the windows?' Kate said. This was, after all, the real reason she'd come along early.

'You'll have to look from outside. They're inside those.' Mel gestured at the two cardboard boxes. 'Or I have photos.'

'Photos would be perfect.' Kate was loath to leave her cosy spot beside the fire.

Mel knelt on the floor beside Kate, and held up her phone screen. 'This is my first Christmas window display. Lovingly crafted by myself and a few of my customers.'

At that initial meeting in the board game café, when she'd first broached the idea of the living Advent calendar, many of the would-be windowers had suggested creating nativity scenes. Kate had said no to most of them, but she'd liked the idea of a knitted Nativity. She was glad she'd said yes to this as she gazed now at the picture of the perfectly crafted figures of Mary in her traditional blue robes and Joseph in beige, leading a grey knitted donkey. A tiny Jesus lay in a manger, complete with real hay, judging from the photo, and there were shepherds and wise men, complete with knitted gold, frankincense and myrrh. But Kate particularly loved the sheep, fashioned out of the fluffiest wool. There was even a knitted star, made out of white wool, with strands of silver running through it.

'Gorgeous,' said Kate. 'It's totally gorgeous.'

It was extra special too, being as how the windows were on a narrowboat.

'And then there's this one.' Mel swiped the screen to reveal a knitted roast turkey, which had a slice or two carved out of it, and a knitted plate bearing roast potatoes, two slices of turkey, stuffing, pigs in blankets, perfect little carrots and tiny sprouts. There was even a knitted jug of gravy and a knitted Christmas pudding.

By six o'clock, there was quite a queue along the towpath waiting for the two windows to be revealed. Peter's rigging wouldn't work tonight – not in the small space inside the boat – so instead, Mel had draped two tarpaulins over the outside of the windows. Nevertheless, Kate had imagined that he'd be here this evening anyway, to help with the unveiling, but he was nowhere to be seen. She couldn't blame him really. With the exception of this and two other displays, he was required every evening up to and including Christmas Eve; it was a big commitment, one he'd made when the two of them were dating, and it was understandable that he hadn't come along tonight when he wasn't officially needed.

Mel was standing on the roof of the boat now, ready to unveil the windows. It would be far better to do them both together. Kate looked round for a second person to help, but there was no sign of Jo or Razz; they'd come along to all of the unveilings so far. Em and Lud would be busy in the café, and the following evening, Taylor's window would be unveiled, so she and Harry would be putting the finishing touches to that. Kate suddenly felt alone, despite the fact that there were a huge number of people here, snaking their way along the towpath. And then she saw Xander. He was about tenth in the queue, but she called his name, and he began to weave his way through towards her.

'Xander!' she said. 'You couldn't help please, could you? Would you mind climbing on the roof and pulling the tarpaulin off one of the windows as Mel pulls the other one?'

'Anything for you, Kate.' He stepped onto the deck of the boat, then sprung up onto the roof, shaking hands as he introduced himself to Mel.

Kate checked the time on her phone and at six o'clock precisely, she began her usual speech, although she felt sure that her voice wouldn't carry all the way along the towpath to the people now joining the back of the queue. She welcomed everyone, reminding them that there were six other windows already on display in nearby Essendale and that the next few would be unveiled in Hebbleswick, and telling them where they could collect a trail map. Then she called for the drum roll, the thigh slapping began, and Mel and Xander lifted the tarpaulins, revealing the knitted displays underneath.

When the last few visitors had finished admiring the windows, and were ambling home along the towpath, Mel said, 'Now, are you two hungry?'

Xander and Kate looked at each other. 'Starving,' he said.

'Come on in then,' said Mel. 'It's nothing fancy, but it'll warm you up.'

They descended the steps into the warmth of the boat. Mel had moved the chair; in its place were three huge floor cushions beside the wood burner. She gestured for them to sit down, then handed them two steaming mugs of tea. Kate wrapped her hands gratefully around her mug.

'I'll fetch the food,' said Mel, disappearing into the galley.

She appeared two minutes later bearing two bowls, handing one to each of them. Inside each of the bowls was a perfectly cooked jacket potato laden with baked beans and melting cheese. She went back into the galley and brought out a third bowl, then settled herself on one of the cushions beside Kate.

'This okay?'

'Delicious.' Xander was already tucking in. 'We were saying only yesterday how much we love a baked potato.'

Kate liked the way he said 'we'.

'Especially with crispy skin,' she added.

'I baked these earlier in there.' Mel gestured towards the wood burner. 'I wrap them in foil and pop them in.'

'I didn't know you could do that,' said Xander.

The towpath was quiet by the time they walked home towards Essendale, their hands stuffed inside their pockets because the wind was biting cold. Kate wished she'd remembered her gloves.

They walked a few steps in silence, before Xander said, 'No Paul again this evening?'

'Peter,' said Kate. 'No, he wasn't needed tonight. Normally he's there to rig up the drapes to conceal the window. He's designed this clever pulley system.'

'Yes, I remember. I thought he might be there to support you.'

'Yeah, well…' She had to tell him now. 'Actually, Xander, Peter and I stopped seeing each other, so it's fair enough that he had a night off.'

'Oh, Kate, I'm sorry. Are you okay?'

'Yes, I'm fine, thank you.'

'Why did you…' he began, before shaking his head, and saying, 'No, forget it. It's none of my business. I won't ask.'

They walked up the steps that led from the towpath onto the street where The Little Board Game Café – Em's first café – had once stood. In its place was a rather soulless, low-rise block of flats, but at least, Kate thought, they weren't holiday lets; the residents were all locals. Most people round here would welcome a few more blocks like that if they provided affordable housing.

'Em's first board game café was here,' she said to Xander. 'Until they bulldozed it.'

'Have you two been friends long?'

'Yeah, since school.'

'Is this where you grew up?'

'No, we grew up in Thornholme. It's about a thirty-minute drive away.'

'Are your parents there still?'

'My dad is. God knows where my mum is.'

She kept her gaze fixed firmly on the street ahead. From the corner of her eye, she saw Xander glance at her, but if he was curious, he didn't ask, and she was grateful for that.

As they approached the centre of town, Xander stopped.

'Wait a moment,' he said. To her surprise, he reached into her pocket and clasped his fingers around hers. 'Look at the place. You've done that, Kate. It's magical.'

She stood beside him, enjoying the feeling of him holding her hand, and stared at Essendale. A few weeks ago, it had looked so drab and boring, with the sparse collection of festive lights that the council had deigned to put up. Now most of the windows had twinkling lights at the very least; most had pictures or baubles or sprayed-on snowflakes too, and several had Christmas trees. Xander was right – it *did* look magical.

'You're a clever woman, Kate,' he said. 'I feel sad that my collection of soldiers got between us.'

He paused. Kate wondered what she should say. That she felt sad too? That she really liked him and that it didn't matter about the soldiers? Only that wouldn't be true, because she couldn't see past them.

'Which window is it on Saturday?' he said.

'Saturday? The craft shop in Hebbleswick.'

'Are you doing anything afterwards?'

'No, I don't think so.'

'Then how about I come along to the grand unveiling

and afterwards, I cook dinner for you again? Not a date. Just… you know, friends. No expectations. I know you've recently split from Peter and you don't date geeky guys who collect model soldiers. But I have a rather special recipe that I'd like to try out on you.'

## 31

The old co-operative stood, not as you might have expected on Hebbleswick's main street, but on a smaller cobbled street overlooking the hills that towered over the town. For much of the twentieth century it had been a shop at the heart of the community, but had ceased trading with the rise of the big out-of-town supermarkets and become an ordinary house. Taylor and Max had set up home there; it was in a state of disrepair at the time, but the young dressmaker had delighted in placing her sewing table in the huge front window and displaying some of her creations alongside it in the hope of attracting new clients. And then the bathroom ceiling had collapsed and Tarquin, who was the letting agent, had decided to pin the blame on her, and all her dreams of running a proper shop with her own designs on sale had ended.

Now, thanks to Kate's powers of persuasion, Taylor's designs hung once more in the window of the old co-operative; the property had been recently refurbished, and the new tenants, a young couple who'd moved to Hebbleswick from London because they loved the community-centred vibe of the place, had agreed that the window could feature in the living Advent calendar. They were especially delighted when they saw that Taylor's new range of Christmas children's clothes would be on display; they'd confided in Kate that they were trying for a baby, so Peter had rigged up the drapes in their front window and Taylor had arranged her clothes behind them and everything was ready for the eighth grand unveiling.

The crowd was even larger than it had been the previous evening at the wool boat, thanks, no doubt, to the ongoing power of #MrBsBaubles. Kate stood outside, trying to count the number of heads, but it was impossible; more people joined every minute.

'Kate!'

Kate saw a hand waving from the back of the crowd, then watched as Em wormed her way to the front.

'Not at the café?'

'I left Lud in charge,' Em said. 'I had to come to see Taylor's window.'

'And it's well worth seeing. It's absolutely gorgeous. It's nearly time.'

Kate left Em, and knocked on the door of the old co-operative before opening it a crack and poking her head in. 'Ready?'

Peter was inside, standing beside the window, ready for the unveiling, with Harry and Max beside him. Taylor was proudly showing her scan photo to the two tenants. She looked up and smiled at Kate. 'Yeah, we're ready.'

'Shall we go outside, Max?' said Harry. 'Watch Mum's window being unveiled?'

Max nodded, and Kate opened the door a little wider for them to pass, then closed it after them.

After the usual drum roll and countdown, the drapes lifted and the crowd edged forward, jostling to get the best view.

Everything on display was second-hand – or pre-loved, as Taylor preferred to call it. With her top-class sewing skills and vivid imagination, the clever seamstress had refashioned the garments, adding Christmassy details here and there. A rabbit wearing a Santa hat had been appliqued onto the front of a child's pinafore dress. The words 'Santa's little helper' were embroidered onto a T-shirt, 'Mummy's Christmas pudding' onto another. There were candy canes, brightly coloured gifts and penguins on an icy landscape decorating various other garments, along with stockings and reindeer. White fur trim had been stitched onto a red dress, and a green dress had been made to look like a Christmas tree with the addition of fabric baubles.

Kate sighed.

Em whispered, 'She's so talented, isn't she?'

Max looked up at Harry and said, 'Isn't Mum clever?'

'She is, Max,' said Harry. 'She really is. Shall we choose one of the outfits for baby Esme to wear next Christmas? Which one do you like?'

'The rabbit one. No, the one with the baubles cos it's sparkly. Do you think Esme will like sparkly things?'

'I'm sure she will.' Harry ruffled Max's hair.

Suddenly Kate remembered standing outside a children's

clothes shop with *her* dad. It would have been around this time of year, and he was offering to buy her a dress for Christmas, and asking her which one she liked the best. She hadn't thought about that for years. Had her mum been there too? Kate thought, casting her mind back, but she had no recollection of the three of them *ever* going shopping together.

She couldn't recall anything about the dress she'd chosen, but the feelings associated with this memory were as vivid as if it were yesterday; she'd felt proud and important inside the shop as she'd tried some of the dresses on, and then watched her father handing over his credit card. She'd felt special. She'd felt loved.

She glanced at Harry and Max again. Max was in front of Harry, leaning against him, and Harry had his arms casually draped around the boy's shoulders. Taylor and Harry had only been together for a few months, but it was clear that Max already had a special bond with his new stepdad.

She felt her eyes welling up and blinked a few times, defying the tears to roll down her cheeks.

'Makes you want a baby, doesn't it?' said Em. 'Imagine dressing them up in those gorgeous clothes.'

'Yeah,' Kate sighed. 'Imagine.'

She'd known Taylor's window would make her long for a baby even more than usual, but she hadn't reckoned on it conjuring up that memory from her past and making her long for her father. Perhaps it wasn't only the window, but seeing Max with Harry.

'Are you okay, Kate?' said Em.

Before Kate could argue, she felt Em's fingers wrap themselves around hers, and she found herself being tugged away from the window, through the crowd, and around the corner onto a quieter street.

'Are you okay?' Em said again.

Kate nodded vaguely.

'Sit down for a minute.' Em gestured at the low wall that surrounded the tiny front garden of one of the houses. 'It's the baby thing, isn't it? I know how you feel. I was hoping Lud and I would be a bit nearer the whole marriage and babies thing by now but...' Her voice trailed away.

'It wasn't that. It was...' Kate could hardly bring herself to say it. 'I suddenly remembered my dad taking me shopping when I was little. How special he made me feel. And then I looked at Harry and Max together, and it made me wish I had a better relationship with my dad.'

'Kate, you still can,' Em said softly. 'If I'm honest, I've never really understood the problem.'

Kate looked at Em in surprise. 'He drove Mum away. If he hadn't ignored her all the time, she wouldn't have left. She was so lonely, Em. I can never forgive him for that.'

There was a knocking sound, and Kate turned to see the resident of the house whose wall they were sitting on knocking on the window and frowning angrily at them, before making a shoo gesture.

'Come on.' Em linked her arm through Kate's and pulled her to her feet. 'Let's walk.'

They ambled down the street, past window after window lit up with fairy lights or adorned with children's Christmassy pictures.

Neither woman spoke for a few minutes, but then, as they turned onto the high street and walked past the hospice shop, Em said, 'When I was going out with Peter, you never liked him.'

Kate harrumphed. 'No, I didn't. I really didn't.'

'But then a few weeks ago, you liked him enough to date him yourself.'

Kate stopped walking. 'What's your point, Em?'

'Why didn't you like him when *I* was dating him? Might it have been the negative things I told you about him? Every time there was an incy-wincy little problem in our relationship, I came running to you, Kate the relationship guru, asking for advice.'

'Yeah, 'spose.'

'So you didn't like him because you only ever heard my side of the story? Is that the case?'

'I guess,' said Kate cautiously, already beginning to suspect where this conversation was heading.

'All those years, before your mum left. You knew their marriage wasn't a happy one?'

'Blimey, Em. I feel like a witness in a court case. The defendant even. What's with all the questions?'

'But you did know that, didn't you?'

'Yeah, I knew that. Mum was always moaning about him.'

'Exactly.' Em punched the air. 'I rest my case, m'lord. Did your dad ever moan about your mum?'

'Well, no.'

'You only *ever* heard your mum's side. You never heard his perspective. Not even after she walked out?'

'No.'

'He didn't criticise her? Blame her for going?'

'He never said a word against her.'

'So all those years, you misjudged Peter because you only ever heard *my* side of the story. What if you've been misjudging your dad, Kate, because you only ever heard hers? It takes two people to make a marriage succeed or fail. Isn't it about time you listened to *his* side?'

Kate paused, mulling over Em's words. She was right, of course. It seemed ridiculous now that she had never talked to her father about any of this, had never given him the chance to explain his point of view.

Although... all those hours in that shed. That look of loneliness on her mother's face.

'I'll talk to him at Christmas,' she said finally, 'when I make the dreaded annual visit.'

'Go tomorrow. It's Saturday. There's no time like the present.' Em sounded uncharacteristically bossy.

Kate wrinkled her nose. 'I'm knackered. I need a rest over the weekend.'

'Either you'll hear his side of things, realise he isn't the terrible person you thought he was, and clear the air,' Em said. 'Then the annual visit won't be dreaded and you can enjoy Christmas together. Or you'll learn that you were right all along, and he's a terrible person who drove your mother away. In which case, you could stop pretending to have any kind of relationship with him, sever all ties and spend Christmas with us instead.'

Kate thought about this. It was a win-win situation. She'd judged her father on what she'd seen as a child growing up, but looking back now, bringing an adult understanding to the situation, she could concede that things mightn't have been as clear-cut as she thought. If he wasn't entirely to blame for her mother leaving, well, maybe she could have a better relationship with him going forwards.

And if he admitted it? Said that he was to blame? There'd be a huge relief in letting herself off the hook, in saying he'd made his own bed, he could lie in it.

'I'd feel like a right gooseberry, spending Christmas with you and Lud,' she said, even though she quite liked the idea. She didn't want Em inviting her because she felt she had to; better to be on her own on Christmas Day if that was the case.

'D'you know what I *really* fancy doing?' said Em, her eyes bright in the way they always were when she'd had an idea. 'Christmas at the board game café. We have decorations, we have food and we have board games. What else do you need for a fabulous Christmas? I could invite everyone. You, obviously. Your dad too if you've patched things up. My dad and Marjory – did you know they were still together? Jo and Razz. Taylor, Harry and Max. Florence, Mr B and Peter – I think Peter needs cheering up. It'll be great fun, Kate, what d'you reckon? I know Lud misses his big family Christmases in Poland, and Mr B probably does too, so they'll both be happy.'

'That's a lot of cooking,' said Kate. 'Won't it be a bit of a busman's holiday for you?'

'Lud and Mr B will muck in and help,' said Em. 'Now are you going to see your dad tomorrow or what?'

## 32

Kate saw him before he saw her. He was standing by a stack of baked beans with one tin in his hand, trying to decide whether to put it in his basket. How could anyone take so long to choose a can of beans? She took a step backwards, wondering if she could hide behind a huge mountain of toilet paper that must have been going cheap at the cash 'n' carry and were now on special offer, occupying a disproportionately large area of Thornholme's small corner shop.

After her conversation with Em, she'd agreed that she would bite the bullet, visit her dad and ask for his side of the story. Em was convinced that the big reconciliation was on the cards, that father and daughter would be happily reunited, and that both would be spending Christmas at the board game café; Kate wasn't so sure.

But here she was. Cowering behind a stack of white, triple-ply bog rolls. She hadn't liked to turn up unannounced *and* empty-handed, so had popped in here for a packet of biscuits.

She peeped over the top of the stack and watched her dad replacing the baked beans and picking up some tinned ravioli instead.

'Can I help you?'

Kate turned to see the shop assistant standing behind her, clearly puzzled at her behaviour.

'Are these quilted?' she whispered, picking up a four-pack of the loo rolls.

'No, I don't think so,' said the shop assistant.

'Oh, well in that case...' Kate shrugged and put the packet back.

'Kate! Why didn't you tell me you were coming?'

Her father was standing beside her now, a tin of spaghetti hoops in his hand.

'Dad!' she said awkwardly. 'I was just passing.'

'You were passing?'

'Yeah, on my way to... a friend's,' she said. Even to her own ears, it sounded unconvincing.

'Don't you have a hug for your old dad?'

He did look old, she realised. His jumper had a hole in it and could have done with a wash. And he was wearing slippers. Slippers in the corner shop. She felt a brief pang of pity for him. Almost strong enough to give him that hug. She knew what it was like to go for ages without any physical contact with another human being. And Dad had probably gone years. She couldn't remember him ever hugging Mum. Perhaps it hadn't happened since the night of her conception. If it had even happened then. Had he rolled off her, pulled on his clothes and gone straight out to the shed?

Reluctantly she put one arm around his shoulders, allowing the top of her body to make contact with his, and turning her face away from him. He put both of his arms around her, the tin of spaghetti hoops still in his hand.

'Have you time for a cup of tea?' he said as she pulled away. 'Or even better, a spot of lunch? I could buy another tin?' He waved the spaghetti hoops at her, as if they were a prized delicacy.

Surely they could do a little better than that.

'We could grab a couple of potatoes to bake instead?'

Why had she suggested that? This was supposed to be a quick visit. One mug of tea whilst she heard him out, then she intended to leave. And unless you microwaved them, jacket potatoes took ages, she thought, recalling that conversation with Xander.

'Lovely,' her dad was saying now. 'I can't remember when I last had a baked potato!'

He went to put the spaghetti hoops back on the shelf, and Kate chose two large spuds from the shop's rather sparse selection of vegetables, a pack of butter and a pack of cheese.

At the till, her father insisted on paying, as if he was treating her to something special, and Kate felt sad for him again. She thought about that shopping expedition and how he'd treated her to a new dress, but then she remembered that she hadn't seen her mum in over fifteen years because of him, hadn't heard from her even, and her sadness turned to anger, and she remembered how, on the day after her sixteenth birthday, she'd resolved to spend as little time with him as possible.

Her sixteenth birthday had fallen on a Saturday. It had felt like any other birthday, with no hint of what was to come. Her parents had taken her and Em out for a meal. It seemed ironic, given what happened soon afterwards, that they had gone out together as a family that day, something they very rarely did.

The atmosphere was tense. Kate couldn't eat her roast chicken fast enough. Once the meal was over, she and Em planned to get the train into Manchester and wander round the shops together. That was the part of her birthday she'd really been looking forward to.

When the empty plates from their main courses had been cleared away, Kate stood up. 'Okay if we go now?'

'What about pudding?' her mum said.

'Too full,' Kate said, rubbing her belly for emphasis.

'Sit down, Kate,' said her dad. He didn't often put his foot down but she recognised that tone of voice. She slid back into her seat.

The waitress appeared at their table then, notepad in hand, pen poised to take their dessert order.

'Can you bring the er...' said her mum.

'Okay,' said the waitress and disappeared back into the kitchen.

About three minutes later, the waitress reappeared, carrying an iced cake with sixteen lit candles. At least, Kate assumed there were sixteen. In her state of embarrassment, she didn't count. The waitress was followed by two of the waiters and a guy in chef whites, all singing, 'Happy birthday to you. Happy birthday...'

Her parents began to join in. People were turning round on other tables, staring at her, some singing along.

Em gave a shrug and began to mumble along too, in much the same way as they used to 'sing' the hymns in assemblies when they were in primary school.

As the song reached the third line, 'Happy birthday, dear...' the waiting staff all hesitated. They hadn't remembered her name, Kate thought. Her parents sang 'Ka-ate' extra loudly, turning her one-syllabled name into two, and the song limped on to its end as the cake was set in front of her.

The entire pub burst into a spontaneous smattering of applause as her mum said, 'Make a wish, Kate.'

Kate wished the ground would swallow her up, that this ordeal was over so that she and Em could make their escape.

The waiting staff looked on, no doubt dying to get back to work.

She blew out the candles so half-heartedly that it took three attempts and Em had to help on the final one. She was sixteen, not six. She loved her mum to bits, but what had she been thinking?

'Have a slice of cake before you go to Manchester,' her mum said.

'Too full.' Kate rubbed her belly again.

Her mum sighed. 'Well, don't be too late back then. We can have a slice before Emily goes home.'

In Manchester, Kate and Em mooched round the shops, trying on various garments that they didn't have the money to buy. They bought cans of Coke and sat on a bench outside the Arndale Centre, hoping that some lads who were messing about nearby might come over and talk to them. The lads didn't show even the slightest interest. As afternoon turned to evening, they watched as the Saturday shoppers went home and the revellers began to appear, girls only a year or two older than them in shorter skirts, lower-cut tops and higher heels.

Kate didn't go out much in the evenings; she always felt she should try to keep her mother company, though it never seemed to be particularly appreciated.

'I need to go home,' she said. She was starting to feel guilty about her mum. Her dad would be in his shed, beavering away on his little radios. Her mother would be staring out of the kitchen window at him. Or maybe staring out of the front window, watching for Kate's return. The birthday cake would be sitting untouched on the table.

'It's only half seven,' Em said. 'And it's your birthday.'

'Yeah, but Mum'll be by herself. She gets lonely, you know.'

They arrived at the station to find they'd missed the train and there wasn't another for almost an hour. When Kate finally arrived home, she found her mother watching television. She barely looked up when Kate entered the room.

'Sorry I'm so late,' Kate said.

'You're sixteen now,' her mother said crisply. 'I guess you'll be doing your own thing more often.'

The next morning, she was gone.

★

She'd left because of him. Because of Dad.

At least, Kate had always told herself that.

But there was a tiny voice in her head, a tiny voice that she tried to ignore, that whispered that she was to blame. If she hadn't stayed out late on her sixteenth birthday, would her mother still have left? Did she decide then that Kate was growing up and had her own life to lead? Is that what made her mother decide that it was time for her to lead hers?

How had she felt, knowing Kate would be going out more in the evenings, leaving her alone, whilst in that bloody shed her father fiddled for hours with his stupid transistors? She must have been dreading the day that Kate went off to uni.

It was a week before Kate accepted that she had gone for good. That she'd never see her again. The realisation unleashed an angry maelstrom in her. She howled. She raged. She shouted at her dad.

'It's all your fault,' she said. 'You've always spent more time in that shed than you have with us! You care more about those damn radios than you do about your own wife and daughter. And that's why she's gone.'

And he didn't deny it.

The irony was that her father padlocked the shed door, and Kate never saw him in there again.

## 33

As her dad filled the kettle, Kate felt herself drawn to the window, drawn to look at the shed. The waterproof roofing felt was torn and missing in places. The pane of glass in the window was cracked. It hadn't had a coat of wood varnish in years and she suspected that it was rotting in places. And the padlock sat firmly bolted, completely rusty now. She suspected that he hadn't been inside since the day Mum had left.

Locking it had been such a pointless gesture, she thought now. Her mother was already gone, the damage already done. If there'd been a time to give up his transistor hobby, it was a year earlier. A month even. A week. A day. Might that have made the difference?

'How's life in Essendale?' said Dad. 'Have you found a nice chap yet?'

Kate thought of Peter. Of her dashed hopes. Okay, so she'd known deep down that the spark wasn't there and that they weren't really right for each other, but she'd still harboured hopes, at the beginning anyway. And she thought of Xander, and how she longed for him, but couldn't get past the image of that table covered in soldiers. Peter. Xander. She wasn't sure her love life had ever been so messy as it had been in recent weeks. Her eyes filled with tears and before she had time to think, her father had seized the opportunity to come in for a proper hug and his arms were around her, enveloping, pulling her in so that her body was completely enfolded by his.

He smelt good, despite the unwashed jumper. Familiar.

She couldn't remember the last time she'd been held by her father like this. Had there been a hug on that sixteenth birthday? Had he held her as she cried over her mother's disappearance? In recent years, Kate had tried to avoid touching him on the rare occasions that they saw one another.

'Oh, Kate,' he said. 'I want you to meet someone and be happy.'

'Yeah,' she mumbled into his jumper. 'You and me both.'

'You can't go through life on your own. It's so…'

'Lonely?'

The kettle reached boiling point and clicked itself off. Kate pulled away from him and slumped into a chair. Her father placed a roll of kitchen towel in front of her.

'I don't have tissues,' he said. 'It's this or toilet paper.'

'I'll take the kitchen roll.' She tore off a sheet and dabbed her eyes.

'I was hoping you'd find yourself a nice boyfriend,' he said. 'Em said you'd split up from Peter.'

Hang on. He knew she'd been dating Peter?

'Em said?'

Her father looked guilty. As if he'd said something he shouldn't. 'She er... look, Kate. I miss you. I worry about you. And Em is kind enough to send me the occasional text to let me know you're okay. She said you'd split from Peter, but there was another chap that you liked. Who seemed to like you. Xander, isn't it?'

'Yeah, I really like him. But it won't work.'

'Whyever not? If you really like him?'

Kate thought of the shed. She thought of the soldiers.

'Because,' she said, looking her father in the eyes, 'he reminds me of you.'

She could see the remark had stung as soon as she'd said it.

Her dad was reaching for the kitchen roll now.

She felt bad that she'd hurt him, but triumphant too. It had been a long time coming. She'd spent her entire adult life wishing she had a mother she could talk to and it was his fault that she hadn't.

'Tell me about him.' He blew his nose.

Kate told him how she'd met Xander. About the awkward date at the V&A – 'sounds like an interesting exhibition,' her dad said – and about the living Advent calendar and how Xander was insisting on doing the final window – 'so proud of you,' he said, 'I'd like to come and see that.'

'We've become friends, Dad,' said Kate. 'He's a great guy, but it wouldn't work romantically. It's lonely being single, but I know from watching you and Mum that being in the wrong relationship can be even lonelier.'

'What makes you think it would be the wrong relationship?'

'One evening, I went back to his place for coffee.'

Her dad shifted uncomfortably in his seat. 'You can skip the sex bit.'

'There was no sex bit. He went to make the coffee, and he was rather a long time, so I went to find him and saw his dining table was covered in toy soldiers, and that's when I decided I wanted to run. That's when I thought about you.'

'I've never had any toy soldiers. Not even as a boy.'

'It wasn't the soldiers themselves, but all the hours he spends painting them. I've spent my whole adult life avoiding men who have time-consuming hobbies. Fishing. Fitness. Computers. And now toy soldiers. I don't want to end up with someone whose hobby borders on obsession. I'd end up even lonelier than I am now. Like Mum was, remember? When you spent night after night in that shed, tinkering with your damn radios. She was so lonely, Dad. She'd stand there for hours, gazing out of that window. Missing you.'

'Kate, that's not how—'

'I'd stay up as late as I could to keep her company, and I was always tired in school next day, and it was hard because I wanted to do well at school. And then when I was a teenager, when my classmates were all going out, I stayed home so Mum wouldn't be on her own. Did you never realise that?'

'I thought you were a bit of a loner,' he said. 'Like me. A bit of an introvert.'

'I'm not,' Kate said. 'I like being with people. You should have been there. We should have been a family in the evenings. Watched TV together. Played board games. Although I don't actually like board games, but anyway... And then, when I'd gone to bed, you should have been with Mum. Spent some time with her. Made her feel loved. Because if you had, she wouldn't have left.'

'Kate, I—'

'Do you know how many times I have longed to talk to her? When relationship after relationship went wrong, how much I needed her? How many times I've wanted her guidance?'

She thought about her pile of self-help books, and how they'd been a poor substitute for being able to ask her mum for advice.

'I wish I could have heard her laugh when I told her about all the terrible dates I went on. Em is brilliant – she's been the best friend anyone could ever wish for – but no-one could ever replace Mum. And she left, Dad. She left because of you.'

The tears were streaming down Kate's cheeks now. She grabbed at the kitchen roll, managing to tear off only a corner. Her dad reached over, tore off a full sheet and silently passed it to her. She remembered that she was here to find out his side of the story, dabbed her eyes with the sheet of kitchen roll, and blew her nose. 'Have I got that right, Dad? *Did* she leave because of you?'

'I'll make more tea,' he said, standing up and filling the kettle.

It seemed to take an age to boil. Neither of them spoke. Kate sat, studying her father, wondering what excuses he was going to come up with. He stared out of the kitchen window at the shed, like her mother used to. Finally, the tea was made, he poured in the milk and placed the steaming mugs on the table.

'I don't know where to start,' he said. 'Your mother…'

your mother was a very sociable woman when I met her. Liked parties. Always the life and soul. Very popular. Loads of friends.'

Kate nodded. She'd inherited her mother's genes.

He took a sip of his tea. 'I wasn't your mother's type. I was a quiet sort, not conventionally good-looking. So different from the men she normally went for. Your mother liked another chap – Garry Somebody-or-Other – but he didn't like her. Well, that's not strictly true. He liked her, but he liked a lot of other women too. These days you'd call him a player. I always suspected she only went out with me to make him jealous.'

'Or maybe she liked you,' Kate said.

He shook his head. 'I don't think she intended to stick with me for long. Just until Garry changed his mind and decided he wanted her, or till someone else – someone better – came along.'

'So, what happened?'

'*You* happened. She got pregnant. We had to get married because of you.'

'Come on, Dad. It was the nineties, not the fifties.'

'Not as far as her parents were concerned. They were rather well off, her parents. And very religious. Your mum had a very strict upbringing. I think that's why she was a bit of a party girl – she was rebelling. Anyway, her father made it very clear that she either married me and got on with it, or she risked being disinherited. She chose the marriage. But then they had a falling-out and the heartless old… well, he disinherited her anyway, so she was saddled with me for nothing.'

He paused for a minute, allowing this to sink in.

As a teenager, Kate had done the maths, had realised that she'd been conceived *before* her parents' wedding, but she'd never realised that it was the *only* reason they'd got married.

'She'd never wanted kids,' her father continued, 'and certainly not with a boring book-keeper in a three-bedroomed terrace. Not when her friends lived in trendy city-centre flats and went out partying. And she blamed me.'

'But I never heard you arguing or anything like that?'

'She wasn't the kind of woman who shouted, but she could be very cruel. Very cutting. In those early years, she made my life a misery. Always reminding me that I wasn't worthy of her. That I'd ruined her life. Always saying that she'd leave one day.'

'Oh, Dad.' She wiped a tear away from her cheek with her hand. 'But she stayed sixteen years. Why didn't she leave before if she was so unhappy?'

'I honestly don't know. I've often asked myself that over the years. Duty, I suspect. The importance of family drilled into her over the years by her folks.'

'Or maybe she loved me?'

Her father paused for that fraction of a second too long.

'She didn't, did she? And I think deep down, I always knew that.' Kate closed her eyes, and bit her lip.

'Oh, Kate. Love. It used to break my heart watching you. Even as a little girl, you were always trying to win her affection. Always trying to be the perfect daughter. You kept your clothes clean. If you fell over, you were upset about the dirt on your dress, not your grazed knees. You had to be top of every spelling test. You knew all your times tables before anyone else in your class. You wanted to make her proud.'

'I wanted to make her love me.'

Kate looked at her dad, his eyes full of concern, and replayed his words in her head. *Trying to win her affection. Be the perfect daughter. Make her proud.*

She was an adult now, but inside she was still that little girl, trying to be perfect in the hope that that would gain her the love she yearned for. Keeping herself fit and healthy, both mentally and physically, with her mindfulness mediation, her ten thousand steps and her ten portions of fruit and veg. Striving for that perfect look, with her shiny bob and her stylish clothes. Always aiming to be the best at work. Saying the right things at the right time and, if she could, making other people laugh. Never forgetting a birthday. And being ever willing to do a favour for a friend.

But no-one was perfect. Look at Em, Jo and Taylor; they all had their little foibles, yet *their* partners still worshipped the ground they walked on.

'If the pair of you were so unhappy together,' she said, 'why didn't you leave?'

'I couldn't leave you. I didn't think she'd want custody, but I couldn't risk it.'

Kate looked at her dad again, and saw suddenly that *he* was the one who loved her. That she'd been anything but the perfect daughter to him, blaming him for all these years for something that wasn't his doing at all, shunning almost all contact with him. She had really hurt him, and yet he loved her.

And her mother never had.

How had she ever believed otherwise? Mothers who loved their daughters didn't leave the minute they turned sixteen, never to get in touch again.

'I've never had so much as a birthday card from her in all these years,' she said. 'Not even a text at Christmas.'

'She didn't have a maternal bone in her body, Kate, but I don't blame her for that, not considering the role models she had. I mean, it's hardly any wonder when you look at how *her* parents acted towards her. They were like something out of the Victorian era. I think she did as much as she could. I was surprised she stayed around for as long as she did. I think when you turned sixteen, she saw you were becoming more independent and seized her chance. Or perhaps she met someone else.'

'I always thought she left because she was lonely. Because you were always in that bloody shed.'

'No. Chicken and egg, Kate, chicken and egg. I built that shed so I could give her space, and to get away from her cruel jibes about how miserable I'd made her. I was never that into the transistors. They were simply something to do, to pass the time. It could have been anything. Model railways. Golf. Fly-fishing. Perhaps even miniature soldiers.'

He gave her a weak smile.

Kate couldn't quite take all this in. Perhaps that wasn't loneliness she'd seen when she'd looked at Mum all those times, staring out of the kitchen window. Perhaps it was resentment.

And her father hadn't spent all that time in the shed because he loved tinkering with his radios. He'd been staying out of her mother's way.

'Men don't always spend time building transistor radios or playing with their Hornby train sets or painting model soldiers because they prefer that to being with their partners,' her dad said. 'Perhaps some do, but not all. They do it because they need a hobby to pass the time.' He took a sip of his tea. 'Kate, do you know what I'm saying here?'

She did know. She always tried to keep busy, to fill her life with activities, because that way, she felt less lonely herself. All the free marketing work she did for her friends, and perhaps even the living Advent calendar too; yes, she wanted to help her mates out, wanted to do something for the local community, but it was also a way of occupying the empty hours.

She nodded, but her dad continued anyway. 'I'm going to spell this out, because I think you might be throwing something good away. If you get together with Xander, you might find he isn't quite so interested in his soldiers. You might find he'd much rather spend time with you. But you'll never know that unless you give him a chance.'

# 34

People often go through life believing the stories they tell themselves, often without questioning whether those stories are actually true. These might be stories about who to love and who to hate, or why to vote a certain way in a general election, or they might be stories about themselves. *I'm still single because I'm too picky about men. If I could lose ten kilos, life would be perfect. I can't sing. I've never been any good at maths.* Even when you know those beliefs are mistaken, it's difficult to change the narrative. Kate knew this – she'd read enough self-help books over the years – but nevertheless, it was hard to shake off the two stories that she'd spent her entire adult life telling herself: that she needed to be perfect to be loved and that her mum had walked out because of her dad's time-consuming hobby, and so she herself should never date anyone with a similar hobby.

Neither of these things were true. She could see that now.

No-one was perfect. No matter how hard she'd tried to be the perfect daughter, her mum hadn't loved her.

She had taken herself off for a walk round Thornholme after their discussion and their jacket potatoes, wanting to get her head around it all. She sat on a bench in the park, staring into space, wondering why her dad hadn't explained things before. Perhaps he'd been trying to protect her; who wants to tell their child that their own mother doesn't love them? Hadn't wanted her in the first place. Kate still couldn't get her head around that.

And why hadn't she *asked* him before? Why on earth had she waited until now to question things? All that anger she'd carried. All that guilt. All that time she'd wasted when she could have had a proper relationship with her one remaining parent: her loyal and loving dad.

She had a chance now to put things right. With him. With Xander.

Give him a chance, Dad had said.

Could she?

And if she did, would Xander give her a chance?

When she got back, her father was upstairs. She could hear him bustling around.

'Stay the night,' he said when he came down. 'I've made up the bed in your old room.'

Kate hesitated. For one thing, she didn't have anything with her. No toothbrush. No PJs. No change of clothes. For another, it was the craft shop's window reveal that evening, so she needed to be in Hebbleswick. Plus Xander was cooking for her afterwards.

'I need to get back for the living Advent calendar.'

'Of course.' He smiled, but she could see the disappointment in his eyes.

All these years, she had neglected this man, had blamed him for something that wasn't his fault. All these years, he hadn't enlightened her, because he knew the truth would hurt her.

Her mother hadn't wanted her.

No matter how many times she heard that sentence in her mind, she couldn't quite take it in. It was going to take a lot of healing – perhaps some counselling even – to get her head around this one.

Her own mother hadn't wanted her.

But her dad did. Always had.

Maybe she *would* stay here tonight.

'I suppose I can miss it this once,' she said. 'It's the craft shop. The owner's pretty clued up. I'm sure they can manage without me. They're doing a display of home-made Christmas gifts.'

'Sounds wonderful. I can see I'm going to have to take a trip to Essendale and Hebbleswick to see all these windows for myself.'

'Come for Christmas.' As soon as the words were out of her mouth, she wondered if she'd been too hasty. After these years of barely speaking to one another, perhaps they both needed more time to slip into a proper father-daughter relationship; this wasn't some slushy film where they would say, 'Fancy that! We've misunderstood each other all along,' and then be best friends again. But then she looked at his face, now bright with excitement. He looked ten years younger than the man she'd met in the corner shop a few hours earlier.

'At yours?' he said.

'No, not at mine.' His face fell, so she quickly added, 'At Em's. In the board game café with her and Ludek – I'm guessing you know about him since you're in touch with Em. There'd be other friends too. What d'you think? You could come on Christmas Eve, see the final window unveiled and stay over at mine, ready for Em's Christmas dinner the following day. Her dad'll be there too. You know him.'

'That'd be a lovely change,' he said. 'Much as I love you, Kate, those Christmas dinners with just the two of us… well, it was never very festive, was it? Every year, I'd ring you to check if you were coming, and if I'm honest, I was always hoping you'd say you had other plans, so I could book myself on a singles cruise or something.'

She gawped at him. 'You're kidding?'

'No. I quite fancy a Christmas cruise, but I didn't want to leave you on your own. Not on Christmas Day. And I'm not keen on those roast-in-the-bag chickens, to be honest.'

The irony.

Kate texted Peter first, explaining that she couldn't make the big reveal at the craft shop and asking if he would mind passing her apologies to the owner, then she messaged Xander, saying that she was visiting her dad and something had come up so she couldn't get back that evening. Can we take a rain check on dinner? she wrote. Tomorrow instead?

Xander responded quickly. Sure. Hope everything's okay.

She began to tap out a reply. All fine. More than okay.

But then she thought better of it. She couldn't explain the events of today in a text. If she felt ready, she would tell him in person about what she'd discovered about her parents' relationship, and how her misunderstanding about their marriage had impacted her own life choices. And at some point, once she'd got her head round all of this, she'd pluck up the courage to come clean with Xander about how this had affected *their* relationship, how if she'd known the truth when the two of them first met, she would never have walked out on him because of a dining table covered in soldiers.

She didn't understand the whole fascination with toy soldiers, but each to his own. If that was what he liked, it was fine with her, as long as they didn't make an appearance in his Christmas Eve window.

Kate slept surprisingly soundly in her old bedroom. When she woke, it was after ten o'clock. Bleary-eyed, she made her way down to the kitchen and found Dad frying bacon and sausages.

A fry-up wasn't something she normally ate – she'd have preferred her food grilled – but maybe just this once.

'Wow,' she said. 'A proper cooked breakfast.'

'I popped to the corner shop first thing. There are hash browns in the oven.'

She hoped he hadn't worn his slippers. 'Yummy. Thanks, Dad.'

They exchanged a hesitant smile.

'We're going to need all our strength today,' he said, 'so I thought we should have a decent breakfast.'

'All our strength? Why? What are we doing?'

'You'll see. Now, one egg or two?'

'Put on some old clothes,' he said later, after they'd devoured their fry-up along with two large mugs of Yorkshire tea. 'If you look in the bottom drawer of the chest in my room, there's some things that might fit.'

She did as she was told, excited to be doing something with her dad after all these years, though hesitant about what that something might be. As he suggested, the bottom drawer of his chest of drawers was full of old clothes – all far too big for her; she'd look terrible in them, but no-one except her dad would see her today. She chose the least paint-splattered pair of jogging bottoms – to her knowledge, her dad had never been jogging in his life so she wasn't sure why he owned any jogging bottoms – and a T-shirt and headed back downstairs.

He was standing in the back garden when she reached the kitchen.

'Come on, Dad, tell me what we're doing,' she said, although she already had an inkling.

'We're demolishing the shed.'

She knew it.

'Are you sure about this?'

'Look at it. It's an eyesore. And I haven't been in there for years. And...'

'And?'

'Well, we're turning over a new chapter, Kate. In our lives. In our relationship. And getting rid of this old thing feels kind of symbolic of that. It'll be cathartic.'

He handed her a sledgehammer. 'Want to strike the first blow?'

'Shouldn't we empty it first?'

'Yeah, probably. If we can get that old padlock open.'

'I'm not sure I fancy going inside,' she said. 'There might be spiders.'

'There will be spiders,' he said. 'But your old Dad's here to rescue you.'

It took the best part of twenty-five minutes and half a can of WD-40 before the old padlock finally yielded and popped open.

'We're in,' said Dad triumphantly, as if he'd cracked the main safe at the Bank of England.

The door opened with a creak. He tried the light switch but nothing happened. The window was so dirty it allowed in little sunshine. They stood in the doorway, peering into the gloom. Dust and cobwebs draped all over the shelves and work benches. Kate jumped to one side as a huge spider scurried along the floor and out to freedom in the garden.

He laid out all the radios on the lawn, and Kate dusted them off before taking them into the house; he said he'd check later to see if any could be salvaged and sold on eBay. Once the shed was empty, Kate took the sledgehammer and swung it at the shed, relishing the sound of the wood splintering. Her dad gave it a whack too, but then said it would probably make less mess if they disassembled it properly, unscrewing screws, prising out nails and removing every piece of wood.

He was right; getting rid of the shed *was* cathartic, although it would have been even more so if they'd bashed it to smithereens with the sledgehammer.

'What'll you do with it all?' Kate asked.

'A bonfire probably. But I'll wait till more of the neighbours have got their washing out.'

She glanced over at him. Was he serious? Or joking? Sad

that she didn't know her own father well enough to tell. Then their eyes met and they burst out laughing.

Later, before Kate got into her car to make the journey back to Essendale, he pulled her in for yet another hug; they'd shared more hugs in the past twenty-four hours than they had in the last sixteen years. Instead of escaping as quickly as possible, Kate held on to him, clung to him, relishing the feeling of safety.

'Now, you give that man another chance,' he said, when they finally pulled apart.

# 35

The enormity of the weekend's revelations didn't hit Kate properly until she closed her own front door behind her and sank into her sofa.

At sixteen, when her mum left, Kate couldn't articulate the overwhelming sense of loss that she felt. At around the same time, Em's mother was killed in a tragic road accident. Kate and Em were already mates, but finding themselves both suddenly motherless had brought them closer together, cementing their bond and turning their ordinary teenage friendship into something that they both knew would endure for life.

Em's tragedy was the greater one – Kate was in no doubt about that. Parents' marriages often broke down, but a mother losing her life in a such a violent and unexpected way was – thankfully – an unusual event. Em's mother was dead and, at the tender age of sixteen, Em was suffering the most enormous grief. Kate's mother had simply legged it, but she was alive and kicking somewhere out there.

But Kate realised something now, as she sat on her sofa cuddling a cushion for comfort. As she and Em had learned to navigate the world without their mums, they had *both* been grieving.

Were you allowed to call it grief when the person you were missing – were mourning even – was still alive?

Sod it, they were her feelings. She could call them what she wanted.

And those exact same feelings were back now.

In some ways, nothing had changed. Her situation was exactly the same as it had been the previous morning when she'd locked her front door and set off for her dad's. She was single, living in a neat, terraced house in the quirky Yorkshire town of Essendale, working in marketing and organising a living Advent calendar to help her local community.

Yet everything had changed. The whole foundation of her life, of her being, had been shaken to its core. Her mother hadn't loved her, had never wanted her. And Kate felt grief all over again. Gnawing, aching, throbbing grief. This time, not for the mother who had left, but for the mother she'd never had in the first place.

She swung her legs onto the sofa, curling up in a ball around the cushion, rocking herself slowly. She ran through the key events of her childhood in her mind, as if she were watching a movie, seeing them all through a new lens – the lens of 'my mother never loved me'. The world of her childhood looked completely different. Young Kate was always there, always trying to please, to be perfect. Wanting to win a kind word or smile or a caress from her mum. Sometimes she'd elicit a nod of approval, but not much more. She thought of how Taylor always ruffled Max's hair, and how he usually batted her away; Max didn't know how lucky he was. Her mum would brush her hair, plait it for school, but she'd never ruffled it.

Full marks in spelling tests, reciting a times table perfectly, moving up a reading level – all of these were met with a 'well done, darling' but there was no real pride in her mother's voice; Kate could see that now.

She'd always regretted that her mum hadn't been around to see her achieve straight As in her GSCEs and A levels, gain that place at her first choice of uni, but what did it matter? Nothing she could have done would have made any difference. A whole lifetime of constantly striving to be the best person she could possibly be, to be perfect Kate... bloody pointless.

Perhaps, she thought sadly, her mum was incapable of love.

Why hadn't he told her before?

Why hadn't she asked?

Her head was throbbing now, struggling with the sheer number of thoughts and memories she was trying to process, and at some point, she must have fallen asleep, because she jolted awake when there was a knock at the door.

Whoever it was knocked again. Kate suddenly remembered that she was supposed to meet Xander tonight outside the board game café. That they were going to walk along the canal to Hebbleswick, visit the previous evening's window, then check that everything was set for tonight's big reveal. And afterwards he'd promised to cook her dinner.

She hauled herself off the sofa, stumbled to the door, and opened it to find Xander wearing a smarter than usual pair of jeans and a cashmere sweater. He'd trimmed his beard and brushed his hair, and there was a distinct whiff of Dior Sauvage in the air around him. Not her personal favourite, but pleasant nonetheless.

'You walk out on me, you ghost me, you cancel our Saturday night plans, and now you've stood me up,' he said, but his tone was light and although his mouth wasn't smiling, his eyes were.

As he waited for her response, he looked her up and down. His expression changed. 'Jesus, Kate. You look terrible. I mean, I'm usually the scruffy one of the two of us, but I think you've got me beaten. Has something happened to your dad? Is that why you cancelled last night? Is he ill?'

Kate ran a hand through her hair. It was still full of dust from demolishing the shed. She'd washed her face and hands at her dad's, but since he'd only had supermarket own brand shampoo and no conditioner, she'd decided to wait till she got home to have a long shower to wash out all the grime. Instead, she had fallen asleep on the sofa, still wearing her dad's old clothes. Still wearing yesterday's knickers. And her eyes were probably red and puffy too. She must look dreadful. Ordinarily, she'd never have allowed anyone, let alone a man she fancied the pants off, to see her in this state, but after the events of this weekend, she suddenly realised she didn't care.

She was fed up with trying so hard to please people. Fed up with being Little Miss Perfect Kate.

Sod perfect Kate.

World, meet imperfect Kate.

Imperfect Kate, who even her own mother didn't love.

'Kate?' Xander reached out and put a hand on her arm,

steering her back inside the house. He guided her into the lounge, pushed her gently onto the sofa and said, 'I'll put the kettle on and you can tell me all about it. If you want to, that is.'

He disappeared into the kitchen, then reappeared moments later with a kitchen roll in his hand. 'I don't know where you keep your tissues, and I thought you might need this.'

Kitchen roll. She thought of her and her father, sitting in his little kitchen. Of his tatty old jumper. Of how old he looked. Of the burden he'd carried alone all these years to protect her from the truth. And she began to bawl.

Xander pulled her into him. In the kitchen, the kettle boiled and switched itself off. He stroked her hair, over and over.

'Oh, Kate,' he murmured. 'Let it all out. I'm here for you.'

When she finally stopped crying, most of the dust from her hair seemed to have transferred itself to Xander's hands. There was a pile of soggy kitchen roll discarded on the carpet, a wet patch on his sweater, and the water in the kettle must have long since cooled down.

'He's not...?' Xander began then stopped himself. 'Do you want to tell me what happened?'

'My dad's fine,' she said. 'Not ill or dead, or anything like that.'

'Well, that's a relief. And your mum...?'

'My mum isn't on the scene. She left when I was sixteen.' Kate hesitated; she had told the old version of events – the incorrect version as it turned out – so many times, but hadn't got her head around this new version yet. She wasn't quite ready, she realised, to tell him everything; not yet. She needed more time to process it herself. Instead, she gave him the potted version. 'I always blamed my dad. They didn't have the best marriage, to be honest. I imagined it must have been a terrible wrench for her to leave her child – me – behind. But yesterday, my dad told me that she never wanted to be a mother. She never wanted me. Never loved me.'

'Shit, Kate. That's huge. You poor thing.'

She nodded, giving him a weak smile. 'What time is it? I need to get to the window unveiling.'

He glanced at his watch. 'Twenty-five to six.'

'Oh God, I'm going to be late. I can't go looking like this, and there's not time to shower, blow-dry my hair, slap on some make-up *and* reach Hebbleswick by six o'clock.'

Xander looked at his hands, still dirty from stroking her hair.

'I was demolishing a shed,' Kate said.

'A shed?' He looked puzzled for a moment, but didn't enquire further. 'Okay, so I agree you need a shower, and a change of clothes wouldn't go amiss, but you can wear a hat over your damp hair and you're every bit as beautiful without make-up. If we hurry, we'll make it.'

Kate hesitated. Okay, so she was fed up with trying so hard to be perfect Kate, but she wasn't quite ready to turn up to the window unveiling if she wasn't looking her best.

'Or they can manage without you for another night,' Xander said. 'You can have a long shower and put on your PJs, and I'll pop back to mine and bring the dinner over here. I happen to have made the perfect comfort food. What d'you reckon? Either way, no make-up or blow-drying necessary.'

She didn't have to think too hard. Yes, she felt bad missing the window reveal for the second evening running, but after everything that had happened this weekend, she could cut herself a little slack.

'You go and grab the food,' she said. 'I'll grab a shower.'

When Xander had gone, she texted Peter to apologise that once again she wasn't able to be there, then went upstairs for the long-awaited and much-needed shower.

'Put on your PJs,' Xander had said.

She liked the thought. But she couldn't. Could she?

Entertain a very fanciable guy in her PJs?

They weren't sexy, silky PJs, but warm, brushed cotton ones, as befitted someone who lived in the Pennines.

Yes, she could. Yes, she fancied Xander – was rather smitten if the truth be told – and under normal circumstances, she wouldn't want him seeing her without flawless make-up and her trademark shiny, blow-dried bob. But these weren't normal circumstances. Right now, it felt like circumstances would never be normal again.

It was time to embrace a *new* normal.

Besides, she'd looked a right mess when he'd first arrived and he hadn't seemed to mind.

She put on her PJs and sat at her dressing table, her fingers twitching over the zip of her make-up bag. She looked at herself in the mirror, her eyes still slightly puffy from all the crying she'd done this weekend, but she'd be able to fix that with the right products. Her gaze drifted upwards to a photo Blu-Tacked to the top of the mirror of her, Em, Jo and Taylor, sitting in the board game café on one of their many evenings together, their faces pressed together. They'd all been so busy recently that the four of them hadn't met up properly since Jo's birthday gathering.

Jo's birthday.

She'd walked out somewhat abruptly because of that silly – *cheesy!* – conversation they'd all been having.

'You're grumpy, but I love you anyway,' Harry had said to Taylor.

'I love you despite your terrible dress sense,' Taylor had replied. Something like that anyway.

Then Jo had said she loved Razz despite him taking her potholing on their first date, and Ludek loved Em even though she refused to go running with him, and Em loved Ludek despite being unable to move at home because of his massive board game collection.

She loved her friends, but none of them were perfect. Didn't even try to be.

She put down the make-up bag. Sod it. Xander could see her in her PJs, with bare skin and messy hair. She wasn't ready to dive headlong into a romance yet anyway; she knew she needed time to process everything she'd learned this weekend. But when she was ready, assuming Xander was willing to give her a second chance, she wanted him to know the real her, the *imperfect* her. And that was going to start this evening.

In any case, he'd already seen her with dirty hair and puffy eyes and wearing her father's old clothes, and he'd said he was coming back, hadn't he?

# 36

'Lamb hotpot,' said Xander, placing a steaming plate of food in front of Kate. 'Complete with that all-important, crispy layer of sliced potatoes. Grandma's recipe.'

'Your gran cooked lamb hotpot? I thought it was more of a northern thing.'

'Gran came from Lancashire,' he said proudly, 'though I suspect I might be better keeping that fact quiet now I live on this side of the Pennines.'

Kate speared one of the potato slices with her fork. 'Very crispy.' She took a bite. 'Very tasty too.'

'Potatoes,' said Xander, 'are the best. So many ways to cook them. They work in stews and curries. Mash. Baked. Chips, of course. Dauphinoise. Rosti. Hash browns. The list is endless. In fact, I reckon they're my favourite thing to cook.'

'My favourite thing to eat.'

'You see? We're a match made in heaven.'

His words seemed to hang in the air. Kate couldn't tell

what he was thinking. Did he still like her? Had he forgiven her for walking out on him all those years earlier? And was she even ready for a relationship if he had?

He must have read her mind as he said suddenly, 'Don't worry, Kate. I'm not trying to railroad you into anything. I know you've only recently split from Paul...'

'Peter.'

'...from Peter. And this stuff about your parents' marriage – I imagine you need a bit of time to get your head straight after learning all that. But I'm here for you. As a friend. Although you seem to have loads of friends round here. You know just about everyone.'

She cut a piece of lamb and paused with her fork halfway to her mouth. 'Knowing people isn't the same as them being friends. I do have friends here. Good friends. But they're all loved up. Taylor and Harry are getting married and having a baby, and I suspect Jo and Razz and Em and Ludek won't be too far behind. I feel like the odd one out sometimes. Perhaps that's why I went out with Peter when I knew we weren't quite right for each other. The spark wasn't there.'

She popped the lamb into her mouth. It was the softest, most tender meat she'd ever tasted. Tasty too. Almost sweet, with the slightest hint of rosemary. She'd always found Xander physically attractive; even more now she knew he could cook.

'Friends then?' he said.

'Friends.'

'Great. You're still the only person I know round here.'

She hoped that didn't mean that he wanted to remain just good friends, that this was his way of telling her that romance was off the cards.

'Did you ever try to find your mother? To track her down?' Xander was saying now. 'Sorry, if you'd prefer not to talk about it...' His voice trailed away.

Kate sighed. 'I don't mind talking about it. When she first left, I wanted my dad to call the police. To report her as a missing person. I thought she might have had an accident and be lying somewhere... or worse. Whenever there was some violent crime against a woman on the news, I'd worry that that had happened to her, but he always said it hadn't. That she'd chosen to leave us. Over the years, I've googled her occasionally. Checked Facebook. But that's as far as I've gone. I think...' she paused, weighing up if the words that had popped into her head were in fact true '... well, deep down, I knew she didn't want to be found.'

Yes, that was the truth. She'd never acknowledged it before, but she'd always suspected that if her mother had wanted her daughter to reconnect one day, she'd have been there on social media, using the same name, with a photo, a profile that was easy to find. Or better still, would have done the conventional thing in the first place, and divorced her husband, rather than going AWOL like she had.

Using a slice of potato, she mopped up some of the delicious gravy from the hotpot. 'I mean, if she wanted to be in touch, she could have reached out, but she didn't. Why would I contact someone who didn't want to be in contact with me? It'd be like messaging someone from Buzzz eighteen times when you know they're ghosting you and they're not interested.'

'I think you'll find it was only seventeen times.'

Kate laughed. 'You did not message me seventeen times, and I didn't ghost you.'

'You didn't reply to my last message.'

'You said not to. Didn't you?' She tried to recall. He'd texted after she'd walked out, saying he assumed that was the end of things, but to get in touch if she changed her mind and wanted to see him again. And once or twice she *had* considered contacting him and saying just that.

'Don't worry, Kate,' Xander said. 'You weren't the only woman who didn't want to go on another date after seeing my little soldiers standing to attention.'

'Now there's a double entendre.' She giggled.

'Soldiers,' he said. 'I said *soldiers*. Not soldier.'

'Now here's the big question,' said Kate when she'd eaten every last morsel of potato. 'Do we do the washing up now? Or leave it till the morning?'

'Ah, the kitchen debate,' said Xander.

She smiled, glad that he'd immediately recognised the reference to their first date at that Cold War exhibition.

'Didn't we agree we'd leave it till the morning?' he said.

'We did, but actually, I *never* do. Luckily I have a dishwasher.' She cleared the table, popping their plates and Xander's casserole dish into the machine. When she returned to the lounge, she found him brandishing a plastic bag with a mischievous look in his eye.

'What are you up to?' she said suspiciously.

'I think you need cheering up. Why don't we go for a little drive?'

'You said to put my PJs on.'

'Yeah, I know. I wanted you to feel relaxed. But I also thought you might like to see yesterday and today's Christmas windows.'

She thought for a second. He was right; she *did* want

to see them. It felt decidedly odd to have missed two of the unveilings after she'd devoted the last few weeks to the living Advent calendar.

'I do,' she said, 'but I'd have to get dressed, and I've no make-up on, and my hair's a mess.'

'You look beautiful. I like you with make-up but I like the natural look too. But I knew you'd say that, so I've come prepared.' He opened the plastic bag and pulled out what appeared to be a bundle of red fabric. 'Ho ho ho. You're going in disguise.'

'A Santa suit? Where did that come from?'

'I wear it every year for my final lecture before the Christmas break,' he said with a grin. 'Silly, I know. Now grab yourself a couple of cushions – you need some padding if you're going as Father Christmas.'

Kate shook her head. 'No, Xander. I couldn't.'

'Ah, go on, go on, go on, go on,' he said, putting on a bad Irish accent, and then, in his normal voice: 'It'll be a laugh. Go on, Kate, you know you want to.'

Holding the cushions in place under her Santa suit, Kate clambered into Xander's car, glancing as she did into the back seat where a tidy-up had clearly taken place since the last time she'd been in here. Had he made an effort for her sake? Or did everyone, even Xander, tidy their car once in a while?

*For heaven's sake, Kate,* she told herself mentally a moment later, *you can't read anything into a man having given the inside of his car a bit of a spruce-up.*

*Or cooking you lamb hotpot, letting you cry on his*

*shoulder and driving you to Hebbleswick because he somehow sensed you'd want to look at the new Christmas windows.*

They drove in companionable silence. Out of the corner of her eye, she saw him occasionally glance at her for a second, before turning his attention back to the road. He turned left into one of the side streets on the outskirts of Hebbleswick and parked outside the library.

'This okay?' he said.

'Yeah, fine. It's not far from here.'

It took longer than usual to walk to the town centre, partly thanks to the cushions and the oversized black boots that Xander had insisted she wore, partly because they stopped at almost every house to admire the twinkling lights and decorations in the windows. The sight took Kate's breath away; she was falling in love – not only with Xander, but with Christmas too.

If you'd told her a few weeks ago that she'd be wandering round Hebbleswick dressed as Santa with no make-up on, getting teary-eyed over a few fairy lights, she would never have believed it.

If you'd told her that the man by her side on this occasion would be Xander, she'd never have believed that either.

Yet here they were.

The disguise had hardly been necessary; by this time on a Sunday night, most people had gone home. Nevertheless, Kate was glad Xander had made her dress up. It was a laugh, and there was something very liberating about walking around in something she'd never normally wear.

The window of the craft shop confirmed what Kate had

thought: she had been right to trust the shop's owner to get on with it. The theme of their display was home-made gifts. There were jars full of cookie mix, beautifully decorated with ribbons and candy canes, sections cut from vintage maps framed to create artworks and candles made from old-fashioned teacups and saucers, plus a selection of jams and chutneys, all in beautifully decorated pots.

'Stunning,' said Xander. 'Do you know if there was a decent crowd for the unveiling?'

Kate shook her head. 'No idea. I'll ask Peter tomorrow. Let's go and check out tonight's window.'

The whole food shop had a somewhat surreal display of giant papier-mâché sprouts, complete with googly eyes and rather menacing smiley mouths.

'They're enough to put kids off sprouts for life,' Kate said.

'Other than that, are you happy with the window?'

She laughed. 'Well, it's different. And I wanted them all to be different. That first meeting, almost everyone was intent on doing a nativity scene. And the vicar! He was so insistent that the honour of doing the Christmas Eve window should go to the church, only it wouldn't be a window – just the usual nativity display on the grass outside. I tried to put my foot down but he wasn't having any of it.' She paused for a moment. 'I'd love to know how you made him change his mind.'

He tapped the side of his nose. 'Can't reveal my methods, I'm afraid.'

'Did you uncover a dirty secret from his past?'

'Nope. If you must know, he simply liked the sound of my display.'

'Which is…?'

'No, Kate. You're not getting that out of me. Like everyone else, you'll have to wait until Christmas Eve.'

'As long as it doesn't feature any toy soldiers,' she laughed.

## 37

The next few days seemed to pass in a whirr of early starts and dashing back from work every day in the nick of time for each unveiling.

On Monday evening, Hebbleswick Primary School revealed their window, which was not Scrabble-related, much to Kate's surprise; everything Jo did tended to involve her favourite word game. They had chosen instead to create a wintry Christmas scene constructed entirely out of Lego, complete with a rather realistic-looking outdoor skating rink.

Next, one of Hebbleswick's many art galleries unveiled a scene of wintry rooftops with chimney pots. There were snow-capped hills in the background and twinkling stars in the sky. Every two minutes, a flying sled laden with gifts, complete with Santa and four reindeer, whizzed across the sky, hanging by an invisible thread. Well, hanging by a barely visible thread anyway.

The following night, the crowds gathered outside

Hebbleswick Library to admire the Christmas trees in the window, all cleverly created out of stacks of books and adorned with fairy lights.

On Thursday, Kompleet Marketing Solutions held their office Christmas party: a boozy lunch followed by the dreaded Secret Santa. Kate limited herself to two glasses of Merlot, wanting to keep a clear head for the evening's window reveal. She gave Jeroen the 'World's Greatest Boss' cufflinks she had found in the Oxfam shop, and enjoyed seeing the look on his face when he read the little card she'd put inside: *These cufflinks may seem a little tacky, but the sentiment is real. Thank you for all your support. Kate.* Okay, so it was supposed to be secret, but she wanted him to know how much she appreciated him. To her surprise, she wasn't given yet another Little Miss Perfect mug, but a notebook. Not just any old notebook; this one was covered with pale blue fabric, with embroidered silver stars.

But the best gift was that when she announced she was leaving early, her colleagues protested far more than she thought they would, saying that they'd have to have an office night out in the New Year, when Kate wasn't so busy.

Then she made a less than elegant dash to Leeds station, catching the train in time to reach Hebbleswick for the unveiling of the bakery's 'Is it cake?' display. Their creations were every bit as clever as the ones on TV. There were a variety of Christmas gifts, but were they really gifts? Or were they rectangular cakes decorated to look like gifts? And that turkey? Surely that *couldn't* be cake. Could it?

By Friday evening, Kate was exhausted. She could barely put one foot in front of the other as she walked to the platform at Leeds station to catch the train home. The train was already waiting, so Kate chose the most empty carriage, tucking herself away in a corner in the hope of catching forty winks on the journey to Hebbleswick.

She dozed as far as Halifax, but then became aware of someone in front of her talking loudly on a mobile phone.

'The whole thing's more popular than ever,' a young female voice was saying. 'Lights everywhere. I don't think anyone cares.'

*Lights everywhere.*

The young woman was quiet for a few moments – the person on the call must have been speaking – and then she said, 'Kate What's-her-name works in marketing so she knows what she's doing. She managed to use my blog post to generate more publicity for her project. It completely backfired.'

*My blog post?*

What the…? Was that EcoEssendale, sitting a few steps away from her?

'Yeah, we thought about a demo, but that might create even more publicity for the Advent calendar,' the woman said. 'And we'd risk being unpopular. People don't want to think about the planet at Christmas. They just want to have a good time.'

*A demo?*

The last thing Kate wanted to deal with right now was a demo.

'No, we've definitely decided against it.'

Thank goodness.

'We need positive action locally, rather than negative. Litter picking mornings. A campaign to generate awareness of nesting birds on the moorland in the summer. Something to encourage more recycling. More upcycling maybe. We wondered about seeing if that woman who did the upcycled fashion show would do another one… Yeah, yeah, okay. We'll talk later. Sure. Bye. Bye.'

As EcoEssendale ended the call, Kate stood up, grabbed her bag and, on impulse, took a few steps down the carriage, plonking herself on the seat opposite the woman. At a guess, she'd have said that EcoEssendale was around a decade younger than her. She wore a thick woollen coat, unbuttoned, and Kate couldn't quite believe her eyes when she realised what she was wearing underneath: a pair of dungarees with a large front pocket fashioned to look like a flowerpot, with embroidered daisies growing out of it. That was one of Taylor's designs. Or rather, *re*designs.

'I like your dungarees,' Kate said.

'Thanks,' said EcoEssendale. 'They're upcycled.'

'I know. My friend Taylor made them.' She held out her hand. 'I'm Kate What's-her-name. Well, Kate Harker, actually. And I'm guessing you're EcoEssendale.'

The young woman's jaw dropped. Her cheeks flushed. She looked flustered for a moment, and then she recovered herself and said defiantly, 'I'm not going to apologise.'

Kate thought for a second. 'Fair enough. You were just doing what you believed in. I get that. I'm doing what I believe in too. I'm trying to support the local economy.'

'Capitalism,' said EcoEssendale, 'is ruining the planet.'

'Yeah, I guess so. I'm no expert on ecology or world politics or economics, but I don't see why looking after our environment and looking after our local businesses need to be mutually exclusive things.'

'There are fairy lights everywhere, consuming masses of electricity and for what? So the towns look *pretty*?'

'And so people feel happy, and to attract more visitors to support the local shops and cafés. Otherwise they'll close down. Isn't shopping local an environmentally friendly thing to do?'

'I guess,' EcoEssendale said grudgingly.

The train was pulling into Hebbleswick now. Kate stood up. 'I didn't mean to eavesdrop on your phone call, but I'm all for litter picking and leaving nesting birds in peace. I did all the publicity for the first upcycled fashion show and would happily do it again if Taylor agrees to a second one, so...' she fumbled in her bag '...so here's my card. If you need any marketing tips for your *positive* campaigns, call me.'

EcoEssendale took the proffered business card, and Kate walked out of the carriage without a backwards glance.

As she stepped onto the platform, she mumbled to herself, 'You must be bonkers, Kate. You've offered to help the woman who tried to ruin the living Advent calendar. Bonkers.'

Then as she stepped outside the station and saw the fairy lights of Hebbleswick twinkling ahead of her, she said to herself, 'Yeah, well it *is* Christmas. Goodwill to all men, women *and* bloggers.'

It was a short walk to the place where that evening's big reveal would take place, and Kate was there in no time. The crowds were already gathering beside a stone wall that ran around the perimeter of one of Hebbleswick's more prestigious dwellings, the old vicarage. It had long since ceased to be the actual vicarage – Reverend Stone occupied a far more modest house a few streets away – and was now the home of one of the valley's most colourful characters, an eccentric artist who'd made a fortune creating cute sculptures for the nation's animal lovers. Kate hadn't hesitated when the artist had offered to do one of the festive displays, even though strictly speaking, it wasn't an actual window that was on offer. Well, not in the conventional sense anyway.

Kate stood in place, waiting for six o'clock and catching snippets of conversation. Everyone was confused; there was no big window concealed with drapes this evening. She was excited; this display was a little bit different and she knew everyone would be delighted when they saw it.

'Good evening, everyone,' she called when it was almost six o'clock. She waited for a few seconds as the crowd fell silent. 'You might be asking yourselves, where's the big window? Well, we haven't got one. But I'm sure you aren't going to be disappointed with what you see this evening, although you *are* going to have to form an orderly queue. We have not one but *three* windows for you tonight and they are tiny.' She held up her right hand, holding her thumb and index finger apart to indicate how small they were. 'So there's no unveiling this evening, but we can still do the drum roll, right?'

Obligingly the crowd began to slap their thighs. When they came to a natural halt, Kate continued. 'I declare tonight's windows open. I'll point them out to you – they're here, here and here.' She pointed to the three small holes in the wall. 'Little people, there are steps for you to see the top one. Please be careful and get an adult to help you on the steps. Big people, I'm afraid you're going to have to bend down to see the two bottom ones – you can always get a little person to help you up. Now who's going to be the first to take a peep?' She picked out Max and two little girls from the crowd. 'Okay, you three, have a look.'

She'd been looking forward to this moment all day, to when the first children gazed through the peepholes and saw the magic inside, and she wasn't disappointed. The little girl looking through the lowest of the three windows immediately turned to her mother with her mouth open, and said, 'It's amazing!'

She then looked at Kate and said, 'It is, isn't it?'

'Yes, it is. But shhh... don't tell anyone what you see, so everybody gets a nice surprise when it's their turn.'

Kate had already looked through each of the peepholes earlier and couldn't believe her eyes. The artist had drilled three holes in her garden wall, installing some kind of lens – wide-angled, presumably – into each of them. Behind the wall, she'd placed three weatherproof boxes, which contained the Christmas displays. They all featured the most gorgeous little families of mice – models, of course, not real mice. In the first, the mouse family were engaged in decorating a Christmas tree in a tiny mouse-sized lounge complete with a sofa and fireplace with a row of tiny stockings hanging up ready for Santa. In another, they were seated around a tiny dinner table, laden with crackers and food. In the final one, they were back in the lounge, this time seated on the sofa. One of the mice had nodded off, whilst the others were avidly watching a tiny television, on which you could clearly see a mouse king, complete with tiny crown, giving his Christmas Day speech.

Kate stood beside the wall, mulling over the conversation on the train and enjoying the reactions to the little mouse tableaus. They were genius, she thought, as she listened to the exclamations of delight as each person pressed their eye to one of the holes. Of all of the displays, this was perhaps her favourite so far, though she would never have admitted that to Em or Taylor.

Then her phone pinged. She pulled it out of her pocket and checked to see who had texted.

Xander.

Sorry I missed the windows this week. Been tying up a few loose ends at work before Christmas. Fancy dinner at mine tomorrow after the unveiling?

# 38

Kate had given up trying to count heads for the window unveilings; it was impossible these days, as there were so many people.

'Thank you, EcoEssendale,' she said quietly under her breath now as she looked at this evening's crowd, all jostling around the hospice shop's window, trying to get the best position. She had wondered afterwards if she'd been a bit too hasty in offering her marketing services to the woman who'd tried to scupper the living Advent calendar, but had decided that, actually, she was happy to help. Going green might even be another way to market the valley to visitors. Ecotourism was very popular these days. Kate was full of ideas for the spring: foraging courses – there was plenty of woodland around – and guerrilla gardening initiative and another upcycling show, although of course Taylor would have a new baby soon, so that mightn't be feasible.

As Kate gave her usual welcome speech, she scanned the faces in the crowd, trying to spot Xander. She initiated the drum roll and waited as inside the shop, Peter did his stuff and began to raise the drapes to reveal the window. The clever volunteers had taken three tailor's dummies, dressing them each in a corset – one red, one white and one pale blue. Each one had a long, tutu-like skirt made out of Christmas tree branches, which were decorated with baubles and ribbons, which matched the colour of the corset. It was like haute couture meets winter wonderland and Kate loved it.

'I'd like to see you wearing one of those,' a voice whispered in her ear.

She turned to see Xander beside her. How he'd got there she wasn't quite sure; he must have weaved his way through the crowd.

'You'd look amazing,' he added.

Kate smiled. 'I'm not sure you could actually wear one. You wouldn't be able to sit down. All those needles.' She winced at the thought. 'You never know where they'd end up.'

'Ouch.' He laughed, a definite twinkle in his eye.

Back at Alessandra's – Xander's now; she had to stop calling the shop by its old name – the boxes were still piled up in the corner of the flat. Xander had rearranged the furniture and there was now a small dining table in the window overlooking the high street. He deftly lit two large candles in the centre of that table, dimmed the main lights of the room and gestured for Kate to take a seat.

He'd said they should be friends, but the atmosphere this evening was definitely romantic.

'Dinner won't be long,' he said. 'I left it in the oven on a timer. Would you like red or white wine?'

'Red please.'

She sat down so that she was looking down the high street towards the board game café whilst Xander went to the kitchen to fetch the wine. From what she could see, there were plenty of customers in this evening, and Em seemed to be bustling about from table to table delivering orders. There were a few groups of people, families mostly, walking along the street too. They were brandishing sheets of paper; she couldn't quite see from here but guessed they were the trail maps. They paused to look in the official windows – the board game café, florist, library and Oxfam shop – and several of the unofficial ones too, before heading off in the direction of the health centre.

'Quite a crowd this evening,' Xander said, reappearing with a bottle of red.

'I know, it was brilliant. We're well over halfway through already. I'm going to collapse with exhaustion on Christmas Day when it's all over.'

He filled her glass. 'What are your plans for the big day?'

'Dad and I are going to the board game café for a big lunch with everyone. Em's cooking so it should be good. You? Do you see your parents?'

She'd told him so much about her parents, but realised suddenly that she didn't know a thing about his.

'No, they're in France,' he said, sitting down opposite her and filling his own glass. 'I sometimes make it over, but not this year. It'll be just me, I'm afraid, but I don't really mind.'

'Come to the café,' Kate said on impulse. She should

probably have checked with the hostess first, but knew Em well enough to be ninety-nine point nine per cent certain that she wouldn't mind.

'No, I couldn't impose.'

'You wouldn't be. Please, come. I'd like it if you were there.'

'Thanks,' he said. 'Can I think about it? And maybe you could check with Em?'

'Sure, but she won't mind. It's a great view from here,' she said, changing the subject. 'I can see people with trail maps looking at the windows. Is it smug that I'm thinking, wow, they wouldn't be here if it weren't for me?'

'Terribly smug,' he said, 'but it's true. You're welcome to come and watch all the visitors from here every evening if you want. And you can be as smug as you like. I have a thing about smug women.'

Kate laughed. Was he flirting with her?

She sipped her wine, racking her brains for something flirtatious to say in reply, but she was too tired to think. Instead she said, 'You won't believe who I met on the train from Leeds.'

'The Dalai Lama?'

'Er... no.'

'Kate Bush.'

'Try again. Last guess.'

'The real Father Christmas.'

'No. EcoEssendale.'

'EcoEssendale?'

'You know, the blogger?'

He shook his head, so Kate outlined the story of

EcoEssendale and her damning words, the rush to swap the Oxfam shop's original offering for the 'How to have a greener Christmas' display and how the local paper, which up until then had shown no interest in the living Advent calendar, suddenly sent along a reporter.

'And that article led to the local TV news deciding to cover it, and Mr B's baubles going viral,' she said.

'And you saw this blogger on the train?'

'Yeah, I overheard her phone call, put two and two together and went over to introduce myself.'

'Blimey, did you tear a strip off her?'

'No, I offered to help her with marketing some green initiatives here in the valley.'

Xander nearly choked on his wine. 'You didn't? Seriously?'

'Yeah, I did. Why not?'

'You're an amazing person – you know that?' he said. 'You do so much for this place.'

She shrugged. 'It's nothing really. Plenty of people do far more.'

'And you're modest too. Not smug at all.'

'That's a shame – given that you have a thing about smug women.'

Their eyes met. Kate bit her lip, wondering what was going through his mind. She wanted him to lean across the table and kiss her, and was sure he was about to, but then a timer went off in the kitchen, and he cleared his throat and said, 'You ready to eat?'

'Yeah. I'm starving.'

He went to fetch the food, returning a minute or two

later wearing oven gloves and carrying two steaming plates. 'Beef casserole with purple sprouting broccoli and...' He paused for dramatic effort. 'Drum roll please.'

Kate obligingly slapped her thighs though it wasn't as good when only one person was doing it.

'Dauphinoise potatoes,' he said, as he placed the plates on the table and sat down opposite her.

She bent over the food and took a long sniff. 'Delicious.'

She loaded her fork with some of the creamy dauphinoise, blew on it to cool it a little then popped it into her mouth.

'Like it?' he said.

She closed her eyes. 'Mmmm.' She swallowed. 'A culinary orgasm.' She opened her eyes again to find him watching her.

'Remember that time...?' he began.

'Harry met Sally! And that young waiter...'

'The poor bloke!'

They laughed for a few seconds, then fell silent. Kate was thinking back to that evening, how they'd eaten that fancy dinner, then shared a bag of chips in the car, the windows steaming up. She'd have bet money that Xander was remembering that too.

'I'm sorry I walked out on you,' she said.

'Kate, it was years ago. There's no need to explain. In all honesty, I wasn't surprised. At the time, I didn't think we were going anywhere, did you?'

'No, I know what you mean.' She paused. Why not be honest? 'Actually, I was very much hoping that we *were* going somewhere. Why did you feel that we weren't?'

Xander looked out of the window, a frown on his face, as if he wasn't sure how to phrase what he wanted to say.

'I didn't know you, Kate. We had five dates, but you were always so perfect. With the exception of that first date, when you showed up late. Always immaculately dressed. Always saying the right things. I couldn't tell if you were really interested in that nuclear bunker or the old docks – and that was when I thought you *were* interested in history. I wondered if you were only being polite, doing what you thought I expected. Does that make sense?'

'You thought I was faking it?'

'Not faking it exactly. You were the perfect date, Kate. A little bit *too* perfect.' He glanced at her, seemingly uncertain about whether to continue. 'I didn't feel I ever got to know the real Kate.'

'And now?'

'Now...' He thought for a moment. 'Now, yeah, I do feel I know you. I've had a glimpse under the surface, seen what's behind that perfect façade that you present to the world. I've seen you all relaxed in your PJs with messy hair and no make-up. I like that you've felt able to be vulnerable with me, to cry on my shoulder. That you were willing to don that daft Santa outfit and sneak along incognito to look at the windows. I feel connected with the you I know now so much more than I did with Perfect Kate.'

'You know how they call me Little Miss Perfect at work? I used to be flattered, but recently... well, I'm not so sure. My colleagues seem a lot more relaxed with me since I made that cock-up the other week.'

It was true; Simone had even asked her if she fancied going out for a drink after Christmas.

He reached across the table and took her hand. 'Oh, Kate.'

'I think my need to be perfect is all tied up with my mum. Since that discussion with Dad, I've been going over and over it. As a child, I think I sensed she didn't love me – not the way my friends' mums loved them anyway. I was always trying to earn her love, by doing well at school, by looking nice, by saying the right things. And I think I've extended that into adulthood. You know, all this dating, trying to find the right person. I thought I had to be perfect for someone to fall in love with me. It seems completely daft now. I mean, look at Peter. Still in love with Em even though she's messy and disorganised and impulsive.'

'Is that why you broke up?'

'Partly.' She paused, wondering whether to add that the other reason – the *main* reason – was because of how she felt about Xander. She couldn't quite pluck up the courage, so said instead, 'I always thought that if I let someone see the real me, warts and all, they wouldn't want me.'

He dropped her hand in mock horror. 'Warts!'

She laughed. 'Just an expression!'

He took it again. 'I know. I was being silly. Warts wouldn't make one jot of difference to how I feel about you. Now, verrucas, that's a different matter. I've had a phobia of verrucas since school swimming lessons. Remember those special socks they used to make you wear? There was one kid in my class who had one on every week.' He grimaced. 'So anyway, Kate, no more Little Miss Perfect. I'm going to think of a new nickname for you. And in the meantime, I toiled for hours over this dinner and it's getting cold. Shall I pop it in the microwave for a minute?'

Xander disappeared back into the kitchen with the

plates, and Kate found herself staring out of the window again, absent-mindedly people-watching.

*Warts wouldn't make one jot of difference to how I feel about you.*

Okay, so perhaps not *the* most romantic sentence ever uttered, but she liked the sentiment.

And toy soldiers, she thought, don't make one jot of difference to how I feel about you, Xander. Was now the time to tell him why his hobby had affected her so much four years ago? How it had reminded her of her dad and *his* hobby, the hobby she'd erroneously blamed for her mother's unhappiness and subsequent disappearance? Was she ready?

Not yet, she decided, but soon. The right moment would present itself and she would confess all then.

He was back now, placing the plates, steaming again, down on the table and slipping into his seat opposite her.

When they finally finished eating, Kate knew she ought to go home. Doing her day job alongside running the living Advent calendar, not to mention all the emotional upheaval recently, was taking its toll.

'I'm exhausted,' she said. 'I've had a lovely evening, but d'you mind if we call it a night?'

'Of course not. Shall I walk you home?'

'Thanks, but I'll be fine. It's only a few minutes.'

She pulled on her coat, then followed Xander down the narrow staircase. He unlatched the door, and they stood together in the doorway, beside the covered-up window of his shop.

Kate loved that delicious moment of uncertainty, of

wondering whether a man she liked was going to kiss her. She lifted her eyes to meet his, and he must have read her thoughts as he said, 'Can I kiss you, Kate?'

He moved towards her. She took a step backwards, so she was leaning up against the window of the shop. He put one arm across her shoulder, placing his hand behind her on the glass, leaning into her, so close she could feel his breath on her cheek, all the while gazing into her eyes.

She could hear footsteps approaching; a group of people on the pavement, chattering excitedly and rustling trail maps. 'This one will be the last window,' someone said, 'so it's still covered over.'

'Is the display already in place, behind there?' Kate said, her eyes still firmly fixed on his.

'It's already started. I'll be spending most of tomorrow on it. I know you like things perfect.'

'Go on, tell me the theme,' she said. 'I'm not kissing you till I know.'

'You tease. I'll have to wait until Christmas Eve then, won't I?'

Kate laughed. 'I guess you will. And I'll only let you then if I really, *really* like your display.'

# 39

The handmade soaps and alpaca jumpers that normally adorned the window of the gift shop in Hebbleswick had been replaced with a potted tree with a variety of stuffed model birds sitting on its branches – a partridge, two doves and four blackbirds. At the foot of the tree were five opened jewellery boxes, each displaying a gold ring. A little notice said, 'Rings kindly provided by Hebbleswick Jewellers'. The jewellers had been one of the few shops that had declined to take part in the living Advent calendar on the grounds that they had already put their Christmas display in the window and didn't wish to replace it.

There'd been quite a large crowd for the unveiling that Sunday evening. Kate had done the usual welcome speech, pointing people in the direction of where they could get a trail map if they didn't have one already, and doing the drum roll and countdown to the drapes lifting. Peter had hurried away early – 'Having dinner this evening with Mother and

Stan' – but Kate had remained outside the shop, listening to all the positive comments people were making about the Advent calendar in general, and this window in particular.

'The "Twelve Days of Christmas"! How clever!'

'Did you see yesterday's window? And the one with the little mice?'

'My favourite was the hangover cures. I'll be trying some of them out on Boxing Day.'

'Yeah, it's good that our local GPs have a sense of humour. Can't be easy working in the NHS these days.'

'Blackbirds?' Are they in the song?'

That last comment was whispered right into her ear. She turned to see Xander; he had sneaked up on her again, and was standing beside her, rubbing his hands together to keep warm.

'I think they're the calling birds,' she said.

Xander pointed at the window. 'Look, they've got soldiers,' he said. 'If they've got soldiers, why can't I have soldiers?'

'They're pipers,' said Kate. 'Eleven pipers piping.'

There were swans and hens too, but no geese. Then she noticed a sign hanging from one of the branches, saying:

If you're looking for the geese, they can usually be found on patrol in Essendale, though they are not currently a-laying.

'Clever,' she said, pointing it out to Xander.

The shop owner had managed to amass a large collection of Cindys, Barbies and Kens, and had fashioned little outfits for the lords-a-leaping and ladies dancing, with their legs pulled into the appropriate positions. There were maids a-milking too – eight of them were sharing two plastic cows – and twelve of the Kens were sitting down behind model drum kits, complete with snares and cymbals, as if they were playing in a band. The dolls were not to scale with the birds and the whole effect was somewhat bonkers.

'It's very kitsch,' said Xander.

'Yeah, but I like it. Do you?'

'I love it. I love all of the windows. Now have you eaten?'

She hadn't. Sleep rather than food had been on her mind today. She didn't realise how hungry she was until Xander placed a plate of rosti with spinach and poached eggs in front of her.

Later, as Kate left, they had the same discussion as they'd had the previous evening, standing on the doorstep.

'May I kiss you?'

'Not until I know the theme of your window.'

'Next week then.'

'Yeah, but only if I like it!'

The following evening's window also had a musical theme. Hebbleswick's pottery studio had devoted their display to Christmas carols. There were little clay models of shepherds watching their flocks, a baby in a manger, good King Wenceslas looking out of a window, three kings bearing gifts and three ships sailing on a cardboard sea. The next night, a glistening white forest landscape was unveiled, tall fir trees made entirely out of cut and folded paper, with white birds and deer and origami snowflakes.

Then it was the turn of the farm shop, situated on a quiet back road that ran between Essendale and Hebbleswick.

Their nativity scene carved out of root vegetables created quite a stir. One of the turnip wise men wasn't quite as well carved as the others, appearing somewhat phallic, if you had that sort of prurient mind, and it certainly seemed that several members of the crowd did. There were giggles and titters and plenty of sharing on Instagram, and Kate found herself hoping for another upsurge in visitor numbers, similar to the #MrBsBaubles effect.

'I promise,' Xander said, 'that there is nothing remotely suggestive in my Christmas window.'

'So what *is* in your window?' Kate said.

'Nice try, Kate. Nice try.' He tapped the side of his nose. 'I've made Bombay potatoes and a chicken curry this evening if you're hungry.'

He had turned up for every single unveiling so far this week, Kate thought as they walked back to Essendale. Cooked for her most evenings too. His model soldiers clearly weren't the all-absorbing, time-consuming hobby she'd once assumed them to be.

The remaining windows were all back in Essendale. If walked in its entirety, and in order, the living Advent calendar trail began at the board game café, took in the florist's, the health centre and some of the other Essendale locations, before going down the towpath past the wool boat, around Hebbleswick, and back along the back road past the farm shop to Essendale Primary.

'It's a bit rough and ready,' said Taylor as the school's gingerbread model of Essendale was unveiled, complete with a gingerbread board game café. Taylor had an intense dislike of the Essendale Primary – especially of its head teacher – since Max had been bullied there and very little had been done to help him. He had recently moved to Hebbleswick Primary, where Jo was the school manager, and he was far, far happier.

'Yeah, very rough and ready,' agreed Jo.

'I told you, it's not a competition,' said Kate.

They did have a point though; the gingerbread houses were all wonky. The gingerbread wool boat on the silver foil canal looked as if it were on the verge of sinking. The primary school had taken even greater liberties with scale than the gift shop had with their Twelve Days of Christmas display: the gingerbread geese were frighteningly large. Nevertheless, the whole thing had a certain charm about it.

'I like it,' Kate declared. 'It's not perfect, but you can see that a huge amount of work has gone into it.'

Her two friends looked at her in amazement. 'Since when were you okay with things not being perfect?' said Jo.

Kate shrugged.

'It's a shame though,' said Taylor. 'With a bit more attention to detail, it could have been so much better.'

Xander, standing in the middle of the three women, had been silent up until now. He sighed and said, 'I hope you lot aren't going to be this critical on Christmas Eve when my window is unveiled.'

'That,' said Kate, fixing him with her eagle eye, 'depends on what it is.'

The window on the twenty-second of December was in a private house. Mr and Mrs Sanderson and their two children had told Kate they were filling their large front window with snowmen. She knew the snowmen wouldn't be real – they'd be a puddle of water after a few hours if they were – but beyond that, she didn't have any expectations of what this display would be like. A few fake snowmen, she supposed, complete with lumps of coal for eyes and buttons, stick arms and carrot noses, with scarves round their necks. She'd never have admitted it, especially not to its creators, but this was the window she was least excited about.

Xander stood alongside her as she made her usual speech. After the customary thigh-slapping drum roll, the drapes lifted and Kate was completely bowled over by what she saw. These were no ordinary fake snowmen; they were *celebrity* fake snowmen. A tall, skinny one caught her eye first, with its red and white stripy bobble hat and jumper, round glasses and a pair of binoculars around its neck.

It must have caught Xander's eye too, as he laughed and said, 'Well, there's Wally!'

Then there was one for the Dr Who fans – a Dalek – and one for the Star Wars fans – a Yoda. There was an Elvis with a dark wig, a microphone and a sparkly jacket, and a Homer Simpson with a bright yellow face and blue jeans.

'It's genius, isn't it?' she said to Xander. 'The people of this valley never cease to amaze me with their creativity and imagination. All of the windows have been so different.'

'You're the genius, Kate,' Xander said. 'This was all your doing. Without you, none of this would have happened. It's been an amazing success. The local businesses must all love you.'

Kate smiled. She was proud of what she'd achieved – of

course she was – but she was kidding herself if she thought this was really going to be enough to turn around the fortunes of the struggling businesses in the two towns. They were busy now, but what would happen when Christmas was over and everyone was skint?

# 40

Two more windows to go.

That was the first thought that flashed through Kate's mind when she opened her eyes that morning. It was Saturday. The day before Christmas Eve. They were almost there. She was going to be relieved when it was all over – she'd be able to breathe again – but sad too. The living Advent calendar had been more fun than she could ever have imagined.

The second thought was that she would be spending the day with Xander.

They were going to walk the trail – his idea – and perhaps spend some time in some of the valley's shops, pubs and cafés along the way.

'As if we're visitors,' he'd said. 'Although I still feel like a visitor here, to be honest.'

'It's a great idea,' she'd said because it was.

And the third thought was concern for the future; come January, the valley would be once more and the businesses would be struggling again. The living Advent calendar had been a good plan, but it hadn't been enough.

Her phone beeped.

**Best wrap up,** Xander had written. **It's snowing.**

Snowing?

Okay, so it was December, but in this valley in recent years they'd seldom had snow in December. In fact, it seemed more common in March and even April.

She scrambled out of bed and went to the window. Xander was right: it *was* snowing, although only a few half-hearted flakes and it didn't appear to be sticking. She glanced at her phone again. It was almost half past ten, and they were meeting at eleven. She dressed quickly in jeans and a cashmere jumper, with her thickest woolly socks, and then set off for the board game café, where she'd agreed to meet Xander.

She was the first to arrive. Downstairs, almost every table was full of parents, grandparents, children, couples and friends, all playing different board games. She noticed that alongside almost every board was a trail map.

'Morning, Kate, what can I get you?' Em looked bright-eyed as usual behind the counter.

'Scrambled eggs please, and a coffee. I didn't have time for breakfast at home.'

'Meeting someone?'

'Xander.'

'Cold War man?'

'Yeah. Cold War man.'

'Hmmm. You seem to be seeing a lot of him. Going well, is it?'

'It is.' Kate suddenly remembered she'd invited him to the café on Christmas Day. 'In fact, I was wondering…'

'Yeah, that's fine.'

'You don't know what I was going to ask.'

Em laughed. 'One more on Christmas Day won't make any difference. Or will it be two more?'

'Yeah, two more. Dad'll be coming.'

'You've patched things up then?'

'Yeah. And I've a bone to pick with you, Em. I hear you were texting him about me.'

Em looked shame-faced. 'Sorry about that. But the poor bloke was desperate to know if you were okay.'

'Doesn't matter. I know you meant well.'

Em smiled, visibly relieved. 'It might be nice to warn Peter about Xander being here for Christmas lunch. You know, with the two of you splitting up so recently. He might be upset at seeing you with another guy this soon.' She turned away from Kate, calling, 'One scrambled eggs, please,' through the serving hatch, then popping some coffee into the machine.

'Yeah, of course I will.' Em had no idea that the sight of her with Xander wouldn't bother Peter in the slightest, whereas the sight of his beloved Emily with Ludek on the other hand...

'So you and Xander, are you dating?' Em said.

'Not yet, but he keeps cooking me dinner.'

'Good cook?'

'The best,' Kate said without thinking. 'Er... *second* best. His dauphinoise potatoes are divine.'

'He cooks dauphinoise potatoes? He's a keeper.'

'He is, isn't he?' Kate felt as if every cell in her body was dancing.

The door of the café opened then, and Kate turned to see

Xander coming in wearing his university scarf tied around his neck so it was covering most of his face.

'It's not that cold,' she said laughing. 'You southerner. Wait till January. You're in for a shock, isn't he, Em?'

'He certainly is. Oh and Xander, you'd be very welcome here on Christmas Day. The more the merrier.'

'Thanks, Em. I'd like that.'

He ordered a coffee and a bacon sandwich, and they sat down at a recently vacated table in the window of the board game café, watching the snow. It wasn't the kind of pretty, white stuff that you got in films, more the slushy grey variety. This was Essendale, after all.

'Do you ever play the games?' Xander asked, nodding towards the board game shelves.

'Not if I can help it.' She laughed.

'Let's try one after breakfast? Before we venture out into the cold?'

'Yeah, if you like.'

'You can choose,' he said.

She looked over towards the shelves. Hadn't Em said something about a game based on the Cold War?

'I'll go and get one,' she said, 'and we can start reading the rules.'

Instead of going straight to the shelves, she slipped behind the counter and whispered to Em, 'Which is the Cold War game you mentioned?'

Em shrugged. 'Thirteen Days. Not sure anyone's ever played it in here.'

'Perfect, thanks.'

'Thirteen Days?' said Xander, when Kate placed the box in front of him on the table. 'Is this what I think it is?'

'Yeah. A board game about the Cold War.' She couldn't keep the triumph out of her voice.

'It's not the only one either.'

They looked up to see Ludek standing by the table with their order. 'Scrambled eggs, which I'm guessing are yours, Kate. And one bacon sandwich. There are several other Cold War games, if that's something you're particularly interested in. I think I have Twilight Struggle at home if you'd like to borrow it.'

'Thanks,' said Xander. 'I might take you up on that.'

'There are games about everything,' Kate said. 'Trains. Crimes. History. Art. Wildlife. Fashion.'

'I never thought I'd see the day when our Kate played a board game on a date.' Ludek hesitated. 'Sorry, I'm just assuming…'

Kate looked from Ludek to Xander and raised her eyebrows.

'This is a date,' Xander said. 'Isn't it?'

She nodded. 'Yeah, it's a date.'

'Okay, I'll leave you both to it.' Ludek began to tiptoe away from their table in an exaggerated way, like a cartoon character. Then he turned back and said, 'Can I get you any ketchup? Brown sauce?'

They laughed, shaking their heads.

When they'd eaten their breakfasts, Xander opened the box and read the rules out loud. He seemed to get them immediately whilst Kate wasn't so sure.

'I don't think I have a gamer's mind,' she said. 'And I don't know much about the Cold War either, despite our visit to that exhibition and the nuclear bunker.'

'It's a card game, and these cubes represent influence around the world.' He gave her a little plastic bag containing a few small red cubes. 'There should be seventeen in there, and three flags too.'

He laid out the game board, which showed a map with nine rectangles, some for geographical places like Cuba and Berlin, one marked 'television' and one for the United Nations.

'Those are all the areas where we want to gain influence,' Xander said. 'And if your counter moves too far up this track, you trigger nuclear war and world obliteration. Oh, and you lose the game.'

'Well, I don't want to be doing that then,' said Kate.

He dealt the cards. She looked through her hand – there was a picture of President Kennedy on one, Che Guevara on another and a man she thought she recognised on a third.

'Is that...?' she held the card up for Xander to see.

'Khrushchev,' he said. 'But you probably shouldn't show me your cards.'

'He's in a board game?' She couldn't believe it. She'd never heard of him until that exhibition.

The game wasn't really Kate's thing; she much preferred Forest Shuffle with its cute animals, but she enjoyed watching Xander, who got really into it, increasing his influence in different spheres and territories across the board, and inevitably winning. It wasn't a long game, and when it was over and packed away back in its box, Kate said, 'I suppose we'd better brave the cold.'

Xander stood up, and began to put on his coat.

They'd agreed to walk the trail in order, so went to the florist's next. There was a group of people gathered outside, making appreciative comments about the window, and several customers came and went from inside the shop too. Andrea was clearly doing a brisk trade.

They walked on to the health centre, and laughed at Razz and Ludek's hangover cures, then dodged the geese to view the Dickens' characters from *A Christmas Carol* in the window of Essendale Library. Then they went to Oxfam and stood outside the hastily thrown together 'how to have a greener Christmas' display.

'This is where it took off,' said Kate. 'The local paper covered this window and then the TV crew tipped up the next evening.'

'Are Mr B's famous baubles still trending on social media?' Xander asked.

'Not exactly trending. But there are new pictures of them almost every day.'

'The mind boggles,' said Xander.

'All down to EcoEssendale. If she hadn't written that blog, we wouldn't have got nearly as much publicity. The whole thing kind of spiralled.'

'Did you ever hear from her after you met her on the train?'

Kate shook her head. 'Nah. And I don't suppose I will now.'

'Shame,' said Xander. 'But the Advent calendar's success isn't down to her. It's down to *you*. Look what a difference it's made. The town's so busy today.'

'It might have been busy anyway right before Christmas.' Kate had been feeling uncharacteristically pessimistic since the previous evening when she'd started thinking about what would happen to the local businesses – particularly the board game café – after Twelfth Night when the visitors stopped coming. 'It's busy now, but in January and February…' Her voice trailed away. 'I was naïve to think that doing this would magically revitalise all the local businesses. It might have given them a bit of a boost, but it's not enough. Not in the long-term.'

'You're one person, Kate. You can only do so much. But you've led the way. You've shown what can be done with a little imagination and some creative thinking, and now other people need to step up and do *their* bit for the local community. Someone else can take the baton now.'

'Oh yeah. And who's going to do that?'

'We all have to. I've already thought of what I might do. Let's take a little diversion off the trail so I can show you.'

They headed out of town now, past where the original board game café once stood, down the steps at the end of the road and onto the towpath, where Xander took Kate's hand and steered her in the opposite direction from where the wool boat was moored.

'Where are we going?' said Kate.

'You'll see.'

Xander was very fond of his little mysteries, she thought. The mystery window display – not long now and she'd get to see what that was – and now a mystery detour too.

He took her gloved hand in his as they walked. A mile or so out of town, he led her over a footbridge beside some locks and through a small field, until they reached a muddy path through the woods with the river running beside it, a few metres below. It was snowing more heavily now; the trees looked like their branches had been dusted with icing sugar.

The air was still. They weren't far from Essendale, but not a car could be heard.

'Now around this bend,' Xander said, 'is our first piece of history.'

He led the way down some steps and pointed at a small, rocky pool, right next to the river.

'What is it?'

'That,' he said 'is Essendale Spa.'

'What? I don't see any fluffy white robes or hunky masseurs.'

'Have a sniff.' He crouched down, lowering his face to the water.

Kate followed suit. 'Urgh, rotten eggs.'

'It's sulphur. People used to come here to take the waters like in Buxton and Bath. Though not in such great numbers.'

'I never even knew it was here.'

'We probably don't have time today and the path's a bit muddy—' Xander glanced down at Kate's flat but not particularly substantial shoes '—but if we carried on up there, we'd find an old waterwheel beside the ruins of a paper mill.'

'Paper mill? Not cotton?'

'Paper mill originally, then it later became a cotton mill. And further up, there's more ruins, and an old mill pond. There are packhorse trails that lead all the way onto the moor to the site of an old workhouse.'

'I hadn't got a clue about any of this.'

Xander smiled. 'And that brings me to my idea. History walks. Maybe once a month on a Saturday afternoon or a Sunday morning. I'd be happy to lead them. I reckon there's loads more places in the area that would be interesting to visitors. I've only scratched the surface.'

'I love that. We could have walking maps printed with information about each place,' said Kate. 'So if people couldn't make your guided walk, they could walk the same route on their own later.'

'Great idea,' Xander said. 'I think we should get back to the living Advent calendar trail now though. We've got to do it all in time for this evening's unveiling.'

'The penultimate one. It's come round so quickly.'

'I've heard they're saving the best till last.'

They stood in the woods for a moment, regarding each other, as the snow fell around them.

'This is the perfect moment for a first kiss,' said Xander.

Strictly speaking, it wouldn't be their first kiss, but she knew what he meant; four years ago felt like a lifetime away. She took a step towards him, putting her face so close to his that their lips were almost touching. Then she put a finger between them and whispered, 'Not till tomorrow. When I've seen that window.'

He laughed and shook his head.

They walked back through the woods and along the towpath to the wool boat. There was quite a crowd gathered outside, peering into the windows and oohing and ahhing over the cosy knits. Kate was surprised to spot a familiar figure amongst them.

'Peter!' she called, as soon as they were close enough.

'Morning, Kate,' he said. 'And Xander, isn't it?'

The two men shook hands, Kate glancing from one to the other to gauge their reactions. She hoped they weren't going to be too awkward around one another, given that they would both be spending Christmas Day in the board game café, but there didn't seem to be any animosity. In fact, Peter seemed in particularly high spirits.

'Are you walking the trail too?' said Kate.

Peter shook his head. 'No, just walking. I often take a stroll along the towpath when I'm mulling something over.'

'What are you mulling over?'

It was none of her business, but she couldn't help being curious.

'Business things. I can't really say yet.' He mimed zipping his lips.

The three of them stood for a moment in silence, looking at the knitted nativity scene.

'Is your window a nativity?' Kate said to Xander. 'Is that why the vicar agreed to it?'

Xander shook his head. 'Nope.'

'Then what is it?'

'I couldn't possibly say.' Xander also mimed zipping his lips, which made Peter laugh.

'No-one's telling me anything today.' She sounded a little exasperated, but in truth, she was just tired from all her hard work in recent weeks.

'Okay, I'll tell you about my plans,' said Peter, 'but it's for your ears only. You can't tell anyone – not even Emily and I know you tell her everything. This is strictly between us.'

'Would you like me to…?' Xander began.

'No, no,' said Peter. 'Strictly between the three of us. How about a chat over a glass of wine?' He glanced at his watch. 'It's almost midday and it is nearly Christmas.'

Kate glanced at Xander. She wasn't sure if he'd want to

go for a drink with the man she had been dating up until recently, albeit briefly, but Xander seemed relaxed about the idea.

'Sounds great,' he said. 'As long as you feel you can trust me with your secret plan. I am, after all, an offcumden.'

Peter shook his head playfully, sucking air between his teeth. 'I don't know, Kate. What d'you reckon? Can we trust this man?'

'Of course we can,' she said decisively. 'We can trust him one hundred per cent.'

# 41

They grabbed a table in Hebbleswick's trendiest – and only – wine bar, where she and Peter had had their first official date, and Peter ordered a bottle of Chablis and a charcuterie board.

'And a large portion of fries, please,' Xander added to the waiter with a smile.

Their order arrived swiftly. The waiter uncorked the wine, pouring a little in a glass for Peter to taste. He sniffed it first, swirling it around in the glass, before trying a little and then pronouncing, 'That's fine, thank you.'

'How are you feeling,' said Peter as the waiter filled their glasses, 'now the living Advent calendar is almost over? Happy?'

Kate paused, wondering whether to be honest or whether to put a positive spin on it. 'Happy in some ways. There are definitely more visitors. Em mentioned that her takings are up.'

Peter nodded. 'I'm glad. I worry for her.'

'Me too.' Kate sighed.

'Why only happy in some ways?' said Peter.

'I think I was a bit of a fool to think that doing something like this could magically transform the town.'

Xander reached across the table and took her hand, as Peter said, 'Oh, Kate, you're not a fool,' and patted her arm.

'Not a fool at all,' Xander echoed. 'You're a hopeful optimist. A hopeful optimist with a heart of gold who worked like a Trojan because she wanted to help the local businesses.'

'Or at least, one local business in particular,' Peter added.

'Yeah, the board game café. I wanted to do this for Em. But it's a drop in the ocean really compared with what's needed. We need more initiatives to keep the tourists coming, and more housing for people to rent, rather than more Airbnbs, so that there are more people actually living here all year round.'

'Nobody said you had to save Essendale all by yourself, Kate,' said Peter. 'You've done your bit. You've shown us the way. Now it's up to other people to do their bit.'

'That's what Xander said, didn't you?'

Kate was about to mention Xander's idea for history walks, but Peter continued. 'And that brings me neatly to my plan.' He glanced around, checking that no-one was listening, and leaned towards them. 'You know that plot of land you told me about?'

For a second, Kate couldn't think what he meant. Then she remembered: the land that Tarquin thought would make an excellent location for yet more holiday homes. 'Yeah, I remember.'

'Well, I've put in an offer.' Peter looked rather pleased with himself.

'You're going to build holiday homes?'

'No, I'm going to build homes. Homes for local people. Affordable homes. I've got an architect looking at it at the moment, but I'm hoping to build about twenty of them.'

'Blimey, Peter. Can you afford that?' She had known he was well off, but not that well off.

'Yeah, I can. The business is doing well again, but Mother and I thought it might be prudent to diversify. We'll sell some of the homes – hopefully with a clause saying they cannot be used for holiday letting – and we'll rent out the others ourselves. At sensible prices to local workers. It's only twenty houses, so it's not going to magically transform things, but it'll help. And in case you're wondering, Kate, I won't be using Tarquin's estate agency to sell them.'

'Twenty houses,' said Xander later, when Peter had headed back to Essendale, and he and Kate were walking to the next stop on the living Advent calendar. 'Wow.'

'Yeah, incredible. I knew he was rich, but not that rich.'

'Do you regret breaking up with him?'

She stopped and looked at him in surprise. 'No, of course not. I wasn't with him because he was wealthy. I liked him. I still like him. But the spark wasn't there. And – keep this to yourself – but he's still in love with Em.'

*And I'm in love with you.*

'Offering history walks seems a bit pathetic compared to building twenty homes.' Xander sounded deflated.

'Don't say that. Your walks will be amazing. I loved those dates you took me on. The exhibition. The nuclear bunker. The docks. You've a real talent for bringing history alive, even for people like me who – let's be honest – have no interest in it whatsoever. And like Peter said, everyone has to do their bit. We aren't all in a position to buy land and build a load of homes, but we can all do something, even if it's just shopping local. Now come on, the old-cooperative is around the corner.'

'This used to be Taylor's home and shop,' she said as they reached the huge window.

A few people were admiring Taylor's upcycled range of children's Christmas clothes, and one of the new residents was patiently explaining that the clothes weren't actually for sale from here, and pointing out the name of Taylor's Etsy store and her Instagram handle clearly displayed in the window.

'Why did she leave?' Xander asked.

'The ceiling fell through and Tarquin – you know, the estate agent – tried to pin the blame on her. It was such a shame. It was practically derelict when she moved in. She transformed the place.'

'So that's why her stuff's on display now at the board game café?' said Xander.

'Yeah, I don't think she could afford to rent another house *and* a shop. She rented Mr B's house initially, did the actual sewing in Harry's dining room, and displayed the clothes at the café. A couple of months later, she moved in with Harry.'

'Does she still want a shop?'

Kate suddenly knew where this line of questioning was going. At least she hoped she knew; it would be brilliant if she was right. 'Yeah, I guess so. As far as I know.'

'Because I know a shop that would be perfect,' said Xander. 'And it's available pretty soon too. From the seventh of January in fact, once its owner has removed an absolutely fantastic Christmas display from its window.'

'You're going to offer Taylor your shop?' she said, wanting to make absolutely certain that that was what he meant.

'Why not?'

'She mightn't be able to afford it with a baby on the way.'

'Mates' rates,' said Xander. 'She can always say no. But I'm definitely giving her first refusal.'

'Wow, that's incredibly generous of you.' Kate put her arm around his waist and gave him a squeeze.

'It's not quite building twenty homes,' he said, 'but it's something.'

'So we're one hundred per cent clear,' she said, 'you are not in competition with Peter. Now come on, we've a whole load of windows to look at and we need to reach Harry's house before six for the penultimate unveiling.'

The snow continued to fall for the rest of the afternoon, no longer grey and slushy, but white and crisp, covering rooftops and roads, and proving far more effective at slowing the traffic than any of the council's traffic-calming measures ever had.

Xander and Kate joined the large number of people who had already traipsed through Harry's back gate and were assembled on the lawn. To Kate's surprise, they were all facing the wrong way; they weren't looking at Harry's shed with its unusually large window. Well, unusually large for a shed anyway. They were admiring the Christmas tree in his and Taylor's dining room window, which was adorned not with conventional baubles, but with reels of different coloured cotton, each one suspended from the tree with a co-ordinating ribbon.

'Have they done the reveal already?' said Xander. 'Are we late?'

'No, that's not the display. The display is in the shed.'

There hadn't been room for Peter's usual mechanism, so instead a huge roller blind had been installed and lowered down to conceal the display inside. Hand in hand, Kate and Xander stood beside the window, she gave her usual welcome speech, then took out her phone and watched the seconds of the final minute tick by so she could begin the drum roll and countdown at precisely the right moment.

The roller blind began to lift, revealing a magical winter landscape inside, complete with snow-topped hills with tiny trees and grazing sheep. The various buildings were all covered in snow too. Tiny people stood in scarves waiting on a station platform. Carol singers were gathered outside the church. On one of the houses, Santa had landed his sleigh, and was about to descend down the chimney. There were miniature shoppers bustling along the street laden with parcels. But best of all, the thing that made this so Harry, was that model trains were speeding their way around this landscape, stopping at signals and stations, disappearing through tunnels and emerging on the other side of the hills.

Kate looked away from the window for a moment, over the heads of the crowd, at the hills that surrounded the town. They were, like the hills in Harry's miniature landscape, covered with snow.

'D'you like it, Kate?'

She looked down to see Taylor's son, Max, standing beside her.

'I helped Dad make it,' he said.

Kate loved that Max called Harry 'Dad'; he wasn't Max's real dad, but the two of them had got on splendidly – as Harry put it – from the word go.

'I love it,' she said. 'I especially love the Father Christmas about to go down the chimney.'

'I don't believe in Father Christmas,' said Max decisively, wrinkling his nose. 'He's a Victorian invention.'

'You're right in a way,' said Xander. 'The image of Father Christmas that we have these days *does* date from Victorian times, but there were versions of him around long before then.'

'Have you googled it too?' said Max.

'No, I'm a history professor at a university.'

'I'm going to study engineering at university and then I can build trains.' And with that, Max was gone, pushing open the door of the shed and disappearing inside.

'That's one magnificent man shed,' said Xander. 'I love a shed. Did your dad buy a new one?'

'My dad?'

'Yeah, that weekend you spent with him. You said you'd been demolishing a shed. You were covered in dust.'

'No, he'll never get another shed,' Kate said.

'Oh? Whyever not?'

'Demolishing the shed was kind of symbolic for both of us.'

'Symbolic? In what way?'

Kate took a deep breath. This was the moment. She was ready. 'I think it's about time I told you everything, but let's go somewhere more private.'

She poked her head inside the door of Harry's shed, where he and Max were sitting at some kind of control unit, operating the model trains, and congratulated them both on a brilliant display. They were so engrossed that they barely registered her presence. Then she and Xander set off on the short walk to the Red Lion, bought a bottle of wine, and tucked themselves into a corner near the roaring open fire.

'I don't know where to start.' She paused. Took a deep breath. 'Earlier, I didn't quite tell you the whole story about my dad. You know I always blamed Dad for my mother leaving.' These days, she found she couldn't bring herself to say the word 'Mum'. 'When I was growing up, he spent all his time in his shed. He was into transistor radios. At least, I thought he was. Night after night. Every weekend too. And she would stand and stare out of the kitchen window sometimes. She seemed so lonely, so isolated. I thought she was longing for him to pay her some attention, and I promised myself then that I would avoid getting involved with guys who had time-consuming hobbies. So that evening, when I came back to your place in London and I saw your soldiers, and then you said about all the hours you spent painting them, I concluded that you were too much like my dad.'

'And that's why you left,' said Xander. 'Not because you thought I was geeky.'

'No, you are geeky, but I like that about you. You see, I'd got it all wrong about my parents. Mum wasn't lonely. She didn't want him to give up the transistors and come inside and spend time with her. The truth was, they didn't get on. They *never* got on. They only got married because she fell pregnant with me. He spent all that time in the shed to keep out of her way. He didn't touch them again once she left. That's why demolishing the shed was symbolic. It felt like Dad and I were starting a new chapter in our relationship.'

'Do you think we can start a new chapter too?' Xander asked.

'I think we can, if you've forgiven me.'

Xander shuffled closer to her. He moved his face towards her left ear as if he were about to nibble it or kiss her neck and she gasped in anticipation, but he did neither.

'I want you to know, Kate,' he said softly, 'that Alessandra's has only the smallest of yards at the back. No garden. So even if I wanted one, there isn't room for a shed.'

She slapped his arm playfully. 'Xander!'

Then she thought for a moment and said, 'Even if you did have a shed, it wouldn't make any difference. I can see now that it's healthy to have hobbies. You know, within a relationship. Not that we... but if we were...'

Her eyes met his. He leaned in towards her again. She was sure he was on the verge of kissing her, and said firmly, 'Not here. And not until tomorrow evening, when I've seen that Christmas window. It had better be good.'

# 42

Kate was excited for that evening's reveal. It was the final window and there would be mince pies, mulled wine and impromptu carols in the board game café afterwards. (Well, the carols would *appear* impromptu but Kate had persuaded Peter with his rich baritone to kick them off.)

But mainly she was excited because she would finally get to see Xander's window – it had to be something special for the vicar to have acquiesced so easily – and then she'd kiss him. And it would feel like their first kiss, she felt sure of it. Yes, they had kissed four years ago in the garden of St Dunstan's in the East, but this would feel different, because this time he knew the real her, the real, imperfect her, rather than that perfect façade she used to work so hard to maintain.

She couldn't fathom what his window might be. Perhaps it was a display of different ways to serve spuds on Christmas Day since he was such an expert on preparing potatoes.

No, that wouldn't have persuaded the vicar to give up his Christmas Eve slot.

Far more likely was that it had a historical theme, only she didn't see why that would have won Reverend Stone over either.

Unless…

Well, might it be about Santa Claus?

Yes, that had to be it.

He'd said something about the history of Father Christmas to Max last night. And wasn't Father Christmas based on an actual Christian saint? If the window told the story of Saint Nicholas, that would not only explain why Xander had wanted the Christmas Eve slot, but also explain why the vicar had agreed; there was a religious element.

Yet Kate had sensed that this window was something that Xander was passionate about. Was he really such a Santa fan? She couldn't see it somehow.

Anyway, in a few hours, all would be revealed and she could hardly wait.

She walked past Alessandra's sixteen times that day. The white geese took to following her, sensing perhaps that something was afoot. Each time she passed the former dress shop, she watched the brown drapes like a hawk for even the slightest twitch of movement, and, let's be honest, hoping for a glimpse of Xander.

'Too busy putting the finishing touches to my display,' he'd said when she'd enquired if he might like to come over for a bite to eat.

'For heaven's sake, Kate, you'll wear the pavement out.'

Kate looked over at the board game café, where Em was standing in the doorway, beckoning her over.

Kate crossed the road, the geese still following.

'What *are* you doing?' said Em.

'Pacing,' said Kate. 'Last-minute nerves about tonight. I haven't seen Xander's window and it needs to be perfect.'

'Nothing *needs* to be perfect,' said Em pointedly. 'But I'm sure it will be good. Why don't you come in out of the cold and perch yourself at that table in the window? You can spy on Xander from there, and I'll bring you a hot chocolate to warm you up.'

'Green tea?'

'Hot chocolate,' said Em. 'Come on. I'm letting all the cold in here.'

With a last glance back towards Alessandra's, Kate stepped into the board game café. The geese tried to follow.

'Not you,' said Em, shooing them away. 'Not unless you want to be on tomorrow's menu.'

'Em!' said Kate, and then to the geese: 'Close your ears. She didn't mean it.'

She shut the door behind her, leaving the geese looking disgruntled on the pavement outside.

'Course I didn't mean it,' Em said. 'We've two massive turkeys. There'll be quite a lot of us tomorrow, but I reckon there'll still be leftovers. Turkey casserole is going to be on the specials board for the entire week after Christmas.'

'So if people haven't had enough of playing board games with their families and eating leftover turkey, they can come here and do the same thing.'

'Exactly,' said Em. 'Even you with your marketing skills couldn't sell that one, could you?'

'Bet I could.' Kate grinned.

★

By twenty to six, there was quite a crowd outside Alessandra's. The air was bitterly cold, but there was a fine array of knitwear on display, along with several upcycled coats that Kate recognised as Taylor's designs. The police had agreed to close the road for a couple of hours as a precaution: a good job, as it happened, given the number of people who were gathering.

Kate was standing with Jo, Razz, Taylor, Harry and little Max. They'd bagged their spot early, and stood with their noses practically pressed up against the glass.

'And you've no idea what it is?' said Jo.

'Not a clue,' Kate said. 'Something historical, I'm guessing, given that history is Xander's passion, but he won't say.'

At five to six, the drapes covering the window twitched. There was a collective gasp of anticipation from the waiting crowd. Xander's head appeared in the middle where two pieces of fabric overlapped. He grinned at the crowd with a twinkle in his eyes, mouthed the words 'five minutes' then disappeared again behind the curtains.

There was a smattering of laughter.

'I like Xander,' said Jo.

'I like Xander too,' said Kate.

'Do you *like* like Xander, Kate?' said Max.

Kate smiled. 'Yeah, I *like* like Xander.'

In fact, she more than *like* liked him; she'd go as far as to say that she was falling in love with him.

She fought the urge to go and bang on the shop door, to demand to be let in so she could tell him there and then.

Instead, she waited on the pavement with her friends for what felt like the longest five minutes of her life.

And waited.

He was probably only a metre away from her, putting the final finishing touches to his display, but a large pane of glass and swathes of fabric separated them. Taylor was talking to Max, so Kate tried to entertain herself with thoughts of Xander and what he would say if she did tell him how she felt. She tried to guess for the umpteenth time what might be revealed when the drapes were removed.

A small child weaved his way between her and Jo, and pushed in front to get a better view. Kate felt a mixture of resentment and longing – resentment that someone was now obscuring her view of the window she most wanted to see, and longing to have a child of her own.

And then it was six o'clock. She wasn't giving an introductory welcome – the vicar wanted to say a few words afterwards instead – so she simply called, 'Drum roll, please' for one final time, and everyone obliged and began to slap their hands on their thighs to create a drum roll effect – well, as best they could given how tightly squashed together they were – and the drapes began to lift.

Kate groaned. 'I might have known!'

In pride of place in the window was Xander's collection of little soldiers, all present and correct in their tiny uniforms. Not only that, but he'd created an entire landscape, a landscape of war. He had even dug trenches, for heaven's sake. These days, Kate had no problem with Xander's hobby, but in this context, it wasn't appropriate. Although she had to concede that he'd made an excellent job of it – under any other circumstances, she'd have been admiring his artistry – but this was supposed to be a Christmas window, and the only festive thing about it was the set of fairy lights twinkling above the battlefield.

There was a huge display screen behind Xander's little army, with a black and white picture of real-life soldiers, and the words '*The Western Front, 1914*'.

What *was* he thinking?

There were families here, with young children. No-one wanted to be thinking of war on Christmas Eve; she should have gone with the vicar and his nativity display outside the church. Okay, so it would have been completely predictable and not very exciting, but a hundred times better than this.

Talking of the vicar, hadn't he known what Xander was planning? And what on earth had he been thinking when he'd agreed that Xander could create this evening's window?

'World War I,' Kate hissed to Taylor. 'It's supposed to be a Christmas display. I'm chuffin' furious.'

She would have used a different word entirely had Max not been within earshot.

# 43

'Genius,' said a familiar voice.

Kate turned to see her dad standing behind her. She forced a smile. She really couldn't see what was genius about this at all.

The shop door opened, and Xander and the vicar appeared in the doorway. Xander smiled at her and gave her a discreet thumbs up. She held her hands up, to indicate that she didn't get it, then turned her eyes back to the screen as the picture changed to a different photo, still black and white, still of soldiers.

Her heart sank further. If the battle scene wasn't bad enough, Xander had gone and prepared a PowerPoint. Kate was a big fan of PowerPoints in the right environment – i.e. work meetings – but *not* as part of her living Advent calendar. She'd worked so hard on this and wanted the finale to be something incredible, something that everyone would talk about and remember for months – if not years – to come.

Soft, string music began to play from a speaker that she hadn't noticed before, which had been rigged up above the window. Some text appeared on the screen.

World War I began on 28 July 1914 and was one of the deadliest wars in history.

*Fabulous. Thanks for that cheery thought, Xander.*
The next slide showed a map of Europe, and explained that by the end of 1914, there was a continuous line of trenches stretching from the English Channel to Switzerland, and that this was known as the Western Front.

'Great,' she said. 'A chuffin' history lesson. I don't see what this has to do with Christmas.'

'I think I can guess,' said her dad. 'And it's chuffin' genius.'

The following slide showed yet another group of soldiers and announced that between fifteen and twenty-two million people died as a result of the war, of whom nine to eleven million were military personnel.

It was a sobering thought and not one you wanted to be thinking on Christmas Eve. Kate dug her fingernails into the palms of her hands. She could hardly bear to watch, and wondered if she might worm her way out through the crowd and hide herself away in the board game café. Thank goodness she'd had the foresight to plan the impromptu carol singing; that would cheer everyone up.

She was about to make her great escape when the next slide appeared.

But during the weeks leading up to Christmas in 1914, something special happened.

Finally, a mention of Christmas.

She glanced at her dad. Their eyes met, and she remembered a scene from years back, when he'd been lending her a hand with some history homework. He hadn't always been in that shed, she thought. And her mum – she never used to ask about Kate's homework, let alone help with it. Xander's window had jogged her memory, and suddenly she knew what his display was about and her dad was right: it *was* genius. Chuffin' genius.

Kate could picture her history book now, the picture she'd drawn of trenches like the ones in Xander's window, and her neat, handwriting underneath, explaining the story of the Christmas Truce of 1914.

She looked at Xander now, staring at him, willing him to meet her gaze. It seemed to take forever, but eventually he did. She widened her eyes and smiled at him, trying to convey that she'd worked it out now and she loved it.

A series of slides and pictures revealed how on Christmas Eve in 1914, some British soldiers saw that their German counterparts had placed lanterns and small fir trees along the trenches, and they heard them singing carols. Both sides shouted messages to each other and next day, they ventured across the trenches to exchange season's greetings and talk. They even exchanged food and souvenirs. Fighting ceased in many places, and there were prisoner swaps and joint burial ceremonies. They famously played football.

Out of the corner of her eye, Kate saw her dad wipe a tear from his eye. She glanced around her at the sea of faces. Many people had their tissues out, and parents were hugging their children close to them.

The string music, that had been playing from the speaker, suddenly stopped.

**Some meetings even ended with the singing of Christmas carols**, read the text on the screen, as from somewhere behind her, Kate heard the sound of a lone trumpet playing 'Silent Night'. She stood on tiptoes, and over the sea of heads around her, she saw one of the players from the local brass band, standing outside the board game café, playing his solo.

The words on the screen now read, **Silent Night, Stille Nacht, Douce Nuit.**

As he finished playing, there were a few seconds of silence, then a woman in the crowd began to sing.

'Silent night, holy night.' The rich alto voice rang through the air, and was gradually joined by other voices. Her dad joined in, hesitantly at first, then Razz and Jo, and Harry and Taylor and Max too. Those who didn't know the words were humming softly and soon it felt as if everyone except her was singing along.

Kate never sang. Never. She'd realised in music lessons at primary school that she hadn't been blessed with a beautiful voice or the ability to stay in tune, so she had given up trying. She didn't even sing along to the radio in the car or in the shower when no-one else was listening; the perfectionist in her wouldn't allow it. But she opened her mouth now, and began to half-speak, half-sing the words, softly at first, then a little louder, praying that the notes came out in the same key as everyone else. And they must have done, as no-one turned to stare.

And to her surprise, she found she enjoyed the sensation of adding to this communal sound. So much so that she was disappointed when, after two verses – or at least, after the first verse sung twice because no-one knew the words to the second verse – the singing ended. Everyone remained silent for a few seconds and then Xander stepped forward to speak.

'Thank you,' he said, 'for coming to see my window display this evening, and thank you, Kate, for having faith in me, and letting me have this night, Christmas Eve.'

He need never know that her faith had wavered for a few minutes, she thought.

'We talk a lot about the magic of Christmas, but my display reflects not the magic, but the *power* of Christmas. Christmas has the power to gather several generations of one family around one table, to bring estranged friends – and maybe estranged lovers – together, and to help soldiers from opposing sides see each other not as enemies, but as human beings. I'm going to hand over to the vicar now, but I wish you all a very happy and peaceful Christmas.'

People glanced at each other. Kate could feel that they wanted to applaud, but there was a stillness in the air since the trumpeter had played, and no-one wanted to break the spell. The vicar stepped forward and cleared his throat.

'When Xander told me he wanted to do the Christmas Eve display,' he said, 'I had my doubts. Like Kate.' He gave her a warm smile. 'Christmas Eve – surely that should be a nativity scene at the church. But then Xander told me what he wanted to do, and the message that his display conveys, one of hope and peace...'

He paused. Kate hoped this wasn't going to become a whole sermon.

The vicar dabbed at his own eyes with a handkerchief

then continued. 'This message that Xander has so creatively shared is one of hope and peace, and isn't that what Christmas is really about? Whether you're a believer or not, as you're opening your gifts tomorrow or eating your turkey, please spare a thought or say a prayer for those regions in the world where people still live under the terrible shadow of war. Let us all hope for a long-lasting truce in those places.'

He paused again, then rearranged his facial features from solemn vicar to someone altogether jollier. 'If anyone *does* have a hankering for a good nativity scene, please pop along to the church in Hebbleswick and fill your boots, as they say. We have Jesus, Mary and the wee donkey. Now all that remains for me to do is to say a huge thank you to Kate for coming up with this wonderful living Advent calendar idea. Have a super day tomorrow, everyone, and if you fancy a mince pie or a glass of non-alcoholic mulled wine, both are available this evening in our wonderful board game café, across the road.'

The crowd began to part. Some people drifted away towards their homes and some towards the station, but the majority, including Kate's very special group of friends, headed for the café. Kate herself remained rooted to the spot, her eyes on the window display. Her hand was wrapped in her father's hand – she wasn't sure quite when that had happened, and then suddenly Xander was beside her too, and she felt his fingers entwining with those of her other hand. She didn't speak as she stood there, between these two men whom she loved.

'It's a wonderful display,' said her dad suddenly, dropping her hand to shake Xander's free hand. 'Inspired. Now, if you don't mind, it's a bit parky out here, so I'm off to the café for a hot chocolate. See you in there.'

When he had gone, Xander said simply, 'Is it okay? I know it's a bit different from your cosy knitted nativities and Mr B's baubles, but I wanted to do something that would move people, that would remind them of the true spirit of Christmas.'

'It's incredible. *You're* incredible.'

She turned towards him, and allowed him to pull her in for a hug. Pressed up against him, she could hear his heart beating through his thick coat, or at least she fancied that she could. She felt safe. Secure.

'I've thought of a new nickname for you,' Xander whispered.

She pulled away from him, looking up into his eyes. 'Go on, then. Tell me.'

'Spudnik.'

'Sputnik?'

'No. *Spud*-nik.'

Kate laughed. 'Because I like potatoes?'

'Exactly. Remember that Cold War exhibition?'

Did she remember? Of course, she remembered. Every little detail. She nodded.

'I told you that Sputnik in Russian means "fellow traveller",' said Xander, 'and that that's what I was looking for. Someone to travel life's journey with me. And I know it's early days for us, Kate. I'm not presuming anything. But I'm hopeful. Very hopeful. Will you be my Spudnik?'

'That's very cheesy. Cute but cheesy.' Then she stood on tiptoes, stretching her face towards his, and lightly brushed her lips against his, just briefly. She shivered with pleasure, and Xander, presumably mistaking this for her being cold, took off his old university scarf and wrapped it around her neck, then back around his own, so that the two of them were effectively tied together.

'This is cosy,' he said, then leaned his face towards her. He lingered, his mouth hovering above hers, moving ever so slightly closer with each passing second. The wait was agony; Kate wanted to grab hold of his scarf and pull him towards her, but at the same time, she wanted him to linger for longer, so that this moment of blissful anticipation lasted forever. And then finally his mouth reached hers. He ran his tongue gently over her lips, teasing her, tormenting her, and Kate thought she would explode, and then a cheer went up from inside the board game café.

They pulled apart.

'Oh God,' said Xander. 'Half of Essendale are gawping at us.'

Kate had her back to the café. She turned and saw that he was right. Em, Ludek, Jo, Razz, Taylor, Harry, Max and her dad were all looking over at them. She waved, and gave them a thumbs up. Then, as if she were shooing one of the white geese, she gestured for them to move away from the window, before turning back to Xander and saying, 'Right, now where were we?'

# Epilogue

If you'd followed the living Advent calendar trail on Christmas morning, you might have looked beyond the first window, the delightful display of gifts underneath the Christmas tree in the board game café, and found your eyes drawn instead to the scene inside. You might have wondered if the smiling people gathered together were part of the display, a kind of a living tableau. The huge table in the centre – Emily had pushed several tables together – was laden with turkey, sprouts, pigs in blankets, and roast potatoes. It looked like a scene from those Christmas TV ads – the ones trying to persuade you that you need to buy your festive goodies from a particular supermarket, the ones that Kate hated. Christmas at the board game café was the epitome of the perfect Christmas.

If you'd stopped and stared – although you probably wouldn't as that would have been rude – you might have wondered how they were related, or indeed if they were related at all. There were three older gentlemen, one of whom was sporting a purple bow tie, and two older ladies – partners of two of the gentlemen presumably – and four younger couples. There was a smartly dressed man with hair so perfect that it looked almost plastic – he was on his own, but he looked cheerful enough – and then there was a boy of about eight or nine. Fifteen guests around the dinner table, yet if you were eagle-eyed, you might have spotted there were sixteen chairs.

Emily hadn't fancied putting hay under the tablecloth to remind her guests that baby Jesus had been born in a stable, but she had set an empty place at the dinner table; this was partly a nod to the Polish tradition that Mr B – the chap in the bow tie – had told her about, and partly it was for her late mother, who had dreamed that she and her daughter would one day run a café like this one together, but who hadn't lived to see it.

You couldn't have known that Emily had asked her best friend Kate in a text early on Christmas morning if she should set *two* empty places, one for each of their mothers. Kate had thanked her but declined.

You also couldn't have known that Kate had decided to turn down Xander's offer to ask one of his students, who had a keen interest in genealogy, if she could attempt to track down Kate's mother or any other relatives on her maternal side. Kate had accepted that her mother didn't want to be part of her life – and never had – and had decided that she had everyone she needed anyway: a loving father, a wonderful new man – she and Xander had woken up together for the very first time that very morning – and the loveliest group of friends that anyone could wish for.

And you couldn't have known that Kate was having the

most perfect day and actually enjoying Christmas for the first time in her adult life.

No, you couldn't have known all that if you'd peered through the window and seen Kate pinching the last roast potato from the serving dish, popping it into her mouth and giving Xander the broadest of smiles because she knew he'd been after it too.

# Acknowledgements

I'm going to begin by thanking someone who will never know that he's had a mention in a book. He was my constant and faithful companion on cold, dark mornings when I rose at 6 a.m. – or sometimes even 5 – to work on this novel. When I was struggling with a plot point or a particularly tricky sentence, rubbing his soft fur or giving his tummy a tickle often did the trick. I've always loved animals, but didn't realise it was possible to love one quite this much. But by the time *Christmas at the Board Game Café* is published, our fox-red Labrador puppy Pete will probably have left us to train with the charity Guide Dogs. We'll miss him terribly but hopefully he'll transform someone's life, and it's been an incredible privilege to have him in *our* lives for the last few months.

A big thank you to all my readers, and especially those who've subscribed to my newsletter for my updates and pupdates. Your messages really spur me on. Four novels in, I still feel that I'm a new author, and am very grateful to everyone who's chosen to pick up one of my books, especially those people who've written Amazon reviews and Instagram posts. Thank you to Rachel Gilbey of Rachel's Random Resources and all the wonderful bloggers who took part on the blog tours for *The Little Board Game Café, Love Letters on Hazel Lane* and *Second Chances at the Board Game Café*.

I've felt wonderfully supported by many readers' groups on Facebook. I can't name them all, but would like to give a mention to the members of Jenny Colgan and More Great Books, including admins Marian Girling and Sarah Price; Wendy Clarke and the team at The Fiction Café Book Club; and Sue Baker who organises legendary virtual publication parties in the group Riveting Reads and Vintage Vibes. I'd also like to thank the Friendly Book Community, especially the wonderful Sarah Kingsnorth; last Christmas, we ran a book auction together in aid of Guide Dogs and we hope to do another one this year – keep your eyes peeled!

I've said it before, but I really feel that I've found my tribe in the wonderful community of writers out there. I'm honoured to be a member of both the Romantic Novelists Association and the Novelistas, and have received so much support and encouragement from both groups.

I am very grateful to everyone at Aria: Holly Humphreys (editorial), Emily Champion (production), Elle Bloom (production), Meg Shepherd (design support), Amy Watson (marketing), Zoe Giles (social media), Jo Liddiard (marketing), Shannon Hewitt (marketing), Yasmeen Doogue-Khan (publicity), Karen Dobbs (sales), Dan

Groenewald (sales), Victoria Eddison (sales), and Nikky Ward (digital sales). A massive thank you to Jessie Price for designing beautiful and eye-catching covers for this book and the first three in the series. Thank you too to copy editor Helena Newton for your helpful suggestions, and to proofreader Carl Smith for all your hard work.

A massive thank you to my wonderful editors Aubrie Artiano and Sophie Dawson, and to my fabulous agent Rebecca Ritchie at AM Heath Literary Agency.

And as usual, I'm very grateful to my mum for being an unofficial extra proofreader, and for spurring me on.

And finally, huge thanks to my wonderful husband. Kate's first date with Xander was inspired by *our* first date; Hermi took me to an exhibition at the glorious Victoria and Albert Museum, and we went there on our second date too. Without you, Hermi, I'd never have discovered the wonderful world of board games and so I'd never have written that first novel about a little board game café in a town called Essendale.

# About the Author

JENNIFER PAGE wrote her first novel – a book about ponies – when she was eight. These days she prefers to write about romance and her debut, *The Little Board Game Café*, was published in 2023, and was followed in 2024 by the second in the series, *Love Letters on Hazel Lane*.

When she isn't writing, Jennifer can usually be found playing board games. She has worked as a television producer, a music teacher and has even run a children's opera company. She lives near Hebden Bridge in West Yorkshire with her husband, his large collection of games and in recent months, Labrador puppy Pete, who will be leaving them soon to train as a guide dog.

For updates and pupdates, you can sign up to Jennifer's newsletter by visiting her website at https://jenniferpage. co.uk. Subscribers will receive a free epilogue of *The Little Board Game Café*.

You can also follow her on social media:

Instagram: @jenniferpagewrites
Facebook: @jenniferpagewrites
X: @jenpagewrites
TikTok: @jenniferpagewrites